food whore

food whore

A NOVEL *of*
DINING *and* DECEIT

Jessica Tom

wm
WILLIAM MORROW
An Imprint of HarperCollins*Publishers*

This is a work of fiction. Names, characters, places, and incidents are products of the author's imagination or are used fictitiously and are not to be construed as real. Any resemblance to actual events, locales, organizations, or persons, living or dead, is entirely coincidental.

HarperCollins books may be purchased for educational, business, or sales promotional use. For information please e-mail the Special Markets Department at SPsales@harpercollins.com.

FIRST EDITION

Designed by Diahann Sturge

Library of Congress Cataloging-in-Publication Data has been applied for.

ISBN 978-0-06-238700-4

15 16 17 18 19 OV/RRD 10 9 8 7 6 5 4 3 2 1

To Mom and Dad

Out comes a gorgeous, fleshy wheel of foie gras, perched on its side like a monument grander than its actual two-inch height. Around it are its minions, smears of savory-sweet onion confit paste and garlic tendrils puffed like Rice Krispies. You slide your knife down, slowly at first. The wheel is murky, muddy, and before you know it, the knife is being sucked to the bottom of the plate as you watch the wheel unpeel from itself.

Out spills a green liquid, as mesmerizing as lava. Go on, take a forkful. Drag the finest, smoothest foie into the absolute essence of pea. Pick up a few pieces from the pool of accents. And taste. Put your fork down and wonder: how could this dish seem so pure and elemental, and yet have a flavor so electric, so challenging?

Bakushan, from the Japanese word *bakku-shan*. A girl who looks pretty from behind, but is ugly in the front.

This dish is not ugly by any means, but it offers that bit of shock, that moment of fear and excitement when the girl turns around and shows you the truth.

Chapter 1

THE RECEPTION WAS MEANT TO BE CASUAL AND FUN, BUT INstead the air vibrated with tension, like a kettle on the verge of boiling. I saw some people in crisp lab coats (the food science researchers), others in tweed jackets (the cultural anthropologists), and a select group in shorts and hoodies who looked about the same age as us (the Internet start-up founders). The room was a convergence of all kinds of food industry professionals, from restaurateurs to packaged-food makers to webseries producers. Students like me jockeyed for position around these would-be mentors, needy moons circling any planet with a vacancy in its orbit.

"Do you see Helen?" I asked Elliott. He already had a job at the New York Botanical Garden in the Bronx, but he'd come with me to the graduate student reception as a show of support.

Even though he had attended three of her speaking engagements with me and knew her face, he checked her picture again before scanning the crowd.

"Helen . . . Helen . . . where are you, Helen?" he said with squinted, searching eyes. "Want me to walk around? I'll text you if I see her."

Before I could say yes, Elliott was off, hunting. He was good like that. Elliott was Elliott—goofy and kind and the type of guy who made me giddy even by standing a little too close. He's a good one.

But one thing Elliott will never be is a person who loves to eat. He isn't opposed to a good meal or annoyingly picky or anything like that. It's just that food doesn't *matter* to him. If a meal ever tried to speak to Elliott, he'd probably excuse himself from the conversation. But that didn't mean he'd bail on helping me out.

Now that I was officially in NYU's master's program in Food Studies, I didn't want to leave Helen to chance. The committee already had my internship application and I'd find out my placement in five days, but maybe—just maybe—I could seal the deal by charming the socks off Helen at this event.

Helen is brilliant. Her work for the *Times* is legendary for its incisive critiques, but I love her memoirs and cookbooks the most. Unshackled by journalistic constraints, her voice grows warm and visceral and pulls you into the heart of every recipe and story. You sit in her blue childhood kitchen in Massachusetts, ache over her short-lived love affair with a chef in France, grit your teeth at her hectic days as a new mother.

Part of my plan included enticing Helen with a batch of my special cashew-almond-walnut-pecan Dacquoise Drops, something to make her take notice of my application essay. Dacquoise Drops were no ordinary cookies. They're what drove me to Helen, though I can't say I planned it that way.

My grandfather had been in the hospital with a weakened heart and rapidly degenerating lungs. For a month, my mom worked nights so she could spend her days with him. My dad visited after work and kept Mom calm.

I took the train from New Haven to Grand Central to Yonkers every Thursday and returned to campus every Monday morning, each trip depressing me more. Never mind the commute—I loathed one rude, forgetful nurse and how her negligence left Grandpa's bed linens scratchy and a little too short. But I was most appalled by the food, which was bad for healthy people, and downright sadistic at the hospital: fried chicken, burgers, fries, salads larded with bacon and creamy dressings. Grandpa had always had a sweet tooth and it pained me to see him eat cookies filled with faux "crème" and cakes with decade-long shelf lives.

So back at campus I developed the Dacquoise Drop: a light, nutty, meringue-based cookie I knew Grandpa would love. I had been cooking with my grandfather since I could reach the stove, but this creation was something else entirely. It was the last thing he ate.

Elliott helped me make them for the funeral, and later, he was the one who convinced me to share my story and recipe in the *Yale Daily News*.

I wrote about one of our last cooking sessions together, right before I went to college. Grandpa taught me how to make Poulet aux Noix de Cajou, a chicken and cashew dish from his native Senegal. We took the train to Little Senegal, a pocket community tucked inside Harlem, and bought unshelled cashews, which are impossible to find anywhere else because the shells contain skin irritants similar to those in poison ivy. Together, we roasted the toxic fluids out, hand-peeled the shells, and then blistered the nuts.

We could have taken twenty different shortcuts, but we took the long way at every step.

I ended the article with my Dacquoise Drops. I bought unshelled nuts and revisited Little Senegal to get the cashews.

Elliott and I detoxed the cashews, then blanched, soaked, and roasted them. And that was just nut prep. The meringues were a whole other painstaking process. They took eight hours to make, but every step was connected to my grandpa. The essay was the most personal thing I had ever written.

The piece was published in the spring of my sophomore year and got a lot of reader attention. The editors gave me a regular food column, where I created original recipes and tied them to my real life. I loved it. One month before school let out for summer, the *New York Times* contacted me for a feature. The reporter said that Helen Lansky had discovered my column online and was reminded of her own writing. This came as the shock of my life. Helen was the master, and to get her vote of approval changed my entire life.

I was supposed to be profiled with other "college chefs," but I ended up being the main story. They even published the Dacquoise Drops recipe, and Helen wrote an editor's note: "These are a creation born of love. Some people write. Others may cook. And some, like Ms. Monroe, are compelled to do both: tell a story through food."

I had been lost, searching for a major and a direction. But after reading those words, it all clicked: food, writing, Helen Lansky. I increased my Yale column to twice a week and spent summers writing for the *New Haven Register*. After that article, I hardly went home, even though my parents lived just one state over.

The day before the graduate student reception, Elliott and I had baked a batch of cookies, and now they were at the peak of their complexity: chewy and crispy and lacquered with the most delicate shell, one that only lasts for eighteen or so hours before humidity steals it away. Now, I clung to the container of cookies, my pride and claim to fame.

"Hey," a big guy said as I surveyed the room for Helen. "You looking for someone?" Between his large red face and flannel checkered shirt, he looked like he had come in from the cold, though it was about eighty degrees out.

"Yeah," I said. "Helen Lansky? She used to be the dining editor for the *New York Times* and was even the critic for a bit. Now she's a cookbook author—"

"Helen! Of course I know Helen!" He looked both insulted and amused that I had assumed otherwise. This was Food Studies graduate school, and these students were serious. "It's weird she isn't here yet, right?" he continued. "Everything about her writing is so immaculate and precise. I would have expected her to be super punctual."

I nodded. "Totally. I hope she's coming. Do you know how internships are typically assigned?"

The guy threw up his hands. "Who knows. This whole process is a black box. I overheard one guy saying selection is a random lottery. They want to 'expose you to different disciplines.' But my friend's sister got her first choice and now she's a professor at UCLA." He shrugged and we both sighed.

I wasn't surprised, though. Who expects anything in New York to be easy?

"Well . . . my name's Kyle Lorimer," the guy said. He held out a hand that was warm and bouncy, like a fresh-baked bagel. He rocked on the balls of his feet as if this were the stop for the Helen Lansky train and all he had to do was wait.

"Tia Monroe," I said before excusing myself. He seemed like a nice guy, but I wasn't going to lose focus now. I only had eyes for Helen.

I texted Elliott: *Anything?*

I waited for the text to send, but the signal wasn't strong enough, so I had to walk outside. As my message finally shot off, I saw her from across the street: a petite, fine-boned woman in a lime-green silk jacket and velvet pants. Her big, bushy black hair nested on top of her head. She was half exotic concubine, half Jewish auntie.

I stepped forward onto the sidewalk and beamed. It was the perfect scenario. I'd leave an impression before the mob of grad students even saw her. I crossed the street before realizing she wasn't alone. A sickly thin gentleman stood across from her in an ill-fitting suit. Helen was on her toes, lecturing him.

Suddenly my nerves ramped up. What was I going to do now? This man—literally—stood in the way.

By the time I crept up behind them, their faces were inches apart and their whispers were loud enough to be heard. I figured the man might spy me hovering or Helen would feel my eyes on her back and turn around. But none of that happened. I just stood there, my smile stiffening and slipping away. I didn't intend to eavesdrop on them, but I had to stay close so I could catch Helen once she stopped talking to the man.

"Now you're not making sense!" Helen screeched. "I'm just trying to help you before you do something you can't undo. I care about your future, even if you don't."

I took one step forward, stretching my ear toward them. What were they talking about?

"To help me, Helen? I wasn't aware that I needed help," huffed the thin man.

"Well, it's increasingly obvious to me. I can read it in your words. I can see it in your physique. And now you want to attend a graduate school reception for no ascertainable reason? The manager of Madison Park Tavern is in there. And plenty of other industry people, too. Any single one of them might recognize you."

She barked the last few words at full volume, then quickly lowered her voice and took a breath. When she spoke again, she sounded scratchy and strained, as if she was on the edge of crying.

"Michael," she began, her words barely reaching me through the hum of the city streets. "You're the *New York Times* restaurant critic. Don't treat this as a game."

I gasped and tripped over my feet. I couldn't help it.

Michael. Michael Saltz, the current *Times* critic. Helen's successor, minus some in-between people. For some, he was New York's most feared person: the man who had the power to make or break any restaurant in town.

I felt a flash of awe. Sure, Helen had been his boss when she worked at the *Times,* but he was a critic who lived in anonymity, and that imparted the sighting with a special taste of the forbidden.

He wanted to attend the NYU reception?

No wonder Helen was so upset. The Food Studies graduate reception was no place for a high-profile anonymous critic. It was like partying with ex-cons while in the witness protection program. Why would you risk it?

Now I was basically on top of them, but they were still so engrossed in their conversation, I didn't think they'd notice. They hadn't paid any attention to me up until then.

And yet.

Michael Saltz's eyes peeled away from Helen and slithered over to mine. He regarded me with the lightest of touches, a nanometer of moisture absorbed into a cloud. But still, he got a read.

A moment later, a city bus arrived behind me and I was separated from the two of them by exiting passengers. I tried to keep Helen in my line of sight until I felt a hand at my elbow and looked up to see Michael Saltz. Helen had left.

"Why, hello," he said. He had a slight lisp, which he didn't attempt to hide. "Looks like you missed your bus."

"Oh, right!" I laughed, as cool as I could manage considering I had been caught eavesdropping on a conversation I'd known full well was private. "Um, I mean, no. I was waiting, but then I realized I have to stay here for a . . . thing." I didn't want to tell him I was attending the same reception Helen had warned him against. His eyes lowered to my NYU name tag, which said, rather unhelpfully, TIA MONROE. YONKERS, NY. YALE UNIVERSITY. FOOD WRITING AND CULTURAL ANTHROPOLOGY.

"So, Tia, you're heading to that venue over there, yes? I see you're a first year . . . an Ivy Leaguer . . . a writer."

"Yes, sir," I admitted.

"Do you know who I am?" He was an odd-looking man. His cheekbones were sharp and knobby like knees. He wore an immaculate suit full of custom bells and whistles—dark silk lining, leather buttons, plaid lines that matched up perfectly at the seams. And yet it didn't fit. What was the point of a tailor-made suit if you swam in it so cartoonishly?

"You're . . ." I looked around for Helen again, but the sidewalk had emptied.

"Go on, you can say it."

"You're Michael Saltz, the *New York Times* dining critic," I said. He wanted the truth and I gave it. What else could I do?

He nodded solemnly. "That is correct. Well done."

But I wasn't congratulating myself. I could tell by the sarcastic lilt to his voice that he didn't want to be ID'd. But he wasn't being discreet, either.

"And are you bringing those . . . cookies . . . to the reception?" he asked, blinking twice at the plastic container cradled under my arm.

"Well, yes," I said. "They're called Dacquoise Drops. They're kind of my specialty . . ."

"Oh!" Michael Saltz said. "*The* Dacquoise Drops? As I remember, that was the top emailed recipe for three months straight. Not developed in-house, but by a college-aged savant named . . ." His eyes lit up, then returned to my name tag. "Tia Monroe. I've been looking for someone like you. So you're the cooking and writing prodigy, hm?"

He was looking for someone like me? In what way? "Oh, I wouldn't say a prodigy, per se. Plus, that article came out a long time ago."

I said it because the situation seemed to call for modesty, but in fact I had never tired of that recognition. My creations were usually a private affair, but that had changed for one glorious moment after the article. I'd been flooded with emails from readers who wanted more recipes, and even gone on local TV for a cooking demo.

But eventually the emails had stopped. Nothing had happened after that TV appearance, and people forgot about it. I had poured myself into each article since, mining every part of my life, sure *that* day's column would be the gem that would return me to the spotlight. Every once in a while, I'd receive a random email or tweet and it'd make my day. But otherwise, silence. And yet I'd persisted on that track. Stay in New Haven, go to class, write for the paper, hope for the best. Hearing that Michael Saltz remembered—I was flabbergasted. The rush of recognition came back, extra sweet because he was so prominent and it had been so long.

"And, let me guess. You'd like to intern for a blog? *Gobbler*? *Diner Nation*?"

"No," I said. "I'm not interested in blogs. I want to write cookbooks and study under—"

"Helen! Now I see. Of course the prodigy would want Helen's internship. As I remember, Helen loved your writing *and* your recipe. Was she the food editor when you were . . . front page, was it?" He closed his eyes and waved his hands in the air, like the end-of-days soothsayer I had seen two blocks down on Sullivan Street. "In the picture, you were sitting in the dining hall with a bowl of cherries."

Bingo. His words glowed on me like a heat lamp and I basked in every second. He wasn't exactly pleasant, but he spoke in the most persuasive way, with a tingling insistence. Still, I realized I was losing valuable time with Helen. I had one chance to talk to her before the placements were announced, and I couldn't waste precious minutes with anyone but her.

And yet, he kept talking and I kept listening.

"Well!" he continued. "You must think that Helen made that happen, yes? Let me guess . . . You came straight from college. Yale, no less. Then came this article . . . all by the hand of Helen, our fearless editor at the time. You never gave yourself a chance to see the outside world." He laughed, not with me, but at me.

I found none of this funny. He sounded a bit like my parents. They loved food and it was their method of choice when showing their love, but graduate school struck them as impractical. Still, I had wanted to go for it.

Plus, Michael Saltz was also making me seem like some obsequious little girl, following her childhood idol with no real-world experience. Maybe I was, but I didn't care. There are things in life that drill into your core. Helen was my idol. She had anointed me into the *New York Times.* She'd been the one to help set me on my path.

"But, cookies?" he replied when I didn't respond. "You think anything in this town gets done because of cookies? No, you must do better than that." He took the Tupperware out of my hands and opened the lid. But as soon as the top was off, Michael Saltz lost his grip and the cookies fell to the ground. A morning of sourcing the best ingredients, an afternoon of blistering four types of nuts, a night of making fifty cookies and keeping only the most perfect dozen. All gone. He had wiped out my best plan to secure Helen.

"What did you do that for?" I screamed and scrambled to pick them up, but they had splayed themselves over the filthy ground.

Immediately, I started thinking about a plan B. Could I dust these off? Make another batch and send them to her in time? Either way, the first step was getting away from Michael Saltz.

"Oh, I'm so sorry," he said, not looking sorry at all. "That was terrible of me."

I had turned away, thinking I'd never say another word to this psychotic man ever again, when he spun me around.

"But tell me," he started. "As I remember, those darling Dacquoise Drops are quite labor-intensive. How many nuts did you use? Three? Four?"

I shot him a glare. He'd destroyed my cookies and now he wanted to hear how I'd made them?

"Four," I said. "And I shelled every one of them."

"Unshelled cashews? How in the world did you manage that? They're related to— "

"Poison ivy, I know. My boyfriend helped me roast out the oils," I said. "And now we'll have to do it again since you ruined this batch. But first I'm going to talk to Helen—with no cookies, thanks to you."

I was ready to storm off when Michael Saltz ran in front of me, standing partially in the street while I stood on the sidewalk. A taxi pulled up so close I thought it might hit him.

"Again, I'm sorry. That was idiotic. But it's become clear that besides being an exemplary cook and writer, you'll take great pains to be with Helen. Am I correct?"

I ached for the Don't Walk sign to change and looked away from him. But from the corner of my eye, I saw that he never wavered, even as a car pulled up two inches away from him.

"Yes," I answered.

"Would you do anything for her?"

Finally, the Walk sign lit up. I stepped from the curb and said, "Yeah, I would."

After I crossed the street, I looked around to see if Michael Saltz had followed me. But he remained in the same spot and now had a wild grin on his face.

ELLIOTT RAN UP the second I stepped into the reception hall.

"Tia, there you are!" he said, winded. "She arrived a couple of minutes ago. Come on! People are already surrounding her! I tried to text you but—"

I had no time to tell Elliott about Michael Saltz. We ran and made a full circle of the room, but neither of us saw Helen anywhere.

"Did we lose her?" Elliott asked me, genuinely distressed.

I spotted Kyle and ran over to him, desperate for info. I'd been so close to Helen. Why had I stayed with Michael Saltz?

"Have you seen Helen?" I wheezed.

"Oh, hey," Kyle said. "Yeah, she was in here for like, five or ten minutes, and then she left. I barely chatted with her."

"You *chatted* with her?"

"Yeah . . . I'm gunning for her internship, so of course I talked to her. At least a dozen people bombarded her with gifts. Did you see her?"

His question sucker-punched me. No, I hadn't. Would I ever? Had I lost Helen, just like that?

I climbed up a set of stairs to get a better view of the room. The room was still crowded with faces, but none was the one I wanted to see.

Then I felt a tap on my leg and looked down to see Elliott, his mouth tight and wary. "Hey," Elliott said. "I was asking around for Helen, and this gentleman said he knows where to find her." He gestured behind him to Michael Saltz, peering at me with those curious, predatory eyes.

"Tia! I'd like to make up for the incident earlier. I'll connect you with Helen. Send me your application essay, and I'll ensure she sees it and makes her desires known to the committee." He took out a pen and scribbled a generic email address, then held out his hand to Elliott. "I must go, but I realized I didn't introduce myself. I'm Paul," Michael Saltz said.

"Elliott," he replied as he shook. With the other hand, Elliott touched the small of my back as if to say, *If this weird guy does anything, I got you.*

I loved that. But at the same time, I was amazed at Michael Saltz's persistence, even after I had stormed away and Helen had expressly warned him against attending this very reception. Amazed, and a little flattered.

"And Tia," Michael Saltz said, turning to me again, "such a pleasure." He held out his hand and as my flesh touched his, he clamped my fingers and swooped down for a kiss. His lips were dry and frail. His cold nose touched my wrist and a chill ran through my bones.

Elliott grabbed my other arm and pulled me away. I looked behind me and saw Michael Saltz smirk his good-bye.

"Ugh, sorry I subjected you to that guy. Who was that creep?"

"He was . . ." My heart was pounding so fast I could hardly breathe.

What could I say to Elliott? He was the *New York Times* restaurant critic. Helen's stubborn friend. An interloper at the reception. A sickly thin man who frightened and aggravated and—I had to admit—fascinated me.

The man who would give my essay to Helen. But what was in it for him? I couldn't quite figure it out, so I echoed the critic's lie, to give myself time. He obviously hadn't wanted to reveal his identity to Elliott, so I didn't give him away. "His name is Paul."

Elliott heaved a sigh of relief, as if that explained everything. "Well, glad we got you out of there."

I made a sound of agreement, but my skin still tingled from Michael Saltz's kiss.

ELLIOTT AND I had planned to wander our new neighborhood for good restaurants, but I didn't want to socialize after the NYU reception disaster. Instead, I made an excuse and stayed in my apartment and thought.

Now my application was out of my hands.

I needed to get the Helen Lansky internship and wanted to start the year on the right foot.

In retrospect, I'd had so many things handed to me in high school and college. But after that article, I'd stagnated, waiting for opportunities to arrive at my doorstep. I'd devoted myself to articles that only a handful of people read.

And I'd thought I'd land a top-tier graduate school internship placement with a batch of cookies.

As much as I didn't want to acknowledge it, Michael Saltz had put something into sharp relief. I couldn't stand idle about my own future now. I had gotten all the way to grad school with one person in mind. Why would I leave my entire future in other people's hands if I had the ability to help things along?

I wasn't thrilled about accepting back-channel help from an erratic, mysterious stranger, but I decided my days of passive waiting were over. This was New York, and if you don't push, you'll be pushed. And I couldn't let that happen.

I pulled Michael Saltz's email address out of my pocket. He had written it on a receipt from a restaurant called Sargasso. The total: $608. Each line was some complicated dish reduced to two words: *offal terrine; rye risotto; papaya choux*. It was a different food world than Helen's. I had fifteen of her books on my bookshelf and not one of them had a recipe for rye risotto. What did rye risotto taste like, anyway?

I typed out the email address—a vague collection of random letters and numbers—pecking at the keys one by one. I kept my message short and sweet, knowing deep down that this was an underground transaction, wrong in some intangible way I couldn't put my finger on.

Hi—I've attached my essay. Please let me know if Helen needs anything else.

But he was the one doing me the favor. So I deleted the last line and started again.

Please let me know if there's anything else I can do for you.

Send.

I still don't know what made him pick me. Maybe my cookies had told him something about the level of my desire. Or maybe he'd know from that one line—*anything else I can do for you*—that I would play by his rules, as long as it got me closer to Helen.

He never responded to my email. The next time he wrote to me, it was under his real name.

Chapter 2

"Hey! Don't you love mangoes?"

Emerald Grace whirled through the door in a backless teal boho maxi dress with three bags and a big leather purse hurled over her shoulder. The straps of her bag tamped down her long hair and I thought she looked quite beautiful and exciting, like an heiress forced out of her mansion by revolutionaries.

My glamorous roommate had returned.

I had moved in two weeks earlier and seen her just three times since, always at weird times when she seemed to be rushing off to somewhere more important. I had found the apartment through Roooomies.com and ultimately chose it because Elliott's new place was two blocks away. He and I had considered living together, but we'd both heard horror stories of college couples who made misguided decisions to cohabitate in New York. Suddenly, you have less space, things cost more, work winds you up. Explosions abound. Besides, there was always next year, and we didn't want to rush it.

And so I'd sublet a room in Emerald's three-bedroom in the East Village. Emerald and I had Facebook friended and chatted a bit. There were a lot of exclamation points and *Can't waits* to soften the blow of the dry logistics: move-in day, what she had and what I needed to bring, deposits and all. Still, I'd thought I had an idea of what to expect: a twenty-five-year-old fashion designer trying to launch her own business.

I was wrong. Charisma doesn't translate that well on the computer. Emerald's real-life presence was a force, something you can only see in the flesh. I enjoyed her online, but now I found myself slightly shrinking as she spoke.

She tossed some mangoes on the couch and one fell onto the floor with a bruising thump. "Are you settling in okay? You must think I'm a deadbeat landlord. Will you forgive me?"

"Uh, sure, I forgive you," I said, trying to play along but not sure where she was leading me.

She laughed. "Ohmigod, don't think of me as a landlord. We're roommates, 'kay? Oh, and I heard from the third girl, Melinda. She's coming in next week from Cleveland. And these are for our living room."

She removed a bouquet of peonies from one of her bags and tossed it on the couch. Then, without a thought as to a vase or brushing her hair or sitting down, she opened up the coat closet and started to put on a large men's suit jacket.

"I'm meeting some friends for drinks now. You wanna come?" she asked.

"Oh, I can't. I'm sorta waiting to hear about this grad school thing I applied for. And my boyfriend is coming over." I'm not sure why I was so vague. With this gorgeous whirling dervish of a roommate, I clammed up.

Right on time, Elliott ambled through our doorway. I could always sense his arrival from the trot-like cadence to his step. It wasn't hugely noticeable, but I knew him so well that even the nuances of his gait were obvious.

"Oh, hey," he said to me before turning to Emerald.

She flashed a toothy smile and took off the big men's coat she had just put on, revealing the elegant line of her naked back.

I got up from the couch and walked over to Elliott. "Emerald, this is Elliott . . ." I said, in a voice I hoped sounded like her cue to exit. But her eyes didn't leave his and her long, thick eyelashes seemed to flutter in slo-mo, all the more tantalizing.

" . . . my boyfriend," I finished.

Her concentration broke. "Your boyfriend? Oh! Your boyfriend! Good for you!" she said.

Elliott didn't seem to notice her subtle condescension. He wrapped his arm around my waist. Immediately, I calmed down.

"Well, Elllllliott," Emerald said, her voice dripping with honey. "Nice to meet you."

He looked at her for two beats, like she was some novelty toy whose function he couldn't figure out. "You work as a fashion designer, right? Tia and I googled you together."

"Yeah, I liked the stuff in your portfolio," I ventured. I really did.

"Why, thank you." Emerald tilted her head and made a flourish with her hand.

Then Elliott adjusted his backpack and I saw him take in the whole Emerald package: the curves, the hair, the twinkling, flirtatious eyes. Elliott was also looking good in a blue long-sleeved tee that hugged his just-right muscles. Those muscles actually seemed a little bigger today. Had he been working out or was it that my perfect and gorgeous roommate had triggered the jealous Neanderthal part of my brain?

I tried to push those insecurities out of my head. I was with Elliott. My Elliott. That was all that mattered.

But then again, I was in New York now, a city populated by models and designers and billionaire socialites. Anything was possible. You felt it in the thrum of the streets, as a spark in the air.

Emerald had the confidence of a native New Yorker. I knew that from our emails, but I could tell it in person, too. She knew what she wanted, and at that moment, I feared that might mean Elliott.

I sat on the couch and distracted myself with my laptop. A new email landed in my NYU inbox, which had been empty moments earlier, save for a very purple welcome email from the University president.

> **SUBJECT:** Fall Graduate Schedule
> **Name:** Tia Monroe
> **Core classes:** Clinical Nutrition Assessment & Intervention, Food Systems: Food and Agriculture in the Twentieth Century
> **Internship:** Madison Park Tavern: Operations, Coat Check

Elliott and Emerald were still talking. Apart from gagging a little, I sat stone-still. What was this? Madison Park Tavern? Coat check? I was going to grad school . . . for coat check?

I tried to calm down and take stock. Helen Lansky was my first choice, but something had happened. I'd been edged out by someone else. But who? Why? I took a deep breath.

Five days ago, Michael Saltz had said he'd put in a good word. He must've forgotten, or maybe he didn't have as much clout as he thought. Maybe Helen was so mad at him that she'd purposely gone against his wishes.

"Hey," I whispered to Elliott, holding my hand out. It swung around languidly, like a heavy piece of underwater kelp.

I tried to telepathically tell him to kick Emerald out, but they were still deep in conversation. Elliott had already talked to my roommate ten times longer than I had. Somehow, they were chatting like old friends.

"Now," Elliott started, locking eyes with Emerald, "here's something I've always wondered: why in the world would anyone pay two hundred dollars for a pair of jeans? Is that a girl thing?"

"There's a huge difference in denim quality," Emerald said, crisp and cocky. "It's like the difference between leather and pleather."

I held out my hand again, this time higher, but Elliott didn't seem to see. This whole thing with Emerald played before my eyes as if I were a cook observing her rising soufflé. The conditions were set. Now everything that happened was beyond my control.

"Pleather! That's another thing I don't get."

"What's not to get?" Emerald raised her perfectly tweezed eyebrows. "It's a synthetic leather. Typically associated with strippers."

"Yeah, but why is it this taboo thing? It's just fabric," Elliott responded, arching his own handsome brow. "There's no scenario in which you and a pole dancer could each live your separate lives and find happiness with clothes made of the same fabric?"

Oh, Elliott, I thought. *Stop! You're falling right for it!*

Emerald thought about this for a moment with mock gravity. "Maybe you're right, Elliott." Then, she wrapped her freckled arms around herself, like a little girl. Her lips curled up in a wry smile, as though she and Elliott were sharing a private joke. "I suppose, under *certain* conditions, strippers could offer me some useful style advice."

Elliott shaded his eyes like he couldn't face some terrible truth, but he was grinning like an idiot. "No, no, no. Don't tell me any more. I think we've just crossed some invisible line into seriously inappropriate material for first conversations."

"Oh, agreed," Emerald said. "We should probably save this discussion until we've known each other for at least fifteen minutes." Then she giggled maniacally and tossed her disturbingly adorable chin, the wind from her hair slapping me across the face.

Suddenly I saw Elliott through a stranger's eyes. Elliott was hot. He wouldn't be seen as the geeky, sweet college kid with the scary encyclopedic knowledge of worms and plants for long. He'd be Elliott Chambers, a naturally handsome guy who charmed naturally lovely girls . . . girls like Emerald Grace.

"Elliott," I finally said in a just-loud-enough squeak. "I didn't get Helen Lansky."

He turned to me, and his beaming smile fizzled into a confused line.

"Who?" he asked.

My jaw dropped. "Are you kidding me?" My voice was louder than it needed to be. I didn't want to lash out in front of Emerald, especially since they were having such a chummy time together. But this was *Helen*. And he was *Elliott*. I'm not super-friendly, and I don't go around trusting everyone. But I trusted Elliott and I never thought I'd ever have to second-guess him, of all people.

"*Helen. Lansky.* My idol?"

"Oh, God, of course. Helen! Sorry, I thought you said something else." He hugged me and became just as puzzled and aggrieved as I was. Finally, we were on the same page again.

But he had scared me a little.

Chapter 3

Dean Chang opened her office door. She was a tall Asian woman who wore a perfectly tailored black skirt suit with a long slit up the side. Maybe it would have looked tawdry on anyone else, but on her and her I-hope-I'll-have-those-when-I'm-forty legs, it looked like pure power.

"Tia. Hello. Nice to meet you." She seemed kind but distracted. "I'm happy to chat with you now if it's urgent, but I'm finishing up some grading. Can this wait?"

"No, it can't," I said, then walked in and took a seat. Dean Chang sighed and went back to her desk.

Her office was a shrine to the classics. Hanging on the wall were old menus featuring dishes like Cherries Jubilee and Lobsters Thermidor, and chummy photos of her and Julia Child, Jacques Pépin, and Alice Waters.

"Dean Chang, I received my placement notification yesterday. May I ask why I didn't get the Helen Lansky internship? I'm so honored to be in this program, I am. But coat check? I don't understand. It doesn't seem like a graduate-level placement."

I wanted to present myself as coming from a place of strength, to negotiate something better from her. But instead, something scared and desperate emerged and I had to fight to remain strong.

"Oh, please don't be upset, Tia," she said, momentarily pushing her papers aside.

I'd talked to her like she was a friend, and it was the wrong approach. She remained administrator-distanced. I began again, this time with more control.

"It's just that the coat check position has nothing to do with food. Or with writing. I was planning on pursuing a different course of study." In that moment, I wished I could be more like Emerald, breezily saying things that sounded calm and clever, but I was just me.

"Tia, I understand your confusion," Dean Chang said with stern warmth, a clear indication she had spent her whole professional career soothing anxious students like me. "Madison Park Tavern is a fabulous restaurant—four stars, among the best in New York, as I'm sure you already know. Your semester will be fantastic, I promise." Then she picked up her heavy pen and looked at me like there was nothing else to say on the matter.

"But why?" I persisted. "I didn't even put any restaurants on my application. I want to be a cookbook writer. Maybe I could be placed with another writer? Or even a blog?" I preferred Helen over every other option, but I was trying to stay open. I liked nice restaurants, sure. But they weren't my passion. When I was growing up, my dad was notorious for his "restaurants are a rip-off" tirade. My parents were inventive cooks and they never considered restaurant food to be worth the cost.

For a moment, Dean Chang looked unsettled. "Wait a second. You didn't select Madison Park Tavern as one of your choices?"

I shook my head. "No, I didn't. I chose Helen. Helen Lansky first and foremost. And then some other publications."

"Oh, but when you resubmitted your essay in that email . . ." She seemed about to open her filing cabinet, but then apparently changed her mind. "I'm afraid the decision has been made. You are a bright young woman, Tia. You'll be fine. If you remember nothing else from this conversation, I want you to remember this: grad school is a marathon, not a sprint."

I fidgeted in my chair. This wasn't how grad school was supposed to happen.

"I mean . . . it's a slow roast rather than a sear," she tried again. I attempted a smile to at least acknowledge her effort, but it came out like a scowl.

"But . . . there's always next semester, right?"

Dean Chang sighed, looking sorry for me. "Right. There's always next semester, and the semester after that, and the semester after that. Though many of our mentors have erratic schedules and I can never know for sure. I can't promise anything, so I think the key is to enjoy the placement you have now."

I left her office in shock.

So, Helen Lansky: not happening. My whole idea of graduate school: rerouted.

And Michael Saltz . . . not only had he hijacked my valuable time with Helen and sabotaged my cookies, but he also hadn't helped in the way he'd said he would. I wished the world would play by my rules, instead of whatever was happening now.

The walk back to my apartment was crowded with incoming NYU undergrads, their parents, and some overflow tourists enjoying the last bits of summer. I sat on a bench in Washington Square Park and watched a baby—too young to walk but old enough to bop up and down—dance to a New Orleans–style brass band. I saw lovers holding hands, friends drinking giant green juices, and three homeless people sunning on the lawn.

I looked again at my course catalog:

Food and Food Management Internship
Practical work experience in food studies or food management tailored to the specific interests & career goals of each student. Work is supported by in-class discussion, written projects & presentations.

I was a twenty-two-year-old graduate student, working coat check. I had failed.

A girl wheeled her ice pop cart through the park toward me. It looked like a traveling Bali, with cool blues that shimmered in the sun, a tasseled white-and-gold parasol, and a bouquet of birds of paradise.

"Pineapple-ginger? Mango with coconut tapioca pearls?"

I tossed the course catalog back into my bag and looked at the menu. "Taro and kemangi leaf? Tamarind-turmeric? Snake fruit with mangosteen gelée? Wow, you're making some amazing stuff."

Her eyes lit up. "*Thank you!*" she squealed. "Have you been to Asia? Are you a chef?" Despite her exotic artisanal ice pops, she was a bubbly blonde with blue doe eyes.

"No, no, I haven't, " I admitted. "But . . . I'd love to. I'm a home cook, though, and in grad school for Food Studies."

"Oh, grad school!" she said, plopping down on the bench beside me. "I had planned on grad school, too. A joint program at London Business School and Oxford. But I decided to travel, and it was the best decision of my life."

"Oh, why?" Only in New York could you find a scholar who'd turned down one of the best educations in the world to hand-sell ice pops.

"Well, I knew that I'd be able to learn more while seeing the world. In school, your life is on hold. Don't get me wrong, learning is essential. But you can learn anywhere. You reap more from the world than from books, especially when that world is New York City."

I stayed quiet and looked out over the park. I had assumed that grad school was right for me. It had seemed the natural, obvious path. But maybe that was the problem. It was a path. It offered no detours or side excursions. And where would it even lead me? Suddenly I felt choked, living in a city of possibility, but with no choices ahead of me.

The girl seemed to pick up on my worry and handed me an ice pop. "Here, this is on the more experimental side of the spectrum. Nutmeg and smoked jackfruit."

I unpeeled the wrapper, looking at the brown, bark-like surface steaming its chill into the late summer air. I look a bite, then spit it out. It tasted like an ashtray mixed with stale marmalade.

The girl shrugged. "You win some, you lose some." We smiled at each other. I had to give her credit for trying. Then she wheeled her cart away, her sandals flip-flopping behind her.

So Madison Park Tavern wasn't what I'd had in mind, but maybe a forced detour could be good. I'd keep Helen Lansky in my heart, but it wouldn't hurt to see what else was out there. Worst case, I could just spit it out like that vile nutmeg and jackfruit ice pop and move on.

Chapter 4

A WEEK LATER, I RECEIVED AN EMAIL ABOUT MY INTERNSHIP.

> **SUBJECT:** Your First Day at Madison Park Tavern
>
> Hello, Tia. My name is Jake Ferguson. I am the maitre d' of Madison Park Tavern. Welcome to the staff. While your first day isn't until tomorrow, we are having a small tasting session this afternoon. I hope you can join us. It's critical to me, Gary Oscars, and Chef Darling that staff members know each new dish. Do you have any allergies? Hope to see you soon.
>
> —JF

He also included some sort of access info to an internal Madison Park Tavern website at the bottom.

I wrote back:

Hi, Jake—Sure, I can come today. I'm allergic to some shellfish—crustaceans and bivalves, specifically.
Sincerely,
Tia Monroe

And then, him again:

You're precise. See you soon.

And just like that, I said hello to the New York dining world.

I FELT LIKE an intruder. First, I had arrived underdressed in jeans, a black V-neck sweater, and loafers with barely attached soles. Second, I had no idea what working at a restaurant entailed. I had spent the last year mapping out my career with Helen: I'd run to the bodega while Helen did the prep work. We'd make a mess in her tiny home kitchen. We'd compare notes over just-out-of-the-oven pound cake, eaten off vintage cloth napkins.

This was not that. The restaurant was all grand dining room and decorum. The aprons were crisp and snow white. The glassware and china pinged with a sharp perfection. The place sparkled with class.

I shot a text to Elliott saying that I was way out of my league. He responded not to worry and that I could choose a restaurant for dinner that night and tell him about my experience then. I instantly relaxed. Even if the afternoon was a disaster, at least I had Elliott.

"Are you Tia?" a small, narrow-hipped man asked. He wore a blue-and-white-striped French-cuffed shirt and a navy sport jacket with a slight nubby texture, like the underside of a thin-crust pizza. "I'm Jake Ferguson. Welcome to the restaurant.

Come this way." He moved his hand toward my elbow, not quite touching it, and I took his lead.

People filed in as Jake showed me the coatroom, the kitchen, and parts of the dining room hidden from public view.

"This is the water station; this is where we hide the washcloths. Here's where we leave notes for the rest of the staff and keep pictures of key critics."

He revealed a cabinet lined with labeled photos of food writers and their media outlets: Kane Hart, critic at *New York,* Richard Callahan at the *Village Voice,* Aria Ramos from the blog *Sexy & Hungry in NYC,* and others. But there was one face and name that took precedence over them all: Michael Saltz, *New York Times.*

They had two pages of bullet points about him and seven photos. But they sure weren't of the same skinny, serpent-like man I had met almost two weeks ago. The Michael Saltz in these pictures was plump, formidable, his shirt barely stretching over his belly. But the pictures were faded. The most recent one was dated from last summer.

"Yes, the Big Guy. Public Enemy Number One, Michael Saltz," Jake said, then closed the cabinet.

Did he realize these photos were totally off?

He gestured toward a banquette and I sat as more people spun themselves through the rotating door. The women wore trim black suits on their identically shaped bodies. They all had different colored hair, but it didn't matter, since they hid any diversity by pulling their hair back tight with rubber bands and gel and bobby pins. They had, literally, not one stray hair. I redid my ponytail self-consciously, but my hair has its moments of thick and thin. When it's not being prickly, it's superfine and flying away.

Next to me sat a girl who was an outlier in every way, too. Her hair was frizzy, her suit was fussy, and she had a busy-bee quality I liked right away. Plus, she didn't make me feel like such a slouch.

The men were more mixed. Among the kitchen staff, there were two Hispanic guys, a large French guy with big hands, and a gangly mustached man. The waiters matched the waitresses—meticulous and precise.

I recognized Matthew Darling and to my surprise, I got a bit of a thrill from seeing him in the flesh. He was just a regular-looking guy, with a round, pale face and buzzed auburn hair.

Helen had profiled him in the *Times* two years ago, when Chef Darling was the executive chef at Vrai and known for microcalibrating the menu to the seasons. Not just tomatoes in the summer, but grape tomatoes in the early summer, because they're more tender in their youth; heirloom tomatoes in the middle of the summer, at the peak of their gnarliness; and then Jersey tomatoes in the late summer, when they've come around to ripeness, like vacationers returning from the beach. Matthew didn't mess with foams and air and such—he was a man of the grill and the hearth.

And now I remembered—Helen had said that Matthew Darling was one of her favorite chefs in New York. He was a purist and a thinker, an unflashy experimentalist. And now he had taken the reins of Madison Park Tavern, a bigger stage. Maybe this wouldn't be so bad.

Chef Darling cleared his throat and Jake moved to cede the floor.

"First up," Chef said, holding a bowl of lustrous burgundy liquid with a rogue white squiggle, "is a cold roasted beet soup, laced with a horseradish crème fraîche." The line cooks passed along teacups filled with the same concoction.

The girl with the frizzy hair handed me mine without looking at me, then cradled the teacup as if the cold soup were warm hot chocolate. She closed her eyes and tipped her head back so the soup coated her top lip.

I did the same, not because I was copying her, but because that's how the soup wanted to be eaten. First, it hit you, cold and bracing. It was almost too vegetal, too pungent. But then you licked your lips, and the soup transformed into something sweet and profound. It pierced you, like a deep back scratch by a warm hand.

Next to me, a waiter with salt-and-pepper hair raised his hand.

"Yes, Angel?" Jake said from across the room.

"Chef, am I tasting heat in here?"

Chef Darling was about to speak when Jake interrupted. "What do you think, Mr. Martinez?"

The waiter didn't miss a beat. "Yes. White pepper. From Ceylon."

Jake started to talk, but this time Chef Darling interrupted. "Correct. Very good."

"Next dish, Chef?" Jake said.

"As you wish, Jacob," Chef Darling said after waiting a few beats, as if he couldn't stand his voice to be that close to Jake's. I felt the tension between the two men, and it seemed like everyone else did, too. We braced ourselves for a confrontation but relaxed when Chef Darling held up a black earthenware pot.

"These are short ribs, black-eyed peas, and kale braised in apple cider and garnished with pistachios and green garlic. Our official fall short-rib dish. After this, I'd like to take a break from short ribs."

"Chef," implored an older waiter. "Chef Tate had a short-rib dish year-round. Will you at least do an appetizer?" He held an elegant notepad and pen.

"No, I'm phasing it out. No short ribs anywhere."

"Phasing it out?" the waiter responded. "That's what everyone who comes here wants to eat."

Chef Darling scratched his head and fumbled for a response. I wanted him to have more confidence. This was his restaurant. Who cared what the previous chef, Anthony Tate, had done? This was Matthew Darling's time.

"Ahem, let's hand the dishes out now, Chef," Jake said.

I had only tasted bite-size Chinese-style short ribs at home, so I was surprised that Matthew's cuts were much bigger and that the meat melted into the kale in the sultry, complete way cheese melts into pasta. The apple cider gave the dish a sweetened edge, somehow making the short ribs and kale more comfortable with their match. I didn't love the dish for reasons I couldn't quite determine. But I appreciated it.

"Do you like it?" the girl next to me asked.

"Oh, yes, I do," I said reflexively. She hadn't looked at me the whole time, and her friendliness caught me off guard.

"I love it," she said, then smiled so widely there was something lusty and embarrassing about it.

Next, we moved to dessert with a bite of berry torte, passed out in shallow bowls meant for sauce.

"There are over fifteen individually prepared components in this," Matthew started.

"And you must know them all!" Jake added.

Matthew cleared his throat. "The important ones are: berry cake, chia seed brittle, mint-honey glaze, preserved orange peel, burnt sugar whipped cream, almond tuiles, almond-Riesling gelato, and rose meringues. Then everything is set ablaze with bay leaf–infused brandy."

"Bay leaf!" the girl next to me whispered to herself in astonishment. She hovered her face over the little bowl and sucked the bite into her mouth, like an alien abduction.

"What's your name?" I asked, but she said nothing, just let the cake and its accoutrements tumble on her tongue. She clearly wasn't going to respond, so I took a forkful of the dessert.

It crackled and melted and oozed. It was special, elaborate, defiantly unusual. I had never tasted anything even remotely like it.

While Chef Darling prepped the next course, the server named Angel introduced himself and the bartender, Chad.

"You like the restaurant?" Angel asked.

"Yeah, it's great. These tastings are incredible. I wish I could be here, where the action is."

"We all started in the coatroom. You pay your dues—like a couple of months or sometimes a year—then you advance. But grad students usually don't do shit," Chad taunted with a smile.

"*You* don't do shit," Angel taunted back. "Don't worry about him. You're in a good spot. The best."

A four-star restaurant in one of the best dining cities in the world. Maybe *the* best dining city in the world. Angel didn't have to convince me.

"And don't be fooled by this imbecile," Angel continued. "He's a softy. And this place is like family. I've been all around this city, and everywhere is family. Restaurant people protect their own."

"Family!" Chad repeated in his best mafioso voice, stroking his soul patch.

"If you work here, then we got you one hundred percent," Angel said, patting my back. "It's a restaurant creed." He held his fist up to his chest and gave what I would later recognize as one of his signature heart-melting Angel smiles.

We sampled the entire menu, jumping from appetizers to desserts and back again, though Jake made it a point to not serve me the paella, which had bivalves and crustaceans. I loved some dishes and wasn't crazy about others, but it didn't matter because the job was more than the food. The restaurant was a community.

Afterward, Jake reviewed non-food developments with the team. We had received new decanters from Kieley Glass, a pricey artisan collaborative in Rhode Island. Some backservers were promoted to waiters, some waiters to captains. The girl next to me advanced from coat check attendant—my position—to backserver. She jumped up and down when she received the white apron, as if it were her college diploma.

"Finally," Jake said to everyone, "this is Tia Monroe. She's our new master's student from NYU and will start tomorrow on the Saturday dinner shift. Please welcome her to Madison Park Tavern, yes? Okay, meeting adjourned."

They looked at me for a second, then the restaurant snapped into action. The dishes were cleared, the tablecloths were readjusted, the wineglasses were positioned just so, catching a glint of the sun. So many staffers said hi, Jake had to shoo them away. So this wasn't writing in Helen's kitchen. But I knew I could make it work. Already, I liked the sense of belonging.

I was about to leave the restaurant when the girl with the frizzy hair stopped me.

"Sorry, I didn't mean to be rude before. My name is Carey," she said, then thrust her surprisingly delicate hand toward me. "Carey Spence. One *R*." She had a wide, earnest look in her eyes, like *she* was the new girl, trying to impress *me*. "I get really into tastings. Like, *really* into them. But Jake told me about you. I'm an NYU Food Studies grad myself. I like your ring, where did you get it?"

"Yeah, I'm Tia. This is my grandmother's ring."

"Oh, it's beautiful. I love jade. I graduated this past May and started in coat check in my final year, but as of, like, five minutes ago, I'm a backserver." She shook her new white apron in front of me.

"What's a backserver?"

"You're not a restaurant person?"

"Um, no. I wanted to get the Helen Lansky internship—"

"Helen Lansky? Oh, I love her. She's great. This is different, but also not. And a backserver is in between the busser and the waiter, status-wise. I also do some side work, like, data warehousing and strategy stuff. Nothing too serious, but Jake lets me dabble."

"What kind of strategy?" I asked. Her words outnumbered mine by such a large margin that I felt compelled to add on, "What do you mean?"

"Strategy . . ." She slowed down a little, which I appreciated. "You have to remember a lot of things. You'll see. Even as a coat checker, you have to know all the permanent dishes and specials. Who raised what pig and what that pig ate. You'll need to memorize which flowers are in the arrangements, who designed the curtains, what soap is in our dispenser. That information is essential and needs to be shared across staff. That's the core function of this industry Wiki I'm working on.

"Each restaurant has its own private access section where they can keep information in a living, online database that select staff can update. I use the Madison Park Tavern area as a rolling log of the restaurant's evolution. I think Jake sent you access info this morning, though as an intern you're read-only. You can't edit or post. I'm not sure how the rest of the NYC restaurant world uses their private access areas because I made sure it's truly private, you know?

"And then there's the public section, where industry types work together to aggregate relevant external information in a public forum. There are about one hundred admins across the city and the site gets about two hundred unique visits a day. Anyone can access it, but it's mostly senior front- and back-of-house people and some deep-digging reporters."

"Wow, that's cool."

"Right? Now I'm expanding my final NYU project: a database where the restaurant can track all the dishes and components, their response as measured by reviews, orders, and—to a lesser extent—the profit margins. I'm also adding information from other restaurants, along with their critical reception. I'm trying to unearth any statistical insights around timing, ingredients, things like that. The idea is that, within the private confines of our Wiki, we can be predictive and therefore preventative."

"Preventative against what?" I had never heard of anyone taking such a data-driven approach to food.

"A bad write-up. Obviously, the end goal is an amazing review. In the *New York Times,* of course. Michael Saltz is due to visit us soon because Matthew started a couple of months ago. And that means we must be on our game. Jake is always worried about being reviewed at any second. He never rests."

Yikes. Michael Saltz. But they had the wrong pictures. Even Carey didn't seem to realize.

"Say, those pictures? Of Michael Saltz? How old are they?"

Carey gnawed at her nails, panic immediately at the surface. "You think they're outdated? Do you know him?"

"Well, no, not really. But I think—"

Suddenly Jake ran up to us, clipboard in hand. "Carey, come on, we have to go. We have two hundred covers tonight, twenty of them PXs." I peeked down at his reservation notes and saw a garble of shorthand I had never seen before: SFN, Bubbles, Whale, Maestro, Mr. Robinson, WFM. Some people had special requests. I saw something about wine served at a balmy seventy-two degrees and a special request called "Kung Pao salad," which wasn't on the menu.

"Okay, well, gotta run," Carey said. "Tell me later!"

Jake cocked his head at me for a split second, as if waiting for me to say that it couldn't wait. But I didn't have the nerve to mention anything, not yet.

"We'll see you tomorrow, Tia," Jake finally said. "Have a good day."

And then they both walked off, eyes buried in their nightly list of boldfaced names. Their notes were so detailed, the degree of personalized service so high, I wouldn't have been surprised if they had bios on every single guest who came through the doors.

Surely Michael Saltz was their top priority, then. They had the experience and resources and motivation to identify him—even if they had outdated photos. Carey had made it her personal mission to predict his next move.

All I had was one encounter. He'd said he would get me Helen, and that hadn't happened. The Michael Saltz I knew was weird and inert, not the powerful man whom Madison Park Tavern and every other restaurant in New York City watched with bated breath.

So I said nothing, convinced that the restaurant knew better than I did.

After leaving work, I opened my apartment door to find a dark-haired girl applying eyeliner in the closet mirror.

"Hey," she said.

"Hey."

"I'm Melinda," she said. "I live over there." She pointed to the third bedroom, the smallest one.

"Cool," I said. "My name is Tia. How did I miss your move-in? Are your things coming later?"

"I just have two suitcases." She shrugged. I peeked inside her room and saw said suitcases and an air mattress.

"Oh," I said. "Yeah, Emerald said that you were coming a little late. How do you know her?"

"Through the magic of the Internet. She's kind of a trip, right?"

I looked around the apartment to confirm Emerald had left. Still, I wasn't going to tell this near-stranger the truth—that I wasn't sure how to communicate with glamorous, gorgeous Emerald. "She's great."

"I mean . . ." Melinda said, and rolled her eyes at me in the mirror. "I think there's something up with her. Just between you and me. This morning when I got here, she came back all disheveled wearing what looked to be last night's clothes. And see that closet over there? It used to be filled with men's coats. I can't imagine that they're all from one boyfriend or hookup. Fine, whatever. I'm not one to judge. But when she saw that I noticed, she moved everything back into her room."

"So? I don't follow."

Melinda took out some iridescent blue-green eye shadow and laughed. "I'm no prude, but that girl is hiding something. Something that goes beyond sleeping with guys."

I had seen how Elliott had responded to her—even with me in the room. I knew Melinda wanted me to think that she was slutty. A gold digger, maybe? I didn't feel great about it, but part of me felt a little smug that there was a dent in Emerald's shiny veneer. But then again, a little part of me was impressed that she was bold enough to be a slut in the first place—if that's what was going on.

"Anyway, it's dark in my room, so I've gotta put my makeup

on in the living room until I buy a lamp. It's all about lighting," she said.

For some reason, the dramatic way she said that made me forget about Emerald and laugh. Melinda laughed, too. "I know that sounds ridiculous. But that's a thing of mine. Lighting, setting, *mood,*" she mused. "I'm into theater and personas and stuff. Faking it."

We caught eyes again.

"Faking it?"

"Fake it till I make it. Try on different people till I find the one I like."

"Oh," I said. Melinda didn't have the eager *hi, how are you, what are you studying* vibe that everyone else seemed to have at NYU. She was reserved and a little mysterious. And I liked that.

"Like you." She turned and looked me up and down. "You have an interesting look. What are you? Mexican? Egyptian?" She picked up a strand of my hair, that mix of straight and shiny, thin and wispy.

"I'm mixed. Half white, a quarter Chinese, a quarter black."

Her eyes skimmed over every inch of my face: the big lips, the wide nose, the frizz at the hairline. She strained for some definition, but I've always defied those. At least when it comes to looks.

"Hm. That's cool. Guys love that."

I burst into laughter. "I can't say I have much experience in that area."

She shrugged. "Well, dude, if I had that exotic thing going on, I'd be working it."

"Yeah, okay," I said dubiously . . . and somewhat flattered.

"What about you, what are you into?" she asked.

"I'm in grad school for Food Studies, doing an independent study, but it's been a confusing couple of weeks—I think I may be forced to reevaluate my entire identity and sense of self over the weekend." I was trying for funny, but Melinda didn't laugh. Instead, she flicked her eyes over my features again.

"Food is cool." She nodded blankly. "And, hell, you're in New York City for the foreseeable future. Welcome to the reinvention capital of the world. Be whoever the fuck you want."

I continued watching her as she dabbed a deep eggplant color on her lips. "Well, I've gotta get ready for dinner." I'd decided that Elliott and I would eat at Bakushan, a brand-new place in our neighborhood that was getting a lot of press. "See you later."

"See ya," she said, studying herself in the mirror.

Fake it till you make it, I repeated to myself. I had always liked that phrase, but now it would come in extra handy.

WHEN I GOT out of the bathroom, Melinda had left the living room and Emerald had come home wearing one of her men's coats. But from where? My new roommate had planted an ugly seed and now my mind was watering it.

She sat on the couch pulling on a piece of tangled T-shirt fabric. "I made this convoluted strappy shirt and now I don't know how to put it on." She picked up a cookie beside her. "Do you want one of these? They're from Health Haven on First Ave. All organic and maybe vegan?"

"No, thanks. Elliott and I are grabbing dinner."

"Your Madison Park Tavern job is so sick, it's incredible," Emerald said. "I bet the fashion is amazing. Madison Park Tavern isn't too far from a lot of magazines and fashion houses. Last year I worked for this jewelry designer named Oji, and she took me there when *Vogue* featured a piece I designed. We had this amazing salad with, like, these corn pieces? But they weren't, like, corn? They were, you know, meatier."

"Hominy?" I answered.

"Whatever. But anyway, those editors and designers love to

go to Madison Park Tavern and schmooze and fool themselves into thinking those salads are low-cal. Have you checked any coats yet? What designers have you seen?"

"I just went for a menu tasting. Tomorrow is my first day." I didn't want to tell her about the people I had met, how I had fallen a little bit in love. It's not like they were real secrets, but I didn't feel like sharing. I didn't want her to compare her New York with mine, because I knew at this point I would lose.

So I changed the subject. "You were in *Vogue*? Then why didn't you stay working with Oji?"

Emerald scoffed and picked up the T-shirt again. "Because I'm looking for the NBT."

"No big thing?" I guessed.

"No!" she said, throwing the T-shirt at me. "Next. Big. Thing. Sure, staying at Oji would have been easy. But, you know, all these people approached me. Investors, photographers, fashion designers, reporters. What was I going to do, just stay there and push Oji's brand? No; my design, my attention. If a magazine wants to feature me and my work, I take them up on it. There's nothing wrong with a little *piston*."

"*Piston*?" I gulped. Emerald was going for it. Like the ice pop girl in the park, she never seemed to waver over her future.

"*Piston* . . . it's French. Literally, a piston. It means string-pulling. And speaking of *piston,* I was wondering—what's your uniform at the restaurant?"

"Everyone wears a suit," I said.

"What kind of suit?"

"A suit. Like a regular, plain suit."

"Let me see yours."

"It's nothing special," I said. I went into my room and returned with the suit my mom and I had bought before I went to college. The cut and fabric weren't great, but it was all I had.

"Oh, that? Is that okay?"

I threw it onto my bed before she asked to see the label. "What do you mean, is it okay? Why wouldn't it be okay? It's a suit."

"I don't know, it's just sort of like—" She scrunched her pretty face. "It's like . . . blah. You're so much better than that . . . thing."

I knew this exact feeling from Yale, and I'd known that it would only get worse in New York. At Yale, tons of girls wore designer everything, as if five-hundred-dollar heels and three-thousand-dollar purses were a God-given right. And for some girls, they were. They were the ones who slept in penthouse apartments rather than tiny dorms. They carried their books in designer handbags and took taxis to class. They all hung out with each other, even if they lived worlds away: New York, L.A., Houston, sure, but also Dubai, Hong Kong, Paris, Santorini. Upon setting foot on campus they knew people like me were not of their kind. They recognized each other through some code embedded in their clothes, their hair, their scent.

Yale had been the first time I paid attention to what I wore. But when I tried to step things up, I usually failed. Though no one ever called me out on it, I knew I'd never been up to snuff. My jeans weren't the right shade. The pattern of my shirt was too outdated. I could follow someone else's outfit exactly, only in a cheaper form, but something always gave me away: the proportions, the fabric.

But Elliott didn't care about that stuff, and as I fell more in love with him, I'd left behind those insecurities. Those other people didn't matter. He liked me as is. And now, I couldn't wait for him to arrive so we could hightail it out of there.

"It's not a fashion magazine, it's a restaurant. And no one bothers with anything fancy. Everyone wears things like this."

"No, they don't." Emerald laughed. "I guarantee it. They're wearing Hugo Boss, Tom Ford, maybe Armani for the older guys. I bet even the bussers are in designer things. They'd probably buy you a suit if you were a full-time employee, but this is a way for you to show initiative. A fab suit."

I wanted to say that was insane. The restaurant was about the food, I thought, echoing a familiar pep talk I'd often given myself at Yale: Yale was about the education.

But I knew that wasn't the complete picture. Yale hadn't gotten its reputation for nothing. Even though those rich kids hardly went to class and spent their nights taking car services to exclusive clubs in New York City, they still got amazing jobs after graduation. They skipped the hard part and went straight to choice placements at hedge funds, law offices, and consulting firms. Others became overnight bestselling authors, entrepreneurs. One girl, the daughter of an ambiguously wealthy family from Switzerland, had become a glossy "lifestyle consultant," growing more and more omnipresent in the media by the day.

Madison Park Tavern wasn't just about the food. Like every other restaurant of its ilk, it was also about the ambiance, the rhythms of the staff, the smallest details—right down to the waitresses' frizz-free buns. It was about the people who came to eat there, who made deals over lunch and whispered secrets over dinner.

And now Emerald wanted to get me a suit, so I could be part of that machinery.

"Well, what do you think?" she asked. "This shouldn't be such a hard decision. Tomorrow we'll go uptown to this thrift store called Trina. You have that small, ass-less Upper East Side body, so those clothes will fit you. We'll buy you a suit on the cheap, and then I can tailor it for you."

"But won't the suits still be five hundred dollars or something?" Of course I wanted to wear designer things. I wished I could be like those girls at Yale who could just borrow the family's credit card and take the train down for a Manhattan shopping spree. But that wasn't me.

"Don't worry about it," Emerald said. "The owner is a family friend, and I've been going there a long time, even though it would take a stick of butter and a prayer for me to fit into most of that stuff."

I had spent so much time in college trying to squelch my curiosity about those things. Clothes. Nightlife. Restaurants. Real Estate. New York's obsessions. I was afraid of cracking the shell I had worked so hard to put up and was about to decline her offer when the door opened.

"Hey, restaurant girl!" Elliott greeted me, just me, with a smile. I held on to that until he looked at Emerald and his attention—along with my resolve—vanished. "And hey to you, too, Emerald. Why does it seem like you have connections with everyone in the city? I just met, like, three people who know you."

"Hey, you're in Manhattan now. It's all about who you know," she said, puffing up her chest, which looked even more robust under a huge silk chiffon scarf.

"Anyway!" I said. The last thing I wanted was to let Emerald go on about her "connections." "Em was just saying how I need to get a new suit for work," I said to Elliott, sure he'd veto any unnecessary suits. "Because she thinks my current one is too 'blah.' "

"Oh, yeah, that's a good idea."

I glared at him, dumbstruck. "Really?"

"I think you'd look nice in a new suit," he said. But did he mean "new"? Or did he mean designer? Something picked out by Emerald?

"See?" Emerald said, basking in her triumph. "Come on, I can even start our consultation tonight. Learn how to take some *piston* and let me give you an outfit for your dinner."

"No. That's unnecessary. We have to—"

"Oh, what's the harm?" Elliott asked. "Just for fun." He followed Emerald into her room and they turned around, waiting for me to follow.

"Come on," Emerald said. "Your boyfriend wants a fresh piece of tail."

I didn't laugh, but I saw Elliott stifle a little bit of a smile. I dragged myself toward Emerald's room, but stood in the doorway, my arms crossed.

"This would be so flattering on you," she said, pulling a dress out of her closet. "It's sort of Halston-like and would show off your cute boobs and accentuate your flat stomach. And then this . . ." She held up a cropped bomber jacket. "It's also from the seventies and, you know, toughens up the look. So you don't look so pretty."

She peered at me, waiting for a response. Elliott sat in Emerald's chartreuse velvet armchair, amused.

"Okay, I'll try it on." I didn't have the energy for Emerald to fawn over me.

I grabbed the hanger and ducked back into my room to slip on the dress, and it was, indeed, flattering. The red fabric gathered at the bust, swept down my sides, and came out in a wispy trumpet shape at my knees. I put on the leather jacket, and though I never would have picked this out myself, again, Emerald was right. I didn't feel so green and scared, but rather strong and protected. No wonder so many women in New York wore leather.

"You look *incredible*!" Emerald jumped up and down when I stepped out into the living room. Then she calmed herself by admiring her work. "Oh, the red looks so good on your skin. And the leather. It's too perfect. Keep those. They don't fit me anymore."

"Wow!" Elliott said. "You look great."

"One last thing," Emerald added. "Take this purse and seal the deal. It's the latest Proenza Schouler bag. The PS1 is done and now they're onto this. It won't be in stores for another year."

I looked down at the purse, a blue, green, and gold rectangle with inlaid triangles and textures. Some pony hair, some leather, maybe snake or skate?

"The purse is a loaner. But don't even think about returning that other stuff."

"Okay," I griped. I hated being put in this situation, but the clothes and especially the purse were so beautiful. I looked better and, in some ways, felt better. Somehow, Emerald, who barely knew me, had cracked the code of fabric and proportions. I had tried so hard to get this right, but she could have done it blindfolded. It was a special magic.

"But no more dress-up after tonight," I said. I couldn't handle anything more than this. Then I turned to my traitorous boyfriend and steered him out of the room. "Come on," I said. "We need to get going."

BAKUSHAN HAD ONLY been open for a couple of months, but expectations were already sky-high. Still, few people had mentioned the food. Instead, everyone was writing about the up-and-coming chef, Pascal Fox. According to nearly every article, he'd dropped out of college and worked at top French restaurants around the world. Then, at twenty-five and on every "30 under 30" list in existence, he had received an offer to take over L'Escalier, a cathedral-ceilinged white-tablecloth institution in Midtown. But just as New York was ready to inaugurate him into a realm of Immortal Chefs synonymous with a certain level of luxurious precision, Pascal had said he would open a place on his own. He didn't have a location or a concept—or so he'd said in his interviews—just a conviction that he didn't want to fall into the trap of being yet another French chef at another fancy restaurant.

So there we were, in front of his brand-new place. It was hard to label it. I had read neo-modernist and Asian-American eclectic. The food was hard to pin down, but the inside was just cool, at least from my sidewalk vantage point. It was 5:45 and already there was a forty-five-minute wait for a spot at one of the communal, no-reservation tables.

I looked at the crowd while we waited and saw a couple of girls dressed in tight, short dresses. One of them held a food magazine with Pascal Fox's face on the cover against a blurred kitchen background. I stole a peek at the photo. His eyes were a deep black-brown with a streak of gold. His hair was charmingly messed up, longish bits going every which way, casting shadows on his sculpted cheekbones.

That was the other thing. Pascal was exceedingly good-looking. I hadn't paid attention to the hype around his looks, but seeing these girls swoon over his photo made his handsomeness hard to ignore. And . . . the pictures. I'm only human.

There was no mistaking it. This was New York dining. Restaurants weren't just the food, but also the attractiveness of the chef, the beat of the music, the wait out the door. And then, there was something else.

As Elliott fiddled around on his phone, I watched a group of women waltz right into the restaurant. Everyone waiting gave them the evil eye as they teetered inside with their sky-high shoes and designer outfits. These weren't the obvious short, tight dresses of the other girls. These women weren't the most beautiful, either. But they were magnetic. An Asian girl wore her hair in purple-gray dreadlocks, complimenting her floral wide-legged pants and crop-top bra. A bald black woman wore a blue knee-length dress with cut-outs across her clavicle, and—

dangerously—over her hips. A full-figured woman had wrapped herself in a black dress and a matching floor-length cape. They walked right in and were seated in the front, a striking sight even through the glass and crowds.

New York restaurants were about the swagger.

I was watching them look over their menus when someone walked up to me, a big red-headed, red-faced man-child. Kyle Lorimer, from the reception. He wore a short-sleeved plaid shirt and came at me with his arms extended.

"Hi, Tia! How's it going!" His gaze switched from me to Elliott, Elliott to me. "I'm Kyle, nice to meet you," he said to Elliott. Elliott shook his hand and introduced himself.

"Guess what?" Kyle continued. "I got the Helen Lansky internship. I heard you got the Madison Park Tavern gig. Congrats!"

A surge of anxiety rushed through me. I may have liked Madison Park Tavern, but the fact that I didn't get Helen, after so much work and buildup, still stung.

"Oh, thanks," I managed. "Congrats to you, too!" I mustered up all the cheeriness I could.

"Yeah, I'm pretty psyched," Kyle said. "Madison Park Tavern should be awesome, too. I've got to head out, but enjoy Bakushan. I've been dying to go."

"Thanks, man," Elliott said.

"See you later," I said, hoping my smile didn't look as fake as it felt.

Kyle left and I returned my gaze to the women in the front window. The beautiful, compelling women who'd walked into one of the hottest restaurants in town and made it theirs.

I looked over every inch of their table. Their hair, their outfits, their shoes. The way they held their menus with the tips of their fingers and drank their cocktails with their lips puckered just so.

They reminded me of similar posses in college, but here those girls—no, women—were different. They weren't born into their privilege. These women looked self-made, women who had formed their looks and identities according to their exact design.

And then my eye landed on something I had in common with the leader of the group, a tall brunette with a long, regal nose and a white padded bustier over a gossamer white strappy dress.

And that's when I walked up to the hostess, a model-in-training wearing inky black leggings, an embroidered vest, and open-toed platform boots. My heart was pounding, but New York City isn't for the weak. Emerald's clothes weren't just armor. They were also a weapon.

"Excuse me," I said, making sure Emerald's straight-off-the-runway purse was in front of me. "How long for the table again?"

Her eyes snapped to the shine of the purse. I straightened up and looked at her imperiously. Faking it until I made it. I wouldn't let Kyle and his giddiness about Helen rattle me. Emerald and her judging eyes wouldn't faze me. I would model myself after those women.

"Of course, Miss," the hostess responded. She closed the reservation book and turned on her six-inch platform. "Follow me."

I called Elliott over and the rest of the crowd collectively huffed that we had cut them all. But I didn't listen to their complaints. Instead, I kept my ear out for the hostess's words.

"By the way, I *love* your purse."

WE SAT IN the front of the restaurant, alongside the crew of mysterious power women.

"We're so exposed," Elliott said, as people tapped at the window, *ooh*ing at our neighbors' dishes. "This place is good, right?"

"Yeah," I said. "It's supposed to be awesome. Though the menu is pretty controversial."

"Controversial, huh? Well, I'll leave it up to you to navigate the terrain."

"Come on, really? Order with me. Please?"

"No, no, don't worry about it," he said. "Go crazy!"

"Okay . . ." I said. "What about . . . gizzard porridge?" That was actually on the menu.

"Sounds fabulous."

I giggled. "Or what about the pork with three sweetbread jellies?"

"Only three? I like at least a half dozen."

I held the menu up like an inspector with her clipboard.

"What about the strawberry ramen with peanut broth?" I challenged.

"Ah, the sweet nectar of my youth."

I spread out my elbows. "Okay, Mr. Chambers. I see your palate is quite sophisticated. Which means you simply *must* have the poached toothfish with nitro-chocolate ribbons."

"Darling, it would be heresy to not."

Elliott and I burst out laughing and a couple sitting next to us gave us dirty looks, which only made us laugh more. This was beginning to feel like old times.

"All right, for real," I said, rubbing his hand from across the table. "What do you want?"

"You decide, T. I trust you."

I gave in and decided on three of the most talked-about dishes: buttermilk Parmesan flan with maple broth, pork and snail dumplings with effervescent chive oil, and beef meatballs with deep-fried cilantro chips. They weren't our typical restaurant orders, but that was the whole point.

While we waited for our food, Elliott told me about his New York Botanical Garden job studying poisons and their medicinal applications. They were getting ready for an exhibit and partnering with Beth Israel Medical Center and Cornell Medical College.

"The doctors visited the lab today and were impressed with our work. It looks like by the time the exhibit comes out we'll have actual case studies from patients. People have been really receptive. Today someone said that his aches and pains have disappeared since we administered treatment. Between the people and the facility and the project, I feel . . ."

"You feel . . . what?" He had me at the edge of my seat.

He gulped. "I feel like I'm living my dream."

"Elliott . . ." I started. I jumped out of my chair and hugged him. "That's so amazing. I'm so happy for you."

"And things are good with you. You like the restaurant."

It wasn't lost on me that he hadn't asked that as a question. He always saw the world in its best light, and though that was the thing that made me love him, I wished in that moment that he could help me with these darker feelings—of insecurity and disappointment. Of doubt and regret.

With my best happy smile, I said, "Yeah, it was great," just as busboys with nose rings poured us more water and our food arrived.

"It's just . . . I don't know. I came in thinking that I'd be with Helen. That was my track, you know? But now I'm kinda doubting my reasoning. We're in New York, having dinner at one of the hottest new restaurants. I'm starting at a four-star restaurant tomorrow. People care about these places. Important people."

"Important people?" he said, tucking his chin.

With Elliott, mentioning status always qualified as a faux pas. Even in college, he'd been so sure of himself. But now I was starting to think that he didn't have the full perspective. Status underlined everything in New York. Even at NYU, people didn't talk about their mentorships as much as what restaurant they'd tried, what club they'd gotten into, what celebrity they'd chatted up on some cool but unknown-to-the-plebeians street.

"I'm thinking this Madison Park Tavern thing is for the best. I can always go back to Helen. And besides, she's not about this sort of stuff," I tried, gesturing to our meal. "I tasted such incredible dishes at work today, and look at what we have here at Bakushan! These dumplings are amazing. It's one thing to have the snail, which is ambitious on its own, then the pork and the effervescent chives? It's genius, right? The sauce is incredible, like a headfirst flavor dive. But Helen Lansky, does she really innovate?"

I thought I was protesting too much after seeing Kyle, overcompensating for some insecurity. But maybe that was me rationalizing. This food truly got to me and my allegiances were starting to slide. I still loved Helen, but the restaurants had their own siren song.

I looked at Elliott's plate and saw it was untouched, minus some half-eaten bites moved way to the side.

Now my mouth dropped in disbelief. "You didn't like what I ordered?"

"Snail? I mean . . ." he said. "It's not my thing. And it tastes kinda sandy? Anyway, we can talk about Helen again. You've changed your mind about her?"

"No, hold on. You didn't eat anything?" I took his uneaten bites personally. I had picked this restaurant, ordered the dishes. Even when my college cooking experiments had gone haywire, he'd still eaten my food.

"We could have ordered other things on the menu," I said, the air yanked out of me.

"I know. But I wanted you to order, since this place is for you."

"I thought you'd like those dishes. Was I totally off?"

Elliott squirmed. "This just isn't my style. Honestly, I like it when you cook stuff from Helen's cookbooks. That's way more edible to me."

I lost my appetite. And then *she* walked in, ignoring the line outside.

Emerald had changed into something different—a low-cut white tank top that fluttered in front of her cleavage, jeans, black knee-high boots, and one of her suspicious men's coats. I was feeling pretty good in this dress, but that confidence vanished the second I saw her.

"My friends got held up, so I thought I'd find you guys!" Emerald said. "The line out there is crazy! Who knew Bakashu would be the place to be?" She leaned in to look at Elliott's plate and I swear he looked down her shirt.

"Bakushan," I corrected her flatly.

"Oh! Haha! Right, I knew that. So what are you eating? This place is cool. I like it." She grabbed a menu from the hostess station, took one quick look at it, and pulled it over her mouth as if she were telling us a secret. "But the menu is weird, isn't it? Snail, chocolate . . . what's screwpine? I guess I'll get the chicken? I'll wipe some of the wacky stuff off." Then she took off her coat and sat at our table.

"I'll get the chicken, too," Elliott said, looking away, then at me, then away again. "Sorry T, I'm pretty hungry."

"You could have said you wanted the chicken . . ." I said, keeping my tone as flat as possible so Emerald couldn't detect that things had gone sour. I looked at Elliott and said as much as possible with my eyes, *Please, let's just have a nice dinner?*

But he didn't see, or didn't care, because he began chatting with Emerald.

"How did you even get in here?" Elliott asked in disturbingly easy tones. "We had to wait."

Emerald shrugged in a way that was at once modest and boastful, *Oh, it's no big deal if you're me.* "Wait, what's the chef's name?" she asked. "I think I read about him in *ELLE*."

"Ooooh, *ELLE*," Elliott mocked. "He must be a big deal, then."

"He is a big deal!" Emerald said, slapping him with the menu. "Or at least he's cute!"

I wanted to yell *Enough*. I wanted to redo the whole night—the outfit from Emerald, seeing Kyle, my orders off the menu.

"His name is Pascal Fox," I said quietly, way too quietly for normal conversation, and unintelligible in this loud restaurant.

The open kitchen's steam and smoke masked Pascal a bit, but I still caught a glimpse. Even though he was getting a lot of media attention, he didn't look like a man who cared about photo shoots and celebrity. He looked like a serious chef with a lot on the line. He sprinted sideways through the narrow galley, threw something out. His chef's jacket was rolled to his elbows, revealing a mural of indecipherable tattoos.

In a faraway place in my mind, I heard the music of the restaurant and Elliott and Emerald, maybe talking about work or liking chicken. I didn't regret coming to Bakushan anymore. Only bringing Elliott there. It was horrible to say, but why had I thought he would enjoy it?

I stabbed a snail-and-pork dumpling, a half-eaten bite that Elliott had probably all-too-happily put back on the serving plate, and ate it. And maybe it was in my head, but this time I tasted a bit of sand.

The waitress came back. "Two chickens . . . for the couple?"

I sneered at the oblivious woman, then looked back at Emerald and Elliott. It was a tone-deaf amateur mistake, but I couldn't blame her. The two of them talked, they laughed. They relaxed while I squirmed. They looked like a couple, cool and easy while I was still stuck in some anxious liminal space where you realize that the choices you've made might not be the right ones.

Just then I looked up to see Chef Pascal standing over our table.

"Excuse me for one moment." He reached over me, and I think Emerald and I both gasped aloud at him. He smelled like bacon and caramelized onions and had a movie-star-perfect face, soft but still chiseled. A little stubble. Dark skin and big eyes with long, thick lashes. And the gold streaks in his eyes? Even better in person, luminous and crackling with light.

Now I felt like Melinda in the living room, asking me what I was. Was he Egyptian? Mexican? Spanish? But of course he wasn't like me at all. He was closer to a model or an actor than anyone like me.

Pascal didn't appear to notice our gawking. He removed the housemade kimchi-ghee hot sauce from our table and replaced it with a new bottle. He gave a soft, barely there smile, then continued to the other tables, leaving almost every girl—and many guys—shivering in his wake.

"Ha!" Emerald said, clearly exhilarated. "That was a rush, huh?"

"Yeah . . ." Elliott struggled. "That guy . . . has a lot of tattoos."

I watched Pascal march back into the kitchen. From the pass, where the dining room met the kitchen, I thought I saw him look back at me, too.

Yeah, right, Tia, I thought just as quickly. Like that could ever happen. He was probably looking at those other women, the important ones, the ones who didn't get their table using borrowed clothes.

Emerald didn't come home after Bakushan, and I spent the night reading everything I could about New York restaurants. I wanted to soak up everything—the places to be, the people to know, the things to say. No more being the ignorant one at the table, the sucker who waited in line in the shoddy outfit. I wouldn't be left behind.

The apartment building quieted and New York briefly rested, but I stayed up.

I visited Carey's Madison Park Tavern Wiki page and ravenously absorbed details about the menu, the flowers, even the soap in the bathroom.

And I looked up those acronyms I'd seen on Jake's reservation sheet, to see what lay on the other side:

LOL: Lots of Love.

SFN: Something for Nothing. Typically an appetizer or dessert.

Bubbles: Champagne upon Arrival.

WFM: Welcome from Manager.

And then, the term that encompassed them all: PX. From the French.

Personne Extraordinaire.

Even as I grew tired, that knowledge strengthened me. By the time I heard the birds singing and the sun had crept up in the sky, I had something to hold on to. Knowledge, authority, direction. And a goal: to become an extraordinary person.

Chapter 5

I AWOKE THREE HOURS LATER TO MY ROOMMATE'S UN-made-up face.

"Hey there, sunshine! Let's go shopping for your suit, then brunch. Tonight's your first night of work, right?"

"Jesus, Emerald. I thought you weren't a morning person. What time is it?"

"I'm excited to doll you up. Did you have fun last night? You looked so good in that dress. Dinner was so-so, though. Did you try my chicken?"

"No. I didn't. And you're not supposed to go to Bakushan for the boring chicken dish. You go there for—"

"Yeah, yeah. So sue me."

She threw the blanket off my body and pulled me out of bed. I was going shopping whether I liked it or not.

THE STORE STOOD on one of those ultra-rich streets lined with brownstones and private garages. Each house evoked a different style. This one was old money—look at the heavy velvet draping, the bulky antique furniture, the oil portraits of unsmiling ancestors on every wall. And this one belonged to a showbiz family—was that a hot tub on the roof? That one was home to serious art collectors who must not have had children because everything visible through the window was white, expensive, and/or precariously perched.

A chime sounded as we entered the store, a narrow slice of a room ringed with tightly packed clothes. Shoes lined the floors, hats and bags overtook the top shelves. The clothes hung according to color, but that was the only sense of order I could see. Within each color, there were summery dresses, heavyweight coats, sequined confections. Other stores rotated their stock with the seasons, but this place seemed like it stayed the same.

"Heeey, Em . . ." the shop owner trilled. She was a big-bosomed woman, with fluffed, feathered hair. "Haven't seen you in forever! Tell me everything that's happening in your life."

"Hey, Sherri. I'm swamped with this new design project and I hardly come uptown anymore."

"Oh. Boo-hoo. So what can I do for you ladies? You have a party to go to or something?" She wiggled her fingers at the word *party,* as if it were magical.

"Ha! I wish. Actually, we're shopping for Tia here. Her clothes are a little lame and she needs a suit for Madison Park Tavern, stat."

Had she really said *lame*? Right. Thanks, Emerald.

"Oh! When are you going?" Sherri asked.

I laughed. Surely more Upper East Side people dined at Madison Park Tavern than worked there. But I didn't correct her. "Tonight, actually."

"I think she's a Jil Sander girl," Emerald yelled as she walked to the black clothes in the back, trailing her fingers across the silks, cashmeres, and leathers. "Like, sorta boring, but with a twist."

"Yes, yes," Sherri said, her eyes widening, though she had the good manners not to repeat the "boring but with a twist" direction.

"Try this one," Emerald said. "And this." She held out a Jil Sander suit and a Diane von Furstenberg suit, which had a ruffled neckline and a tie around the waist. I had heard of Diane von Furstenberg, but of course had never worn her or Jil Sander. As much as I had hated the fact that Emerald had dragged me here, trying on these clothes excited me. But I wouldn't give her the satisfaction.

"You'll hate this DVF one. But you should try it on. It'll be good for you."

I grabbed both hangers from her.

"Fine," I said. "But I don't understand why I can't wear my Banana Republic suit." Damn. I had tried to keep the brand a secret from her. I entered the fitting room, undressed, and started to put on one of the suits. "And if you were going to give me so much grief, I could have come myself. The 6 train isn't hard to find."

"Whatever, Tia. You would have walked into Ann Taylor and bought a regular mall outfit. What an upgrade. Seriously, though. You don't want the guests at Madison Park Tavern to shade their eyes when they turn over their coats."

"I don't care," I replied, zipping up the Jil Sander skirt. "I never asked for your help anyway." I stepped out with a dramatic thud, to show her that I hated coming here.

But suddenly I didn't. I saw my reflection in the three-way mirror. I had put on the dressing room's spare set of heels and pulled my hair up in a bun, like the waitresses at work. The suit shined like gunmetal, sleek as sharkskin. It was thin and pliant, shaping me in the right spots and letting the curves hang out in others. It was a thing of beauty. The person who looked back at me was sophisticated and poised, as if she belonged at a place like Madison Park Tavern.

Emerald came up behind me.

"Look, you're gorgeous, okay? I realize I interrupted your dinner last night. That was a jerk move of me. I'm sorry." She spoke into my ear and I began to sweat inside this beautiful suit by a designer I had learned about five minutes ago.

"Elliott and I were trying to catch up," I said. "He works all the way in the Bronx, and I hardly see him."

"But you guys love each other, right? What's worrying you?"

"I guess I just feel a little lost," I admitted. "And . . ."

Then her phone rang and Emerald clammed up. "Oh, Tia, I totally forgot I have an event! And now I'm late. The suit's fifty dollars, I already worked it out with Sherri."

She left so fast the bells on the door smacked across the glass. I thought back to what Melinda had implied—that Emerald was a flake and a flirt, someone to be wary of. Melinda was on to something. Emerald had something sketchy to hide.

The suit still had its original tags: $2,500. The store had marked it down to $700, and then Emerald got me a $650 discount. She had really hooked me up.

Sherri rang up the skirt and jacket, then put them in a bag. "Sweetie . . ." she said after inspecting my face, likely soured by Emerald's hasty exit. "I've known Emerald since she was a little girl. She's had a hard life and I'm sure she's doing the best she can to be a good friend." She handed me my bag. "Enjoy your suit. It's a fabulous one."

I didn't doubt the suit's fabulousness. But a very hard life? As far as I could tell, it didn't seem very difficult to be beautiful and talented and connected. All I had seen from Emerald was glossiness and unexpected generosity and an ease in the city that made me so tense.

I didn't thank her for the beautiful suit and never asked where she ran off to. I needed to keep my distance, so she wouldn't have such a hold on me, wouldn't make me feel so uncool and dull and common.

THAT NIGHT, SEPTEMBER turned from summer into fall.

I slid through the revolving door and found the restaurant had already transformed to match. My first official night at Madison Park Tavern. A tall bouquet hung over the front foyer: winding tapering sticks, eucalyptus leaves, tiny bells hanging on wayward stems, exotic berry-colored flowers the shape of lily pads, purple-veined curly kale, featherlight white poppies ringed on the inside with black, like a goth girl's eyeliner. I smoothed my Jil Sander skirt against my hips and walked up to the dining room. The fireplace crackled and the linens were a tad more gold, not the crisp white of newness, but something with a more weathered patina.

"Happy first day," Carey said. "Are you excited?"

I paused to get my bearings. Even though from coat check I couldn't see anyone eating or smell the aromas from the kitchen, I could still appreciate where I was: Madison Park Tavern, a four-star restaurant in New York City.

"Yeah, really excited," I replied.

The cooler temperatures outside made coat check the place to be. I coddled every coat and bag, warmly welcomed every guest. There were big potbellied men and soft-in-the-shoulders women who looked like the adoring and generous Pop-Pop and Grammy children love to visit. There were younger men who shoved their packages in my face. One gave me a twenty-dollar tip in front of his guests, who didn't look all that impressed. I got a small thrill taking the coats of some local news anchors and one big-time news anchor, and an even bigger thrill when about ten reality TV show contestants came in to celebrate something.

But of all the faces and facelifts, one man caught my attention. He handed me his coat with two hands, as if handing a flag to a fallen soldier's family. I mirrored his movements and his cold fingers touched the insides of my wrists. I watched his skinny silhouette walk upstairs, his slacks hitting more air than leg. He wore a linen shirt with a Nehru collar, the look of a genteel Indian diplomat, which threw me off. But something about him seemed familiar.

When I got a free moment—between a fur-collared jacket from MaxMara and a bag from Ferragamo—I looked at his coat again, in case it provided a clue. Even in my short coat check career, I knew cashmere was normally just the shell of the coat, with silk or wool for the lining. His coat had cashmere inside and out. It was cold out, but not that cold. Though if I had a coat this soft, I'd find any excuse to wear it.

A note dropped out.

Good evening. Stay on your toes tonight.

A tingle ran down my spine as I turned the velvety blue cardstock in my hands. *Stay on your toes?* Who should stay on their toes? For what?

I heard a cough at the coat check opening, then turned and held out my hands.

It was Jake. "Oh. Hi, sorry, I thought you were a guest."

"Tia. I have a couple questions for you." Jake's usually composed hands moved double-time and a cowlick was showing itself on top of his otherwise perfectly styled hair.

"Okay, what do you need?"

"I don't need anything. I want to know what you know. How is the shrimp toast prepared?"

"Oh, um," I said, collecting myself. "Brioche is marinated

overnight in shrimp stock, then caked with Indian prawn and langoustine mousse." I had read that in Carey's Wiki last night.

"Where are the langoustines from?"

"Montauk."

"And how would you recommend serving the salmon?"

"Which salmon?"

"Both salmons. The sous-vide and the salad."

"The sous-vide should be served well." I remembered reading that sometime between two and three A.M. "Because it stays moist in the pouch no matter what and the greater cooking time allows the flavors to infuse longer. Medium-rare to rare for the salad, to show off the quality of the product."

"And where do you put the bone bowl for the frog legs in tarragon gremolata?"

"What do you mean?"

"Do you put the bowl on the right or left of the guest?"

"Neither. The frog legs are deboned. No bowl is necessary."

"Good answer," he said, visibly relaxing. "Listen, we have a full house and thirty PX tables, most of them unexpected. We're in the weeds in there. This is a very unusual circumstance and I need your help. Will you backserve regular tables so we can concentrate on the PXs? You'll trail Henri on half his tables and we'll let the hostess do coat check."

"Backserve tonight? You mean work in the dining room?" My voice must have jumped an octave.

"Yes, work in the dining room. My God, let's not say everything twice, okay?"

I immediately lost interest in the mystery note and stuffed it in my pocket.

"Of course," I said. "Whatever you need."

As Jake handed me my white apron, I saw that Jake's idea of "in the weeds" would have looked serene to 98 percent of other restaurants. But I had already gotten a sense of the staff's collective competence, and indeed the air had turned tense. In the back, a couple of waiters were sorting out the chits, little cheat sheets on tables' preferences.

"No! Dean Chariss is on table nine," a waiter whispered.

"No, that's Frank Harris. He's a friend of Yael Jean."

I saw a waitress anxiously watching a wine chiller water bath, waiting for a bottle of champagne to come to the guest's exact preferred temperature.

Jake was already in service mode, smiling and shaking hands, patting backs and pouring wine.

I only had to watch Angel, the wait captain, to learn how to act. I hadn't yet seen him on the dining room stage and found he moved with a regal grace, his usual swagger tightened to a light-footed march.

Henri flagged me and led the way toward the "regular" tables. Each table silently screamed for a fresh this, a folded that. As backserver, I was to set the table (with the right silverware), take away the plates (without rushing the guests), and perform a variety of hand-touches—grating cheese, pouring soup, ladling sauce. Steaks needed a steak knife. A fish dish required a fish fork and fish spoon, and a fish soup needed yet another designated spoon. Surf and turf was a bridge I'd cross when I got to it.

"Here's place one, two, three, four," Henri said pointedly. "Two and four are the same. Don't get them mixed up."

I loved the food at my fingertips and the smells in my nostrils. I loved being inside the meticulous clockwork, and for the first time since I had arrived in New York, I hit my stride.

During a short lull in service, Jake gave me and a couple other waiters and backservers a quick run-down of the PXs, most of whom I hadn't recognized at coat check. "It's a perfect storm. A third of these people used fake names and another third dropped in after the *New Yorker* Festival. They weren't on the books and we had to open up the private dining room."

Saveur magazine editors doing a tasting at table 7. There, at table 3, a kindhearted food science expert. Tucked in the corner, a chef with a ten-restaurant empire in Chicago, eating with his family. Then, at table 12, a celebrity news anchor and her famous director husband. I had noticed her at coat check, but not her date. At table 1, a disgusting lecher of a man with a prostitute dressed in red lace. No one wanted to sit next to him, but he always spent more than $5,000 on dinner for two, making him the most important—and therefore most pampered—guest that night. Barring few exceptions, money put the *extraordinaire* in *personne extraordinaire.*

A couple of diplomats, some restaurant investors, wine importers. They all needed varying degrees of special treatment. For some, the whole meal was comped; for others, just a glass of champagne.

I moved around the room, picking up bread baskets, refilling water. My suit had an obvious air of quality to it. Guests respected my space and my actions, though at the end of the day, I was the one serving them. I mimicked the other backservers and soon I got into their rhythm. The dining room was my dance floor and I was enjoying myself.

"You're doing great," Angel said in passing. He rushed away before I could say anything back.

I enjoyed Angel's approval and knew that Jake had been watching me all night. If I played my cards right, maybe he'd promote me and I'd be in the dining room after all.

Then Henri nodded his head and I followed him to a table in the private dining room, where the mystery man from the coat check sat.

Strangely, Jake hadn't mentioned him. He sat tucked in a dark corner of the room, which was too small to have a "view," only a narrow line of sight into the main dining room. His three dining companions looked mild-mannered and a little serious. I couldn't get a good look at his face.

I lowered their midmeal palate cleansers to the table as Henri walked away.

"Excuse me? Can you tell me what this is?" asked one man, not the mystery guy.

Instead of pointing, I gestured with my whole hand as Jake had taught me. "This is a grapefruit terrine with pickled borage flower." I felt the mystery man studying me as I tried to keep my voice steady.

"Thank you," a woman said. "Looks delicious."

Was he from Yonkers? Someone I had seen around NYU? I rotated to the other side of the table to make sure the silverware was ready for their next course. And then my eyes met his. Eye-liner rimmed his eyes and I think he was wearing some sort of dark foundation. But I recognized him.

Of course, he looked nothing like his pictures in the restaurant, big-cheeked and round-gutted. This man was thin, frail, the same man who had touched his cold nose to my wrist. Here he was—the *New York Times* restaurant critic, *Michael Saltz*—eating out in makeup. He was keeping me on my toes—but who was that note meant for? Surely not me.

But what if it was?

And yet it seemed preposterous that he was there reviewing the restaurant. Jake knew all the PXs in the house—their names, occupations, favorite wines, and even some random story he'd casually drop, a hint to say, *I see you, I know you, you're in good hands.*

But even I knew that he couldn't know everything. He hadn't known that the restaurant would be slammed with PXs tonight, or that we'd have to open the private dining room.

After the table ordered more wine, Henri returned to the kitchen but I stayed behind in the doorway between the private and main dining rooms, figuring out how I could tell someone.

Angel and Henri had been instructing me with grunts and urgent commands, unable to chat for any length of time. Carey was sorting out silverware at the other end of the restaurant. The hostess was away from her post, working her charm on an elderly couple lugging their heavy and unsightly bags, not content with their prime table by the window. No one knew.

Then I remembered his note and looked at it again. Even though it seemed farfetched that he'd come to the restaurant to see me and give me that note, part of me thrilled at the thought. What would he want to do with me, anyway?

I looked up and saw him staring at me. He winked and brought his finger to his lips. To anyone else, it might have looked like he was wiping his mouth, but to me, the message was very different.

Keep quiet.

So I did. The dining room went on without me. The world didn't end. I focused on my job and avoided eye contact with Jake, Angel, and the rest of them. They couldn't see the guilt in my eyes. I had to see what Michael Saltz had in store for me.

Once the crowd had died down around eleven, Jake told me I could take a break, then return to the coatroom to finish out the night. I took one last look at the private dining room, to absorb my first day working in a restaurant. And then Michael Saltz's eyes met mine again and he put down his napkin.

He was ready to talk.

I brainstormed for a place to hide, then decided on the basement, knowing full well he would follow me. We had to be fast since the staff could figure out Michael Saltz's presence at any time. But then again, the last of the PX tables were still keeping them busy. They didn't realize their number one target was already dining among them.

"Hello, Tia. Good to see you again," he said when he arrived in the basement, as if we'd bumped into each other on the street. The hallway was dark and severe, white concrete walls and red doors leading to the boiler room and storage. You never would have known we were in a fine-dining restaurant.

"Good to see you, too, sir." I thought for a brief second that nothing good would come out of this basement conversation, that I should get out now. But then he spoke, and his riptide pulled me in.

"Well, I'm very happy to see you again. And I wanted to ask your opinion. Seeing as you're the college cooking prodigy and all. Did you serve a good meal tonight?" he asked, his voice slinking up like a snake in the grass.

The college cooking prodigy . . . At the time, it had seemed like such a big deal, but now it was just an old title, a trophy losing its luster. Though I still liked the sound of it.

"I think your amuse-bouche . . ." I started slowly. Sure, I had opinions about it, but when it came to Michael Saltz, I couldn't say much. I bit my nails and stared off into the hallway, imagining Jake catching on. Surely he must have suspected something?

"Yes, my amuse-bouche what?"

I finally met his eyes and saw he was genuinely interested. I could tell him a little bit. Talking about food was the thing that made me *me*. What made me shine.

"The edamame puree with clementines and endives is genius. It's bright and bitter, soulful and singing. It's a summer dish with autumn actors."

"Oh, yes? That's a lovely turn of phrase. Tell me more."

I felt only vaguely aware of who I was talking to. If I really thought about it, I'd have stopped. He was too important and I couldn't imagine his motives. But I was also flattered. Shocked, really. Michael Saltz remembered *me*. Sure, it had been an oddly indelible first encounter, but I was just a grad student and he was the *New York Times* restaurant critic. He shouldn't have given me a second thought. But he was. More than a thought. He was listening to me.

"I've read that when he was a line cook at Vrai, Chef Darling would cook the most amazing staff meals—daring, audacious flavor combinations. This amuse-bouche is more reckless than anything else on the menu, and is probably a taste of his cuisine before he took on leadership positions." I was basically paraphrasing Helen's article, but there was power in her words coming from my lips.

"I see. You seem to know a lot about Chef Darling. And his food. What else did you like?" Michael Saltz asked, arching his brows.

The words rushed out of me. I feared someone would find us, but maybe more than that I feared that this moment would end and I'd lose this audience. And then I'd be back to square one. That wasn't the end of the world, but it wasn't the NBT.

"Well, the opposite of the amuse-bouche is the short rib with kale and black-eyed peas. From the most fundamental taste perspective, I find it . . . flawed. The black-eyed peas have a funk to them that clashes with the short ribs. Short ribs are soft, smooth, fatty—like vanilla. And black-eyed peas . . . they taste like dirt, and not in a good way. The two don't harmonize. I think Chef has been phoning these plates in. Short ribs are the restaurant's signatures, but I don't think Chef Darling wants to step into someone else's shoes. He's having adjustment issues and it's obvious."

I hadn't admitted this to myself during the staff tasting, but now in the basement, the thought sprang forward. Things I was afraid to think or say or do surfaced in the dark. Was I going against the restaurant? Yes. But it felt so good to just talk. My roommate was a mystery. Things had been feeling funky with Elliott. Michael Saltz may have been a stranger—a very sketchy stranger—but having him listen satisfied some deep, aching part of me. A part that must have been starving for a while, because I leaped into his attention like my life depended on it.

"And the chicken? What's your opinion on that?"

"I think the chicken is very good," I said, my voice steadying and my volume growing. "It comes from a local farm where we also get our eggs. If you taste carefully, you can detect a slight herbaciousness in the meat. Matthew doesn't add that, that's in the product. It's very subtle, but I'm sure you—"

"Yes, yes, that's right . . ." He took out a tall, skinny pad of paper and furiously wrote something in mangled handwriting. "And the cassoulet?"

"The cassoulet is one of my favorites," I said, gaining steam. "We use fresh, not dried, white beans, and homemade rabbit sausage. It's only stewed for an hour or two, so it retains lovely freshness."

"Yes, yes, freshness," he said. "Now tell me about the seafood paella."

"Well, I'm allergic to some types of shellfish, so I didn't try the paella at our menu meeting."

He looked up from his pad abruptly. "Allergic?" He looked mad for a moment, then suddenly, he let out a giant grin that seemed to unhinge his jaw. "That's not ideal. But I have a rather complicated relationship to certain shellfish dishes, so I'll take that as a sign." He looked down at his pad again, excited. "What did you think of the pork loin? Enlighten me!"

Here he was, Michael Saltz, writing down *my* thoughts about food. It was unreal. Insane. A dream I didn't know I wanted, come true.

"You got the pork with the ras el hanout?" I asked. There were two pork preparations that night—one homier preparation with carrots, corn, and okra on the regular menu, and a pork loin with Middle Eastern spices, butternut squash, and radicchio on the specials menu.

"Yes . . . yes, that's the one. What do you think of it?"

"The one with the roasted butternut squash and caramelized radicchio, right? Not the one with the carrots and corn? They sound similar, but they're very different."

"The ras el hanout. The first one you described."

"Okay." I filled my lungs and let it all out. I was onstage, just me, performing for Michael Saltz. This was the climax.

"I think it's awful. The pork is overdone and the dry spice rub accents that. Ras el hanout has a beautiful bouquet of tastes, but when overcooked the spices wick all the moisture out of your mouth. Then the radicchio furthers the dryness. The butternut squash adds a dose of heart and lusciousness, but there's not enough of it to save the dish."

I knew I was betraying the restaurant, but I tried to shed that self-doubt. I wanted to forget about the meek girl who never believed in her voice and thoughts. In that dark basement, with the EXIT light flickering, I made myself heard.

He wrote for several more seconds before looking up at me. "Thank you. You're impressing me a great deal."

"Is that what you thought of it?"

"Absolutely. The ras el hanout was too strong. I can still taste it." His dry lips split as he talked. "And the desserts?"

The meal we were reviewing was coming to a close and I was feeling as if I'd said too much. But I continued anyway.

Call it inertia. My words didn't want to stop.

Or call it hunger. I craved the recognition.

Or call it searching for the NBT. The New York way. Would Emerald or the ice pop girl have done any differently?

"Desserts . . . did you have the sweet potato cassava pie with the hazelnut praline crunch?" I asked.

"Yes, I had the cassava pie."

"What did you think of it?"

He closed his eyes and swayed into the wall. "Tell me what *you* thought of it."

I heard footsteps above us. "We should get going. Maybe you can email me? Can this wait?"

"Why?" he asked. "You've held nothing back so far. Tell me what's on your mind." He smiled. Though he'd been smiling up a storm, the expression looked unnatural and pasted on.

"I . . . I don't know." Surely someone would show up any minute now. My heart sped up again. I didn't know what he wanted out of this conversation, but whatever it was, I knew I had just cheated on my new restaurant family. Irreversibly.

"Yes, you do. Don't be afraid of your opinions. Tell me."

Now I could hear the sounds from upstairs with unsettling clarity. People walking, people worrying. People searching for the man standing in front of me right now?

"I can't. I shouldn't be talking to you like this," I said, wishing I could turn back time. And short of that, I wished Michael Saltz was so drunk that he'd forget this ever happened. I didn't want to be a traitor. I just wanted my moment.

He pursed his lips and for a second I saw the wheels turning, his mind clicking on a decision.

"I read your essay, you know. Before I gave it to Helen. I couldn't resist."

"Oh!" I said, yet another puff of wind blown beneath my wings. My heart slowed down. I hadn't thought he'd bother to read my application.

"It was fabulous. You have a way with words, and as I can tell from this conversation, a way with thoughtful criticism. I have to say, I'm glad you received this placement over Helen. She can be an aggressive, demanding boss. I should know. You're lucky you're here. *I'm* lucky you're here."

"Oh, well, thanks?" I said, but I didn't understand the meaning behind his words. I still didn't have Helen. And why was this situation lucky for *him*?

"You owe it to yourself to be heard," he said, interrupting my thought. "It would be a shame to go your whole life without sharing your gifts. Don't you think, Tia? You were quite the star in college. Front page of the *New York Times* Food section. But it's too easy to get left behind in New York City. There are thousands of people like you. Some make it. Some disappear. And some get an opportunity like this . . . to be heard."

His voice was low, vibrating, and pointed in its aim. He got under my skin. "Now, I'll ask you again. Tell me about the dessert."

"Well, the dessert . . . I think it's interesting," I started. "The pie has sweet potato for the sweetness and cassava for the body and heft, but what gives it its unusual taste and structure is kabocha."

"Kabocha! Fascinating."

"Oh, so you noticed the kabocha?" I asked. "It's subtle. But, yeah, of course you would notice."

" . . . I did notice. It was much firmer? That's what gives it the dryness?" he said.

I made a face. Was he joking? "No, that's the thing, right? The kabocha ties the cassava and the sweet potato, and together it feels substantial, yet cloudlike and souffléed."

"Indeed. You are correct. I've had way too much wine. Much too much wine. And the strudel?" His head tilted and he quickly righted it. "Tell me about that one."

Now that my nerves had settled, I could see Michael Saltz more clearly. He had a pointed nose and a head of dark, thin hair sharpened by a widow's peak on his forehead. He fiddled with the edge of his linen shirt.

In fact, if you looked closely, his disguise was utterly unconvincing. You could tell he wasn't a diplomat or even a rich guy with a penchant for "Eastern cultures." His eyeliner hovered too far from his eyelashes so he looked more like a kid playing in his mom's makeup bag than a foreign gentleman.

"I find the berries too tart and the walnut brittle too sweet," I said. "It's gummy and heavy."

Now I could hear someone down the hall. Someone was in the basement.

"Meet me upstairs! At coat check!" Michael Saltz whispered, just as Carey rounded the corner. I turned away as fast as I could, but still saw Carey's face freeze the second she saw us. Her shaking hands told me everything: she knew who he was.

What had I done? Did I really say all that to Michael Saltz? *The* Michael Saltz, the guy the whole restaurant obsessed over?

"Oh, hey," she said to me. Then she looked at Michael Saltz. Then back at me.

"Oh, I didn't realize you were there, sir," I said to Michael Saltz. Then, to Carey, "I had to pick something up from my locker, and I think this gentleman took a wrong turn looking for the restroom." Out of the corner of my eye, I saw Michael Saltz silently gleam at my diversion tactic.

Carey chuckled hesitantly. "Well . . ." she started. "Sir, can I show you back upstairs?"

"You may," he said. He didn't look at me. To do so would suggest that we knew each other, and Carey was watching us closely. I followed Michael Saltz's lead and walked away.

From the end of the hallway, I heard Carey say to him, "I hope you had a good dinner?" Anxiety had crept into her voice.

Part of me wanted to cry out, *Don't let him see you sweat!*

But there was another part that reveled in the thought—*He's hiding from Carey. From everyone. But not me.*

Finally, the last thing I heard was Michael Saltz saying, "The dinner here was quite nice. I'm in town for a conference, and this was a lovely respite."

They went upstairs, then I followed up a couple of minutes afterward. I didn't want people to suspect I'd been with Michael Saltz the whole time and I hoped Carey wouldn't tell anyone she had seen me with him. It was bad enough I'd spotted him and told no one. What I'd said to him in the basement . . . that was treason.

I went back to the coatroom and gathered my composure. Five minutes later, he arrived at the booth with his guests behind him, waiting. Jake had positioned himself at the top of the dining room stairs, looking down at me and Michael Saltz's back.

I handed him his coat with a smile and a slight nod.

He took it and reached into his pants, as if retrieving a tip.

"Tia," he mumbled, the sound articulating inside his mouth but not on his lips. "You did a good job downstairs. I want to see you again. You're qualified."

I repositioned myself so Jake wouldn't be able to see me from the landing. Qualified for what? He handed me a piece of paper: his dinner receipt with his email address written on the back.

"Thank you . . ." I said, as the reality of the last few minutes sank in. The *New York Times* restaurant critic wanted *me* to contact *him*. And not through a random throwaway email anymore, but his actual *New York Times* address. I had graduated somehow.

"*Shh . . .*" he whispered, then he was out the door.

I shoved the receipt in my suit jacket as Jake ran down.

"Did Carey tell you who that was? What did he say? Did he say anything about the dinner?"

"No," I said. "He didn't say a thing."

It was true—he hadn't said anything. Only I had.

Chapter 6

Two days later, I still didn't know what I wanted to say to Michael Saltz. It all boiled down to: *What do you want from me?*

Jake called an emergency all-staff meeting at Madison Park Tavern. A photographer from the *New York Times* had called to shoot eight dishes between three thirty and four P.M. on Monday, when the restaurant was closed to the public. We gathered at five past four to debrief and strategize. When everyone arrived, Jake cleared this throat and began.

"Listen, people. We're in the crosshairs." He gestured to the bar, where the eight dishes had been laid out for the photographer. "This is what unprepared looks like. We all failed on Saturday." He stalked through the dining room, winding between tables and looking every staff member in the eye. "It's a travesty we recognized Michael Saltz so late, but kudos to Carey for bringing him to our attention." Some people gave Carey soft smiles. I did my best to follow their lead, even though I was the one who had first noticed him. Revealing him was another story.

Jake quickened his gait, his face reddening. "What I don't understand is how the most important critic in the world can walk into our restaurant and not be fucking ID'd. His 'disguise' was bogus, so that's not an excuse. Believe me, I blame myself more than anyone. But no one in this room gets a pass. Why do we have multiple pictures of the guy in the dining room and in the kitchen? Hasn't his image been seared into your minds by now? If we don't notice Michael Saltz—fat, skinny, bald, even if he's got a fucking eye patch—then I shudder to think who else we are missing. We're clearly being reviewed now, and the four stars are ours to lose. We must treat him like a king. But it is us against him."

Jake sat down among us. He adjusted his tie clip and sighed. "The photographs are already done. That means the review can be printed as soon as this week. This restaurant and everyone in this room relies on that man's words. You and I know that Madison Park Tavern is one of the best. But if we lose that focus, we will die."

Jake shook, as if possessed by something much stronger than him. He was a man who took offense when the fork was in the wrong place, suffered shame when a host or hostess didn't say good-bye to a guest. And his pain now? Practically visible from space.

I bit my nails and let his words sink in. *The four stars are ours to lose.* I hoped that wouldn't happen. I hoped that my conversation was a little side thing. We just happened upon each other.

But I knew he'd had a plan to see me. The memory of that night burned so hot into my heart that I was sure my face gave me away. That, or a scarlet *MS* blazed on my chest.

"Come on, let's eat these dishes before they get too cold. Let's get a sense of what Mr. Saltz experienced."

In sports, the coaches analyze the tapes, but we were going

to experience the game in real time. We sampled all the dishes the photographer had requested. These would be the targets in Michael Saltz's review.

As I tasted the food and listened to everyone hypothesize how Michael Saltz could have perceived it, I reviewed my strange conversation with him. I carefully controlled my face in case someone could see that my focus lay elsewhere. I needed to make sense of our basement chat before I reached out to him. He'd started as a reporter, so maybe that was why he was questioning me. He was getting an outside opinion, right? People always ask their waiter or waitress about ingredients or recommendations. Looking at it that way, perhaps the whole thing wasn't so bizarre.

While people crowded around the bar, I stole a peek at Michael Saltz's receipt to see what he'd decided not to photograph. And then I knew my theory was wrong.

There on the marble counter was the pork with ras el hanout. But the receipt told a different story: Saltz had ordered the pork loin from the main menu. The other, homier one. One dish could never be mistaken for the other.

Then why did Michael Saltz tell me and the photographer he got the ras el hanout one?

After we ate everything, Jake adjourned the meeting, then walked toward my table.

"Tia, I wanted to let you know that I'm glad it was you who backserved Michael Saltz for a short time on Saturday. This whole thing?" He waved his finger in a circular motion around the dining room, which was at the height of its grandeur in the dying afternoon light. "This is a big deal in this city. And you're an important part of it. You're doing an outstanding job."

I clasped my hands so tightly, both my arms trembled. It was a prayer, of sorts. I wished he couldn't see my guilt. I wished what

I'd done wouldn't change anything. And as I squeezed harder and harder, I wished that I could keep this episode contained. No leaks, no betrayal. No messiness.

He gave me one last look, a fond one even, then walked away. I felt so relieved that I collapsed onto the banquette and closed my eyes. I wanted to freeze time for a little while, to help my mind catch up with reality, to preserve Jake's gratitude for the sliver of good I'd done, despite the sliver of transgression afterward. Though my sorry heart knew it had been more than a sliver.

Carey ran up to me and I tensed as she approached. "Wait, so what was the deal on Saturday?" Her stare was so intense, I had to avert my eyes.

"I forgot something in my locker. Jake said that I could have a break before I went back to the coatroom."

That wasn't too bad a fib. Anyone could have done the same.

"Everyone thinks I saved the day, that I spotted him first," Carey said, her eyes sharp and frighteningly alert. Carey was the queen of data capture, and I could tell that I was now under her microscope. "But I just stumbled on him. How long were you standing there? Why didn't you recognize him?"

"Recognize him?" My voice quivered, so I slowed it down, became conscious of my exhalations as I lied. "It was my first day on the job, and I'm not a restaurant person. I didn't even know what he looked like."

Carey backed off, but not without a slow squint that stopped my breath, heart, and head.

"Okay," she said. "I believe you."

It occurred to me that I should have sounded baffled and out of my depth, but I worried I couldn't get the tenor right. Better to keep quiet, let the moment pass, and let Carey come to her own conclusions with as little information from me as possible.

We stayed there in silence for a couple more seconds, then she shook her head as if she had thought better of what she was about to do, and walked away.

THAT NIGHT I emailed Michael Saltz. I needed to get everything out on the table so I could put this saga to rest: What did he want from me? What was he doing at the restaurant?

Then I'd be done with it.

> Hi, Michael. Today the team at Madison Park Tavern met about your meal on Saturday. I shouldn't be emailing you. But can you tell me why you were there and why you asked me so many questions? I'm confused as to why you wanted to talk.

He replied immediately.

> Tia, don't be afraid to shine. Things are about to get good.

Chapter 7

THE NEXT NIGHT, MADISON PARK TAVERN'S OWNER, GARY Oscars, was dining at the restaurant with a laptop. We never would have allowed guests to do that, but of course he was an exception. He owned six restaurants across the city and typically only tended to the new ones because they got the most press. But tonight, Madison Park Tavern had his full attention. Chef Darling and his cooks could hide in the kitchen, but Jake and the waitstaff had to bear the brunt of Gary's manic energy.

I poked into the dining room a couple of times and saw him calling for poor Jake, who had to run over while still looking calm in front of the guests. Angel, Chad, and Henri checked their phones compulsively. Chef Darling left the kitchen more often than usual, especially given that Gary was in the house. He kept checking in with the hostess, who would shake her head and tap her foot, sharing whatever anxiety he had. I saw Carey run up to Chef Darling, nod, then check her phone, too.

"What's going on? Why aren't people at their stations?" I asked Carey.

Carey shot me an incredulous look. "The *New York Times* review? It comes out tonight."

"But it's Tuesday. Aren't the reviews published on Wednesdays?"

"Yeah, in the paper. But it'll be posted online sometime tonight," she said, eyeing Chef Darling through a small window in the kitchen door.

We spent the night totally distracted. Everyone wore a look of worry, from the dishwashers to the line cooks to the hostess with her perma-smile. I heard some guests mumble that the service had gone downhill. But if only they knew the *Times* review was upon us. Even Jake had turned his attention away from service and toward the final judgment. Everything was out of our hands.

But I didn't let on. To the extent that I could—which wasn't very much—I tried to make up wherever the service was lacking. I grinned extra wide. I took the hands of people who wanted to be touched and demurred respectfully from the ones who preferred to be left alone. I did my small part so I didn't have to see the restaurant slide so slipshod. But even I knew it was too little, too late.

I left at eleven and walked slowly back to the apartment. It was the perfect fall night: air that refreshed, leaves that lullabied, weather in which everyone was comfortable. Except me. I didn't know what the review would say, but I knew what I had done and said. I couldn't take it back. All I could do was wait and see, just like everyone else.

Emerald and Melinda weren't home, to my relief. I opened my laptop and saw an email from Carey, subject line: *SHIT.*

I clicked the link to nytimes.com and read.

Famous Farmhouse Goes to Pasture
by MICHAEL SALTZ

If you are in possession of a coatrack, you might want to give it to Madison Park Tavern. The Flatiron mainstay is in need of a fresh concept and a place to hang its hat.

When my predecessor reviewed this restaurant four years ago, the establishment had a dynamite idea. The brash young chef Anthony Tate had the groundbreaking insight to use fresh, local produce in his cooking. He wouldn't veil these ingredients with words like "rustic" or "home-style." The menu put no qualifications around its products and made no apologies for serving them in a high-end atmosphere. The idea spread through Manhattan like organic dandelion greens, and soon our fair city of asphalt and car exhaust turned a little bit country.

But that was four years, and four stars, ago. The Madison Park Tavern of today has a new chef, Matthew Darling, formerly of Vrai, and the idea of "local ingredients" can no longer carry a restaurant. What was so revolutionary about Madison Park Tavern yesterday is a given today, if not a total cliché. There are a host of innovative restaurants—Bakushan, Alltop Peaks, Yop Factory—that use local, fresh ingredients, employing them with abandon and excitement, not reverent tiptoeing.

Indeed, there are some lovely, delicious moments at Darling's Madison Park Tavern. One night, I had a delightful amuse-bouche of edamame puree, clementines, and endives. It took my breath away with its notes of bright and bitter, soulful and singing. This is daring food that transcends seasons, something that comes all too infrequently. Matthew Darling has a very popular, very seasonal restaurant to lose, so transgressions are relegated to one bite. Most dishes seem to beat you over the head with their capital-C Concept. Even the dining room could double as a movie set for a "market-to-table restaurant," so obvious, so caricature-like is its premise.

I liked the roast chicken with potatoes six ways, a clever way to dress up a classic. While the potato morphs in every which rich, fried, and gratinéed way, the chicken works its own special magic. Chew carefully and you will taste a slight herbaciousness in the meat. This is a chicken who has eaten well, and here the tranquility of the farm is spun into fireworks on the plate. The rabbit cassoulet approaches the tongue with unexpected freshness. It is not the familiar mush, but another toothsome thing.

Yet much of the menu ranges from not-so-bad to what's the point? The pork loin with ras el hanout, a special one night, was alarmingly off-balance. The spices wicked the moisture out of my mouth, and imparted little of their beautiful bouquet of flavor.

Yet the biggest slight of all is the short-rib dish. Short ribs have always been a standard at Madison Park Tavern, ever since the days of Anthony Tate. But Matthew Darling doesn't seem interested in using them to articulate his own vision. In the days of Chef Tate, the short ribs spoke volumes about the transformative powers of well-aimed and well-executed technique, and Tate was like an athlete at the top of his game. Five years ago, I couldn't get enough of his interpretations. There was the unctuous, exotic beauty that was the short ribs glazed with hoisin and beer and served atop a chervil-leek puree. And another masterpiece: short ribs wrapped in savoy cabbage and paper-thin disks of turnip and pancetta.

The short ribs of today's Madison Park Tavern feel like a halfhearted remake. The current kale and black-eyed pea preparation is flawed at the most fundamental level. The black-eyed peas, darling little things that they are, add a discordant whiff of dirt. They are the mud to the short ribs' soft and smooth vanilla, a combination that hits you in the gut in the worst possible way.

Of the desserts, the sweet potato–cassava cake with praline crunch is a pleasant surprise. The sweet potato offers sweetness, while kabocha provides an unusual, almost souffléed dimension and structure. Yet the berry-walnut strudel with thyme-infused rice gelato suffered from too-tart fruits and too-sweet walnut brittle.

The service is, like at all of Gary Oscars's restaurants, impeccable. The dining room is a masterpiece of good-looking staff conducting elaborate choreography.

One danger of passing the torch is that the newest torch-bearer is burdened with the agenda of his predecessor. Matthew Darling is a fine chef, but one who appears to be driving the restaurant down a road to irrelevance. Madison Park Tavern used to be a transcendent experience, one of the best. Now it's just one of the good.

TWO out of FOUR stars

Once I finished, I started again. I lapped it up over and over. I couldn't believe it. Two stars? That was one thing—a shocking thing.

But even more shocking—Michael Saltz had used my exact words. Reading the article, I heard my own voice talking back.

I thought for a second that this was a joke. Maybe someone had created a fake website to fool me. I clicked around and got to other *New York Times* articles. Tomorrow, these words would be distributed in printed papers all over the country. The whole world could reach this page. These words. These thoughts. Mine.

But as much as I liked seeing my words in the paper, the truth was that he had stolen them right out of my mouth. There was no other way to look at it. He had lured me into the basement with that note, solicited my opinions, and pawned them off as his own. He had a lot of explaining to do, and I was ready to confront him when I saw a new email. From Michael Saltz. I opened it with trepidation, a cliffjumper's look over the edge.

> **SUBJECT:** Let's Talk
>
> I assume you've seen the review by now. You have a special talent. Come to my apartment, 257 Central Park West. Tomorrow we will discuss everything.

Damn right we would. I had seen my words in the *New York Times* once before, and that time I hadn't made the most of it. Now I knew the value of my voice, and I wouldn't let someone else take it without a fight.

Chapter 8

People came ready to gossip about the review at my internship seminar.

"I bet everyone *freaked,*" said Rachel, a thirty-year-old former banker interning at a sustainable fishing advocacy group.

"Reviews are over, anyway. Do people still care about those?" Geo asked. He was working at a kitchen incubator geared toward low-income immigrant women.

Even our seminar leader, a Food Studies postdoc researching the link between obesity and methamphetamine use, weighed in. "Authority will never die. It may change platforms, it may shift voices, but there will always be room for the guru," she said, with a doleful nod. "And Tia, what do you think?" she asked.

My classmates looked at me with disinterest. I'd be skeptical about my insight, too. From what I'd heard about the internships, the early weeks were about busy work. Students came in with these ideas and directions for the future, only to have them squashed by protocol, status quo, and moody staffers who made sure the grad student didn't feel too privileged.

"Well . . ." I said. "It'll be tough to recover, I'm sure. I was there when it happened and I saw him." I stopped and watched them slip to the edges of their seats. Just for kicks, I waited a beat longer to see their eyes widen even more. "We even talked."

"You *talked* to Michael Saltz?" Rachel squawked. "About *what*?"

"Oh," I said, slow and easy, knowing that all ten of them at the seminar table were hanging on my every word. On some level, they must have known they were merely gossiping earlier. Idle academic chatter.

But I couldn't tell them about my real role, not until Michael Saltz gave me an explanation. "I just gave his table their palate cleansers," I said reluctantly.

And then the spell broke. Rachel leaned back. Geo rolled his eyes. Even our seminar leader sighed audibly.

"Okay," she snapped. "Let's talk about our actual work."

Easy come, easy go. I opened my notebook, a journal of my internship experience. Already the words were reading like a farce, a sanitized shell of intellectualized blabber. Just like this seminar. Just like grad school. A play-area separated from what mattered. *Who* mattered.

AFTER SEMINAR, I rode the C train to Michael Saltz's Upper West Side apartment, a beautiful high-rise with a fountain and a rounded driveway in the front, like a hotel.

"I'm here to see Michael Saltz, please," I said to the man at the front desk. The lobby dripped baroque—marbles and golds and heavy drapery—and I felt too young and poor and disheveled for the surroundings. Why hadn't I worn my Jil Sander suit?

The man at the front desk had a long face and boxy chin and eyed me through wire-rimmed glasses. "And your name is?"

"Tia Monroe. He's expecting me."

Without hiding his grimace, he dialed a number, then turned away and whispered in the phone. He spun around. "Thirty-five Q. Elevators are over there," he said, without showing me where "there" was. I took the elevator up and stood in front of 35Q for a split second, clenched my jaw, and knocked. I vowed that whatever he said, I'd hold my ground. He'd stolen my words, and I needed to find out why.

Michael Saltz opened his door slowly at first, then swung it wide open.

"Come in, come in," he insisted. He grabbed my elbow so tightly, I was sure he couldn't know his own strength. Strangers don't touch other strangers like this. I swallowed hard as he pulled me into his living room.

As expected, his thirty-fifth-floor apartment had a stunning view of Central Park. But what I didn't expect was the smell. I picked out smoke and meat, spices and herbs. Eggs and bananas and cheese. Not bad separately—delicious, even—but the combined vile stink of everything meant I spent the first five minutes trying to figure out how to will my nostrils shut.

Michael Saltz looked like a different man from the one I had seen on the street and at the restaurant. Sober and in the light, he looked sharp and intimidating, despite the oppressive stench. He was quite tall and slinked onto his long, white leather couch with a calm, collected fluidity. I knew he was a very important man. I knew I was alone with him in his apartment. But I didn't know what he wanted from me, and that was the gravelly grind inside my throat.

I sat down on another couch. In front of us stood a coffee table topped with various jars. In fact, jars covered every surface of the apartment, all of them closed except for a few by a laptop on the dining room table.

I leaned back on the couch and my cardigan slipped down

at the shoulder, revealing my tank top and a little bit of my bra strap. I yanked it back up.

"Don't worry about that." Michael Saltz laughed. "I'm flaming."

"Oh," I said. That relaxed me, but only a little. I wanted to confront him about stealing my words, but already I felt scared.

"You're not here for a booty call, that's for sure. But I'll tell you why I invited you in a moment, I just want to get one thing." He picked up a beige-gray ceramic jar from the far corner of the coffee table. He circled his fingertips around the lid gingerly, as if the jar held a tiny animal that needed to be coaxed out.

Was he going to drug me? Show me something disgusting? It seemed like he was taunting me, flaunting how much control he had.

Finally he revealed a brilliant tangle of saffron. I could tell it was excellent quality by the long, elegant strands and the way it had stained the unglazed jar its same shade of burnt red.

He swirled the jar in front of his nose. "But before I go into that whole mess, isn't this magnificent?" He poked his finger inside the saffron, mashing the valuable threads, and brought the jar up to his nose. "People forget that saffron is the backbone of a flower," he said, still sniffing. "They get so preoccupied with saffron's cost that they forget what saffron really is."

"My boyfriend used to study crocuses in college," I said, unsure where the conversation was going, but determined to set it on stable ground. "He harvested the strands for a pilot dining hall program, but gave me the best ones to cook with."

"A match made in heaven."

"Yeah," I said. "He's great . . ." But we weren't here to discuss my love life. What *were* we here to discuss?

"And what did you make with the saffron?" Michael Saltz asked.

"My specialty is a rice stew with ginger and flounder." He had brought the conversation back to food and I felt more at ease.

"Like a paella?"

"No, not like a paella. I don't use shellfish, because . . ."

"Oh, right, allergic! Yes, how could I forget?"

He had an excellent memory. Or maybe just for me.

"It has an Asian flair," I continued. "The saffron adds a taste of the sun. You have the pillowy sea element of the flounder and the earthiness of the rice, and I think the farminess of the saffron—that rustic, rough flavor—brings the dish together."

"That sounds wonderful," Michael Saltz said. "Simply wonderful. Will you excuse me for a moment?"

"Fine, but I wanted to talk to you about—" But he wasn't listening.

He walked to a cabinet underneath his wide expanse of windows. "I bought this from an old library in Paris," he said, running his fingers across the labeled drawers until he came across the one he wanted. He opened it and plucked out a lined white card. He brought it back to the table, and wrote in slow, tortured script:

Saffron rice with ginger and flounder: haylike, sea, land.

He put the card back on the coffee table and looked at me blankly, as if he hadn't just sucked the words right out of my mouth.

"Wait a second," I said. I was willing to hear him out by coming to his apartment, and was even willing to let him delay his explanation. But I wouldn't let him make a habit of stealing everything I uttered.

"Tell me what you want from me," I said. "I'm not talking about food until I get some answers."

"Answers!" he said, as if they were at the tip of his tongue all along. "Yes, that's what we're here for. I'm quoting your words for my archives."

"Archives . . . so you have dishes to refer to when you try new things?"

Michael Saltz laughed a long, disturbing laugh. He turned bright red and said, with tears in his eyes, "No. Wouldn't that be nice. Actually, that's why I've asked you here."

Finally—this was the moment. Maybe he had some news about Helen? Or he wanted to apologize for not securing her internship for me?

"There are no new dishes to me," Michael Saltz continued. "That card catalog of tastes, that's all I have. My memories, and the memories of others."

"Oh . . . because you forget flavor combinations?" I guessed. I thought of the ras el hanout pork. He had clearly forgotten what that tasted like, or else he wouldn't have mistaken it for the regular salt-and-pepper version.

"You can't forget what you've never had," he said. "But here, let me demonstrate." He opened a drawer in the coffee table and handed me a bottle of red liquid wrapped at the base with aluminum foil. The bottle looked like it belonged in a lab more than in a living room.

"See this? This is made from one of the hottest chilis in the world, bhut jolokia. There are some farmers who say they've grown a hotter pepper, but the bhut is the most natural—the gentleman's hot pepper, I'd say. Open it."

I twisted the small cap, and immediately my hands burned and my eyes teared.

He snatched the bottle away from me, tilted his head back, and shook the bottle into his mouth until a sinister-looking pool of sauce collected on his tongue.

He closed his mouth and sucked his cheeks in. After about

thirty seconds of what felt like a private freak show, he stuck his tongue out and revealed a quarter-sized welt that pulsed with anger.

"This is my favorite 'taste.' But it's not really a taste. I can only feel the burn. These are volatile, violent oils. But that's all."

Suddenly, I understood. His apartment's funk, his skeletal frame, his inability to differentiate those two porks.

"It's gone," he said. "All gone. Sweet, spicy, sour, bitter . . . the flavors mean nothing. The most finely calibrated soups taste like sewer water, an elegant filet is cardboard. I'm the unluckiest man in the world, or so I thought . . . until I found you. I need your help and your exquisite palate."

My eyes were still tearing from the tiny whiff of bhut jolokia I'd caught, and I was sure the sauce had singed a hole in my cardigan, but I didn't care. This was huge. Michael Saltz, the world's most powerful food critic, couldn't *taste*. He couldn't do his job at the most basic level, and now, for some reason, he wanted my help.

"I'm just a shell of what I used to be, robbed of what I loved most in life," he said. But then his eyes lit up. "But my grief is your opportunity. I want your assistance. You are a true food mind, someone who understands flavors and honors the craft enough to pursue it at all costs. I want you to become my sense of taste. You will be my protégée and accompany me on my meals—the best and newest places. You will know about them all, experience them all . . . rule on them all. If you're up to the challenge."

My mouth dropped as I struggled to understand. "You want me . . . to eat meals with you . . . and write about them? Me?" I thought he had invited me to his home to apologize. But he'd done something even better.

Michael Saltz opened his hands, palms up, as if to say, *Of course you.* "And there are perks," he quickly added. "I have a personal account with Bergdorf Goodman, unrelated to the *New York Times*. I want you to go there. You can use my personal shopper, Giada. She will take good care of you."

Bergdorf: the grand mecca of designer clothing. This was going a bit too fast and all I could do was repeat what he was saying, even though the words were fantastical and strange coming out of my mouth. "So . . . I get to go with you to these restaurants? *And* pick out my own outfit at Bergdorf Goodman?"

"Not an outfit. A whole wardrobe! Giada will help you. This will be a wonderful change for you."

I felt delirious. It seemed like a joke. And yet the intense smell of the apartment and Michael Saltz himself, staring at me with his beady-eyed gaze, convinced me. Amazingly, this was real life.

My mind raced through every fancy dinner I had ever had. I could count them on one hand, and they'd always been apologetic affairs, excursions where I felt underdressed and left hungry for more. The only time my family had gone out to eat had been when we were on vacation, and still my parents would complain how they could make those dishes better at home.

The first time I'd felt like I belonged at a fancy restaurant had been less than a week ago at Madison Park Tavern's tasting. But now I'd be on the other side, dining and not serving. I wouldn't have to worry about not dressing the part. My personal shopper at Bergdorf Goodman would take care of that.

I could even get my own Prenza Schooler purse, or whatever the brand was called.

"Just one small thing," he continued. "It probably doesn't even need to be said."

"Oh, what's that?" I asked, breathless over this new chapter.

"This has to be a secret. If anyone found out I was working under these . . . unsuitable . . . conditions, the whole food world would have a fit. It'd be journalistic fraud, which is a very serious offense. I ask for your discretion, and in return you get dinners and clothes and an education unlike anything you can get in any school."

"Discretion . . . So I can't tell . . . anyone?" My mind clicked. Of course, a catch.

"Not a soul. Remember—free dinners, clothes, and, occasionally, your words in the *Times* blended with mine. That is your compensation, and our secret. Now that we've become involved, no one must know where you're going or what you're writing."

Now that we were involved? I had agreed to come to his apartment, but I didn't remember signing a contract.

"Mr. Saltz . . ." I said.

"Please, we're partners now. Call me Michael."

"Okay . . . Michael. 'Our secret'? I still haven't said yes to anything."

Michael Saltz scowled, his face an asterisk of wrinkles. Then he spoke, bringing his face so close to mine that I saw the veins in his eyes, wild branches of red that crowded his pupils.

"But don't you see? You have. You talked to me in the basement and didn't tell anyone you saw me, not then and not after. You probably didn't even tell anyone you were coming here."

He had me there, yet again. I had told no one. But I couldn't put my finger on why. I guess I'd wanted to keep this to myself, to incubate it away from insistent eyes. Just for a little while.

"That's nothing to be ashamed of," he continued. "You were being judicious."

If my parents or Elliott or anyone knew what was happening, surely they'd encourage me to explore the opportunity. Explore and negotiate. I had to be smart about the offer. Michael Saltz was asking me to sacrifice something tremendous—my identity. Now I recognized his enthusiasm at the door as desperation. It would be ridiculous to do this gigantic favor for him without securing a prize of equal value for myself. Wouldn't it?

I must have made a thoughtful face or hesitated too long, because when Saltz spoke again there was an edge to his voice.

"What's wrong?" he asked sourly. "Is this generous offer not to your liking?"

"No. I mean, yes, it is. It's amazing. I'm just wondering about one thing." I was afraid to say it, afraid he'd withdraw his proposal. But what did I have to lose? He may have been playing tough, but I saw the hopeful, embarrassed look in his eyes. I had leverage and I had a dream, one I hadn't let go, even with my Madison Park Tavern assignment.

"Helen Lansky," I said.

"Yes, Helen. The fine woman who brought us together."

"Right. You said you'd help me get that internship before, but now it's gone. Dean Chang at NYU said there are no guarantees that Helen will serve as a mentor again. If I'm working with you, and keeping all of this secret, I won't be able to concentrate on building my résumé if and when Helen accepts applications again."

Michael Saltz looked around his apartment. I followed his gaze, but couldn't tell what he was looking at or thinking.

"Helen, Helen. How could I forget about Helen? I should have known you'd still want to work alongside her after being placed at Madison Park Tavern. She has quite the pull. Well, in that case, I'll tell you the full story. I neglected to mention that I'm planning to undergo taste-correction surgery later this fall—January, at the latest—pending approval from my ENT doctor, my neurosurgeon at New York–Presbyterian, and the FDA. It's an experimental surgery, and I'm up next in the trial. So this is only for the current semester. After that, I'll make sure you and

Helen Lansky connect." He spoke with a certainty and crispness that sounded like fact.

"Didn't you promise that the first time around? That you would get me Helen?"

He waved his hand. "Yes, but that was for *school.* That's not the real world. The world doesn't act on committees and applications. It acts on this." He jerked his hand between our bodies. "Personal relationships. Influence. Access. You know I know Helen and that I can get you into any restaurant. And you know your opinions will matter to me. The one thing you need is faith."

"Faith." I squinted my eyes and thought. "Say I were to believe you. What would come next?"

Michael Saltz raised his eyebrow, a gesture of *game on.* "Well, you can still work at Madison Park Tavern, if it's necessary for your degree. But for the purposes of this relationship, it's unnecessary. A liability, even. After we finish up this semester, I'll just call Helen and you can work with her in the spring."

"Work with her. As a recipe tester or research assistant or something?"

"Recipe tester?" he scoffed. "You've been spending too much time in your graduate school bubble. No trivial work for you. No fake 'exercises' that count for nothing in the real world. This is real, true, the biggest of the big leagues. As I said earlier, you are an unusual talent, Tia. If you prove as much to Helen and work very, very hard, she is the sort of fair-minded person who will want to reward you accordingly. I would think that, under the right conditions—and with the right introduction from me—Helen would consider crediting you as a coauthor on her forthcoming cookbook. Your name would appear on the cover below hers. Think about it, Tia. This is a chance of a lifetime, the finest education in food writing you could ask for. This autumn, you'll serve as my protégée. Then, you'll work with Helen in the spring. Your whole career will just fall into place after that. It's rather simple. An easy decision, if you ask me. You'll leave behind your other, more mundane life for something extraordinary."

Extraordinary. My heart raced; my palms began to sweat. Could I do this? Manage this second life, without telling a soul?

"Well?" he asked.

With one word, I'd get closer to Helen. I could walk into any New York restaurant with my head held high. I'd have something, like that girl with the ice pops and the women at Bakushan, that made me shine above all others.

"Yes," I said.

And so it began.

Michael Saltz gave a slow, conspiratorial smile. "Wonderful. Come, let's toast! I have just the thing."

He opened his cabinet, and I thought he would take out one of his many bottles of wine there, but instead he reached in the back and brought out a large foil bag. As he opened it, a strong coffee aroma rolled through the air. He ran his fingers through the beans and the smell amplified. It smelled like a million coffee shops in one. The purest expression of a roasty, toasty coffee flavor.

"Nice, right?" said Michael Saltz. "I love this. It's called kopi luwak. The rarest coffee in the world. Goes for a hundred dollars a cup. Thankfully I can at least smell it."

I reached for the bag so I could hold a handful under my nose. I couldn't get enough of it.

"A civet cat has already digested and fermented the beans," Michael Saltz continued. I pulled my hand away. It was already *digested*? By a *cat*?

"But perhaps I love it so much because I've never had the chance to taste it." His face was clear and open. "Every cup is like water to me. So now I just brew it and smell it. Heat creates another dimension of smell. It amplifies and deepens and . . ." he hesitated, looking for the right word by waving his pointy white fingers. "Pierces. But, come. I want you to tell me how this coffee tastes."

We walked into the kitchen, a room littered with spices and herbs and jars of what looked like dried fish and wrinkled brown citrus peels. There was a fresh pineapple on the counter, split open with the exposed yellow part desiccated away. A wasabi root the size of a child's shoe sat perched on a porcelain grater, its smell prickling the air.

"It's an obsession, I know. All these jars, they're the reason I can get by. I've spent thousands of dollars to recapture through smell what I've lost in taste." He smiled abruptly. "But now I have the surgery lined up. And I have you!"

He pulled out a shiny Italian grinder and poured some beans into it. Grinding the beans released even more incredible aromas. Then he tamped the grounds and screwed the portafilter into the espresso machine. The coffee came out in a rusty, rushed stream. He inhaled it longingly before he handed the tiny cup to me.

"Go on, taste."

I didn't even like coffee that much, but even I could tell this was exceptional. It was easy to forget that it had come from the inside of a cat and figure out why people paid so much for it.

"Well? Does it taste like it smells? Or is it even more amazing?" He started idly combing through the beans, rustling up their scent.

The coffee did smell amazing. But the truth of it was: it tasted even better. It had a sudden, violent character, hitting you over the head and grabbing you by the throat. It was a full, lusty drink that needed all the senses, but especially taste. That's what made the coffee exceptional.

"Yes," I said to him. "It tastes like it smells." My first lie. It came out accidentally. Something in me wanted to put his mind at ease.

Michael Saltz took his hand out of the coffee bag, stopping the search for whatever he yearned for. "Really?"

"Really. Exactly the way it smells." My second lie. This time it came more easily.

He lifted his eyes to the ceiling, his mouth slackened, and the wrinkle in his forehead smoothed out. I had never seen a man so relieved by a coffee description. "I've been wondering about that for so long. Thank you," he whispered.

"What else do you miss?"

Michael Saltz's eyes softened. "Everything," he said with resignation. "It's torture to go to these restaurants and not be able to experience them. But I also miss the simple things. Coffee in the morning. Popcorn at the movie theater. A fresh bagel on a Sunday."

I nodded. I'd miss those things, too. Take away the rituals of eating and you remove the bones of the day, your connections to others.

"And . . . when did you lose your taste?"

Now Michael Saltz had fallen fully into a reverie. "I lost it about three months ago," he said. "It turned off like a switch. For a while, I was in denial, but . . ." He rolled his eyes and threw his hands in the air. "This condition isn't easily treated through medical means, so I've been treating it using my own tactics."

I didn't dare ask how he'd published a weekly review for the past three months, afraid that the question would make him angry and he'd rescind his offer. Had he really been faking it the whole time?

"Is there a name for what you have?"

"Well, that's an interesting question." He grated the wasabi, holding his nose to the porcelain spikes where the pungent smell collected. "When you lose your sight, you're blind. When you lose your hearing, you're deaf. When most people lose their sense of taste, they're actually losing their sense of smell. There's a name for that, too. But my brain tangles tastes, sometimes nullifies them. If I'm lucky, things just taste like nothing. But other times they taste like sawdust or cardboard, or like something else entirely. I'm one of the unlucky ones. And there's no name for what I have."

"Why is that?"

Michael Saltz took a long time to answer. "Maybe because it's too terrible." He put his hand on my shoulder, the smell of the coffee beans still stuck to his skin. "But let's not dwell on that ugly past. This is an exciting arrangement, for both of us."

"I agree," I said. Then he opened a kitchen drawer and gave me a wad of hundred-dollar bills.

"Here's some pocket money for miscellaneous expenses. Remember, use my personal shopper at Bergdorf Goodman and don't mention the *New York Times.* Just ask for Giada Fabrizio and put it on my tab. It's family money, and it's of no object to me. I'm not your typical restaurant reviewer, and this is not a typical arrangement."

"Yes, I realize." I exhaled. "I'm looking forward to starting."

Michael Saltz shook his head. "No, no, don't look at it like that. You've already started. You're already *in.*"

Again with his insistence that we were more involved than we were.

"Okay, then. Yes. I'm in," I said. I didn't say it with confidence, a *yes* clenching its conviction. No, I said it like a question in the dark, hoping someone would catch it. I had no idea how this would work, and already he expected me to be fully committed. But I'd go along. I'd catch up with him eventually.

"Very good," he said. "It's very important you think about this in immediate, immersive terms. I need absolute discretion. Even your saffron-harvesting boyfriend cannot know. It's usually the ones closest to you that hold you back. Especially ones from a prior, simpler life. Do you understand?"

"I understand," I said.

"You understand . . . what?"

"I understand . . . I have to be careful. And not tell my boyfriend."

"Because why?"

"Because . . . you have to look out for the ones who are closest to you."

"No, that's not what I said. I said the ones closest to you are the ones who hold you back."

"Right," I said. "That's what I meant." Perhaps they were one and the same. You just had to pay attention to the people in your life. I convinced myself that Elliott would be fine. No casualties.

Michael Saltz smiled a sweet but devilish smile. "Good. I'm glad we're on the same page. Now, going forward, keep your schedule flexible. I will call you when I need you." I wasn't sure how a graduate student with major obligations could remain "flexible," but it was the price I had to pay for this arrangement.

"Yes, sir," I said. "Thank you?" It came out like a question, but Michael Saltz softened, as if he empathized.

"I'll call you to schedule our next dinner. You may not have time to go to Bergdorf beforehand, so I guessed your size and got you this."

He unzipped a garment bag labeled *Prabal Gurung* and revealed a silk sheath dress in a golden peacock print. Then he opened a shoebox of copper strappy stiletto sandals embellished with little gems.

I had never touched clothing this exquisite, much less worn it.

This was the world I was stepping into, and it couldn't have come at a better time.

"This is just to tide you over until you make it to Bergdorf. I will see you soon."

I rushed out of the apartment and found the hotel-like smell of the hallway cleansing after the stench of Michael Saltz's place. When the elevator door closed, I collapsed to the floor and screamed. For thirty-five floors, all I could say was "*Yes, yes, yes!*"

I made sure the Bergdorf bag was in clear view as I entered the lobby, and just as I expected, the doorman—the stupid doorman who couldn't be bothered to even smile thirty minutes before—ran to open the door for me.

Helen and the *Times* were cemented into my future. The city was my playground. I'd be heard. I couldn't have imagined a better scenario. Walking to the subway, I realized I held my head higher. I wasn't afraid of this cacophonous city or intimidated by the achievements of others. And I even put aside my worry about what would happen to Madison Park Tavern after that two-star review. A rush of possibility flooded my heart, and I rode the wave all the way home.

Chapter 9

In the twenty-four hours that followed my meeting with Michael Saltz, I did as he said and didn't tell a soul. I woke up and did my reading about food systems in Australia. I wore my regular clothes and went to my internship seminar and talked about modes of leadership.

But the whole time, our conversation tingled. Here I was, sitting in a concrete cell, talking about drab assignments. My classmate Rachel was studying canned mackerel and brought five tins to class, one of which had leaked foul-smelling oil into her new purse. Geo thought he'd be recruiting a new class of bakers into the incubator, but was spending all his time doing paperwork thirty blocks away from the actual space.

They had accepted this as their lot, and I don't think they were even unhappy. It was what they had asked for, and they'd gotten it.

I was glad I wasn't in their shoes.

After my morning class, I went to visit Elliott. We had yet to find a good rhythm to our days. My classes and internship shifts were scattered and herky-jerky. And though he had a full-time job, that didn't mean he had a regular schedule, either. Experiments went long, fund-raising events held him captive. Sometimes he worked the night shift and returned home on sleepy subways taking their time making all local stops.

But today, we had found time.

"Tia!" Elliott said as he opened the door and gave me a hug. "I got a thing! For the apartment!"

I looked in the farthest corner of the room, a mere five feet away in Elliott's tiny studio, and saw an end table. He'd even hung a wreath on the window behind it.

Elliott was determined to get "real person" furniture—no funky hand-me-downs and no bottom-of-the-line IKEA. Lucky for him, his studio was so small it didn't take much to fill the space. In college, we had both lived on-campus and never bought anything that couldn't be abandoned at the end of the year. Now I was pleased to see the adult Elliott coming to the forefront. An adult Elliott who like hardwood end tables and sage and lavender wreaths.

Though he still hadn't gotten chairs, so we stood awkwardly in his space.

"I love it!" I replied, then gave him a hug and a kiss.

"Good, I'm glad you said that. Because maybe in a year or so, we can find a place and . . ."

I hugged him again. He was shopping for our future apartment! So Elliott.

"How was your day?" he asked.

"Oh, you know, class, things." I felt my meeting with Michael Saltz pushing itself into my consciousness and I focused on forcing it out. "How are you?"

"Great. So great. Today we harvested our first samples from those South American specimens I told you about."

I didn't remember him telling me about any South American specimens, but I stayed quiet as he continued. The thoughts about Michael Saltz had bubbled over and now all I could think about was my first dinner. My clothes. My words in the paper. Those three things cycled in my brain so fast I felt like I was hovering over real life, disconnected by the ecstasy of excitement.

"Tia . . . hello?" Elliott said, and I snapped to attention. "Did you space out? I just said you've barely been over since we got here."

"I know, I know, I'm sorry," I said. "It's just . . ." But where could I start? I wanted to tell him so badly, but I couldn't. I had never kept anything from Elliott in our four years of dating.

"Hold on a sec . . . I *did* get something else. Close your eyes!" Elliott tiptoed his fingers over my shoulders and closed my eyes with his palm. Even with my eyes closed, I could feel his excitement. I loved Elliott's surprises.

I heard the *tap-tap* of his feet and the sound of things hitting the floor.

"Okay, open!"

Elliott gestured toward the queen-size bed, which took up a third of the room. His messenger bag and folders had been thrown to the ground.

"New. Sheets. Five hundred thread count."

"Hooray!" I said.

For the longest time, Elliott had said that thread count was a hoax. The human body can't detect thread density, he'd said. But then we'd stayed in a hotel in D.C. that had 750-thread-count sheets, and he was converted. We'd had amazing sex that night, and he—scientific mind that he was—deduced that it was the sheets. I didn't think the linens had anything to do with it (more likely a delicious dinner, perfect weather, and drinks that buzzed us just enough), but there was no point in bursting his bubble. Elliott was happiest when he had a problem to solve.

"Well?" he said. "You may approach the sheets."

I bent over and ran my fingers across the fabric. They were white and very smooth but reeked of the vinyl packaging. You could see still see the crease marks from the folds. But on the whole, they were nice. I ran my hand across the duvet as Elliott came up behind me and kissed the back of my neck.

"Want to give it a go?"

I gasped as if I couldn't believe how louche he was being, even though I loved every second.

"Should I?" I teased.

"You should," Elliott said, nodding with his whole head and torso. "In fact, you have to."

"Oh, is that so?" I said, my fingers tucked into the front of his jeans.

Elliott stepped forward and I stepped back, but his binoculars were in the way and I ended up tripping and hitting the bed with not just an unsexy collapse, but a mood-killing *thud*.

Elliott fumbled down right after me and then we were kissing and grappling all over those sheets. I guessed they did have magical powers. I'm sure we didn't look very sexy or competent, but we were enjoying each other. It occurred to me for a fleeting second that we'd been in New York for more than a month and hadn't had sex yet. There were some days when we didn't even make contact with each other.

But his touch erased any distance. Elliott and his perfect body, the ideal size for me, the right height and boniness and flesh and heat and hair. I couldn't have fashioned a man better fit for my hands and hugs than Elliott. I'd missed him.

His fingers slipped under my T-shirt. Suddenly, I wished I had something from Bergdorf at that second—anything to replace the boring stuff I was wearing. Lately, Elliott seemed to be caring more about nice things. And I was, too.

Elliott started kissing me on the nose. I nudged myself closer and we kissed faster, deeper. He unbuttoned my jeans, then swept his hands up my shirt and under my bra, barely touching my breasts but just holding them, understanding their shape.

I could hear the next-door neighbor playing the keyboard, repeating the same lines in a manic tumble that sounded like marbles falling down the stairs. She kept on going, laboring over and over that part.

We rolled around more, but I couldn't block out the neighbor. Why couldn't she just move on? The thrashing of her keyboard drilled in my head.

Elliott took off my top and then started on his. I looked at him while his face was hidden and cringed for some reason. But by the time he got his shirt off, I was ready to embrace him again. Whatever that feeling was, I had shaken it off.

He unlatched my bra with minimal struggle, and I looped my big toes around his white athletic socks and peeled them off. He pressed his chest against mine and that feeling overcame me again. Heartache. Fear. I buried my face in his neck—a neck and body that had been so good to me for so long—and winced. I was sure he felt my face change against his skin, but he kept going. He kept kissing me and moving his hands across my shoulders. It was the same tempo and sequence as always. Kissing, undressing, him on top, done. Perfectly fine. But this was different in other ways. Suddenly everything filled me with an inexplicable sadness.

Elliott's sheets reeking of vinyl. His tiny studio with barely any light. The belongings he'd triumphantly swept off the bed. The fact that he'd thought this would be a wonderful surprise pinched my heart. He seemed so ravenous for me, while I was holding my breath, waiting to be seized by another wave of sorrow.

My phone rang on that new end table. Rescue. I picked it up.

MISSED CALL: MICHAEL SALTZ

And then, a text:

Call me now.

I put the phone down—a little too loudly—as Elliott realized that he had lost me in the moment.

"Hey, what, who," he said, panting, his hands hovering over my topless body as if I were radioactive. "What is . . . ?"

"Oh, Elliott. I— It's just—" I jumped out of bed and kissed him on the forehead to make up for the abruptness, but of course that didn't help.

He let out a ruffled, pained sound and wrinkled his face like he was talking to the sun. "Tia, come back. What are you doing?"

"I have to—"

"Seriously, Tia? Please come back to bed. I miss you. I want you." So he'd noticed our lack of sex, too.

"Elliott, I have to do this thing . . ."

"Come on! Can't it wait? Who was that?"

"No one," I said, putting on my bra and shirt. "I just remembered I forgot to write up my report for my internship seminar. Which is in an hour. And that will take me at least an hour to do."

Elliott looked at my phone on the table, and I swiped it away. Nothing I said seemed to stick with him. He kept looking at me, expecting me to say something that would register. But I couldn't do that for him.

Still lying on the bed, Elliott slammed the wall.

I'm sorry, I mouthed, as if uttering a sound would make this a real problem. This was a little blip. I was adjusting to Michael Saltz, and soon everything would settle into place.

Elliott propped himself up on his new sheets and stared at me with round, searching eyes. The tiniest of frowns crossed over his face. "It's okay. Let me know if you need help." But he said it as an afterthought.

"Thanks, I will," I said.

I called Michael Saltz back the second I got onto the street.

"Okay, I'm returning your call." My eyes climbed to the fourth floor of Elliott's building. I wasn't sure which window was his.

"Well, hello to you, too," he said. "Are you free Wednesday night? I'd like to go to Panh Ho."

Elliott and I were supposed to hang out that night and I had an internship report due on Thursday, but now that I had it within my grasp, I needed to get the NBT. Everything else would have to wait.

"Yes, I'm free," I said. "And . . ." I was searching for the little bead that had changed things with Elliott. "I want to go to Bergdorf, too," I said, just to try it on for size.

"Go anytime you want!" Michael Saltz said. "You have free rein over my account."

A rich and luscious relief washed over me. It came out of nowhere, as sudden as the wave of sadness in Elliott's apartment. It rushed in like fresh air, something new and invigorating.

As I hung up, I noticed Elliot's wreath in the fourth-floor window and ran down the street to the subway that would take me uptown to Bergdorf Goodman. I had to get away.

Bergdorf was unlike any store I had ever seen, more like a museum than a place to buy clothes. I didn't see cashiers, or lines, or even many people. Each designer had his or her own little boutique with its own type of carpet and mannequins and salespeople. The Chanel boutique was black-and-white Parisian elegance. The Roberto Cavalli boutique screamed with color and print and leg. The Chanel saleslady wore a prim black sheath and cardigan, while the Cavalli woman wore a whipped tropical number slit to her upper thigh.

A tiny, impeccably dressed Italian woman approached me. She wore towering black patent leather ankle boots and had very arched eyebrows, the best-looking woman in sight.

"May I help you?" she asked. She had no name tag, nothing that would puncture a hole in her beautiful blouse.

"Yes, I'm looking for Giada Fabrizio? Michael Saltz sent me."

"Ah, I am Giada! Signore Michelangelo is very nice. Come with me to lingerie, yes?"

"Lingerie! No, no."

"You don't want something . . . pretty?" Just then I saw the obvious: older man sends young woman to "get some nice things" with his money . . . I shuddered at the thought.

"I need something that will make me look polished and sophisticated."

"Of course," she said, though she looked disappointed. "Is it for special occasion? What sort of thing you like? We go polished and tough, perhaps Balenciaga? Or polished and modern like Prada? Or do you like the polished and . . . how do you say . . . girly? Like a Temperley or Matthew Williamson, do you suppose?"

"Oh! Um, well, I don't know." I suddenly wished Emerald could help me with this. "I need to look older and more professional."

"Okay, do not worry. I will get you something so beautiful. I gather clothes for you, and I call you into room when I am ready."

I sat on a taupe suede couch and watched her walk away, two long zippers trailing down the backs of her boots like silver invitations. She was born to be a lingerie personal shopper.

I got to my feet and made a little tour of the floor, focusing on each designer name and committing the different looks to memory. Each boutique was its own little stage, mini lifestyles living side by side, ripe for the choosing. If I was going to play the part of the elegant diner, this was a world I needed to know.

I watched older women inspecting the seams of each garment and younger women holding slinky dresses against their bodies. Husbands sitting on the couches, playing games on their cell phones. Gorgeous six-foot models listening to the advice of their gay best friends. Two women wore their sunglasses even though we were very much inside and argued where they would spend Thanksgiving, the one's house in Southampton, or the other's house in Bridgehampton.

And then, at the far end of the store, someone caught my eye, a woman sitting in a leather armchair in the Michael Kors boutique. She was hugging her arms around herself and rocking slowly, strangely. It looked like she needed help.

When I stepped closer, the woman's eyes darted around like those of a caged animal. She sank back inside the chair, a tiny plant among a forest of faceless mannequins.

"Excuse me, ma'am?" I said to the woman, crouching down to eye level. The Michael Kors boutique smelled different from the rest of the store, of white flowers like jasmine and gardenia. "Is everything all right? Are you here with someone?" I looked for her companion. I couldn't imagine that she'd have come here on her own; she seemed afraid to move.

The woman said nothing. She actually wasn't an old woman at all, maybe in her forties or early fifties. She had a beautiful face and a dignified look to her, if you could imagine a time in which she didn't look so fearful. Her hair was high and tight like a ballerina's, a style that called attention to her hollowed cheeks but also gave her a look of strength and grace. She wore a pink cashmere sweater decorated with delicate crocheted flowers and two rings with large ruby stones. They must have been a weighty burden on her weak fingers.

Then I heard a worried voice from some faraway Bergdorf chamber. "Mom? Mom, where are you? Mom?"

The woman looked up and shrank even farther into her chair. She pulled the neck of her sweater up to her mouth. I didn't know how to help her, whether it was best to reveal the woman to her daughter, or hide her instead.

Still, I couldn't see the girl, just hear her voice.

"Mom? Mom? Excuse me, miss? Have you seen my mom? She was sitting right here. Her name is Janelle. If you see her, can you tell her that Emerald is looking for her?"

Five boutiques away, I saw her gesturing wildly at a saleswoman. Emerald. I took another look at the woman in the armchair and ran off to the Dolce & Gabbana boutique, where I hid behind a rack of large wrap sweaters.

Emerald couldn't see me in Bergdorf Goodman. She knew this wasn't my kind of place. We'd be put in some awkward situation that wouldn't benefit either of us. She had her secret, and I had mine. Facing her would rattle the divisions we'd created. So I remained hidden, poking out from behind a large sweater threaded with frazzled yarn that leaped out like rainbow eyelashes.

From there I saw Emerald spot her mother, then grab her with a force that surprised me. "Mom! I told you to stay where you were! Why did you move?! I told you to stay, I told you to stay!"

This had to be the "hard life" Sherri at the thrift shop had been talking about.

The woman looked up at Emerald blankly. "Mom, please, please don't do this again," Emerald said. The woman rose out of her chair and hid her face, as if ashamed.

They passed the Dolce & Gabbana boutique and Emerald

had tears in her eyes as she mouthed the word *fuck* over and over again. Her mother looked back at me and I almost knocked down a mannequin dressed in a stretchy black dress covered with silver ziti-shaped tubing.

I waited until they entered the elevator, then turned around to find Giada behind me as close as my shadow.

"Are you ready now? I think I have everything you need," she said. "I had lots of fun with the bedroom things, even though you say you don't like."

Now didn't seem like the time to try on clothes—much less lingerie.

"Would you be able to send the outfits to my home?" I said. "I can just return them if they don't fit."

"Of course, miss. I have it couriered to you tomorrow morning, and we can pick them up if you do not like."

"Great. But the delivery must be discreet," I said, echoing Michael Saltz.

"Say no more, miss. I understand."

I wrote down my name, address, and cell phone number on a cream linen card.

"Ah, very nice, Miss Monroe," Giada said. "We have another delivery to the East Village tomorrow morning. I will tell the courier, Piotr, to call you when he is outside your building."

I nodded, then took the escalators down. Outside Bergdorf's, tourists had taken over Fifth Avenue. Emerald and her mother were nowhere to be seen.

Chapter 10

My cell phone rang at nine the next morning.

"Hello, Tia Monroe? This is Piotr from Bergdorf Goodman."

"Okay, I'll be down in a second." I threw on a hoodie, picked up a laundry bag, and ran downstairs, thinking I'd hurry everything into my room while Emerald and Melinda slept. But when I arrived in the lobby, I saw an entire rack of garment bags and boxes next to a big man. He dressed like a bellhop but looked strong and sharp-eyed enough to be secret service. Both he and the doorman looked unfazed. I guessed they had seen weirder things.

My laundry bag wouldn't even fit a quarter of the stuff. The delivery was crazy. I hadn't asked Giada for this much. She, or maybe Michael Saltz, must have taken liberties with my request.

"Okay, well, I suppose the garment rack has to come up. But we have to be quiet so my roommates don't wake up," I whispered to Piotr.

"Very good, miss," he said. We took everything into the elevator and I wanted him to break the spell and say the truth, that this was strange. But he didn't. I made him stay in the hallway while I peeked inside our living room.

The coast was clear, but Emerald's door was now a little open. Had it been open when I left? Or had she left and gone down another elevator? I hadn't seen her in the lobby, but maybe I'd missed her. Or maybe she hadn't spent the night at the apartment at all.

After Piotr left, I locked my bedroom door and put everything away, but Emerald stayed in the back of my mind. When would she come back? Could she have seen Piotr and this mountain of clothing?

There was so much in the delivery, I didn't know where to start. So I started everywhere. I opened garment bags stuffed with four or five things, then took something out of a tall bag, then something from a box. Inside one garment bag I found a navy suit with an ever-so-faint paisley design woven into it. The tag said *Valentino*. Got it. An Italian name, with luxe flair.

And then I uncovered two sleeveless silk shirts, structured with expert-looking pleats around the shoulders and bust. These were by a guy named Narciso Rodriguez. Or was that a woman? They were subtle and somehow mathematical, something an architect would wear for herself and not necessarily for others.

Next, a white Carolina Herrera blouse. A female designer, that I could understand. But what I couldn't understand—its buttery weight, a silkiness that enveloped your hands. This woman is casually wealthy. She may roll up her sleeves, but the blouses are dry-cleaned and steamed the second she takes them off.

I marveled at a blazer by Missoni. It was black on the outside, but lined with what I would later learn were the house's signature zigzags. This one seemed like a stretch for me, but that made me like it more.

A round, pumpkin-orange box labeled *Hermès* beckoned. I

didn't know whether to expect earmuffs or a necklace or a bathing suit. It was none of those things: a beautiful silk scarf patterned with hot-air balloons. Now I remembered what Hermès stood for. Scarves, yes, but also bags. Could I get my hands on one of those?

I crouched down and found a navy shoebox etched with a silver triangle and discovered a pair of red patent leather slingbacks. *Prada*. They were clean and sturdy, yet subversive. There was a lone spike on the underside of the sole, in the space where the toes vault up to the heel.

I worked to internalize everything as if it were a dream that might fade away. With each garment, I studied the tag—who made it, where it came from, what materials. Like the restaurant dishes at Madison Park Tavern, I wanted to learn everything. There was security in that complete knowledge.

I turned my attention to three dresses that were definitely not made for dining. They were going-out things, dancing looks. One was a swingy black dress made of a wet suit–like material, with a high neck and stiff A-line skirt. *Alexander McQueen*. Another was a red Gucci with little loops of textured fringe. It should have looked Elmo-like, but the sophisticated shape overrode the thought. I twisted the dress on the hanger, and the skirt rose and fell like the swelling of the ocean. The last dress was surprisingly heavy even though it was the shortest, narrowest, lowest-cut garment in that day's shipment. The tag said *Hervé Léger* and the dress was ribbed like a mummy, a very tight, shiny, green-and-gold mummy.

I skipped three other boxes and opened the big one on the bottom, a white box sealed with satiny tape labeled *Jimmy Choo*. Inside was a pair of black knee-high boots in a beautiful glossy crocodile pattern. I wondered if they could really be crocodile, and then realized I had never touched crocodile before. I looked at the side of the box, but couldn't find the price tag. Not that I knew how much crocodile cost, anyway.

I didn't know how much anything cost, and that added to the surreality of it all.

The last thing I opened was a classic trench coat with sharp, precise lapels, whimsical hooks and snaps, and a silk lining that spoke something about me that I was not. In coat check, I never saw coats with so much detail and beauty. I tried it on and it lay on me as a new identity would, heavy and complete and consuming. I wanted to live in this coat and have it do all the talking for me. The label said *Burberry.* At that moment, the name meant little aside from shiny magazine ads and Chinatown knock-off scarves. I could only pay attention to the quality, the luxuriousness of the thing itself.

I used to think that fashion was a disguise. People depended on those bells and whistles to prove something about themselves. I still felt that way, but was it so bad? It was like speaking many languages. Each one gave you a new entryway into the world. That's what clothing could do for me. I could step out as someone different.

There were so many brands I didn't know, so many things—like brooches and clutches and silk neck scarves—that totally stumped me. Millions of women would have killed for this, all this *stuff,* all this possibility. I didn't have to pinch myself to prove it was real—I just had to touch it, press it against my face, spritz it on the inside of my wrist.

I looked at the rest of my bounty and realized that it would take me a good part of the morning to open everything and put it away. And actually, I had miscalculated how much closet space I had. Even though I had received a flood of clothes, more than I had ever bought in my life, I still fit everything in my closet. It had started big and empty. But now it was full, finally full.

I took out one last package and unwrapped it on the bed. Out came black lingerie with laser-cut lace, beautiful pieces that were romantic yet strong. Modern and sexy. Giada had left a note on another of Bergdorf's signature cream linen cards: *Enjoy your new clothes.*

THAT AFTERNOON, I took my Nutrition test wearing my new lingerie. No one saw it, but it made me feel better. I left class thinking I had done really well.

Chapter 11

The Financial District was empty when I arrived on Wednesday night. There were huge buildings, blocky statues, streetlights that managed nonexistent traffic. Thick pillars of steam rose from the sewers, like the ground sighing after a long day.

After getting lost on streets I didn't know existed—Beaver and Bank and Gold, nothing like the easy grids of Midtown or the familiar tangle around NYU—I made it to the restaurant. I wore Michael Saltz's original Prabal Gurung dress and gemstone sandals. When I had first put it on, I couldn't help but think that the dress gilded something—or someone—quite ordinary. But instead of shrinking from the grandeur of the clothes, I made myself rise to them.

Michael Saltz sat in the front waiting area on a red satin couch beneath a lurching, voluptuous orchid. "Hello, Tia," he said. "Welcome to our first meal together. Why are you standing like that?"

"Like what?"

"Like you're in a police lineup." He took me by the shoulders and jolted me back. I teetered on my high heels, let my chest jut out and my butt move back.

"There, that's better," he said as I acquainted myself with the new S-shape of my body. I had a lot to learn.

The waiting area veered off in three directions. Each hallway had a fish tank recessed into the floor. I supposed one path led to the bathroom. Another to the coatroom. The last to the dining room. I couldn't see much beyond the koi.

"May I take your bag?" a woman asked. She didn't sneer at my tote, though I immediately regretted carrying it. Had I really brought a canvas tote to this restaurant? What had I been thinking when Giada had delivered so many other beautiful bags?

"Thank you, miss," she said, taking my bag as if it were a newborn baby, with delicacy and respect. She was a coat check master.

"Now remember," Michael Saltz whispered. "I order, you eat. You tell me what you think. This is a dry-run dinner. I want you to enjoy yourself, but not too much. Always assume we are under watch."

I nodded silently.

"Ready?" A hostess had appeared out of nowhere. I wondered if he had rented the entire restaurant for us. It was so quiet. Too quiet.

Michael Saltz put out his arm for me hold, but I didn't take it. He wore a gray checkered shirt, a navy V-neck sweater, and khakis, a hedge fund manager's casual look.

"Remember, I'm gay. And I'm helping you—in more ways than one."

I wrapped my arm in his and he gave me a fierce, satisfied look. The bones of his arm poked through his sweater and I gulped as we walked into the dining room, my stilettos clicking uneasily on the black marble. The NBT had begun and there was no looking back now.

"That dress looks good on you. Giada told me she gave you more like this. I'm glad. This is a vast improvement."

I let out a brief chuckle, a vague sound of agreement. A part of me wanted to rebel against his words—*What was wrong with me in the first place?*—but this wasn't the place. And, more than that, I had to admit he was right.

We sat and looked over the menu. Michael Saltz ordered a reasonable number of dishes. Perhaps on the high side, but nothing that would arouse suspicion.

A couple of minutes later, the hostess laid what looked to be a flower on each of our bread plates.

"Compliments of the chef. This is an olive oil sweet potato tulip croquant. Inside are 'stamens' made of black sesame and honey."

I twirled the stem in the light of the candle. Michael chomped on his and let out a small, contented noise.

"Hm. Crunchy," he said. Then, with his head lowered, "How does it taste?"

It seemed a shame to eat such a gorgeous thing.

"Don't be precious. Eat it."

"Okay," I said. I took out my phone. It was so lovely and well constructed, I wanted to preserve the memory.

"Whoa, whoa, whoa. What's happening here?"

"Oh, sorry. It's just so beautiful. I wasn't going to post it or anything."

"Put your phone down. Now," he said. His face had reddened, and we hadn't even ordered drinks yet. I did what he asked.

"Let's go through the reasons why you shouldn't do that," Michael Saltz said, his skeletal fingers waving close to my face.

"First, taking a picture draws unnecessary attention to yourself. You must blend in. You must go undetected."

"I understand. No pictures."

"We have professional photographers for that," he continued. "You don't have to use your phone, for goodness' sake. Second, what if someone saw that photo on the phone. Or, even worse, you were stupid enough to send it to someone or post it online. How would you have explained your meal here?"

"Well—" I stammered.

"Have you even thought that far ahead?"

"It was just a picture for myself, I swear," I said, though under any other circumstance I'd have definitely sent this photo to Elliott. He would have loved sweet potato that looked like a flower. That was a dish he could get into.

Michael lowered his fork back to his plate. "Tia? Do you know where we are?"

"Um, Panh Ho?"

"Have you heard of this place before?"

"Yes."

"But did you think you'd come here, ever?"

"No."

"Have you ever worn anything as exquisite as that Prabal Gurung?"

"No. I've never worn anything this nice."

"Have you ever seen anything as exceptional as that sweet potato flower?"

"No." Okay, I got his point. He didn't have to be such a patronizing jackass about it.

"Precisely. You have been here not ten minutes, and already you have become a worldlier person. Why would you deny yourself that by reverting to your past and emailing your college boyfriend?" His face soured at those last words. "Look at me. Look at these surroundings. You are a grown woman. Don't look back. Not when you have me and this right in front of you."

I went to put the phone back in my purse, but Michael Saltz stopped me. "No. Leave it on the table, face up. I want to see who calls you and how you manage these situations."

I did as he asked and tried to mask my extreme annoyance. Was this a job or detention? I couldn't believe what a jerk this guy was. He could have been nicer, considering I was his "protégée," not his punching bag.

Around us, the dining room was filling up, elegant women with frizz-free chignons and white fur stoles. Dapper men in suits constructed to their long, lean bodies. An extremely attractive waiter walked toward our table with our appetizers, and Michael clamped his mouth shut but glared at me as if to say, *I'm not done with you yet.*

The waiter stood about six foot three and had wavy chin-length hair. I think he was half black, but I didn't know what the other part could be. Whatever it was, it combined into something staggeringly handsome.

"For the lady," he said, "a poached quail egg inside a wonton cabbage 'purse.' And for the gentleman, pork meatball on a bed of braised endives and demi-glace 'roe.' "

I punctured the cabbage and a bright orange yolk spilled onto the greens. I imagined Elliott inspecting each dish. He might've liked a meal like this, playful and smart, with a little touch of botany mixed in.

But then again, he'd hate the pomp. The cost. The ceremony of every little thing. I couldn't be sure that he'd eat anything on the menu.

That's when my phone rang. I extended my hand, ready to silence it.

"Don't touch. Who is it?" he asked.

But I knew he knew. This was a test.

"No one," I said. "I won't answer it." But the phone kept ringing.

Michael put his hand out. "Give me your phone. Before it stops ringing."

"No, I'll just turn it off."

"Maybe you will, but you don't want to." He lifted my hand off the phone. "Elliott," he read. "I remember him from the reception. Well?" He nudged the phone toward me. "Answer it now before he hangs up."

"But what do I say?"

"Say what you think you need to say." But he didn't mean that. He wanted me to say what he wanted me to say.

I answered the phone.

"Hey," I said.

"Hey," Elliott said. "Um . . . can you talk now?"

"Well, not really. I mean, for a second . . ."

Michael Saltz gave me a stern, but not forbidding look—like I could do better.

"Let me know if you want to get together later, okay? I want to see you."

Shit.

"Probably not tonight—I'm at the library struggling with this paper. But I'll call you tomorrow." I looked up at Michael Saltz, who was smiling for the first time that night. I smiled back, a tiny bit content that I had pleased him.

"Seriously? Tia, I—"

"Sorry, Elliott, gotta go." I remembered I was supposed to be in the library. "I can't talk now," I whispered, and then hung up. Just like that.

"Excellent work, Tia. See, you're a natural! That wasn't so hard, was it?"

I still held the warm phone. Farther uptown, Elliott was wondering what was up. Did he even believe I was in the library? Maybe he'd stop by to find me. He'd ask me the best studying spots and I wouldn't be able to tell him. It was a good thing I was all the way down in the Financial District. He wouldn't bump into me here.

"No, not hard," I said as my main arrived, braised veal over hand-pulled noodles, artichokes, and mint.

I put my phone back on the table. In a way, I was glad Michael Saltz had forced me to avoid Elliott. We hadn't seen each other since our awkward non-sexcapade last week. Our schedules rarely lined up, though now it was probably better that way. I wouldn't have to lie to his face.

"Good! Now let's toast," he said, lifting his wineglass.

I lifted mine and we barely, briefly touched glasses. But the *ping* sent shivers through my arm.

"Cheers," he said. "In October, we'll try Tellicherry. That will be your first review. To leaving the past, and starting the future."

"To starting the future," I said, then took a sip of the wine. It was dark and dusty-tasting and I had a hard time keeping it down. A little beeping noise beckoned from my phone. Michael Saltz didn't hear it and I pretended not to notice. But it pinged away inside me, a tap-tapping upon my heart.

Michael Saltz was too busy gulping down his wine. He had been insistent on a full-bodied Bordeaux. I guess that's what was most palatable to him. Plus, it had a high alcohol content.

"Well, Tia Monroe," he said. "Your time in New York City just got a whole lot more interesting."

We ate our desserts, refined mochi balls made with a finger lime curd. Then, as we were walking out of Panh Ho, I thought I heard a click, an old-fashioned shutter sound but with modern clarity. Even though Michael Saltz was rushing me out, I looked around. I just saw the dining room, operating as normal. Except for one person rushing behind a red velvet curtain, gilded with elaborate embroidery.

That must have been when they photographed my face.

Chapter 12

THE NEXT AFTERNOON, THURSDAY, I REPORTED TO MADISON Park Tavern at four wearing my old Jil Sander. I was dying to wear my new clothes, but I couldn't arouse suspicion. I was looking forward to getting back to work, though transitioning from Panh Ho to Madison Park Tavern left me disoriented, a whiplash of perspective.

Jake clearly wanted to rebound from the two-star with a vengeance. It had been nine days since the review came out. The floral arrangements had quadrupled in size and the curtains had been freshly pressed. He'd put out better silverware, which clanged on the stemware with a more crystalline, exquisite sound.

I went downstairs to the locker room to drop off my coat and purse and took a moment to absorb it all: the white-tiled basement floor, the metal mesh lockers—tiny ones assigned to waiters, and even tinier ones for the bussers and backservers—the smell of sweat and food and coffee, lots of coffee. Garment bags from Calvin Klein, Armani, and Paul Smith covered the walls.

Emerald had been right about all the waitstaff dressing in designer suits. Now that I had my own windfall of designer clothes, I finally noticed.

A bunch of staffers came in all at once with one of the assistant managers trailing behind them yelling, "Get moving, first seating in thirty-five minutes. Now, now, now."

I crammed everything into my little locker.

Carey stood in front of a mirror and smoothed out her frizzy hair with an extra-strong hair gel. Angel wiped his sweating forehead with a festively colored handkerchief. Chad was rescheduling something on the phone, saying, "The next couple weeks are fucked and Monday I'm stacking interviews back to back."

Outside, I heard Jake and Gary walking into the prep kitchen, Gary talking in unintelligible but triumphant garble like he had just landed a hole-in-one.

Someone had posted a picture of the new, skinny Michael Saltz on our staff corkboard, and it had already been defaced with a mustache, devil horns, buckteeth, a hairy mole, and an ax severing his skull. A grading rubric had also appeared. The waitstaff was now evaluated on personal presentation, menu expertise, client emotional intelligence, and something called "CTD." As a new backserver, Carey barely made it onto the board, but she had the highest CTD score.

"You're lucky you're not subjected to this shit," Chad said, nodding to the grid. Chad rated high on client emotional intelligence and menu expertise, but was below average in personal presentation and CTD. Now, I noticed he had shaved his goatee and put on moisturizer or something. He looked younger and smoother. I'd liked him better before.

"Hey, what are you doing?" Carey asked, seeing me in my daze.

"Oops, sorry. I'm just feeling out of it." Two stars. That was big—huge. Seeing it in writing, it felt so distant. But standing here, bumping up against the people it affected, I could see it was more than a grade. It was lives. I was beginning to really like these people, a thought that clashed with my Michael Saltz dealings. They were two sides of the same coin, always opposites, always opponents.

"You worried about the review?" Angel asked. "Nothing we can do about it now. Tonight, we kill it."

"Yeah," Chad said. "That shitface Michael Saltz doesn't know a thing."

That shitface knew *some* things, I thought, stabbed with a dagger of guilt.

Then Chef Darling barged into the locker room, took out a flask, and chugged. Carey ran up to him.

"What happened, Chef?" a waiter asked.

"This shit's fucked. I'm on probation. Gary is on the warpath."

The locker room quieted as everyone crowded around Chef Darling, asking him questions and trying to comfort him.

"Come on, Matthew," Carey said carefully. His body radiated anger. "Don't drink any more. You'll be fine. We'll be fine," she crooned. By now, she was stroking his leg. He had calmed down and even lowered his flask.

Then the locker room door creaked open, and Jake inserted his lightly gelled head inside. "Tia," he whispered. "Gary and I would like to see you in his office."

"Oh!" I said, panic prickling up my spine. Shit.

Of course they would find out. What had I been thinking—that I'd get away with this Michael Saltz arrangement? Someone had spotted me exiting his building. Or maybe I had dropped his note. Maybe they'd read our emails. Had I been on the restaurant's Wi-Fi that whole time?

I followed Jake down the hall and up two sets of stairs to the offices. I had never ventured upstairs and saw that the finesse and elegance of the restaurant didn't continue up there. The rug said "institutional" and the walls cracked with old, carelessly applied paint. I ran my fingers across them and realized they were hollow and cheap.

I'd been arriving at work on time, and Jake had said I was doing a good job, so they had to know about Michael Saltz. Our every correspondence rushed through my head. What would be the thing that did me in, and how could I talk my way out of it? How could I diminish what I'd done?

I had no idea who he was.

Didn't realize he'd use my words.

Wasn't thinking when I wrote back to him, and went to his apartment, and took his money.

All lies, of course. I'd known what I was doing, I realized with a thump of nausea. Ultimately, I'd put myself before people I liked and cared about. I could have looked out for them, but instead I'd looked out for myself.

That was bad, but was it a crime if my intentions were pure?

We passed Jake's office and I caught sight of a tube of Pringles, some paperwork, and a pile of large black binders. He had taped a picture of a woman with two tiny babies on the shelf behind his desk. Chef Darling's office was filled with books and magazines, dirty tissues, and opened bags of gummy bears—nothing like his immaculate kitchen. The reservationist's room must have originally been a walk-in closet, because a closet rod and shelves hovered over her tiny desk.

We continued to the only room that had any windows: Gary Oscars's office. If the dining room were a hotel lobby, Jake's and Matthew's offices would be the custodial closets, and Gary's office would be the penthouse. Gary sat at a humongous wooden desk, leaning back in an expensive-looking leather chair.

And there, sitting across from him, was Dean Chang. Now I knew I was in big trouble. She folded her hands on her tweed pencil skirt. Jake sat down and gestured for me to do the same.

"Hello, Tia," Dean Chang said coolly.

"Hello, Dean Chang," I returned. I heard myself breathing and felt faint. Suddenly I wished I could have erased everything with Michael Saltz. So far, I had nothing to show for it, just clothes and secrets piling up.

"Tia," Jake said. "We have something very serious to discuss with you." He wouldn't meet my eyes.

But if Gary could have fired me with his stares, he would have already done it ten times over. His face was sweaty, red, and speckled. Every time he inhaled, the front of his shirt gaped so I could see bits of his undershirt.

"Tia Monroe, NYU graduate student," Gary started. "Many people consider Madison Park Tavern one of the best restaurants in New York. Do you agree?"

"I agree," I said.

"Of course you'd agree. Not that you've been to many," he said. "How could you? You're just a twenty-two-year-old girl from . . ." He looked down at a piece of paper, which must have been from my employee file. "Yonkers? How quaint. No restaurant experience. No industry connections. Tia Monroe, allergic to crustaceans and bivalves." He jerked his gaze toward Jake. "Seriously?"

I sat up straight, waiting for the ax to come down.

"Gary, please. Don't torture her," Jake said.

"Just tell her," Dean Chang said, though she wouldn't look at me, either.

Gary took us in. "I don't know why we let people like you work in this restaurant. You're a child in a grown person's job. I cannot take children on staff. Especially wicked children like you."

The room closed in and a cacophony of smells slammed into

me—the rottenness of Michael Saltz's apartment, the ambiguously sandy dumplings at Bakushan. I smelled gingery perfume off Dean Chang, a powdery scent from Jake's freshly cleaned suit, an odor of cigars and dark wood and leather on Gary Oscars.

Gary punched a button on his computer keyboard and turned the screen toward us. I saw a black-and-white movie of me talking to Michael Saltz in the basement. It was crude and pixelated, but it was clearly me.

"Would you mind telling us what is happening here?" Gary asked.

I just stared at the screen, a grainy image of me held captive by a thin man who still had such immense strength. It looked like a scene out of a cop show, where all the viewers know *this is a moment of danger.* It hadn't felt that way, but from the outside, it was obvious.

"We also have footage of you going to the basement, and Michael Saltz following you soon after."

Dean Chang put her hand on my shoulder and I snapped away. "Tia, what happened between you and Michael Saltz?"

Jake crossed his arms, gazed at his shoes, and said nothing.

"Yes, Tia," Gary said, "what happened? Because you have an unusual relationship with the *New York Times* restaurant critic."

They all waited for me, their collective authority seeming like an impossibly high wall fringed with barbed wire. But in one second, my outlook changed and I tried hard not to smile.

They only had this tape. They had no idea Michael Saltz had used my words in his review. They didn't know about my visit to his apartment, Bergdorf, Panh Ho. Though the image had at first alarmed me, it was nothing compared to the truth. Gary Oscars could call me a child all he wanted, but he knew nothing.

"Tia, tell us," Dean Chang said. "Is Michael Saltz bribing you? Is he . . . taking advantage of you?"

"Oh, that's bullshit," Gary said, spitting at me. "She's not the victim here."

"No, none of that happened," I lied. "This is all a misunderstanding. I've never worked in a restaurant before and that was my first night on the job. I didn't know who he was."

All three of them looked at one another. Dean Chang shrugged slightly, as if to say *Hey, she's got a point.*

But Gary Oscars couldn't be swayed. "But you *talked* to him. For five minutes. He was scribbling notes after you spoke. What in the world were you discussing?"

"Five minutes?" I said. It had actually felt much longer than that, but of course I wouldn't let on. "I honestly don't remember what I said. Maybe he just had a random thought and wanted to write it down? I didn't say anything important. I'm just a student."

"We realize that you couldn't have affected the reviews," Dean Chang said, "but this is still—"

"Insubordination," Gary Oscars finished.

"—not adding up," Dean Chang continued. "Is there something you're not telling us?"

I looked at each of them. I was going to make it out of this okay, I just had to get through this conversation. "No, I told you everything."

Dean Chang smiled, apparently relieved that I wasn't as evil as Gary had made me out to be.

My heart twisted again. It was easy to lie to Gary, someone who didn't know me and wasn't a particularly nice person. But Dean Chang and Jake were different. In this moment, they were placing their bets on me. They could have backed Gary, the path of least resistance. But they were willing to give me the benefit of the doubt. I was amazed and touched and guilt-ridden. Did I deserve that kind of loyalty from them?

I was sure I didn't. I was lying to them just by sitting there silently, letting them believe a better side of me.

"You can still work here, but we'll be pulling back your hours and putting you on probation." Dean Chang sighed. "This is your last warning. If we have another . . . breach of trust . . . then we'll have to reevaluate your graduate candidacy and scholarship. Best-case scenario, things run smoothly from here. Worst-case scenario, you'll lose the generous funding we've given you and be placed in a more structured program with traditional classes and check-ins with an academic advisor."

That sounded terrible. It sounded belittling, more like middle school than grad school, though grad school wasn't so great, either. They glorified it like some great privilege, but thus far, it had only held me back.

Gary leaned over the desk, his pudgy, hairy forearms streaking grease on the surface.

"This is the real world," he said. "There are no grades or empty probationary periods. You either fucked us or you didn't. And I think you fucked us."

Jake cringed. "Gary, there's no evidence to suggest that. We can only take Tia's word and give her a warning."

"Hm," Gary said, drilling his eyes into mine. I stayed still and strong.

"Her *word,*" he continued. "Tricky thing with words, though. You can't trust a liar's word. But I suppose that's all we have." He inhaled and for a second, despite his intimidation tactics, I thought he was giving me the benefit of the doubt. He briefly let his head-honcho guard down and I didn't think he really believed I was as wicked as he said. But of course he was oblivious.

"Thank you for letting me stay at the restaurant," I said.

Dean Chang shook her head and looked out the window. Jake got up out of his chair and held out his arm with the slightest bow, just as he had when he'd first welcomed me into Madison Park Tavern.

"Come on, Tia. I think it's time you leave. You don't have to work tonight."

"Make sure you stay out of my sight!" Gary called after me.

The whole encounter only took a couple of minutes, from the locker room to the office to the dismissal. I had gotten away with it. Nothing had changed. The rush caught up to me and suddenly I was gasping for air. Somehow, the restaurant knew—maybe not the people, but something in the walls, the twinkle of the glass, the marble of the stairs. If I wouldn't be punished by Gary, Dean Chang, or Jake, then maybe the restaurant would have its own karmic retribution.

I retrieved my things from the locker room and was about to escape when Carey called after me from the dining room. "Hey! What are you doing? Service starts in twenty minutes."

"I . . . I'm not working tonight." I held on to the wall for balance.

"Oh, gosh, Tia. Are you sick? I'll call you tonight after service. Or we can talk about it now?"

"No," I replied, softening my voice to a whisper. "Don't. It's better if you don't know. Or, rather, I don't want to get you sick." I reached for the rotating door, but it was rotating too fast, and I couldn't keep up. I thought it would tear my hand off.

She looked at me, confused, then gave me a hug. I was sure my body was pulsating with tension and guilt, but maybe my coat was too thick, because she didn't seem to notice.

"Okay, Tia," she said. "I'll see you later." Then she ran back up into the dining room.

I walked into Madison Square Park and sat on a bench. Gary Oscars pulled away in a town car. Guests arrived for dinner. I hoped to the ends of the earth that the review wouldn't affect business. I hoped Chef Darling would prove himself to the world and that Carey and Angel and Chad and the whole gang would make it out unscathed.

And I hoped I'd be able to pull off this balancing act.

Chapter 13

THE NEXT DAY I DID EVERYTHING BY THE BOOK. I WENT TO class, did my reading. I texted Elliott, but he didn't text me back. I wrote extra-precise notes about my internship and sent them off to my seminar leader two hours early. Everything would be just fine.

Around seven, Melinda and I got hungry and walked to a fancy bodega near NYU. I wandered around the buffet and served myself a smattering of arugula leaves, a spoonful of canned tuna, and some other small bites. Moving between worlds—NYU, Madison Park Tavern, Michael Saltz—was a shock to the system, like an astronaut blazing into a new planet's atmosphere every couple of hours.

"Were your classes today as boring as mine?" Melinda said as she scribbled in her hummus with a carrot.

Her voice spun in the air until it landed with a flat, incomprehensible thump on my head. Class! As much as I had tried to focus, that was still the last thing on my mind. "Classes? You're taking classes?" Last I heard, Melinda was working on her acting career.

"Yeah, I'm taking figure drawing classes. They're okay. I'm quitting soon, I think."

"Oh, yeah. That sucks, they suck," I said, mirroring her apathy. I smooshed everything together on my plate—olives, peas, arugula, mustard.

"Yep." Melinda sighed.

I looked down and saw I had accidentally made a tuna niçoise. This tiny autopilot act grounded me a little.

I mixed and tasted and went back for other ingredients until the tuna salad was near perfect. It was filling and bracing and pickled. It didn't taste like bodega food at all. The simple act of cooking and tasting calmed me like nothing else.

We sat in Washington Square Park and picked at our food. It felt nice to be outside, where no one expected me to be anyone or say anything. But apparently we picked the wrong park to sit in, because I saw Dean Chang walk out of her office right across the street.

Twilight had turned to night and the park twinkled with streetlamps and stringed lights. Our gazes caught and she walked toward me, a tempered pace like she was deciding how it'd go.

"Tia, it's nice to see you here. How . . . how are you?" she asked, searching my face, presumably for distress or any other reaction from yesterday.

Melinda looked at her blankly, then went back to taking baby bites of her steamed broccoli.

"I'm okay. It's been an eventful couple days. As you know," I said, digging into my salad. The truth was, I already felt like I was juggling one too many things, and I hadn't even officially reviewed restaurants with Michael Saltz yet. Something would fall through the cracks, so I had to tighten up ship. There was no other choice.

"I see," she said, looking at Melinda, who didn't look back at her, which was crazy because Dean Chang was tall and imperious, a woman who commanded attention. "Can I talk to you for a moment?"

I turned toward Melinda, but she didn't signal approval or otherwise. She gave me a perfect *whatever* face. "I've gotta go," she said. "See ya, Tia." And then she left, taking a pack of cigarettes out of her purse after she threw away her food.

Dean Chang gracefully settled on the bench wearing a long black silk skirt with tiny pleats and an asymmetrical hemline. Issey Miyake, I realized with satisfaction.

She started, "Yesterday afternoon disappointed me, and I would like you to tell me, in confidence, what happened at the restaurant."

"I don't know," I said, mimicking the tone I had taken with her yesterday, but with greater conviction. Practice makes perfect.

"What do you mean you don't know? Why were you with Michael Saltz in the basement? And before they received that disastrous review? Something isn't right."

"I didn't—"

"Tia. Please, talk to me. Did he do anything to you?" She bent her head, confidentially, motherly, filled with a warmth that, despite my efforts to remain hardened, broke my heart.

"Who cares about the review," she continued. "I only care about you. I want to help, but you have to tell me what happened."

"Nothing happened." I stiffened. I wished she would lay off. This had nothing to do with her.

"Oh, Tia. Fine. Keep your secret. But I hope you realize how lucky you've been up to this point. Have you noticed how few first-year grad students are even allowed into the self-directed internship program? This is the best program in the country, filled with students of staggering caliber. We picked you and placed you at one of the finest restaurants in the world. Think about what you've learned in just a few short weeks: food, culture, consumption . . . interior design, sociology, even floral arrangements! In no other place are you going to rub elbows with dishwashers and fishmongers and CEOs and celebrities."

She was right. I had learned about those things, but it was hard to trace the origin. Was it the restaurant or Carey's Wiki page or Michael Saltz's access? I couldn't quite define the outlines in my life anymore. The mind wants things clear-cut, but instead everything blurred.

She stood up and continued, "Don't derail your academic—and professional—career now. Graduate school is a place for you to plant the seeds of your entire life. I've seen very promising students set terrible precedents for themselves. It's unfortunate, and I don't want that to happen to you."

This was going to work out fine. Life had gotten mixed up, but there'd be plenty of time to sort it out. I shouldn't have been surprised that there were some transitional bumps. Surely the girl who sold ice pops had overcome some hurdles before she'd made her dream come true. Looking at it that way, of course I could survive a little restaurant interrogation.

Sorry, Dean Chang, I wanted to say. *I'm building my foundation, but it's not according to your blueprint.*

I saw some girls in the corner of my eye watching my exchange with Dean Chang with rapt attention. One guy was creeping up to us, eavesdropping. It wasn't comfortable, but at that moment, my resolve to push through became stronger than ever.

I'd thought I had my future figured out. I'd get good grades. Get into a good college. Pursue food and writing in grad school. People had tried to tell me that grad school wasn't necessary, but I hadn't listened. That degree was a badge. Validation.

But now I realized that was naïve. Nothing is handed to you.

I had learned as much with Helen. You could want something so bad that your feverish desire was practically a neon sign on your forehead. You could work hard, do all the right things, and still not succeed. You weren't better than anyone else and you didn't have a claim on rewards that everyone else wanted, too.

So instead of telling the world that you wanted those prizes, instead of wearing your best dress and your most cloying smile, it was better to just grab them. Beat your way to the front of the line.

Your best intentions aren't enough.

Dean Chang's words clarified this for me. She was nice and helpful and well-meaning—but she was dealing me bad hands, telling me adversity made me stronger and then wondering why I was struggling.

The proof was in the pudding. Or, in this case, my two-hundred-dollar La Perla bra and five-hundred-dollar Hermès cuff. My dinner with Michael Saltz. My words in the *New York Times.* That was the real, in-the-hand jackpot. I just had to be strong and careful. Dean Chang talked about the unsurpassed education I would receive working at Madison Park Tavern, but with Michael Saltz, I was on the better side of the table. I'd receive food, not serve it. I'd judge instead of being judged. The choice was so clear.

"I'll only ask you one more time. What does Michael Saltz want from you?"

"He doesn't want anything from me," I said, like she was stupid and this was the most obvious thing in the world.

"You have real talents, Tia," she said. "I don't want you to waste them. If that's what you say about Michael Saltz, I believe you." Then she spun on her high-heeled shoe and left.

I sighed and returned to my clever tuna niçoise salad, now looking more wilted and wan.

Strong and careful, I thought. I ate my salad by myself.

Chapter 14

One week later, Michael Saltz and I did our first review together. Tellicherry was not a subtle restaurant. It was loud, crowded, and white-hot cool.

I had spent the week reading up on everything about the chef, Christian Rhodes, and all the go-to dishes. Several bloggers and reporters—the ones who weren't anonymous and who could accept invites to dinners and launch parties—had already reviewed the restaurant. I read these with curiosity and just a little bit of self-satisfaction. They and I both knew that many people considered the *New York Times* the final word.

I had also read every review Michael Saltz had ever written, studying the last three months extra carefully. After he lost his sense of taste, he must have enlisted some friends, gotten them drunk and talking about the food, and just used their impressions. Reading them now, I could tell the difference. The critiques felt surface, like assessing the costume design rather than the play. Michael Saltz must have known that was unacceptable in the long term. So here I was.

At Tellicherry, Michael Saltz wore a realistic strawberry-blond toupee that made up for all the other ridiculous toupees in the world. It turned him from a neurotic rich guy into an all-around good guy. To complete the look, he'd worn khaki pants, a purple-and-white-checked shirt, and pointed brown shoes. He looked like a guy you'd ask for directions, someone who'd happily let you take his cab. I hardly recognized him.

We did not match at all. I wore an emerald long-sleeved dress by Vivienne Tam and a pair of tangerine Christian Louboutins. I had seen the same look in one of Emerald's *Vogues* and asked Giada to overnight it. I learned quickly, though I wasn't very original. I'd changed in a coffee shop next to my apartment, then hopped into a cab.

"Next time we must coordinate outfits beforehand," Michael whispered as we sat down. "I was going for 'salt of the earth' today."

"Oh, I wanted to match the décor," I said.

Tellicherry felt like a sexy, sinister jewel box. A rich sapphire blue stained the walls in large, meandering splotches, like dye dropped into water. Bronze silk leaped and dipped in the cushions. The waitresses wore black dresses with seductive lace panels revealing flesh-colored bits, and the waiters slinked in semi-sheer pajama-like outfits, conjuring bedtime escapades, none of which involved sleeping.

Michael Saltz shook his head. "Wrong approach. Consider this—would a restaurant critic look like I do now? Like a dad from Bergen County?"

"No, I guess not." I leaned over the table so no one could hear me. "Should I always dress the opposite of the décor?"

"Not always. Think strategically. Sometimes you want to blend in. Sometimes you want to look like an aberration. When making multiple trips, you have to change your plan of attack every time."

"Oh, that makes sense," I said, hiding my clutch, the same sapphire blue as the walls. "So, I wanted to tell you in person that things have gotten a little crazy for me. I got put on probation at Madison Park Tavern."

"Is that right?" he said, surprised, even though he was the reason I'd gotten in trouble in the first place.

"Yeah. They think there's something fishy with the review. They saw you and me in the basement on the security tapes, and—"

"Wait, what? Do they know about us?" He put his napkin on the table as if ready to leave.

"No! Gary and Jake don't think that. Neither does the director of the program. I told them we didn't discuss anything important and that I had no idea who you were."

He tapped his fingers on the table, then flattened them with a slap when a very handsome waiter came over. The way he introduced the food, I could tell he was a nerd, though a hot nerd. Like a nerd who could also throw around a football and model for a sporting goods company.

"Well, I suppose that was the best you could do," Michael Saltz said after we ordered. "But a probationary period isn't good for maintaining secrecy. Your behavior will be under stricter scrutiny. Which reminds me, where's your phone? I thought I made it clear that I'd like it on the table, face up, when we have our dinners."

I brought it out and Michael Saltz nodded in acknowledgment and appreciation. Strangely, he seemed more worried about my incoming phone calls than the possibility of someone at Madison Park Tavern discovering our arrangement.

"So, this is what I think so far," Michael Saltz said. "I think . . ." He looked up, averted his eyes from a passing guest, then whispered under the Euro-beat music, "I think Tellicherry has the makings of a three-star restaurant."

"How do you know?" I asked.

Michael Saltz blinked his eyes ten or so times. Every once in a while, he did these weird sensory wake-ups, the way people scratch their head to get their ideas flowing. "You get a second sense about these things."

The waiter returned with a pre-appetizer amuse-bouche, a soup spoon filled with diced radishes, shortbread crumbs, and a black pepper gastrique. After the waiter left, Michael Saltz said, "They're trying. Hard."

The flavors surged. The radishes had been pickled, articulating their peppery bite and giving them a sharpened edge. The shortbread grounded the bite with a bready, buttery mouthful and the black pepper–vinegar sauce finished it with an elegant and seductive wisp of sweet, salty, and spicy.

"This is very, very good," I said.

"I know. I can see and smell the craftsmanship. You can tell where this restaurant is shooting," he said, his spoon suspended in the air like a conductor's wand. "It wants to be a three-star restaurant."

But judging from the amuse-bouche, this food was sensational—why couldn't it be four stars if the food was that great?

Our waiter approached with several more dishes, and I adjusted my dress.

"Here is the monkfish wrapped in yuba," the waiter said. "Underneath you'll find a gingerbread vinegar puree tossed with a cranberry bean 'soil.' And this is the rutabaga–duck confit terrine with licorice lace wrapped around an orange-scented breadstick."

"Fantastic, thank you so much for this," I said, eager for the next bite.

"My pleasure. I'm Felix. What's your name?"

"Hi, Felix. I'm Tia," I said.

Michael Saltz kicked me.

"I mean, Mia," I lied, clutching the table.

"Very good, Mia," he said, and I thought he had a twinkle in his eye, almost as if he was flirting with me.

"Why would he want to know your name?" Michael Saltz shook his head as Felix left. "And, Mia? You must do better than that next time." He cut through the monkfish with the side of his fork and plunged it into his mouth.

"What do you think?" I asked.

"I'm starving, but it all tastes like boiled potatoes to me, which is sadly the most appealing taste I've had all day. The wrinkly texture of the yuba is interesting. Does it add much to the flavor though?"

I took my first bite. "Hm. Yes, I think so. It's very thin and crackled, almost like chicken skin. And, look, it's bonded to the fish somehow. But what I really like is this gingerbread puree and cranberry bean soil. It's so unique. The gingerbread spices sort of unlock the monkfish's meatiness and muscle. Then the bean soil scratches your tongue and sort of forces the flavors into deeper levels of taste. And I love how you can't place it. It's not ethnic, it's not market-driven, it's its own thing."

"Good, good. Let's continue." He passed the rutabaga and duck terrine toward me with the tips of his fingers. "Isn't this a little odd?"

I wanted to like it, I did. I pushed the ingredients around

with my knife and fork, trying to understand it and formulate an opinion.

Then Felix swooped in. "Oh, miss. Pardon me, I was helping another table. That's supposed to be served with something else." He looked at Michael Saltz sheepishly, and Michael Saltz turned his toupeed head away. "We added this dish today, and I'm still getting used to serving it. The proper preparation includes just a bit of truffle."

He took out a fist-size beige knot from underneath a white napkin. The shavings rained down in ruffled, translucent strands. Felix backed away as I poked my fork through the tangle of truffles, into the terrine.

I had read about truffles—their taste, their hormonal, almost sexual aromas, their exorbitant cost—but I had never even seen a truffle in person before, and had a hard time understanding why people paid thousands of dollars an ounce for something so humble-looking.

But at Tellicherry, I understood. I melted in my chair.

"Mmm . . ." I couldn't stop saying it. "Mmmm."

Michael Saltz, excited too, picked up a large pinch of truffle shavings and held them to his nose. "These are very good. The finest."

"Oh God," I said, in a state of delirium. "This makes the dish so much better. Why aren't truffles on everything?" I had forgotten about the funky terrine. Now it was just a vehicle for the magical urgings of the truffle.

A few minutes later, Felix came out again. "Here's your next dish, potato pearls with black, green, and crimson caviar in a cauliflower cream nage."

The caviar shined like little jewels among the equal-sized potatoes. They bobbed around in the soup, glistening as if illuminated from within. I took a small spoonful and in surged a soft, sweet ribbon of cauliflower essence. I popped the caviar eggs one by one. *Pop,* went one, a silken fishiness. *Pop,* went another, a sharp, tangy brine. *Pop,* went a seductive one, dark and mysterious and deep.

Michael Saltz rolled the caviar in his mouth, too. "This is quite nice, isn't it?"

"Really nice," I said, feeling a million well-fed miles away from that bodega salad bar and my idiotic tuna niçoise.

The rest of the night proceeded like this. It didn't seem real. We found our table filled with dishes of sausages and mousses, soups and salads, deep fried balls of this, grilled à la plancha that. None of my online research had prepared me for the quality and imagination of this restaurant. You could never completely describe the real thing, and I thought myself silly that I had thought otherwise.

Michael Saltz barely ate anything, but after a while, I stopped feeling self-conscious about it and devoured every dish. After each one, Michael Saltz made me render some ruling, guiding me along the way, asking me to be more precise in my wording, more rigorous with my logic.

Needs to be sweeter, or more pumpkiny.

The fish's velvety sweetness is tempered by the ashy bleu cheese.

Fabulous char on this. They must have an excellent stove and the finest, heaviest cast-iron pans.

My stomach felt like it was about to burst. But we still had dessert.

"Wonderful, this is excellent material for the review," Michael Saltz said, finishing yet another glass of Bordeaux.

"It is? That's great," I said, genuinely pleased that I was doing a good job.

We had ordered the shaved ice and candied tropical fruits, the curry ice cream with mini brioche puffs, and the lemon basil profiteroles with blueberry-oatmeal brittle. But a small army of servers brought out even more: chocolate fondant sandwiched in coconut crisps, cinnamon apple churros with maple syrup tapioca, chocolates, macarons, marshmallows. Felix delivered the petit fours himself, and whispered to me, "I'm sorry for the delay with the truffles. Try the lavender-peach macarons. They're my favorite." Then he smoothed his bangs back and gave me an extra-long look that made my hair stand on end.

Michael Saltz didn't notice. "Any good?" he asked, once the fleet of servers had left.

"Yes, very good," I said, the dough of a churro still wedged in my cheek. "Is this the way it always is?"

"Well, the extra desserts are a little suspect. Perhaps he was making up for being late with the truffles?" He looked around. "I can't decide if we've been made."

"'Made'?"

"Yes, when a spy's cover has been blown, he—or she—has been 'made.'"

"Oh," I said, looking around the room. Everything seemed to be operating normally. No one was staring at us or taking our picture or anything. The restaurant looked routine, but then again, I had only ever eaten at a few fancy restaurants before I met Michael Saltz.

Michael Saltz wiped his mouth with a satisfied grin. "I'm going to the bathroom. Don't eat it all," he said with a wink.

I ate a coconut crisp and the whole thing shriveled in my mouth, evaporating into nothing but pure taste. I held another up to the golden light as someone sat down across from me.

"I can't figure out this cooking technique. Do you think it's a meringue?" I asked.

"Actually, I believe it's freeze-dried."

My gaze leaped from the coconut crisp to the source of the

foreign-sounding voice, smoother and younger than Michael Saltz's agitated lisp. Pascal Fox.

"They make a conventional cookie, then, *shoop,* in it goes with dry ice, and the thing is a mere shadow of what was before."

His black hair was slightly matted and spiked, hair that was—amazingly—a bit like mine, thick and straight in places, wispy and fine in others. He wore a cobalt-blue button-down shirt with the sleeves rolled up, exposing his tattoos. In the semi-dark, I made out a mural of forks and knives, cows and pigs, carrots and eggplants and squashes and melons, like a super-hot, toned supermarket. He seemed to be showing off the whole mural to me.

"Oh, hi!" I said.

"I remember you. You came to my restaurant about three weeks ago, right?"

"Wow," I said. "You have a good memory." I couldn't stop blushing and I regretted eating all that food. It was hard to feel pretty when I felt nine months pregnant.

"I don't remember everyone. Just the special people." He nudged his body an inch toward mine and my breath caught in my throat. Up close, I noticed he had a slightly crooked smile and somewhat stained teeth. I liked that he wasn't the perfect model he appeared to be in all the magazines. He was almost a regular person.

"What's your name?"

"Tia," I said, knowing full well that Michael Saltz would have wanted me to say Deirdre or Emily. But when you enter a raffle, you don't write the wrong phone number. The odds aren't in your favor anyway, so what's the harm?

"Are you eating dinner here?" I asked him.

"No," he said. "I took tonight off—first night since the restaurant opened two months ago—and I wanted to say hi to my friend Christian before I go out to dinner with some friends."

"Chef Christian Rhodes?" I asked, in a voice that came out way too geeky.

"Yes, Chef Rhodes." He laughed. "You know your stuff, don't you?"

"Oh, I just saw it written on the menu," I said. I had told him my name, but I knew I shouldn't take it too far. *You must be incognito, discreet.* Things I didn't want to be in front of a hot guy showing interest in me.

"I really like your restaurant," I said.

I really like your restaurant? For real? Why hadn't I said, *Everything was so yummy in my tummy*? "Thank you, I appreciate that. Coming from someone like you." He looked down at the massacre of dessert plates on the table. "You here with a boyfriend?"

"A friend! A friend!" I said a little too loudly and quickly. I stuffed Elliott and Michael Saltz toward the back of my mind, making way for Pascal's hotness and attention. It was just for a couple of minutes. I'd get back to reality soon enough.

"Oh," he said. "You should invite him—or her—to Bakushan. It'd be great to see you again. I have some new things on the menu that I think you'd like."

I spotted Michael Saltz in the bathroom hallway, waiting anxiously for Pascal Fox to get out of his chair.

"Ask for me, and I'll make sure you get seated right away. There's a chef's table, you know. Right in the kitchen with me. It's the best seat in the house."

My mind did some quick computations. The stylish women at Bakushan—they'd only sat in the front window. Little had I known, there was better currency, better social clout. You just had to know the chef. That was the ultimate in.

"It was nice seeing you again," Pascal continued. He stood up, walked around the table, and gave me a little kiss on my left cheek. He stayed there for a bit, and my face burned so much I was sure his lips would singe from the molten heat of my blushing.

Then he walked out the door.

I couldn't move. I still sensed Pascal's stubble on my cheek, the smell of meat and toast from his skin. "What the hell was that?" I said to myself, my lips moving, but not a sound coming out.

I ran over the entire interaction in my mind. Partly to make sure that I hadn't accidentally cheated on Elliott. And partly to relive Pascal's singular magic.

Michael Saltz returned and shoved his chair in so tight the table pummeled his hollowed-out stomach.

"I don't want you talking to people at restaurants if you don't have to," he said, his voice a swift jet of wind. "It draws attention to yourself. And Pascal Fox! Do you think I go around talking to chefs?"

"Well, I . . . he came up to me. I didn't mean to hold you up at the bathroom, but—"

Michael Saltz surveyed our table, locking eyes with my phone and every plate and bowl. "And don't you have a boyfriend?"

"Yes, I do," I said with a pang of regret. But did I regret what had happened, or just that I'd gotten caught? "It wasn't like that. I didn't call out to Pascal or anything."

Michael Saltz gave me a look like, *Sure, it may not have been your fault, but you liked it all the same.* "Listen. I'll only say this once, because I know you're a smart young woman. This is not a joke or some idiotic after-school program. This is my job and my name. If a single soul finds out about our arrangement, I will lose everything. That would be bad for me, and disastrous for you."

I suddenly felt woozy. All that food and Pascal and now this—something that sounded like a threat.

"If my position is compromised, I will have no choice but to bring you down with me," he continued. "I have far-reaching connections and will not hesitate to end your career before it's even begun. I can do that one hundred times over."

His words opened like switchblades in that raucous jewel box of a restaurant. Sure, he had given me an opportunity, but he had also trapped me.

But despite his anger, I felt relatively calm. Like he had said, we were partners, and by then I knew that he wouldn't accept any errors from me. I'd always known this would take some necessary sacrifices.

His stare drilled into me. "Do you understand?"

"Yes," I said. "I understand completely, so you don't have to threaten me."

"Well, I'm just reminding you for your sake and mine. Not to mention the sake of your dear boyfriend. We'll reconvene tomorrow to go over the review. Can you have some notes written by then?"

"Tomorrow?" I was supposed to meet up with Elliott later. It was Friday and I was going to use the weekend to write a paper for my Twentieth-Century Food Systems class, due on Monday.

"Sure, I guess." What else could I say, especially after I had just pissed him off by talking to Pascal? I'd have to make the time.

Michael Saltz took out a fancy pen to sign the check under a fake name. I guessed the credit card bill went right to the *Times*. "Good." He released his pen with a heavy thud.

Outside Tellicherry, I trailed behind Michael Saltz as we walked to the corner. He raised his hand to hail a cab.

"This was not a good first run. That Pascal Fox incident could have been disastrous. Remember that for me, okay?" Michael Saltz said, his voice like live wires at the edges, like he might zap me at any moment. He stood so close, the tips of our shoes touched. "You can order anything you want, you can buy anything you want, but you must be careful. Don't trust anyone with our secret. Too much is at risk."

His voice was soft, almost gentle. He seemed to be making up for his tone earlier, but I wasn't too sure he had that apologetic streak in him.

"I understand," I said, and I really did. I didn't want to screw this up.

"Talk to you tomorrow," he said. Then he put me in a cab, slammed the door, and I sped away.

I CALLED ELLIOTT and told him that I wasn't going to be able to hang out that night.

"Work stuff," I said. "I'm so sorry."

His end of the line went quiet. "Okay, whatever you say," he said. Then he hung up.

Shit, I thought. Elliott had never once hung up on me. Was he busy at the lab? Was his boss around?

Or was he so annoyed that he had nothing to say?

I wrote the review but picked up my phone every couple of minutes, thinking that I'd text him *hey* or something.

But eventually, the writing carried me away and I forgot about Elliott. I was so worked up about the night's food, seeing Pascal, and Michael's warnings that I stayed up until four in the morning, hammering out an entire review. I started:

> Tellicherry blossoms like an electric kiss, tempting you along the way with everything it can: truffles and caviar, yes, but also an old-fashioned, sweep-you-off-your-feet seduction. For hedonists, Tellicherry is a paradise, full of fragrance, boldness, and refined sensuality.

Spellbound, I wrote about the headiness of the food and its power to save you. Why bother with some other boring, less tasty fate?

> The meal comes to a crescendo at dessert. The shaved ice with candied tropical fruits takes you on a sumptuous vacation, and the curry ice cream with mini brioche puffs will make you want to tear up the return tickets.
>
> Tellicherry comes at you unexpectedly, with a new aroma at every corner. It's a restaurant that foretells a new future, and should be closely watched and lavishly commended.

FOUR out of FOUR STARS

By the end, I'd written myself into conviction. I loved Tellicherry. I hoped Michael Saltz would read the certainty in my review and agree. As for the inherent dangers of flirting with Pascal, there was no getting Michael Saltz's or Elliott's agreement on that.

And yet.

The mere thought of Pascal sent electricity through my body. Pascal sitting across from me, his lips on my cheek, an inch away from my own. The adorable way he'd said *shoop!* The thoughts reverberated, each cycle becoming stronger, more defined, more calming.

I sent the review to Michael Saltz without reading it over, then went to sleep fantasizing about a world in which I could have turned my head ever so slightly to meet Pascal's kiss.

Chapter 15

The next morning, I woke to my phone ringing.

"Hello, Tia, are you up yet?" Michael Saltz said from the end of the line.

"Um, yeah? I am now."

"I read your piece," he said. "I asked for notes, not the whole damn thing."

"Oh, I'm sorry," I said. "I didn't mean to be presumptuous. It just came out of me. Delete it if you want."

"No, it's fine, for the most part."

I sank into the recesses of my bed, relieved. Had I really sent my words to Michael Saltz, thinking he'd be okay with that? But amazingly, he was.

"Great. I'm glad you liked it. I don't think I captured everything, but I know you'll put it in your own words. I was just trying to weave it all together."

He went silent for a while, which I took to mean he was thinking. "Like I said, it's fine. I'm going to make some adjustments to it but I'm more than able to write a column."

"Okay . . ." I said, not expecting such defensiveness. I had figured he'd tweak the review. He was the mentor, and I was the protégée. How else would it be?

He kept breathing heavily, and in the background I heard the faint sounds of his mouse tapping and glassware pinging.

"Well . . . I should be going now," I finally said.

"Wait!" he said, snapping to life. "I have another meal for us. Can you do lunch on Thursday? I'm visiting a place on the Upper East Side."

"Next Thursday? Oh, I have my internship seminar then. I have to go or else Dean Chang might find out, and my scholarship—" I rambled.

"Eugh," Michael Saltz grumbled. "Tia, tell me. Why are you still so insistent on this program when I'm offering you a far superior experience? I never should have told you I was ambivalent about your enrollment."

"Oh . . ." I responded weakly. If you compared them side by side, Michael Saltz's "internship" was obviously better—a wider reach, more restaurant exposure, more contact with a true leader in the field. But what was I supposed to do, abandon NYU for a whole other life—a secret life, no less?

"Have you heard of Le Brittane?" he asked.

Everyone had heard of Le Brittane. The restaurant was among the handful of New York four-stars, the elite group that Madison Park Tavern had once been in. Within that group, each had its special realm of distinction. Sakura was ascetic, even severe, but served the most heartbreakingly fresh sushi outside of Japan. Alici served luscious Italian food in a baroque, palatial setting. Le Brittane wasn't so extreme. It specialized in seafood and was elegant and posh. If you were in a fifty-mile radius and wanted to propose, entertain a dignitary, or have some other experience smooth in every respect, you went to Le Brittane.

"I'm re-reviewing them. I've gone for dinner many times over the years and now I'd like to experience the lunch. You'll get to be my polished Upper East Side niece. How does that sound?"

"That sounds . . ." I thought about it for a millisecond, a quick calculus of weighing the pros and cons, this life versus that. It was certainly worth missing a class or two. "Okay, I'll go."

"I sense hesitation. Is Le Brittane beneath you?"

"No, no, I meant . . . I mean, it's great. Thank you." I tried to sound grateful and be in-the-moment, but I couldn't stop thinking about how I'd fit this in my schedule. I was already on thin ice and I couldn't disappoint Dean Chang, Jake, or Elliott any more.

"Your time will be rewarded, I promise. I hope you'll see that this is worth more than some silly classes."

"Mmhmm," I said, as if to say, *They're stupid classes.* But were they? Now I wasn't so sure.

"How do you think I should dress?" I asked.

"Well, it will be midday and you'll be my niece. Pick a career."

"I want to be . . ." I thought for a second. "An actress." That'd be the only way I could lead these multiple lives. I had to become someone else.

"Oh yes? Well, you're already an actress when you're out with me." He laughed. "But I like where your head is. You're getting into the spirit of disguise."

"Ha. I guess I am," I said, already fantasizing about what I'd wear, imagining how it'd make me feel. "Le Brittane on Thursday, then. When does the Tellicherry review come out?"

"This Wednesday."

"This coming Wednesday? Like, in four days?"

"Yes, that's what Wednesday means."

"Sorry. I guess I'm surprised everything's happening so fast."

"The process of reviewing may be slow. Earlier in my career,

I'd visit a restaurant at least three times. But once I send the review, it's done. It'll get fact-checked first thing on Monday, sent to the printer on Tuesday, published on Wednesday morning. It's practically a done deal."

"Oh, okay." When I'd written the review the night before, I hadn't thought my words would be published in a matter of hours. Now, I was second-guessing my monkfish judgment. Had I talked too much about the truffles? Not enough? And was it really a four-star? How did I even know what the best of the best was?

Michael Saltz had said he was going to tweak the review. But in what direction? I had written it was a four-star, but he had a lower opinion. At Madison Park Tavern, I had seen what a review could do to a restaurant. So many people worked so hard, just for a single person's ruling.

We must treat him like a king, Jake had said. *But it is us against him.*

"You came through nicely, Tia Monroe," Michael Saltz said in glowing tones. "Keep up the good work."

"Thanks," I replied, and all self-doubt dissipated. I accepted the comment for what it was. I was good at something . . . and I wasn't going to apologize for it.

Chapter 16

MELINDA KICKED OPEN MY DOOR ON SUNDAY NIGHT. "HEY, you wanna take a little study break with me?" she asked. "I brought snacks."

"Sure." I had been studying up on clothes and restaurants and food—not working on my Twentieth-Century Food Systems paper.

Emerald was gone, so Melinda and I moved to the living room and plopped down on the floor with a box of Triscuits and a jar of mayonnaise.

"It's tarragon . . ." She turned the jar to read the label. "Dijon garlic? I don't know. It was an impulse buy at Food Emporium. Trashy and delicious," Melinda said, before she threw a whole Triscuit in her mouth.

"Ha, come to think of it, I studied straight through dinner. I'm starving!" Sometimes I found reading about food could almost replace eating it.

"Seriously? You are working way too hard, then. Follow my lead and chill out." She smiled. Melinda rarely smiled, but when she did, you got a sense of the girl underneath her too-cool-for-school exterior. She was kind of a goofball.

I opened a napkin, laid out some Triscuits, spread the mayo on top, then remembered I had a leftover salad in the fridge and added some lettuce for an extra dose of freshness.

Melinda told me about her haphazard job search; her mom, who was about to get remarried; the amazing and terrible acts at a comedy show she'd snuck into. She spoke fast and in a list-like way. Next, next, next.

"But anyway," Melinda said, in her screen diva voice, "what's happening in the world of Tia?"

"Well . . ." I started. Melinda was chomping away at the Triscuits. I thought I could let out a bit of tension. That wouldn't be so bad. It might even help me live a more stable life. "The other day my dean put me on probation." This I knew was okay to say and the words hissed out of me like air out of a tire.

"Probation? Isn't that sort of a big deal?"

"Yeah. It is . . . but it isn't," I said. The Tellicherry review was coming out that week and I'd get that surge of exhilaration again. Even thinking about it, my energy picked up, my posture straightened. My words in the paper had an unmistakable effect on me.

Melinda went back to pondering the thatching on a Triscuit. It didn't seem like she wanted to hear any more, but I went on anyway. "What if I told you that . . . I got a really great job that I can't tell anyone else about. I just started, but it's more than I ever could have imagined."

Melinda leaned back. "Go on . . ." she said skeptically.

I stammered, already at an impasse. That was all I could say, and hearing it come from my mouth, I realized it wasn't much and that it raised more questions than it answered.

Just then Emerald walked in, still on the phone. "Hey, Mom?

I gotta go. Tia and Melinda are here," she said, then hung up. "Hey." She nodded to us before making her way toward her room.

Melinda and I didn't even have time to say hey back before she closed the door.

"She's the worst," Melinda whispered. "So what have you found out about her life?"

"Uh . . . I did see something weird." I knew the Bergdorf incident was fair game, though I hadn't intended to make it a big deal. I guess I wanted to talk to someone about something *real*. I felt bad that it was gossip about Emerald, but I knew this was the type of thing Melinda would be interested in.

Melinda's eyes widened. "Really?"

"Well . . ." I lowered my voice, more lip-synching than sound. "I think there's something up with her mom. About two weeks ago, I saw them at a store together, and Emerald's mom was—"

"A store? What store?"

"Oh, I forget the name of it," I lied. "It's in Midtown."

"Hm . . ." That explanation didn't satisfy Melinda, so I hurried up with the meat.

"Her mother is . . . not all there . . . I don't know why."

"I thought you were gonna say something about her having a sugar daddy or something." Melinda shrugged her shoulders, scanning the room, bored. "I'm getting sleepy anyway," she said, picking up her things. "Let me know if Miss Big Boobs does something crazy. The mom thing isn't doing anything for me."

Her nastiness pained me, but I didn't let on. "Yeah, for sure," I said. "Good night."

Why did I feel the need to talk shit about Emerald? She was by no means my best friend, but suddenly I felt shameful and dirty.

After Melinda went back to her room, I tried to resume my restaurant research, but the conversation bothered me. I didn't want to be that "mean girl," but it seemed Melinda and I only had two modes: gossiping or some half friendship of incomplete sentences and barely there stories.

The story about Emerald's mom wasn't nice, and I shouldn't have been the one spreading it. But at least it was tangible and tellable, two things I had in short supply.

Chapter 17

After class on Tuesday, I stopped into Whole Foods to escape and relax. I had made a habit of wandering around the city's markets after class. I didn't have to walk far. On one block, you'd have a Greek grocery store, stocked with salty triangles of feta peeking out of a barrel, every color of olive in every iteration—pitted, brined, and herbed. There was the Indian market with six shelves devoted to turmeric. And finally, Chinatown and its cacophonous cross section of humanity—the grandma bargaining for vegetables, the kid poking mischievously at the dried fish, the newlyweds piling their cart for their first home-cooked dinner with their parents.

Whole Foods wasn't that exotic, but it was my Tuesday and Thursday spot. After my internship seminar, I went to the Lower East Side location, which I liked because it was roomier and less chaotic than the Union Square one. I walked through the aisles and unwound without tourists colliding into me.

I stopped in the produce aisle to look at their selection of exotic eggs. They had white eggs, brown eggs, large, extra-large, and jumbo. They also had tiny quail eggs, weighty duck eggs, and a giant forty-dollar ostrich egg.

I picked up the ostrich egg and felt the viscous insides slosh around. I flipped it over and over in my hands like a Magic 8 Ball.

First, I'd loved Helen Lansky. She was why I came to NYU.

I didn't get the Helen internship. I got Madison Park Tavern.

But then Michael Saltz had given me the opportunity to work with him. He would ensure I'd be set up with Helen. Which brought me back to the beginning.

I had to keep sight of that. Lately, with everything happening, I'd started to forget why I'd agreed to this whole arrangement. The clothes, the fine dining, the hot waiters and chefs—they all threatened to cloud the real reason I was jeopardizing my personal relationships and my place in grad school.

You're doing this for the right reasons, I told myself. *Steady on.*

Around and around the egg went, and now the insides had taken on their own momentum, whirlpooling around.

Then someone bumped me on the hip and the giant ostrich egg fell to the ground.

"*Merde!*" Pascal Fox said.

I didn't have time to react to his presence. We just watched the egg. At first, it seemed like it'd be okay. But then a crack wiggled its way from the bottom to the top, and the insides took their cue, oozing out with a definitive *blurp.*

"My, my," Pascal said.

We watched as the white spread fast and loose, while the bright orange yolk moved with purpose, like a paramecium.

"Kinda sexy, no?" he remarked, more to the egg than to me, but I blushed four thousand degrees anyway.

Oh. My. God.

A manager came rushing over.

"Oh! Chef! Good to see you. Don't worry about this at all. We'll take care of it right now."

"Thanks, Frank," he said. I was surprised that he knew the manager—who wasn't wearing a name tag—personally, and that he was taking the blame for the egg. But I was even more surprised when he stuck around with me and smiled a full, toothy, letter-D-shaped movie star grin.

The magazines said he was only twenty-eight, which was young for an executive chef but felt old to me. He looked like a man. Even when Elliott turned twenty-eight, I doubted he would look as manly as Pascal. Somehow, in the supermarket lighting, Pascal seemed hotter—more capable and more real. In restaurants, he blended in with the scenery of the meal. But here, holding his basket just like everyone else, looking at the discounted produce, getting lost in the aisles, his presence became even more magical, as if I were seeing a beautiful, powerful animal in the wild instead of at the zoo.

"Where's your boyfriend?" he teased.

"I was eating with my friend at Tellicherry," I said, which was kind of true. Michael Saltz was most certainly not a boyfriend. I hoped Pascal wouldn't mention a "boyfriend" again so we could continue like this, talking in a safe, cordoned-off ring away from Elliott and Michael Saltz. Could Michael Saltz blame me for running into him here?

"Girls' night at Tellicherry? You know how to live, then. Aren't you in school?"

"Well . . . yeah . . ." I started, wondering how he'd known. I was wearing regular jeans, a toggle coat, and ballet flats—standard grad school wear. And it was midday, so clearly I wasn't at work. "School's okay," I said, "but I prefer being around this stuff."

"Gigantic cracked eggs?"

I giggled, a high-pitched girly trill, an uncharacteristic sound that momentarily startled me. Was he really talking to me this much? Again? "No, I mean I like being around food and learning about it and stuff."

Learning about it and stuff? Apparently I always had grade-A babble for Pascal.

"Yeah, me too," he said. He spoke like he was just another NYU student, low-key and modest, some guy shopping for groceries. Not some super-hot celebrity chef, the preferred topic for every food magazine and blog.

"Well, see you around," he said, then bowed his head in the courtly manner that I knew from Madison Park Tavern was the mark of a fine restaurant.

"Yeah." I gulped. "See you around."

He picked up his basket of mushrooms, herbs, and heavy cream, and walked away.

I looked down at my outfit. It was one thing to see him in the dark lights of Tellicherry when I'd worn that Vivienne Tam, but unlike Pascal, supermarket lighting wasn't doing me any favors. Michael Saltz didn't want me wearing my Bergdorf clothing out, but how would he know? I had a whole closet of shiny, new, sexy, impressive things that deserved to be seen. It wasn't like I was telling people where I was eating dinner. No one besides Elliott knew that I had barely touched designer clothing. Emerald and Melinda were somewhat aware I was a fashion dilettante, but they were two people in a city of 8.5 million. I just needed to keep them at arm's length. Everyone else would assume I had always had these privileges.

But I could only self-loathe for a second or two because then I saw Pascal Fox turn back toward me, like he'd just thought of something. Maybe he wanted yams, or cauliflower, or oranges. Not me again.

"Hey, Tia," he said.

He remembered my name. Now I felt like that ostrich egg, rolling around, oozing goo. He whistled slightly as he spoke, a part of his accent that made him seem like he was whispering something to me and only me.

I suddenly thought of Elliott. He and I had started dating in freshman year. He was my first love, my first—and only—lover. Early in our relationship, he had given me a list titled: "59 Reasons Elliott Loves Tia." Once I had read it, I'd recited a list of my own, right off the cuff. Fifty-nine to his fifty-nine, and we kept building on that list in our minds and in our hearts for the next four years.

This was fresh in my mind as Pascal inched nearer, every millimeter burning into that memory. When was the last time I'd had these red-hot feelings for Elliott? Maybe never. We had started as friends, temperate water that had worked itself to a simmer.

But with Pascal, I was already at a full boil.

"Yes?"

"Can I get your opinion on something?" He bit his lip and sounded adorably unsure. His chef's coat was unbuttoned at the top, and I was disappointed to see a T-shirt instead of his bare skin.

"Sure," I said.

"Come on." He nodded his head toward the spice aisle and I followed, practically skipping behind him because apparently my feet didn't know how to play it cool.

"I'm working on a new dish with fluke and lovage, but it's falling a little flat for me," he said. "What do you think?"

I scanned the spices. Something to pull them together . . . "Hmm, okay. Let me think."

We stayed silent for a while, pondering the selection.

"You know what lovage is, yes?" he asked finally.

I shot him a face. "Um, yeah. It's been written up all over the place."

He laughed. "Sure. I should have known you'd know. But do you like it?"

"Well . . . actually." Normally, in any room, I was the food expert. But this was New York City. And here was Pascal Fox. And I was just one of thousands of people like me, people who had curiosity and a computer. "I've never had lovage," I admitted. "I know it's like celery, but milder. And I know it looks like fennel. And I know it comes in giant stalks and . . ."

"Whoa, whoa, hold on right there! You can talk all you want, but that doesn't tell you everything about love—"

I kept expecting him to finish the word, but he let it hang until I interjected, my voice trapped in my throat. "Lovage?" I said.

"Love-age." He smiled. "What do your book smarts tell you goes well with lovage?"

I felt him watching me as I reconsidered the spices, trying—and failing—to keep my heartbeat soft and steady. "You said fluke, right? Well, I'd stay away from the stronger spices that would otherwise pair with lovage—cumin, coriander, etc. And I see you already have dill in your basket." As I thought, I got calmer. I didn't even need to look at him; I felt Pascal warming up, smiling at my knowledge.

God, I loved that—being challenged and appreciated and heard. As much fun as I had with Elliott, I could never talk to him directly about food. He'd listen, sure. He'd try to understand, of course. But I'd always hold back, curbing my passion. What if I didn't have to?

"So I think . . ." I picked up a jar from the spice rack. "Nigella."

"Nigella! A daring pick. Why nigella?" Pascal asked, taking the jar from my hands.

"Because the oniony flavors will complement the lovage.

Onion, celery, fennel. It all goes. And it has that sort of prickly pungency to it. The taste matches the texture." I looked up at him, but he kept his lips tightly sealed, as if words were about ready to come out . . . but didn't. Did he want to correct me? Say "never mind"?

"But . . ." I looked back on the shelf. "If you're not looking for textural contrast, maybe a whisper of white peppercorn?" Strain had entered my voice because he wasn't giving me any feedback. He was the chef, not me.

Finally, he put me at ease. "Why did you stop?" he asked. "You were giving me free ideas!"

I blushed. "Oh, I guess I didn't know if you liked my suggestions."

He shook his head in disbelief. "I liked them very much. Pretty good for never having tasted love-age ever."

I bit the inside of my cheek, trying not to beam. All I thought was, *Thank you, you get it.*

"Well, why don't we pop your lovage cherry?" he said.

Under any other circumstances combining lovage and cherries would have repulsed me, but now I simply melted.

"Come to Bakushan now. I'll try out the dish and you tell me what you think."

I gasped and leaped up in the air. "Really?"

He touched me on the shoulder and a chill zipped to my toes. "Really," he said.

Before I knew it, we were in the checkout line together. I briefly checked my phone to see if Elliott or Michael Saltz had called or texted, but thankfully neither had. For now, I pretended that I was in another world without them.

"OKAY, GIVE ME fifteen minutes," he said. "Study up, book smarts girl!"

The restaurant was closed until five P.M., so it was only us plus some prep cooks in the back. The dining room looked oddly inert and uncool in the light. I heaved my books up and tried to do my reading, but I couldn't concentrate, not with Pascal clanking around in the open kitchen.

I kept my head down and my eyes up, watching him. The situation was at once strange and homey. We barely knew each other and yet the moment now felt tender, like he was my boyfriend making me breakfast while I worked.

I closed my book and walked up to the kitchen pass.

"Hey, brainiac," he said upon seeing me. "Sick of the books and wanting to do some hard labor, huh?"

"Ha! Yes. Over books any day," I said, and walked in. I saw him take me in, from head to toe. Not the once-over that I'd gotten at Yale or from Emerald, but another sort of thing, a look that said, *I'm glad you're here.*

He put me to work.

"Smaller," he said, looking at my lovage chunks. "Like this." His knife vibrated up and down, and before I knew it he'd tada-ed a mound of perfect translucent green cubes.

"Oh, jeez! I've never learned knife skills. I guess I've sort of faked it this whole time."

He leaned his hand on the counter and looked at me curiously, licking his soft, ribbonlike lips in thought. I had to hold on to the ledge for balance.

Then he came up behind me, so we were both facing the counter. "Well, faking it is fine for amateurs. But I know you're a professional. I'll show you. Get the knife," he whispered in my ear. He picked up a stalk of lovage, holding on to my shoulder as he side-stepped. We gripped the knife together. With his thumb, he pressed my thumb against the blade, as if the knife were a fanned deck of cards. "Just light pressure. Always come back to the tip. Use the curvature and keep rocking."

We practiced, the knife dipping in and out over the cutting board, his hand pressing harder as we swept into the downswings. Then he put the lovage underneath our knife and we started. The knife slipped through it like skis on snow, not like the *clomp clomp* of my regular slicing.

"See? Easy."

He pulled away and—just like at our meeting at Tellicherry—my skin sizzled with the memory of his touch. I still felt his chest against my shoulder blades, my butt against his hips, his arm curved around mine.

I couldn't decipher what he was doing with me. We had accidentally bumped into each other at Tellicherry and Whole Foods, but this, now, was intentional. But on whose part? The way he talked to me, looked at me . . . This morning, I never would have thought that I'd end up here, in Bakushan, with Chef Pascal Fox practically spooning me while teaching me knife skills.

I heard my phone ring in the dining room but decided not to answer it. I didn't want to break the spell. All the other cooks had left, the calm before the dinner storm. The kitchen bloomed with the full smells of roasting onions and garlic. In the back, a duck on a spit. Where Michael Saltz's apartment was prickly and cacophonous, here everything swelled and harmonized.

While he sautéed the lovage, my eye caught on a framed newspaper article. It was just two lines, but it was the only thing in the room not designed to make or serve food, and it had choice placement on the door between the kitchen and the dining room, next to the two-person chef's table.

PASCAL FOX of Antoinette has left his Executive Chef position to pursue other projects. Chef Fox says multiple investors have approached him and he is weighing options.

"Why did you frame this article?" I asked.

"Well, why not?"

"Because it doesn't really say anything."

He stopped tending the stove and looked back at me. "Actually," he said, "it's what it *doesn't* say that matters. What comes next? What are the possibilities? It's easy to rest on your laurels, but this tiny mention inspires me."

"Right. Because you're on the line to do something good and prove yourself." I thought of the reviews—so many people lived on those words: the diners, the chefs, the owners, the waitstaff.

"No, no," he said. "I don't need to prove anything to anyone. Just me." He pointed to his chest and he would have sounded cheesy had he not seemed so genuine. "But, here," he said. "Try this." He handed me a fork.

I poked the fluke, a cube of lovage, and hay-like strands of some dried root vegetable, and dragged it through a sauce studded with nigella.

Before I took my bite, I asked, "Did you try? What did you think?"

He grinned and took off his apron. "I don't care what I think, I care what you think."

"Sounds like you want to prove something to me," I teased. Where I was coming up with this saucy tone?

"Maybe I do," he said with an arched brow, his gaze never leaving mine.

I tasted. "It's great," I squeaked. What did I think? I thought he was the hottest guy I had ever talked to, maybe even seen. It didn't matter what I thought of the dish.

I heard my phone ring again and groaned. Not now! I just wanted this moment a little longer. Who knew if I'd ever live anything like this dream again?

"Is that you?" he asked.

"Yeah, but it's fine," I said as the ringing stopped. I took another bite. It didn't follow any normal standards. The fluke was slippery, cold. The lovage's potency poked through, funked it up. But it felt incomplete.

"It's missing something . . . right?" Pascal asked, reading my mind.

I tipped back on my heels and considered him. He barely knew me and yet he seemed in tune with my thoughts. Even in the tiny kitchen, we somehow danced around each other without stepping on each other's toes.

"Right," I said. "But I'm not sure what it is."

Pascal put his hand on his hip. "Come now, Tia. This is the creative process and I want your input. We have to remember those words on that wall."

We? We *who*? We the restaurant, or we *us*? Like, him and me?

"Who wrote that, anyway?"

"A woman named Helen Lansky."

"Helen?" I nearly hiccupped. I studied the article again, but it was still two lines, the same two lines I had read before. Of course Helen Lansky knew who he was. He wasn't some random grad student like me. "You know Helen?"

"Yes," he said. "She's a prize unto herself, separate from restaurant reviews and that blogger shit." Annoyance overtook his voice, but he shook it off. "Helen is *magnifique*. I have all her cookbooks; her flavor combinations are classic, eternal."

I couldn't help staring at him, slurping up every atom and utterance and whistle in his voice. He'd become more relaxed in the kitchen, relaxed yet assertive. He bit his thumb in thought and the contrast between his big, strong hands and this adorable, boyish habit made me woozy.

"Well . . . what are we doing with this dish?"

"Let me think," I said, letting my exhalations calm me down yet again. "I think the dish needs something more to ground it. Something earthy."

"That's the lovage," he said, now looking in the fridge, his jean-clad butt poking out.

"No, the lovage is the wild card," I said, as steadily as I could, even though I was intensely distracted and slightly astonished that a man's butt excited me so much.

"That flavor remains suspended in your mouth," I continued. "You need something that goes deeper." As I said it, he slowly approached me. I lifted my hand to make way for him but he caught it midair.

"I *need* something?" he asked, tightening his grip with a little smile and a little threat. He walked one inch closer and that inch set my heart fluttering again, the air between us compressed and tickling.

"Yes. Um, I mean . . ."

Still holding my hand, he grabbed a bowl of toasted almonds. "Like this?" He dropped one in my mouth with his free hand, his fingers barely touching my lips.

I didn't feel like eating. I felt like either running back to my apartment and hiding under the covers, or maybe just pretending I was someone else and kissing him right then and there.

But I ate the almond and resigned myself to imagining his lips on mine. His hand was still around my wrist . . . his finger on my lips . . .

"Or, maybe this." He gripped me tighter and, with his other hand, picked up a frond of dehydrated kale, as big and light as a feather. He touched the end of my lips, but when I opened my mouth, he pulled it away. "Careful," he said. "It crumbles." He placed it on my lips once more and I took a bite, little flakes of kale falling like green fairy dust.

Now my heart was taking off and I was gripping his hand, too. Was this what cheating felt like? Like the wind is being sucked out of you and replaced with something volatile and hot, something that saps you but leaves you invigorated all the same? My breaths shortened. I leaned all my weight on the wall. One nudge and I'd fall to the ground—or into Pascal's arms.

"Or this might do the trick." He reached for a plastic container and plunged his pointer finger in. Out came a puff of white on the tip of his finger. "It's a sesame-yogurt mousse, with a hint of sumac."

Yes, that would go well with the dish, that was perfect. Cheating tasted like helium. You can breathe it, but it makes your insides go awry. It flushes out the oxygen to make way for something new, something false.

But maybe if you're starved for air, you'll breathe anything.

And before I knew it, the tip of his finger was against the side of my mouth, the mousse cooling my skin. I turned my head to get a full taste, but he moved his finger away so I only got a tiny wisp of the mousse, not enough to know it.

"Hey, come on," I said. "Let me taste it."

He took another step forward, and I took the tiniest of steps back, pressing us both against the wall, Helen's write-up just over my left shoulder. "Oh? You think this is what's missing?"

I chased his finger with my lips. He had only grabbed one of my hands, so I could have brought his hand to my mouth, but I stayed there, transfixed, like a bug pinned down for inspection. Finally, the flat of my tongue and the tip of his finger met. He gently pushed it inside my mouth, and I tasted the yogurt at last. It was surprising in every way—airy yet hearty, sunny yet earthy. The final piece. He kept his finger in my mouth even after I finished tasting it, my tongue against the ridges on the underside of his finger, coarse from cooking, I suppose, but more likely from being a man. Pascal was a man.

He pulled his finger out and my lips made a suctioned *pop* sound.

Maybe Pascal was the oxygen. Maybe he was what I should have been breathing.

He tilted his head, let go of my hand, and took a step back. "Yes, I think that'll do the trick." He handed me his phone. "Can I get your number?"

I was still woozy, hungering for Pascal's body and face and breath. This was 110 percent unacceptable to Elliott and Michael Saltz, but I went through with it anyway.

As I entered my number in his phone, I kept on messing up and deleting, messing up and deleting. Whenever I gave my number to a guy, it was always to collaborate on a school project or something. But this was different. Pascal—for some reason—desired me.

I had to imagine this was how things happened when a boy meets a girl in a restaurant or bar. I didn't have much experience.

By the end, I had forgotten about Elliott and Michael Saltz. Pascal's touch had taken over. Pascal and his body and his cooking and the way he understood and listened to me.

"*Parfait,*" he said when I finished typing. "I can't wait to see you again."

I WALKED HOME with my body singing. In my mind I re-created the warmth of his hands, the proportions of his body, the tip of his finger. Even though we'd had our clothes on, I had never felt so sexy, so electrified by another person's presence.

But that was just my body. My mind knew better. By the time

I got home, I was on the verge of vomiting. I looked at my phone and saw Elliott had called me three times, texted once, and left a voicemail. Who leaves a voicemail?

The text said, *where r u?,* which sounded fine enough. Standard. But the voicemail. He'd said those same three words, but they had come out mean and scared and annoyed, a voice laced with distrust.

I texted Elliott back and asked when we could get together. He said he'd be at Barnes & Noble the next day to study. His boss had put him on the lab's night shift and he wouldn't need to go in until seven P.M., so we could hang out while doing some work.

Theoretically, the timing was perfect. The Tellicherry review was coming out online that night, but I was thinking about waiting for the print version the next morning, so I could experience it for the first time as a physical object. At Barnes & Noble, I could pick up a hard copy and share it with Elliott.

But that was just in theory. He couldn't know the truth. Instead of looking forward to seeing Elliott, I began to dread it. And I kept thinking about Pascal.

Chapter 18

THE NEXT MORNING AT BARNES & NOBLE, ELLIOTT AND I SAT across from each other in the café section. He'd brought ten botany journals and one textbook, which stood between us like a wall. The bottom of my stomach rumbled with the taste of that sesame-yogurt mousse, of Pascal against me in Bakushan. I shook the memories out of my head.

"What are you doing?" I asked warmly, trying to be sweet and open to his affection.

"Studying evaporation rates in tropical versus tundra climates," he said, his head already buried in his books.

"Oh, cool," I said. I looked down at my books and tapped the table. "Do you want to tell me about it?"

He glared at me for a quick second before he returned to his work. "I can't now. Moishe wants this report before I come in. Sorry, Tia, I'll explain it to you later."

"Oh, okay," I said, playfully tapping his foot. He pulled it away.

I took a deep breath. Elliott wasn't even noticing my efforts, so I went to find the newspaper without him.

There in a wire bin next to the entrance, I spotted them. I peeled away to the Food section and saw a beautiful picture of Tellicherry's jewel-like dining room, centered around the best table, where Michael Saltz and I had sat and Pascal had paid a visit.

I read it slowly and carefully, ingesting each word before I moved on to the next.

Some parts of my review were left out or skewed. For one, I had raved about the lavender-peach macarons, but Michael Saltz had decided they didn't make the cut. I had also written favorably about Tellicherry's varied menu, but Michael Saltz's review tweaked my words so that the menu selections came off as flighty and indecisive instead of agile and joyous. It made the thrilling will-he-or-won't-he danger of the dishes something to be frightened of.

But those were subtle matters of punctuation and syntax, slight connotation shifts. More important, there were two major things that caught my attention.

First, just like the Madison Park Tavern review, Michael Saltz had used my exact words in the vast majority of his column. As he had said on the phone, he was perfectly able to write his own review, even if he was using my thoughts. So why had he bothered to use my wording? I loved some of my turns of phrase, but I couldn't imagine why he had used them, especially given that this was Michael Saltz—his ego and name were so precious to him.

And then there was the big type across the bottom of the review: THREE STARS, as Michael Saltz had said it would be. He'd had it in his head from the beginning, and that's why he'd made it so. My words, his judgment call.

But even with the star rating changed and those other minor tweaks, I still felt I owned that piece of writing. My words were in the *New York Times,* and that was an intoxicating, sky-high rush, the type that makes you want to scream from the rooftops and tell everyone you know. But of course I couldn't tell a soul. All that energy ricocheted back inside me and I felt radioactive, so excited and pent up I might have burst.

I ran back to sit with Elliott and made a big show of opening and shutting the paper, spreading it wide over my face, crinkling the edges, folding and unfolding. He kept working.

I didn't want it to, but my mind turned to Pascal again. I couldn't help it. What would he say if he saw this review? If I wrote one about him, would he hang it up in his kitchen? Would he celebrate with Chef Rhodes, because after all, three stars was pretty good?

Elliott sat there while I thought of another man's hands on me, his finger in my mouth, his smell of caramelized onions and brown butter and sage. Thankfully, Elliott would never find out about Pascal. We weren't in college anymore. In New York City, millions of people went about their business on separate tracks, going to work, going to bed, having sex.

Yikes, sex. I tried to refocus, away from Tellicherry and the review and a certain someone's tattooed arms.

"How's it going?" I asked Elliott, my heart still fluttering like a hummingbird after a candy binge.

He pursed his lips and hit his book with the end of a pen. "It's okay. I'm thinking about a problem. Give me a couple moments."

"Um . . . sure," I said, my heart sinking. He was studying a molecular diagram and drawing out his own. His head turned from side to side as he compared the diagrams, his lips skewed in thought. I had always liked Elliott's hard-core study sessions. He dove into everything he did, and that passion, that disregard for what anyone thought of his intensity, had attracted me. But now he looked pained, his eyebrows at an angry slant, his fingernails scraping at the table.

Fact was, Elliott could never match Pascal. He and I didn't share the same passions. Elliott didn't light up around esoteric veggies. Elliott didn't have his own restaurant and a staff who reported to him. And, frankly, frighteningly . . . Elliott didn't turn me on like Pascal had. I had always thought I just wasn't a sexual person, but . . . Pascal. Pascal and his strong arms. His hair mussed just so. His hands rough and firm and . . . large. Part of the appeal was Pascal's size. Not that he was a giant or anything, but he had stature.

I took a walk to cool off. Studying was impossible. So I kept quiet, choking on my happiness. Every now and again, I looked back at Elliott, still engrossed by those molecular diagrams. I monitored the newspaper bin and tried to eavesdrop on people reading the review:

"Have you read the review of that new place on Bond Street? Sounds like Michael Saltz got his groove back."

"Dude sounded like he was losing it for a while. His old reviews were so boring."

"Tellicherry sounds interesting, we should go."

"This licorice breadstick sounds so cool."

Perhaps people were quoting my words in their emails and would talk about them over dinner. Perhaps a young girl had brought my review to school and read it in class while her teachers weren't looking. Perhaps she dreamed that she could write this column, too.

I wished *I* could write this column and have it to myself.

I didn't attempt to lure Elliott out of his shell again. Instead, I listened to the chatter. I walked past a *Bon Appétit* magazine with Pascal Fox on the cover, holding a plate toward the public.

Oh, Pascal, I thought, as if we were two old hats working at the famous foodie game. I imagined him right there in the bookstore with me, holding me from behind, his chest so warm and broad in my imagination that I got too hot and took off my cardigan. I shook my head—yet again—to rid myself of these thoughts. I had a boyfriend. But thinking about Pascal wasn't cheating. Especially if Elliott was already being so distant. I liked Elliott when he was passionate, but those passions had usually included me. Now I didn't know where I stood.

Finally, I returned to our table. "Hey, are you hungry?" I asked.

"Hungry?" Elliott said gruffly. "We just got here."

I looked at my watch. "No, not really. It's one thirty. We've been here two hours."

"*Eugh,* yeah, you're right," he said. "Let's go, then." He began to put everything in his backpack. "How about that falafel place?"

"Falafel?" I scrunched my nose. "Actually, what do you think about going to Tellicherry?"

"What's Tellicherry?"

"It's a new restaurant. The *New York Times* reviewed it today." I opened the paper and showed him the page. My page. It was my last effort to connect.

Please, I thought. *Please like this. Please please please.*

It was relationship voodoo. If he liked it, everything would be okay. If he loved me on a fundamental level, he'd somehow be able to recognize this as mine—knowing nothing about it. He'd feel it in his bones.

He quickly glanced at the article. "Really? That place? Eh . . . that's not us."

My hands dropped with the newspaper. I reworked my voodoo. If he realized the importance after a little coaxing—after all, he couldn't read my mind—then we were right for each other.

But part of me knew that was an impossible challenge. Maybe I wanted him to fail.

"Come on, read it," I said, meaning to sound breezy, but my voice came out a little mean and annoyed, a voice laced with distrust.

Elliott sighed and took the paper. I watched him expectantly.

I wanted him to love it so we could share this moment, even in the weakest of ways. That would be better than nothing. Yet I also wanted him to hate it, to absolve me of my Pascal thoughts, to give me permission to think new ones.

"Yuba stick?" he said with a small note of disgust in his voice. "Curry ice cream? Sounds pretentious, doesn't it? And gross, frankly."

I staggered back as if he had struck me. One last chance. "You're missing the point. Read it again."

"I don't want to read it again," Elliott said with finality. "I want to eat lunch." He took me by the hand but I yanked it away.

"I don't want falafel," I said. "I want to go to Tellicherry."

"Okay!" Elliott replied with his hands up, as if I were holding him hostage. "Let's go. I definitely want to spend my nonexistent money there. Maybe it'll be as good as Bakushan."

The word from his lips paralyzed me for a second and I felt protective over Pascal and his restaurant.

"Fine, I'll go by myself." It'd be a mistake to take him there anyway. What did he know about food? Why did I need to tolerate this attitude? I'd given him a shot, but I wouldn't pretend that the review didn't matter to me.

By now people were looking at us, shoppers and tourists and kids and parents. The newspaper stack had diminished considerably. God, couldn't they get more papers here? People wanted to read the review! Where was the floor manager?

Tellicherry was never the type of place for Elliott. I don't know why I even bothered to ask him in the first place, especially after Bakushan.

I'd find someone else to go to Tellicherry with me. At least one guy would be game. I let my mind escape to that fantasy. He'd go with me to any restaurant in the city. He was the ultimate insider, tastemaker, key-holder. Everything about Pascal excited me—the roughness of his skin, the clench of his hand, the lullaby that was his knife slicing through the lovage.

I didn't have to fantasize for long, though. Just then, Pascal texted me a picture of that fluke, lovage, and yogurt mousse dish along with a caption:

IT'S A HIT!

I smiled and didn't even bother to hide it from Elliott, who was loading up his backpack with his mountain of books.

"Sorry, I mean . . . I just don't feel like going out to a fancy lunch." He smiled in a long-suffering kind of way. "I guess I'm stressed. And I remembered I have to head out anyway. I have this thing—"

"Sure," I said, relieved, actually. Elliott picked up his bag and walked away without saying good-bye. I waited for him to turn around and wave back at me, in case a small part of "us" was still there. He descended on the escalator, walked through the crowd, and left through the revolving door.

I realized then that my relationship voodoo was juvenile. There were no cryptic signs. It was either there or it wasn't.

LATER THAT AFTERNOON, I got another text from my new friend. He really wanted to see me again.

HEY. I NEED TO THANK YOU FOR THAT LOVAGE INSPIRATION. DINNER?

But before I had a chance to think about it, I got an email from Elliott. A mass email.

Dear Friends,

Come one, come all to the botany symposium—tomorrow! A couple of us will present our work, ranging from cryptozoology to chemosynthesis, and we'll also show a sneak peek of our Poison exhibit.

I'll be your honorary emcee and will also present my project, eco-friendly pest control via carnivorous plant enzymes. It sounds sexy because it is sexy. I'll be introducing our awesome speaker, Dr. Mohammed Zalmai, who'll speak about the New York Botanical Garden's partnership with Beth Israel Medical Center.

The symposium is tomorrow at 3:00 P.M. in Weill Auditorium, 1300 York Ave and 69th St. Hope to see you all there.

Cheers,
Elliott

Had he been planning the symposium at the bookstore? Had he told me about it? Wasn't he studying something about the Arctic? I looked at my phone, then at my computer. I made an effort to get back to Elliott first, even though I wanted to flood Pascal's inbox with *Yes, what time, I've been thinking about you every second*. But I focused on Elliott's message. I had scheduled lunch at Le Brittane with Michael Saltz, but Elliott's thing wasn't until three. And then I had to report to Madison Park Tavern at five thirty. It would be tight, but it seemed doable.

Hey. This sounds really exciting! I'll be there.

Elliott's email *was* exciting. I was proud of him and happy that he was happy. And yet. After I pressed Send, the words looked so sterile and forced. They didn't look different from any other email I had sent to Elliott, even when we were at the height of our love. And yet those days seemed so far away.

In New York, my best moments had been at Madison Park Tavern, Tellicherry, Bakushan. The people I liked most were food people, who lived and breathed it like me. Maybe all the times Elliott had chased a food adventure with me in college, he'd just been playing along because he couldn't think of anything better to do. But now we had options besides each other.

And so I turned my attention to Pascal's texts. Where would we have dinner? My mind raced to what I'd wear and what I'd order.

But Michael Saltz wouldn't approve of me texting back and would forbid me from seeing him, so I did nothing. For now.

Still, Pascal Fox had texted me. That was something. I savored it, and for the time being, that was enough.

Chapter 19

My Le Brittane–symposium–Madison Park Tavern triple-header started at one thirty. After class, I walked to a coffee shop and went straight to the bathroom.

I took off my jeans and sweater and jumped into a fitted Carolina Herrera skirt and a chiffon Moschino blouse with a patterned sash wrapped around the waist. Ballet flats, off. Red Prada slingbacks, on. I'd put my Burberry trench coat on later. I stuffed my old clothes in my Goyard tote and checked myself in the mirror.

Today I was playing an actress. I had a lot on my plate, but the key was to own the part. For the next couple of hours with Michael Saltz, I put my old self aside.

I had some extra time, so I ordered a coffee and sat down with my schoolwork. I think some people looked twice and I imagined them thinking things like, *Why is the woman buried in books? What if she gets highlighter on her nice blouse? Surely she must be "someone."*

I let them wonder and pretended to study my Nutrition notes

like they were the lease on my Monaco house, handling them delicately, as if my nails were freshly manicured.

WHILE MADISON PARK Tavern was tall and bustling, like an haute indoor greenmarket, Le Brittane was rather dim and cozy. Some restaurants make you feel like you're on top of the world with sweeping views of street and sky. Le Brittane, on the other hand, seduces you into believing you're part of an exclusive club, a luxurious world of Upper East Side ivory moldings and gilded purse hooks.

I passed my Burberry to the coat check woman. Michael Saltz was already sitting at a circular banquette in the middle of the room. He wore pewter-gray slacks, a dark blue button-down, frameless glasses, and a smug sense of ease. He looked like an uncle of the renegade type, the naughty rich one who never got married. All his disguises must have been some variation of rich, powerful guy—he couldn't play anyone else.

"Hello, Tia," Michael Saltz said. "You look like quite the uptown lady. Nice work."

"Thank you," I said, pleased.

"Now?"

I took my phone out of my purse and placed it, face up, on the table. As much as I hated being watched like this, I had to accept it as standard procedure.

"Good afternoon, my name is Hugo," a tall, gray-haired waiter said. He wore a gray vest tight across his narrow chest, and despite his hair, he didn't look old, more like an exotic cat or a black-and-white Calvin Klein ad. He handed us the menus, beautiful, narrow pieces of paper, periwinkle blue and letterpressed with gold foil.

"Let's start the tasting menu, if you please," Michael Saltz said, leaning back in his chair.

I tried to silently catch his attention. Le Brittane was the most seafoody of seafood restaurants. Looking at the menu, I noted a variety of possible pitfalls—an oyster and sea bean salad, langoustine cream, clam-miso emulsion.

"Very good, sir," the waiter said. "Is this your first time?"

"Yes, first time," Michael Saltz said quickly.

I was about to cancel the order so I could spend more time with the menu when he edged me out.

"Her first time, too."

"Excellent," Hugo said. "Chef will take good care of you." He took the menus from the table and walked away.

"Hey," I said. "We can't just get the tasting menu. I'm allergic to crustaceans and bivalves. Remember?"

Michael Saltz slapped his face in despair. "I realize that. But we're here for the tasting menu and that's the end of the story. You can eat around certain components."

"But if I can't eat it . . . and you can't . . ."

He sneered and put his hand up to silence me. "Don't say it. Eat what you can and make up the rest. We have to see the dish in its original preparation. What are they supposed to do, substitute bacon for oysters? If neither of us can taste it, then we at least have to see it for the review."

"I don't know, Michael," I said. "I don't want to risk anything because I have a thing right after this and I don't want to get sick."

"How sick?"

"Not fatally sick, but close enough. It's pretty dire. Sick!"

"Okay, okay. Noted. I'm not making you eat anything you can't," he said. "But we need to get the unadulterated menu. Once you make substitutions, you're tarnishing the chef's original vision."

Sure, I got that. But I wasn't ready to risk my life for a chef's vision. Hugo approached and set down the first course. Before he left, I asked for the menu again so I knew what I was eating. Hugo graciously obliged.

"What are you doing?" Michael Saltz hissed. "Now they know we're paying extra attention to the food, instead of eating it like normal people."

Really? He left me speechless with how little he seemed to care about me, when I was supposed to be his precious, treasured protégée.

"Don't pout," he said. "Now that you have the menu, tell me what this is."

"Tuna, vanilla brioche crumbs, and a bruléed disk of monkfish liver."

"Ah, monkfish liver. Foie gras of the sea!" Michael Saltz said, lifting his cup in a toast. I refused to join him and just tipped the bite back like a shot, letting the mouthful take shape all at once.

Michael Saltz squinted at me while I set the cup down. If he disregarded me, then I'd disregard him.

Next, Hugo brought out a single octopus tentacle, roasted to bring out the burgundy speckles in its skin, painted with sweet, sea-infused balsamic squid ink and framed by two quarters of a ruddy pear.

We stayed silent as I ate.

Skate came wading in a chorizo broth, a cap of seaweed poking through the surface like an island paradise. Like always, Michael Saltz barely ate anything. This whole menu was on me.

I processed every dish the moment it hit the table. Daring. Subtle. Safe. Classic. I didn't eat the oysters or clams, but I tasted what the chef wanted to convey. And whatever I couldn't taste, we'd just make up. Still, I felt bad for the readers. They thought they were getting thoughtful criticism, but they got us: a disabled critic and his "protégée" who couldn't eat a third of the menu. It'd be better if I could take over: choose the restaurants, order the dishes, write the review. I wanted to have it all.

In between courses, I went to the bathroom to regroup. It shouldn't have been a surprise that Michael Saltz didn't care about my well-being. He was an egomaniac hell-bent on protecting his identity. What else did I expect? But maybe Michael Saltz and I were just getting used to each other. Of course there'd be some bumps in the road. I took a deep breath and went back out.

White-haired couples and men in suits watched me walk by. I could feel their curiosity swirl as my heels clicked on the pink marble tiles. Le Brittane was a gorgeous restaurant, and the people had a sophisticated uptown look. White pants, even in the fall. Smooth sweaters with not one pill. Clothes from legacy designers who had dressed First Ladies. I told myself to enjoy.

But as I walked back to the table I saw that Michael Saltz had a stern look on his face. And he was holding something: my phone.

"Whose number is this?"

He showed me a text, still on the lock screen.

YOU, ME, BAKUSHAN . . . TONIGHT?

Luckily, I hadn't put Pascal's name in my phone, so it was just a phone number.

"Oh, that's my roommate," I improvised.

I was ready to take it out of his hands when the phone chimed with another text.

I'M HERE ALL NIGHT. COME & I'LL TREAT YOU TO THE CHEF'S TABLE.

Michael Saltz cocked his head and reread the texts. I quickly tried to think of it from his point of view. Would my roommate really be at Bakushan? And be in a position to get us chef's table seats? In truth, no. But did he see that? I braced myself for an interrogation.

" 'I'm here all night . . . I'll treat you'?" he repeated. " 'I'll treat you'? What does that mean?"

I couldn't tell if he was playing dumb or if he genuinely didn't know.

Hugo returned to our table. "Chef is thrilled you're visiting us today," he said. "The first time is always the most special." He grinned with an air of suggestion in his eye and held out a dish. "On the house, a little interlude: ginger-infused egg custard." He left out two tiny spoons with luminous mother-of-pearl handles. The dish itself looked rather plain, a yellow jiggly surface like every other custard I had seen, even in my less-than-four-star life.

I kept my eye on Michael Saltz, who still seemed like he was pondering the damning texts. How could he not see it? Was he testing me? Or was he that dense? Was he planning how he was going to offload me?

And would he make good on what he had said—if I brought him down, he'd bring me down with him? At the time, it had seemed like an abstract thing to say, a bluff. But now that I had spent some time around him, I wasn't so sure.

"Are you ready to talk now?" he asked. Talk? He wanted a confession out of me? Now? I wrapped my arms around myself as armor, as a brace, to touch these clothes one last time. I had just gotten used to them.

Would Michael Saltz tell Elliott about Pascal? He'd have to find a way to condemn me without condemning himself. It seemed difficult to pull off, but I didn't doubt Michael Saltz could do it if he wanted. He'd said he could end my career before it began. Maybe ending my personal life came with the package.

He was still looking at me with disturbing calm, waiting for me to explain myself.

"Well . . . I didn't do it on purpose!" I said, almost crying. "He came up to me again at—"

Michael Saltz took a big gulp of his wine and laughed. "Tia—"

"I didn't think he'd call me. I wouldn't do that to Elliott. Or to you."

Michael Saltz scratched his widow's peak and shook his head gravely. Who was I kidding? He didn't need me. He could drop me just as fast as he'd picked me up. I had no doubt that he'd have another person doing my job in two days.

"Tia, I think you're overworked," he said. "If your roommate wants to take you to dinner, that's his choice. I'm surprised you have a male roommate, that's all."

The worries racing through my head halted. Really? He had no idea that was Pascal on my phone. Pascal Fox, maybe the second-most discussed man in food, after him. His texts and our Whole Foods shopping and our steamy Bakushan cooking lesson—those all remained hidden.

The relief knocked me out.

"Never mind!" I said, hoping my voice would obey my commands to be steady and breezy even when I was anything but.

"Okay, well, eat your thing. I didn't catch what it was, did you?"

I hadn't. But I was too worked up to think about the components of this little jiggly cup. I plunged in with no expectations but for something smooth, something creamy, something to set the stage for the rather spectacular-sounding next course: the escolar and Kobe beef surf and turf.

The custard slipped down my throat like a fish down a stream. I liked its muscular, silken force, until my throat seized and my face inflated like an emergency raft. I tried to reach for some water, but my eyes clouded and suddenly I slid into the banquette. The mother-of-pearl spoon catapulted under my forearm onto the floor.

A pair of hands cradled my head as the dizziness mounted.

I had almost lost this job and my shot with Helen.

I felt a cold piece of fabric on my forehead, then the taste of artificial strawberry sizzling on my tongue.

I had almost lost Elliott.

Someone had fished one of the allergy pills from my purse and placed it in my mouth. Finally, I felt my heart begin to take it easy, telling my blood to slow down, like it was a rambunctious child during recess. I guessed there were benefits to Michael Saltz being nosy.

My eyes opened and I saw nothing but a bright sheet of white, the tablecloth draped over me like a blanket. I swatted it away and saw Michael Saltz was now sitting next to me in the banquette. He looked up and around, then brought his face close to mine, wet cloth napkin in hand and a brow furrowed with a blend of anger and worry.

"Shellfish, huh?" he said. "That was dramatic."

I slowly sat and Michael Saltz propped me up as we stepped out of the banquette, looking as natural as possible. Lunch business was slowing down and few people were in the dining room. We made our way to the women's bathroom and after I told him the coast was clear, Michael Saltz entered and locked the door behind him. I stayed at the sink for a long time until I vomited. My face was scarlet from my hairline to my neck. Michael Saltz held my hair as I splashed water on my face.

After all this, I thought that maybe he wasn't as bad as I'd feared. Maybe he'd threatened my career because it seemed like the thing to do, the last checkmark when you're sealing that sort of deal.

We looked at each other in the bathroom mirror, the illustrious critic and his protégée.

When we returned to the table, I touched my face every second, hoping it had magically deflated through a vent in the back of my head. I checked my reflection in the back of my spoon, but that made my face look fatter and redder. Michael Saltz stayed nearly silent the whole time, just looking at me and waiting for me to recover so I could do his work.

Hugo rushed to our table. "Oh, dear!" he said. "Are you allergic to shellfish?"

I didn't have to answer. He knew.

Hugo took a deep breath, and his face turned bright red, maybe as red as mine.

"I should have told you that there's a lobster gelée on the bottom of the custard cup."

"Of course you should have told us!" Michael Saltz said, in the most direct voice I had ever heard him use to address a waiter.

"This is my fault entirely. I'm so sorry. It's Chef's play on 'fruit on the bottom' yogurt. The bill will be on us, naturally," Hugo said, though I think Michael Saltz had already assumed it would. "Please let me know if there's anything I can do to make this up to you." He closed his eyes as he spoke. I wanted to give him a hug and tell him I was fine, that it wasn't his mistake. The onus was on me to tell them of my allergy. It was my fault I had been distracted enough to eat that custard.

"Let's go," Michael Saltz said. "*Now.*"

I wondered if Hugo would be fired that night. Certainly by the time the review came out. Michael Saltz had the power to end his career. And to some extent, I did, too.

"That was a disgrace," Michael Saltz grunted when we left the restaurant. The day was misty, and taxis made a slurping noise as they zipped their way over fallen leaves and across Sixty-Eighth Street. "I would have liked you to finish the meal."

Seriously? I couldn't believe I had thought for one second that he cared about me. He'd only taken care of me because I'd have blown his cover if he hadn't done anything. Sure, he had taken care of me. But he'd also looked put-upon, like I was a chore.

He'd never be my ally and I told myself never to think that was a possibility ever again. When it came down to it, I was just as alone as before.

"Oh, well," I countered. "I'm terribly sorry to have inconvenienced you with my near-death experience. You wouldn't even let me tell them that I was allergic. Why didn't *you* eat the regular menu while I got a modified one?"

"Oh, yes, I'll eat the regular menu. Me. Fuck *me*. Do you . . ." He grabbed the top of his pants and shook them around his sickly thin legs. "Do you understand that all food is cardboard to me? That these riches are nothing more than calories? Of course you wouldn't. You're young. You're healthy. What I've been through . . . what I'm going through . . ."

His mouth hung in exhaustion, and amazingly, I felt bad for him again. But was his pain genuine or a trick?

Michael Saltz shook his head, spooked. Something about the episode had hit a nerve.

"I'm free tomorrow, if you want to come back," I finally said. I didn't have to love Michael Saltz, I just had to tolerate him. Until spring semester, I'd play by the rules. Then Helen would be mine and maybe I'd be able to return to some degree of normalcy.

"Don't bother," he said. "Where did you say you needed to go?" He just wanted to dispose of me.

"My boyfriend is hosting a botany symposium at three."

"Three?" Michael Saltz pulled up his sleeve and looked at his watch. "It's three ten now."

"Shit!" I cried and touched my face. Still swollen. I looked at my reflection in a silver plaque on the side of the building. Not only had the swelling not gone down, but the cold had made my face even redder. I pushed my cheeks in with the heels of my hands, as if I could shape my face into something acceptable. I pushed and pushed, knowing I was likely making the situation worse.

Michael Saltz threw his hand up to hail a cab. "Go. He won't notice." He wore that long, touchable cashmere coat, the double-sided one I'd taken from him that cold night at Madison Park Tavern. It was amazing how a man sheathed in something so soft could turn so hard.

"He'll definitely notice my tomato face," I said. "How could he not?"

"Believe me," Michael Saltz said. "Most men don't notice things like that. Most people are ignorant of their senses."

Maybe he was right. The sear of a steak, the crumb of a piece of bread, the precision of a diced carrot—only certain types of people paid attention to those things. But at the end of the day, I wasn't sure that meant a whole lot.

I hopped in the next cab and Michael Saltz gave the driver a twenty, even though I was only going a couple of blocks away.

"I'll need your thoughts as soon as possible, Tia."

"Yes, of course, sir," I said. I ran the lunch over in my head again. It may not have gone well, but thinking about my writing put me in a better mood. I thought of clever phrases I wanted to use: *Oceanic epiphany. Silken aromas.*

He slammed the door so hard the cabbie cursed him as we drove away.

Traffic was terrible. I thought about getting out and walking, but my face needed time to de-redden. When we approached Weill Auditorium, I made the driver circle the block twice to give myself even more time. I adjusted my skirt, retied the sash around my waist, and buttoned up my coat.

It took me about fifteen minutes to even find the auditorium. I ran up and down stairs, got lost in satellite wings. Finally, at

4:15, I spotted Elliott coming out of the auditorium, laughing with about ten people I didn't recognize. Everyone in the crowd seemed like science types, bookish and a little mischievous. But *she* stood out like anyone would've expected: a fashion designer at a botany symposium. Emerald was talking to another girl at the bottom of the ramp. She raised her hands in crazy motions and the other girl nodded and shrugged her shoulders.

What in the world was Emerald doing on the Upper East Side, going to Elliott's symposium? She never came up here. She had said as much when we'd made the trek to shop at Trina. Had she come all this way to listen to him? Had Elliott actually invited her?

After the cab pulled away, I watched Elliott in his suit looking capable and smart and happy. He carried a basket of mushrooms and handed them to a guy who patted him on the back. Another girl with a notepad and a pen asked him some questions and Elliott stopped and talked to her while she scribbled.

There was a time when I never would have missed anything as a big as Elliott's symposium. I would have altered my entire schedule for a special event like this, as he would have done for me. Why hadn't I asked Michael Saltz to reschedule?

In an alternate universe, the one I had imagined for us when we first arrived here, I'd have been standing there with him, chatting with his friends, getting to know his research deep enough that I could actually help him.

He walked toward me then and pain sliced through me. None of those things had happened. I didn't know about his job. I didn't know his friends. I didn't really have any friends myself.

I suddenly remembered my ugly swollen face and thought he might wonder what I was doing in this obviously new and expensive coat and skirt and shoes.

"Hey," he said, seeing me finally. "There you are." He didn't seem to notice my bogus clothes or my bloated face, and that killed me, too. Maybe he just didn't care.

"How did everything go? I'm so, so sorry I'm late. I had this thing, and it took much longer than I thought. And then I had an allergic reaction. I'm sorry. I know this is important to you, and I should have been here. Things have been crazy for me, and—"

"Things have been crazy for me, too, Tia. Don't worry about it," he said. He gave a small, closed-mouth smile—not an Elliott smile at all, but the smile of someone else. "Let's meet up later. I don't want to talk about this . . . here." A couple of the senior scientists were walking up behind him, looking about ready to congratulate him. "I'll see you later," he said, turning toward them. As he did, his body opened and he smiled a large, goofy smile, like a kid. That was the real him, not the stiff, distracted Elliott he had shown me.

I saw Emerald give him a big hug and they walked together with a bigger group down the street. They left without me. A rotten taste built up in my mouth, something worse than the vomit at Le Brittane. He looked so comfortable with her as they moved in rhythm along the sidewalk. An ugly idea popped into my brain, one so vivid I couldn't believe I hadn't thought of it earlier.

What if they were secretly seeing each other when I was at class or with Michael Saltz? Was Emerald actually with Elliott every time she went out late at night? Were they laughing about me and the "pretentious" food I always ordered? The questions piled up in my head.

I sat down on a stone bench. I had been paranoid about Michael Saltz picking up on Pascal's text, and I hoped I was being paranoid now.

Once Jake dismissed me from Madison Park Tavern, I texted Elliott, asking if I could stop by. He said sure and I rushed over.

Elliott opened the door and I hardly recognized the place. He had gotten more plants and a desk. The wreath had been replaced with a bouquet of flowers, the type of bouquet you'd give your girlfriend or maybe one you'd receive from a would-be girlfriend trying to woo you. I willed myself not to think that way. That'd get us nowhere.

"Hey," he said as we awkwardly hugged.

He stared at some distant place in the hall. "So, why did you get to the symposium so late?" His voice sounded hollow and hoarse, devoid of warmth.

"I was tied up with something else. I'm really sorry. The day just crept up on me," I said, pleading. "Can I . . . can I come in?"

He paused for a second, like he was thinking, like he'd actually consider not letting his own girlfriend in his apartment. "Sure," he said finally, then he sat in his desk chair. "Come on in. So you were caught up with . . . something else. Like, work? A paper?"

"Like . . . an event. It was for work. A last-minute thing for the restaurant."

"Oh. I guess I didn't give you much notice. I'm not sure I told you about it in advance," he said, again in that flattened voice that was freaking me out. So I hadn't forgotten about the event. Not that his omission made me feel any better. In fact, it made me feel worse.

"It's just . . . it's just that I never got the chance, you know?" Now his volume was rising and an edge sharpened in his voice. "You . . . you're not around." He talked to the wall. "You're always running away."

I thought about taking him by the shoulders and saying, *Hey! I haven't been great—in more ways than I'll ever be able to admit to you—but I love you. And you're my Elliott. And I don't want to lose you.* But something in his posture told me that if I said that, he wouldn't hear it. Elliott was a scientist. He needed proof and all I had were words.

So I had to find the facts. "When have I been running away?" I asked.

He exhaled sharply and the sweet face I knew turned sour, offended. "Running into your apartment. Out of your apartment. Running out on our phone conversations," he said, rubbing his forehead. "Or like that time you high-tailed it out of here and immediately jumped on your phone. Once you thought you were in the clear, you called someone back. Who was it?"

For the first time that night, he looked me straight in the eye as he said those last three words.

Who. Was. It.

I knew he'd only accept one answer—the truth. But I couldn't do it.

"Who was . . . who?" I asked in my best confused voice.

"Don't patronize me, please, Tia." He went back to staring at the wall.

"Elliott . . ."

"Why are you keeping this from me?" He sounded defeated, tired. Old. He had been spending nights in the lab. Did I ever ask him how he was holding up? Did he ever tell me? We had never been like this, ever. Before we were a couple, we were friends. Now we were barely acquaintances.

"And every time I touch you," he continued, "you cringe somehow. You're shrinking away from me."

"Elliott . . . I . . ." But I wasn't sure what I could say.

"Tell me something." He closed his eyes, a full pressing of the lids. A wet, tear-licked seam. "Do you still love me?"

I made myself hold his gaze when his eyes opened.

I did what Elliott wanted me to. I looked at the facts.

I thought about how hurt I'd been when he'd pushed aside that Bakushan dumpling. How he hadn't opposed Emerald's suit idea. The way he'd looked at me hungrily in her clothes, a new me that wasn't the Tia he had fallen in love with. I thought about his face when I'd told him I didn't get the Helen Lansky internship, that blankness. His swift dismissal of the Tellicherry review even though he'd never read it. I remembered that I'd never really believed he would be into it anyway. It had been a long shot asking him to eat with me there.

It was a long shot to ask him to be interested. It was a long shot to think he could understand everything that was happening, and that's why I was withdrawing. That's why I was running away.

What would I do if I lost him? We had been through so much together. College had formed us, and we'd thought we would come to New York and continue growing together, become the people we were meant to be. I looked at Elliott's end table. He must have paid three hundred dollars for it and he had been so proud. Now three plants had spilled their soil on it. A water stain peeked from underneath a wide unruly vine. So much for our big New York plans. You could plan and plan, but ultimately, life takes over. Choices get made.

"I guess I'm figuring things out," I said. "And . . . I'm a bit hurt that I haven't been able to share the things I love with you. Like that time we went to that restaurant, or when I tried to show you that review in the newspaper . . ."

"Review in the newspaper? That thing you showed me at the bookstore? You know I've never been into that stuff. I try, I've always tried. Come on, you can't make me the bad guy here."

"I know you're not a bad guy," I stammered. "But even you

have to agree that we haven't been that attentive to each other lately."

"Attentive, right," he said, pinching the bridge of his nose. "I've been trying to figure out what's going on with us. I guess I was pissed that you couldn't make the symposium, but I'm not sure I even told you about it. That won't happen again. We can do better. Like, go out? I want to try Madison Park Tavern. It sounds . . . great? Whatever, even if it was some disgusting roadside shack, I'd still want to go with you." He looked around for a second and I tried to follow his line of sight. I was in my work clothes, but then realized I'd brought my Goyard. My paranoia rushed out again. Would he notice? Now that he was in New York, did he realize how much those cost?

Instead, Elliott looked at his corkboard of pictures.

He took a pushpin out of a snapshot of me posing with a Helen Lansky cookbook.

"I love this picture of you. I guess I never told you that I'm sorry you didn't get the Helen Lansky internship. That must've sucked for you."

My heart plummeted a mile. Part of me wanted him to deny everything I had just said about our distance. I wanted him to say that I was wrong, that it was all in my head.

He continued, "And I'm sorry I was passive-aggressive at Bakushan."

"Mm-hmm," I said, biting my lip and closing my eyes. His apologies should have stitched us together, but instead they did the opposite. Each word snipped us farther apart.

People say you should never keep secrets from your partner, but that's all I'd been doing since we got to New York. I could have disobeyed Michael Saltz and told Elliott the truth about the reviews and all of it. And then we'd be Tia and Elliott again. But I didn't. I didn't think he'd understand why I was putting myself through Michael Saltz's intimidation and abuse. He wouldn't understand the failure I'd feel if I didn't go after this with every ounce of my being.

In the end, I didn't want to be on the same page again. That was the truth of it.

I took the photo out of his hands and laid it on his end table. "Elliott," I started. "I'm sorry. I never thought New York would be like this, either. I know you didn't mean to hurt me. And I didn't mean to hurt you, but—" I took one last look at that Helen Lansky picture and gulped. That was ages ago, whole identities ago. With my eyes down, I said, "I know I've been a jerk lately. But I just don't think—" I stopped again and bit my lip.

I hadn't planned on doing this, but this is where life's momentum had taken us. We couldn't make each other happy anymore.

I looked back up at him. "I think we should take a break."

Elliott's shoulders dropped a millimeter but his eyes stayed focused on mine.

"Is that what you want?" he asked. To my surprise, his voice was steady. As steady as I was forcing mine to be.

I steeled myself again. This was so hard, excruciatingly hard, but I had to do it so we could get on with our lives.

"Yes," I said. "Not a breakup . . . a break."

I saw his tears collect, yet he didn't let one drop. He straightened up and walked over to me. He held me for a long time. We stood there, quietly rocking.

"Okay," he said. We didn't fight for each other. He deserved better. And so did I.

I GOT HOME a little after midnight, and found Emerald's program from the symposium on our coffee table. She had circled Elliott's presentation.

I quickly escaped to my bedroom, catching my breath.

I remembered my best times with Elliott: puzzling over econ problem sets while playing footsie. Him tagging along gamely as we visited farmers' markets across town. Trekking to our favorite deli way off campus and picnicking in the park. Sitting in his dorm room drinking cheap wine and nibbling on whatever my latest project was—caramel corn, flaxseed crackers, coconut macaroons with some exotic spice.

I opened my wallet and took out a small piece of paper, now faded and creased to oblivion: *59 Reasons Elliott Loves Tia.*

But we were in New York City now, which burned with an activity and excitement that eclipsed those memories, all fifty-nine of them.

I put that out of my mind and wrote Le Brittane's review in one sitting. We hadn't even finished the meal, but what I didn't know, I made up. I had gotten the hang of the rhythm, and the words banged out of me easily, even the wholesale fabrications.

TWO STARS

I knew what a downgrade from four to two stars would mean. I knew that the soul of the restaurant would change, that morale would plummet, and that I was bringing an end to a New York institution.

But in my room, I didn't see those things. It felt small pressing the Send button, not like I was throwing a grenade into the New York dining world. It just felt like this was the only way I could untangle my emotions after a very long, very hard day.

By sunrise, my review and everything that had pained me that night were in Michael Saltz's hands.

Chapter 20

"Are you sure?" Michael Saltz asked the next morning on the phone. "Two stars, huh? That's a big thing. People will talk."

I sat in the living room in my pajamas, my eyes crusted with fatigue. Emerald and Melinda were still sleeping.

"I didn't enjoy it that much."

"Are you talking about the experience, or the actual meal?"

"The meal, of course."

"Do you want to try it again?" he offered. "No shellfish this time, and we'll make sure the scheduling is less problematic."

"No," I said. "I'm set in my decision. I think it can run as is."

"Well . . ." he said. Then a couple of seconds later, "Okay. We didn't finish the meal, but that might be okay. *Scandal*. The news will be everywhere."

"Right." I gulped. "It's your call, obviously. It's your byline."

Though I wished it was mine.

I imagined Michael Saltz in his big apartment overlooking Central Park. I tried to guess what he was sniffing. Perhaps a roasted seed from Bhutan, or a fermented bean paste from China, or a fatty pâté from southern France. Whatever he was doing, he had it so easy. It was *my* life that was fragmenting into little pieces. Helen and my words in the *New York Times* were the only things keeping me going until spring.

"Two stars, that would make a splash," he said. "It's an interesting thought. What did your boyfriend say when you got to his presentation late?"

It sounded like a riddle, another trap. I waited until the wave of emotions had retreated. "It was fine," I lied.

Another pause. "We have a good thing going here. Don't forget that. Sometimes you have to struggle to gain clarity."

Struggle! That was the key word for my life these days. His concerned, earnest tone caught me off guard, but he was the one who knew the most about my life—my double life, that was. And in that way, he was more than a boss or mentor—he was my best friend. As much as I disliked him for his sneakiness, the sense that I was never quite getting the full story, I couldn't hate him.

"Why did you agree to the lunch if you knew you had another commitment?"

I looked around the room, squinting, looking for some knowledge that I never had.

"I thought I could do both," I said, and nearly gagged, because at the time, that had been true. But now I realized I had been lying to myself, as brazen a lie as telling Michael Saltz I was "fine."

"Watch out for that," he said, with what I thought was empathy.

"How do you keep everything balanced?" I heard popping in the background.

"Sorry, making popcorn," he said. "To start, I have a lot of secrets. I can't taste. I'm hiding you. And I'm the supposedly anonymous *New York Times* restaurant critic. After a certain point, these secrets don't register anymore. They just become second nature."

"Second nature," I repeated. I imagined a life of this being the status quo. Getting to things late, changing in the bathroom, lying to people I cared about.

It wasn't what I wanted long term. Absolutely not. But I had gotten this far, and I couldn't give up yet. Spring would be here in no time, and then I'd be able to file this semester away as simply paying my dues. Getting to the NBT would make up for everything.

"Hey, I've been meaning to ask, when is your surgery scheduled?" I asked.

"Oh, yes, *that,*" he said, like it was the last thing he wanted to talk about.

"Is everything going okay?"

"Well . . ." He sighed. "It's been a battery of tests. Grueling, actually. Brain surgery is never a bet easily taken, and psychosurgery, that's another story."

"Are you excited? Scared?"

"Um, well. Not scared. It's, um . . ." Michael Saltz was usually so articulate, I took his stammering to mean that he felt real terror. "The other patients in the trial have had success, so that's quite promising. I just need to hear back from New York–Presbyterian on timing, and they're waiting on the FDA for approval, and my test results and the like. It is a bit . . . harrowing, in a way."

I had never heard him speak so frankly. On the other end of the line, I imagined his posture changing, the slouching of a bewildered patient in front of his doctor.

"But what are you saying? Do you think you might not get the surgery?" I had visions of having the column to myself, with my name as the byline. Maybe Michael Saltz would pass it on to me. It'd make history.

"No, no, it will happen," he said. And then, as if reading my mind, "Don't dance on my grave yet, Tia Monroe."

THE LE BRITTANE review was the top emailed story on the *New York Times* website. The comments section exploded. Hordes of people tweeted about it, reposted it. And then, just a few hours later, there were articles about the article, and then comments about the articles about the articles.

The review took on a life of its own. There were arguments about the role of white tablecloth restaurants, about Michael Saltz's refreshed writing style, even about responsible fish farming. I had given birth to something big and I felt like a conductor before her orchestra. Read! Reflect! Rebel! It's shocking how easily you can shake people up, even if you can never control what they say.

Mostly the conversation centered around the downfall of another restaurant. Like Madison Park Tavern, Le Brittane was an institution, and New York with two fewer four-star restaurants was like a basketball team without two of its star players, a city stripped of its iconic landmarks. Only three four-star restaurants remained. I had changed the character of New York, not once, but twice.

I went through all the avenues of the Internet, chasing down articles and blog entries and tweets. The Le Brittane Wikipedia page added the watershed *New York Times* two-star review. Then a new section emerged: Controversy.

The reactions to the review exhilarated me. I was alone in my room and yet I felt like I had company. Out there, these people were talking to me. They listened to me. It was the most gratifying conversation I'd had in weeks, though they never knew my name.

Chapter 21

OVER THE NEXT THREE WEEKS, MICHAEL SALTZ AND I WENT to three different restaurants. Harpsichord, a restaurant inspired by the Appalachian trail and where the waiters carried walking sticks. (The food was surprisingly refined, yet hearty. Perfect for late autumn weather. Two stars.) Crangteen, a greenhouse-inspired restaurant where guests could request herbs plucked off the walls. (Fresh and delightful. Three stars.) On Halloween we went to XB5, a modernist restaurant promising a new style of molecular gastronomy featuring neurological taste triggers administered by various stimuli and actual dishes. Michael Saltz was excited about this one, but it felt more like a Disney-fied hospital cafeteria, which horrified us both. The *Times* rarely gave zero stars—if it's not worth at least one star, it's not worth a review—but Michael Saltz was so appalled by the execution that he wrote most of the column and used it to make sure XB5 would be closed within a month.

Michael Saltz had told me that critics typically visited restaurants at least three or four times, but we only went once before we dealt our rulings. Michael Saltz didn't see the need for multiple visits. He was strict as always and made me keep my phone on the table. He insulted my outfits. Threatened me and my career.

But he kept on using my words and inviting me to meals. And I kept going with him so I could get to Helen.

I had kept my life stable, but only by doing three things: school, restaurant, and dining with Michael Saltz. Plus some clothing requests to Giada, who basically just shipped my wish lists.

After the scare at Le Brittane, I had learned how paranoia could overtake me. So I kept my world small and contained. I was friendly and agreeable in class, but never went out of my way to hang out or show an interest in anyone. I avoided Emerald altogether. We saw each other for less than ten minutes a day—if at all—and we mostly never said a word to each other.

Finally, one day in early November, Michael Saltz asked me about the one restaurant I had been dreading.

"Bakushan?" I repeated on the phone.

"Yes, Bakushan. The kitchen should be up and running smoothly . . . Or so we'll find out."

I was getting out of class and swerved into a more private hallway. "I guess," I whispered, "but it's still so new. I don't think it should be reviewed now. Pascal—or, Chef Fox—probably needs more time."

"I give them three months, that's my rule and we will follow it. We saw Pascal Fox taking a night off at Tellicherry a month ago, so obviously he's at a point where he can relax. Besides, I've heard some rumblings that the service is snobby and the cooking is sloppy. It looks good on paper, but taste is a different story. We need to get in there and organize the masses."

"Organize the masses?"

"Yes, add direction and clarity to the conversation."

I knew what he meant, in theory, but I had no direction or

clarity to give when it came to Bakushan. In my mind, it existed away from my world with Michael Saltz, as a place where I wasn't a critic but a girl. Every week or so, Pascal would text me new dishes that reminded him of me. One day, it was a freeze-dried lemon square. Another time, it was an ostrich omelet for six. He made me laugh and I felt close to him. I never answered any of his texts, but he kept sending them for some reason. But I drew the line at seeing him again, alone.

Every time Pascal texted me, I texted Elliott. Most times he never responded, or replied with a curt "ha" or "k." But I kept checking in anyway. Call it love. Call it guilt. All I knew was that I wasn't ready to let him go.

"I disagree," I said. "Bakushan's not ready." But maybe it was. I just didn't want to do this, the whole "disguise and judge" thing. I wanted to have his texts, his attention in pocket form that I could control and hide. I wanted to see him so badly, but I couldn't. So I just stalked him on the Internet and read every single thing ever written about Pascal Fox.

"If you want it done, I think it's better if you go without me," I said.

"Don't be absurd. You need to go with me," Michael Saltz snapped. "Eight P.M. Next Tuesday. Don't be late."

"Wait!" I said. If I couldn't avoid this dinner, then I'd have to remove myself in another way. I had four days. "Should I get a new look for Bakushan?" I was going to explain why—that Pascal might recognize me from Tellicherry, that I thought it would help me separate my food critic "character" from my grad student reality—but Michael Saltz didn't need to hear any of it.

"Oh! That's a brilliant idea. Highlights and a fresh cut. I'll refer you to my stylist now."

It was one thing for me to think I needed a makeover, and quite another for someone else to agree so immediately. But Michael Saltz was never one to spare my feelings. At least he and I were in agreement. It was time for a true transformation.

I took a walk to Mercer Street later that day and entered a gigantic salon that soared up and sank low from the entrance. A tall, handsome man greeted me as I walked in.

"Tia, right? Let's get freaky." He ushered me to the back, where the daytime clientele of trophy wives were getting their blowouts and manicures.

He treated me no differently, even though we both knew I was there on someone else's dime. I suppose, to him, it was a regular thing, five-hundred-dollar cut-and-colors given as gifts. He played with my hair, lifted a strand then let it fall, rubbed his fingers at my scalp to measure the density. He circled around me like a sculptor in front of marble, or in the case of my unruly hair, maybe a matador in front of a bull.

"Tell me what you want, sweetheart."

I realized then that he, too, was gorgeous—tall, dark, chiseled jaw, hair tied into a surprisingly alluring man-bun. Yet another specimen in a disorienting stream of hunky men. Was it New York? Or was it me, attracting them with some force? Two months ago, that would have been ludicrous. And yet since arriving in the city, ludicrous had become the norm: strikingly handsome men, four-star meals, an unlimited expense account at one of the world's most glamorous stores.

"Well," I started soft, like I was apologizing.

When Pascal had first met me, I was just a scared girl. But now, with some reviews under my belt, I had grown. Theoretically, this makeover was so I'd disappear in front of him. That's what I had told Michael Saltz.

But, really, I wanted him to notice me. I wanted him to see how far I'd come in terms of clothing and looks and restaurant cred.

My volume grew. "I don't want to be a kid anymore. I want to command attention and be beautiful and sexy and powerful." My hair had fallen in my face as I got worked up.

The stylist pushed my hair aside and looked at me in the mirror. "Honey, you're already all those things. I can just give you a nice hairdo."

In the end, he transformed my black hair to a dark brown with subtle auburn highlights. My erratic straight hair plus frizzy waves inflated into a voluminous va-va-voom thing. I never in my life had imagined myself with dyed hair. What was the point when you were born with perfectly good coloring?

But those weren't the same eyes looking back at me in the reflection. In the last few months, I'd had a couple of moments like this: getting dressed by Emerald before Bakushan and by Giada at Bergdorf. The moment I had decided it was okay to return to Bakushan with Pascal and give him my number. And now this.

I was ready to see Pascal again, ready to step out as a new person. I had already changed on the inside, and now the outside had caught up.

ON THE WAY back home, I felt people's eyes on me. My hair made me look bolder, sassier. I was dressed head-to-toe-to-underwear in designer. My stilettos navigated cobblestones and ragged asphalt. I didn't particularly care when the tip of my heel got stuck in a grate—I could always get a new pair or ten.

I detoured to the SoHo Prada store and admired a fur coat.

Not one, but two attendants rushed to me. They were practically groveling: their spines curved, their hands pressed in pleas.

"Good afternoon, miss," one said.

"Would you like me to take your coat?" the other said.

Just two months ago I would have laughed nervously and

said no. I was a normal girl! But this time, I let them take it away while I browsed the store. I couldn't buy anything—I only had the expense account at Bergdorf—but they didn't know that, and I didn't give anything away.

THAT EVENING I was slated to work at Madison Park Tavern. I had long abandoned my trusty Jil Sander and now had a rotation of luxe but unflashy suits. Today I wore an Armani with a moonstone brooch in the shape of a star.

"Hottie alert!" Chad whistled when I got to the restaurant. He circled around me, stroking his chin.

Angel yelled at him from across the dining room, "Let the girl go!"

Chad grinned goofily and punched me in the shoulder. "You know I'm fucking with you, right? You look good. Different."

Angel came over and looked me up and down. I had worn this suit to work before—had even worn other, nicer suits—and they never said anything. My hair was also pulled back and gelled, so they wouldn't have been able to see my new hairdo, either.

"You do look good. Not like a schlumpy grad student anymore."

I had to chuckle to myself. I was glad they had finally noticed something was different. I wanted to be better in all parts of my life, not just with Pascal and Michael Saltz.

Carey spotted us and gave me a hug. "Here, try this." We walked away from the rest of the team and she handed me a cube that looked like a marshmallow covered in sawdust.

"What is it?"

"It's Chef Darling's 'Fuck You, Michael Saltz' dish."

"That's what's written on the menu?" I gagged.

"Ha! You're too funny. It's in the subtext." Carey smiled. "He's been perfecting an alternate menu since the review, and is now rolling out his new creations. People have been going crazy over this one."

I popped it into my mouth. The outside was soft like a marshmallow, but it got progressively harder toward the core. It had the vision of Chef Darling's best dishes—of vegetables and sun and tilling the fields. But I couldn't quite place the flavor. It was part artichoke, part bitter green, part creamy something or other.

"What is this?" I asked.

Carey raised her eyebrows. "Have you been reading the Wiki?"

"Yes!" I laughed. How many nights had I spent on that site, clicking on links to ingredients, to other restaurants, to NYC lore? It was the best resource out there.

"Well, this is a throwback to Chef Darling's work at Vrai," Carey offered.

"Okay, okay, don't tell me," I said. I rolled the wood-chip-like elements in my mouth. They had the taste of hazelnuts, but the ephemerality of chocolate flakes.

"Hazelnut. Artichoke. And mustard green?"

"Fava bean, actually." Carey beamed.

"Nice! I remember reading about this now."

Carey went straight and solemn, a sudden shift in tone that unnerved me. I stopped smiling. "You should," she said. "Maybe that review was a good thing. Matthew is cooking the best food of his life now. It should be recognized."

"I'm sure he will be," I said. "This is really good."

Carey shook her head, like I wasn't understanding.

"This is *incredible,* Tia. I know you know that." She handed me a piece of paper with a URL and password written on it. "That's admin access to the Wiki. I know you have your eyes and ears open just as much as I do. So, I'm putting you on data duty. You can now post on the site." She gave a long, meaningful pause, and all I could do was gulp and hope she'd change the subject.

"But anyway," Carey said finally, her tone ramping up to her usual level of intellect and intensity. "We missed you at the tasting!"

"There was a tasting?" I asked. "I guess I'm not included anymore." After Gary Oscars had put me on probation, I had been invited to fewer events. Some days I'd get to coat check, do my thing, and leave without speaking to anyone on staff. I'd also called in sick a couple of nights when I had to eat out with Michael Saltz or I was in a rush to get him my notes.

"Oh," Carey said. "Sorry . . . I mean . . ." Chad and Angel walked up to us and she looked at them as if to say, *Can one of you guys help me here?*

"No, it's okay," I said, but inside I felt that familiar pinch, of missing out on something good. "I was wondering when I'd stop being invited to everything altogether."

"Gary Oscars is a bastard who'd hold a grudge against his asshole," Chad said.

Angel would never say anything so crass in the restaurant, but I could tell he agreed. "Don't sweat it, Tia. One day, you'll get what you deserve."

He was trying to be nice but a chill came over me. I'd get what I deserved? I wasn't sure what that would be.

Chapter 22

THE NEXT NIGHT, MELINDA AND I WENT FOR DRINKS AT A rooftop bar warmed by heaters every couple of feet. The evening felt fresh and unadulterated, like breathing the sky itself rather than the thick, angsty air below. Melinda and I didn't even need to talk. The drinks were enough. Solitude under the stars was enough.

Melinda and I walked back to the apartment and saw Emerald reading a magazine in the living room.

"Hey, guys," she said. "Do you know where Elliott is tonight? I'm supposed to go to the Botanical Gardens tomorrow, but the Bedford Park Boulevard station is closed."

Blood rushed to my face and my breath got jerky. I tried to remind myself that we had been on a break for a month. I was no longer entitled to feel possessive, and this relationship between Emerald and Elliott was all in my head. But then again . . . why was she going to Elliott's work? And why was she asking me how to get there—to mess with my head?

Luckily, Melinda jumped in while I worked on calming down.

"Jesus, Em. You have a phone. Why don't you call him yourself?" I wasn't sure if she was being bitchy to protect me, or if she just despised Emerald and was a little drunk. Either way, I liked that she'd said it.

"Ooookay," Emerald said, rolling her eyes. "I'm taking off anyway. See you guys later."

She picked up one of her men's coats and a fedora and left. Melinda and I went to my room and I collapsed on my bed while Melinda sat in my desk chair, swiveling. Emerald's question about Elliott had rattled me.

Maybe it was time to reassess. We were just on a break, not a breakup. Things had somewhat stabilized in my life. Though that was mainly because without Elliot, I didn't have to lie anymore. No one looked out for me or worried about me. My life alternated between freedom and loneliness. I had survived without him, but that didn't mean I didn't miss him.

I'd think of Elliott suddenly and randomly, like when I caught myself twirling my pen just like he did—three swings and a pause, three swings and a pause. Or when I passed volunteers at a community garden, jamming to a live guitarist and eating chicken skewers. He came to mind every time I looked at my NYU books, because he had been so supportive throughout the application process.

But despite all those fond memories, I still wasn't ready to talk about what was next for us. I didn't know if I could make our relationship work. And even if we could, was that what I wanted?

I groaned and covered my face with my hands.

"Hey, dude," Melinda said, handing me a glass of wine. "Let it go. Seriously. This is New York City. You're looking hotter than ever. I don't know what's happening with you, and you don't have to tell me. But take my advice: the best way to get over something—or someone—is to start over."

She barely knew Elliott and I'd barely spoken to her about him. But she was trying, in her vague way, and I had to appreciate her effort.

"The mind is like a body of water," she continued, holding up her wineglass. "It always wants to be at the same height. If a tide goes out"—she took a big gulp then immediately topped herself off—"you should let something else rush in. Your mind won't know the difference."

Maybe your mind wouldn't, but what about your heart? I didn't say anything, but then I got a text.

WHAT DO I HAVE TO DO TO GET YOUR ATTN? MEET ME AT RYE LOUNGE.

Melinda grabbed the phone out of my hands.

"Unknown number? Now that's not sketchy at all."

I had never texted Pascal back. But why not? Why was I keeping myself at low tide? Especially when there was a perfectly good wave waiting to come to shore.

"Oh, that's a guy named . . . Pascal? He's . . . a friend."

". . . A friend? Well, go to, lady! Get outta here and have fun, okay?" She stood up and started for her room. "Take your hot ass out on the town."

I looked back at Pascal's text. It'd be nice to go out. Finally answer his texts. See him again. Michael Saltz had put more trust in me over the last month, and he'd never suspect I'd correspond with Pascal.

It'd be nice to not be lonely.

Before I overthought it, I texted that I'd meet him there, put on skinny jeans and a Tibi chiffon top, and left the apartment.

On my way out, I bumped into Emerald, returning from wherever she'd gone.

"Whoa there, hot stuff! You're leaving now?" She caught me by the shoulders, like I was a mental patient on the run.

"Yes! I'm going out," I said, a little too proudly. I'd never left for a social thing after Emerald had returned. "To Rye Lounge."

"Rye Lounge? I've never heard of it."

Neither had I, but it felt good knowing something Emerald didn't. "Oh, it's new."

"Cool," she said. "Well, see you later."

I got excited with every step I took. I eyed other girls, as if to pick up cues from their social behavior—was I chill? Excitable? Should I unbutton my coat even though it was freezing out? I felt stupid for not knowing these basic things, but Elliott and I had started going out freshman year and been in our little New Haven bubble. I didn't know what it meant to "go out" in NYC, but now I wanted to find out . . . bar by bar, restaurant by restaurant.

I finally arrived and spotted Pascal hunched over his drink in a booth. The bar was dark and straightforward. Nothing gimmicky or shiny. No light shows or designer outfits on the bartenders. It seemed to be filled with low-key locals and restaurant people getting off work. I didn't have to worry about bumping into Michael Saltz here, that was for sure. Still, I felt overdressed in this place, a compact bar that didn't feel particularly special—just basic booze and some pictures of old New York.

He didn't see me at first, so I just watched him slumped over in the shadows.

I guess people always look at models and celebrity chefs and famous people and think of those cover stories—movies and restaurant openings and looking glamorous. But now his handsomeness took a backseat to what looked a lot like loneliness. That made me like him more.

It wasn't until I lightly tapped Pascal on the shoulder that he noticed me. "Oh!" he said as he jumped up and hugged me, his energy suddenly at the surface. I felt his heart beating through his leather jacket. Or maybe that was my heart.

"Tia! What a treat to see you tonight. You look beautiful! Sit, sit. Did you have a good day?" He nodded to the bartender, who started mixing me a drink. He had shed his funk and was now all smiles and mussed-up hair and tattoos that tantalized from his open cuffs.

I recomposed myself. I *loved* that he asked about me. I *loved* that he had a drink at the ready for me and that we were here, sitting next to each other with the purpose of . . . what? *To chat, to chat,* I drilled into myself. I didn't let myself think in terms beyond that. I kept those definitions—a date? a precursor to something more?—fuzzy and at the periphery, but close enough that I could take joy in them.

"Well, grad school is sort of a drag," I said as a waitress delivered my drink. "It probably seems like a waste of time to someone like you. It feels that way to me sometimes."

"Wait, wait. Why are you putting yourself down like that? NYU's a great school. I've heard it's the best Food Studies program in the country."

When did I tell him I went to NYU?

The thought occurred to me in a flash, and then it disappeared, making way for Pascal's attention.

He had put his drink down and was looking at me with concern. Why *was* I putting myself down? Pascal made me want to be a better version of me—more confident, more sure. But also prettier, better dressed, more in-the-know about the world in which he was a player. I liked who I became in his eyes.

"Yeah." I sighed. "I'm lucky, I guess. I have a cool internship now. That's rare for a first-year."

He nudged toward me and his face opened up in a way you rarely see from handsome faces. You expect those faces to look perfect, an encapsulation of a single pure moment for the outside viewer to appreciate from afar. But his expression intertwined with mine, reflecting my emotions, amplifying them, eliciting them. I nudged toward him, too.

"You like food a lot, don't you? Is that what you want to do with your life?"

"I want to *write* about food," I said matter-of-factly. And then, less so, "I want people . . . to listen to me." The moment I said it, I felt embarrassed. It seemed so crass. Of course everyone wanted to be heard.

But his eyebrows softened. He rested an elbow on the table and looked at me with undivided attention.

Why was I even telling him all this? I didn't tell anyone this stuff—not Elliott, my friends, my family—no one.

Pascal let a smile creep over his face.

"What, do you think that's funny?" I started sweating right through my chiffon top.

"No, no, I don't. I like your passion. It makes me happy to meet people who know what they want and are going for it. Especially when those people are beautiful, like you."

I retreated into the shadow of the banquette. Man, he made me feel so good.

"It can be scary to pursue your dream, but I think the key is to surround yourself with people who support you," he said. "My parents love to cook. My mom is Filipino and my dad is French—both food cultures. They put me on this cooking track and I never looked back."

"Oh!" I said. So that's why he looked a little like me. "I'm also mixed," I said.

He smiled shyly. "I know," he said. And then I blushed, too.

"When I was in school, I never partied or went out with my friends," he said. "I preferred to stay home and cook. And I guess when I was younger, I thought that made me weird. But then I realized that was my purpose in this world, and I owed it to myself to see it through." Here his accent became not quite French, but something dreamy around the edges.

I picked up my drink, a brown whiskey-based thing that was much stronger than what I was used to, but somehow went down easily. I let Pascal's knee touch mine.

"Did you always want to be a chef?"

Pascal bit his nails. Bit his nails! He was so cute, so real. All those articles about him made him seem like some cocky man-about-town. But here he was modest and measured, talking in thoughtful tones. "I think so, yes. If not a chef, then maybe a food writer like you. Have you always wanted to be a writer?"

The power of someone listening startled me. I had gone through the semester without a single real, deep conversation. But why? What did I think was so bad down there?

For the first time in months, I let myself look into that darkness.

"Yeah, I've always wanted to be a writer. But more than that, I've always wanted to have a *thing*. Something that defined me."

Ugh, that sounded so lame. The second I spoke, I regretted the desperation of it. I wished I could have tossed out something hollow like Melinda, or something assertive and sure like Emerald. But Pascal put his hand on my leg, and I knew right then that what I'd said was okay and he understood.

". . . something that validated me," I finished.

He squeezed my knee. "You're not alone."

As steamy as our Bakushan episode had been, this time we hardly touched. We talked into the night. In the same way I'd spilled my heart to Michael Saltz in the restaurant basement, I gave myself to Pascal. I talked about my dreams, the raw stuff. I wasn't sure if this was okay during my break with Elliott, and

I was positive that this was unacceptable to Michael Saltz, but I pushed them out of my mind. It was easier to throw myself into this, this ecstasy of being heard, of being magnetic to someone you admire.

Of course I liked that he was famous and hot. But I hadn't realized until then how tense I had been all fall. With him, I let go.

I drank that drink and ordered another. And when the bartender made last call at 3:45, I ordered another. Pascal and I talked the whole night, and at the end of it, he walked me back to my apartment. We were tired, yet not as drunk as I would have thought. I wanted to touch him and felt like he wanted to touch me, too. The air in the late, late night was thin and hallucinatory, like we were at a high altitude.

Outside my apartment, Pascal sighed and took me by the waist. He was much taller than I and swung me from side to side. He tipped his lips down as I tipped my lips up. And then, without a care in the world, we kissed.

His lips were surprisingly soft. I had only kissed Elliott for the past four years, and every kiss before that had been embarrassingly bad. Pascal's lips were so *different,* full yet muscular. He held me by the back of my head, then slid his hands down to my neck, kneading as he went, so by the time his hands were at the small of my back, my insides had melted.

Elliott had a shallow way of kissing, lips that moved like an ant on a leaf. Pascal was all push and pull, suck and lick. Every bit of pressure corresponded with another withdrawal, leaving me panting and yearning. With each second, I felt more and more out of my body, out of my mind. I felt, blissfully, like a totally different person.

And that's when I heard him.

"Tia!" yelled a voice from down the street, a silhouette with a slightly off-balance movement.

It was so late, I didn't think it could be him. But I had been made. And not by Melinda or Emerald or Michael Saltz, but by someone I actually cared about.

He was probably returning from one of his night shifts at the lab. He held a basket of flowers. Crocuses and saffron, I thought, but that could have been some hallucinatory guilt. I thought if I stayed still he wouldn't know it was me. But just like I knew his walk, he knew the lines of my movement. I couldn't even look back to see what Pascal was doing. I just stayed still, waiting for him to walk away, to think we were just some strangers in the night.

Elliott. He looked for a second longer, and of course I knew more about him than just his walk. I also knew this face he was making now, a frown and a gulp and a punch in the stomach. And then he turned away.

What had I done?

"Elliott!" I called back, but my voice cracked and fell midair. I left Pascal and ran to him, my stomach balling up and my breath quivering in the cold.

He snapped back, his blue eyes sparkling with tears. "So you wanted to go on a break, huh? To do this?" He'd started at a whisper but ramped up to a yell. I hadn't seen him in a month. Had barely talked to him. It crushed me that his face and his body and his voice felt vaguely foreign to me. We had lost something real.

"Elliott, I . . ."

"What is a break to you anyway? You know, *I* thought it was so we could get our heads on straight. Do some thinking on our own. But if I had known that you wanted to use this opportunity to—"

"Elliott. I . . . it's just . . ."

"Who is . . ." He pointed to Pascal on the other side of the street, who had his hands in his pockets and was looking down at the sidewalk.

"He's just . . . a chef."

"A chef . . ." Elliott said. And then something clicked for him. "Oh, right. Right! Why didn't I fucking see this before? That's the Bakushan dude who makes the fucking amazing snail bonbons and sauerkraut ice cream."

I closed my eyes and stayed stone-still, scrambling for the right words to say.

"It all makes fucking sense now. All fall you've had this weirdness about you that I couldn't put my finger on. It was Helen, or me, or school, or Emerald, I don't know! But apparently this guy makes you happy."

I couldn't respond because the answer was yes.

He stopped and regained his composure, standing to his full height, six or so inches above me, as if to intimidate me, to show me his worth.

"I get it now. This is who you are."

The lone shadow across the street turned away. Pascal had made his exit.

Now it was up to me to say something. But what could I say?

That night, I had kissed another man and let him into my heart. I was hiding my life from Elliott and could see no end to that.

"I give up," Elliott said. "Forget this break. You're a terrible person and I'm done with you."

As I WALKED upstairs, I thought about Elliott's tears falling in a sudden downpour.

How Pascal stared at me in the dark bar.

How Elliott had been with me through thick and thin.

How Pascal rested his hand on my knee.

The look on Elliott's face when he saw me kissing someone else. Every time I thought about it, my heart twisted. Just a couple of months ago, I'd been in love with Elliott. New York was going to be our place, where we'd become our true selves.

But that was an old plan. That was an old Tia.

As much as I hated hurting Elliott, I also felt relieved. It was good that he'd let me go. A break was too weak. Because, really, I had let go of him the moment Michael Saltz laid eyes on me.

When I got back to my room, I saw that Pascal had texted me.

:(IS THERE ANYTHING I CAN DO TO HELP?

Yeah. I texted back:

Can you come over?

I didn't want to stumble into my life anymore. I wanted to take charge and control my destiny. In thirty minutes, Pascal was at my door with a bag of beignets he had freshly fried. We ate them in my bed, getting powdered sugar on our clothes, and then on our underwear, and then on our naked bodies.

"Who was that out there?" he said, his tongue edging up from my collarbone, to my neck, to the curve of my ear. His hands were on my butt, and my hands were on his. We were pressing into each other as much as we could, as much as was possible until we were finally one.

"No one," I said, as he began pushing into me.

No one, I repeated to myself. *No one. No one.*

Inside, a mountain of tension squeezed tighter and tighter before crunching into a tiny crystalline diamond. That diamond shattered into a billion pieces of wonder and I came harder than I'd ever come before. I was broken, but I was also new.

I silently cried myself to sleep with Pascal beside me. But when I woke up, I felt much better. Kissing Pascal had made me feel like another person. And after having sex with him, I knew that the change was finally complete.

Chapter 23

MICHAEL SALTZ GOT US A GUARANTEED TABLE AT BAKUSHAN, even though they didn't take reservations. Instead, he got a "holder" who waited in line for him, then passed the table on to us when we arrived.

"Thanks for waiting, Hank."

"No problem," Hank said in a giddy way, like it was an immense honor to wait in a long line so someone else could eat dinner in his name. "Have a good night . . . *Hank*." He winked and Michael Saltz and I smiled back awkwardly.

The wait wasn't terrible, though. After the initial excitement, people had said that Bakushan wasn't worth the hype, and as Michael Saltz had said, the staff was snobby, and the food uneven. But to me, that was in one ear, out the other.

As I put my phone on the table, I saw Pascal in the kitchen and felt an intense sense of longing for him. What was he thinking? When would we see each other again? I wanted Pascal to whisk me away to fabulous restaurants, show me secret underground bars that only industry people knew. I didn't want to disappear anymore. It seemed crazy that just three nights before, we were revealing the deepest parts of our souls, and now I was at his restaurant wearing my most ridiculous disguise yet: a staid pant suit to match Michael Saltz's even more conservative suit. We would have passed at an investment bank, but here in the East Village, at Bakushan, we looked pitifully uncool.

The menu had changed radically since I had eaten there with Elliott and Emerald. If the dish wasn't entirely new, it was an old dish with new ingredients. I was disappointed that the fluke and lovage dish wasn't on the menu, but maybe he was saving it for a special one night.

"This is how you order at a place like this," Michael Saltz said, in a professorial mood. "You get all the must-haves. The obvious picks that bring people in. Everyone who reads about Bakushan wants to know about certain dishes. Then you get the most expensive and the cheapest, because that gives you range. You get the token vegetarian dish, the trendiest dish, the most loved, and the most hated. And then you get something like this." He angled his menu toward me and pointed to the page.

"Beef Wellington?" I read out loud. All the other items on the menu had much longer descriptions, but this one was conspicuously spare.

"Right, something is up with this one. And this one here," he said, pointing to another line.

"Celery soda lemon pie with pine nuts and guanciale," I read. Guanciale, bacon made from the pig's jowl. I had read it was the "new bacon," but had never tried it.

"The flavor sounds foul, right?" Michael Saltz said, then looked over at Pascal Fox, as if to size him up.

I wanted to say, *But I bet it's amazing!* or *That's the most creative dish I've ever seen on a menu!*, because I believed that and I wanted to shield Pascal. I had the power to protect him.

"But that's why you get it," Michael Saltz concluded. "You get the one where the chef is reaching for the stars."

"Pascal is good at that," I said, sitting up tall. My voice came out in a steady, authoritative stream. No more of that quiver, and I felt proud that words bent more easily to my will these days.

"Pascal? You get a new hairdo and now you're all chummy with the chefs? I forgot you had that little flirtation with him at Tellicherry." Michael Saltz shuddered. "Yes, well, *Pascal* wasn't known for his adventurousness at his previous posts. This is brand new for him. There's a lot at stake here."

I crinkled my nose, playing along with him. "I know, we dodged a bullet there. But it's just . . . I get a four-star vibe here. I can tell the difference now. You were right about Tellicherry being three stars."

Michael Saltz's smile was instant and blinding. "Oh! Good, good. You're learning. I've never trusted the hoi polloi. Maybe this place is . . ." He looked around and I laid it on thicker. Michael Saltz ran on ego like cars ran on gas, but because his job required him to be a ghost, he only had me to show off to. I was about to use that to my advantage.

"What were Pascal's other restaurants like? I've read about them, but I never got around to going. You have the most impressive dining history." I made it sound like I hadn't gone because the restaurants had just been a little bit out of the way, not the real reason, which was that not too long ago I was a girl from Yonkers with parents who thought restaurants were the world's biggest scam. I did it to protect my own ego, sure, but also to make Michael Saltz feel that he was talking to a fawning acolyte.

"Oh, Tia. They were *classic*—to the book," he said, playing right into my charms. "Beautiful food, my goodness. But the creative latitude was about this wide." He held his hands about two inches apart. "And the menu here is like this." He opened his hands to the width of the table and shrugged his shoulders as if to say, *So what's he got?*

I watched Pascal from our table. He never hesitated over a dish or doubled back over something he forgot. I could see his mouth moving, and then understood why the music was so loud—so the patrons wouldn't hear his constant yelling. By then I had a sense of his musculature and the complex ways he moved through space. His motions were slick and fast, like a seal in the water. For a second he stared at something outside of my sight and I wondered if he was daydreaming of me in that moment. I wished I could have walked right up to the pass and kissed him, but all I could do was stay in my chair, in a pant suit that made me feel ten years older, and make his day in another way.

The food arrived. The snail and pork dumpling had new, thinner dough. I placed it in my mouth but instead of melting away, the skin suctioned to my mouth like a piece of plastic. I gulped it down and noticed a gravelly feeling across the roof of my mouth. Sand.

Then, a pea shoot and foie gras wheel with a small butter knife. Michael Saltz and I stared at it, confounded by how it worked. It stood on its side like an ancient monument, with various crinkly and crackly things at its base.

"Just cut it," the waiter said kindly. He looked like Pascal Lite, not as exotic or statuesque, but with a bit of Pascal's twinkle and good-boy-with-a-lot-of-tattoos edge.

I slid the knife down. At first nothing happened. The foie gras clung to itself, until it peeled apart sleepily and a green, milky liquid bled out.

"Wow," I said.

"Wow," Michael Saltz said.

I took a soft forkful of foie gras and dragged it through the pea shoot sauce and the brown crumbles and white flakes. I rubbed the foie gras against the roof of my mouth, and it stuck there with a sticky stubbornness, then melted away. The taste coursed through my body, a slippery, moody, gutsy smoothness that slithered and pushed and screamed down my throat.

Oh, Pascal, I thought. If I couldn't be with him, this came close. I flashed back to three nights ago and the pleasure cascaded through me once more.

And then came the celery soda lemon pie with pine nuts and guanciale. It didn't look like a pie, more like a pudding. The pine nuts gave it roundness and body, and the guanciale a lurid, sweaty moodiness. But the soda effervescence was rather unnerving.

"Well, how do you like it?" Michael Saltz asked, picking at its jiggle.

I tried to silence a pine nut–celery–lemon–pork burp. It was . . . interesting.

But it didn't matter. For the purposes of this dinner, I loved it. I loved more than "it"—I loved the whole orbit of genius that linked the food to the space to the man.

"Four stars, for sure," I said while imagining Pascal's joy and what would become of us.

"Four stars, oh, yes?" Michael Saltz said. "That's a bold statement, but I shouldn't be surprised, coming from you. You know, I've heard rumblings that Le Brittane is cleaning shop."

"Cleaning shop?" I gulped.

"Firing all the staff and starting fresh. They were blindsided." Michael Saltz cleared his throat and his face got stern. "We did a number on that restaurant. I sometimes wonder if they deserved it." He looked at me for a long time, but not in an accusing way, just pondering, reflective. Even though he didn't care much for me or typical journalistic integrity, he still had his own moral compass when it came to the reviews.

Shit. Le Brittane hadn't deserved it. They hadn't lost two stars because the food had fallen or the service failed. That day, with Elliott, I had fallen. I had failed. And now people were losing their jobs. I thought of our waiter, Hugo. He was probably the first to get fired. Did he have a wife? Kids? A mortgage? I realized with a wallop of regret that he probably had all three.

Writing the review had made me feel powerful, sure. But I never wanted to abuse it again. Back then, I had let the pains of my life affect the stars. But I wouldn't make that mistake again. People's lives were on the line, and starting with this review, my impact would be more positive.

"Bakushan deserves four stars," I said. "Absolutely." I sat up, ready to flatter Michael Saltz again if that's what it'd take to give Pascal what I wanted.

"Building something up requires more effort than taking it down," he said matter-of-factly. "In this city, ninety percent of all restaurants fail. Another restaurant failing might make news for a couple days, until the next week's review gets people up in a lather. But a restaurant reaching four stars, rising above ninety percent of the failures and ninety-eight percent of the mediocres, then that's something to seriously consider."

"Well, I think Bakushan is up there. You said Pascal never showed his creative range at his earlier restaurants, but look at how far he's come. He's pushing cuisine, and—"

Michael Saltz nodded. "Okay, okay, you don't have to convince me. I agree. Bakushan certainly has the bones of a four-star, but let's take this one day at a time. I haven't awarded four stars since . . . since, you know. The experience has to absolutely merit it and I have to be able to stand by the claim."

"I understand," I said. "But I stand by it. I've used everything I've learned from you and I really feel that this is it."

Michael Saltz lifted his fork, then thought better of it and put it down. After all, the food was cardboard to him anyway. "Well, we can keep that in mind. For a four-star, I'd like to come back again, to check for consistency. I wish I could experience it with you, just so I could know for myself." He brought his napkin up to his mouth and kept it there for a while, like he was going to cough. "I'm lucky that I've got you."

I liked the compliment but something about the way he said "got you" made me shiver.

"Thanks," I said, shaking that off. "I'm glad you've got me, too."

As we left, I popped a stick of gum to mask the lingering effects of that porky soda pie. Pascal never spotted us.

Chapter 24

EVEN THOUGH MICHAEL SALTZ WANTED TO VISIT BAKUSHAN for a second time, I started writing the review. *Four stars. Obviously genius. World-class.* I agonized over every word since I knew that this document, these sentences, would come to define the restaurant and set in motion a whole other chain of events. Expansion. Investments. Cookbook deals. When I wasn't in class or working at Madison Park Tavern, I was crafting the Bakushan review.

After class on Wednesday, I power-walked back to the apartment to get ready for work and found Emerald sitting on the couch in a black silk taffeta gown and dangly gold earrings. A big bouquet of lilies lay nearby and a guy I didn't know stood next to her.

"Um, hi?" I said to Emerald, even though she had her head buried in her knees. The guy wore a hoodie over a suit and looked nice, down-to-earth.

Emerald lifted her head and said, "Sorry Tia, I didn't think you'd be home this early." She put her hand on the small of the guy's back, in a place you don't touch friends of the opposite sex. "You should go now," she whispered, a voice that had none of Emerald's usual honeyed swagger.

The guy smiled at me, then left. And then I saw that Emerald's face was red and swollen, her makeup streaky.

"That's Charlie, my boyfriend," she said flatly.

"You have a boyfriend?"

"Yeah. We just made it official last week. He's great." Talking about him seemed to brighten her mood, but barely. She was oddly still, like she'd been sedated.

"Elliott introduced us," she said. "Charlie works at the Botanical Gardens."

"Oh!" I said, pretending that Elliott's name in her story didn't startle me. So that was why she'd wanted to go to the Botanical Gardens the other day.

"Do you want to know what I was doing today?" she asked in resignation.

The flowers, the dress. I had no idea what other surprises she had in store for me. "Sure. What were you doing today?"

She pursed her lips and leaned her head away, like a buoy tipping far from shore. "You know, I thought we'd be friends. I saw your Facebook profile and you seemed nice, like really *real*. And then you get here, and . . . I don't know what happened. We don't even know each other. I don't know why I even expected we would be buddy-buddy. It's perfectly fine that we aren't, as long as you pay the bills, I guess. But . . . it's hard living here with you and Melinda, like I'm not welcome in my own home." She shook her head. Happy, sexy, confident Emerald looked totally hopeless.

Of course she was right. We didn't know each other. But I just didn't know how to relate to her. She looked at me, through me, grasping at a connection we didn't have. Her grief filled the room, and I felt suffocated by her earnestness, not ready for what came next.

"I was at the cemetery today, Tia."

"The cemetery?" I repeated numbly.

"Yes. I go every week. But today was—"

"Wait, what?" I didn't feel equipped to be here with sad Emerald. I couldn't even handle happy Emerald.

She collapsed back on the couch, the black ball gown poofing upward like a cloud of dust. "Never mind."

"No . . . really," I said. I approached her as if she were an injured animal: concerned but cautious, ready to jump back at any moment.

She eyed me with suspicion and as her tears dried up, I saw the Emerald I knew come into being. Emerald's essence was in her posture. Her spine, sure. But also her alert lips, her demonstrative hands, her hair elevated just so. Even her boobs had poise.

"A memorial service," she said, and in her eyes I detected something similar to what I'd been doing a lot of lately—a computation of what can be disclosed, and to whom.

"Oh," I said. "For . . . who?"

Emerald scrunched up her face and just went for it. "My brother and father. They died four years ago."

Sherri's hint of a "hard life." The sighting at Bergdorf with her bewildered, weak mother. I realized with a shock that I had had a chance to step in and ask her about those things. I could have been there for her instead of gossiping behind her back. At the very least, I could have thanked her for the suit, the suit that had made me feel like I could actually belong at the type of restaurant I now visited every week.

"You didn't know that about me, did you?"

"Oh, Emerald," I said. I walked closer, but stopped myself as a matter of habit. All semester, I had avoided closeness—physical and emotional—with her. We had never spoken about our families, but we could have. It seemed so obvious and right, to be friends with your roommate. It would have made New York a whole lot easier and more fun.

She took a deep breath and blurted out the rest in one long go, like coming up for air after being underwater. "My parents were finalizing the divorce. Dad picked up Peter from Yale for our last Thanksgiving as a family." Her voice squeaked on the word *family*. She talked to the wall behind me as if she were reading off a teleprompter, so her voice seemed delivered to the space in the living room, not to me. "They were going down I-95 and a sixteen-wheeler swerved. The fucking driver fell asleep at the wheel. The road was icy and he threw them off, right into a ditch."

I gasped so hard it felt like a hiccup. Emerald sighed.

"Every day I miss them. I guess I'm okay for the most part. I guess I'm past it all. But sometimes I think funny stuff, like they're gonna come back. Like Peter's gonna write me an email out of the blue and tell me that he has a lacrosse game on Friday and maybe I can take the train to New Haven."

"Emerald," I started. "I don't know how . . ."

"You went to Yale, right?" she asked. Her voice had regained its typical lushness, but there was still a sorrowful lethargy about it.

"Yeah, I went to Yale," I said. I knew we had done the requisite research on each other, but it still surprised me that she remembered that. I'd thought I was a nobody to her, but now she seemed to be going out of her way to show me otherwise.

"I went to NYU for undergrad, you know," she said. "Two of my college friends lived with me until they moved to L.A. Is Regina Chang your dean?"

"Yeah . . ." I said. Did she really pay this much attention to me and I so little to her? I was sure I would have remembered that she'd gone to NYU, but somehow it had slipped my mind. I guess I was too focused on myself.

"I saw you at Bergdorf," Emerald said suddenly and I accidentally kicked a chair in surprise. She turned her head to me and for the first time during the conversation, we truly locked eyes. "I don't hide what happened with my dad and Peter, even if I never told you. But my mom . . . she fell apart after the accident and she's never been the same. I never talk about that—to anyone. It kills me to have her like this and it's too much for me to explain."

She looked at me softly, strangely. "You knew my real secret. So, congratulations. I've lived in New York my whole life and yet I can count the people who know about her on one hand. It's funny that you're part of that group." She brushed her hair back and smiled her Emerald smile.

Then she walked into her room and, without shutting the door, changed into a high-collared red-and-white-check wrap dress that hugged her amazing curves and showcased her face, beautiful even after all the crying.

I averted my eyes and waited for her to finish.

"Emerald?" I tried.

"Yeah?"

"I'm sorry about your dad and brother. And I know I saw you at Bergdorf, but it's just that—" I stopped myself. I wished I could have matched Emerald's bravery. "I was too distracted by work things to stop and say hello." That wasn't technically a lie, but it felt so cheap compared to what Emerald had just told me.

But Emerald didn't seem to notice. "Badass." She nodded. "From day one, you've always been a badass about this food thing."

I had to laugh at that. Emerald understood. That's all I'd ever wanted out of this situation: to be badass at something. "Thanks,

Emerald," I said. "The internship has been great. And . . . thank you for the suit. I wear it all the time at the restaurant."

Emerald laughed uproariously. "That old thing? I'm surprised you still bother with it. Don't think I haven't noticed all your new goodies. I see you at Bergdorf once and you come back with a never-ending wardrobe."

I tensed and looked away. "Oh, but that was a one-time visit. My new clothes are nothing . . . H&M and stuff."

Emerald chuckled, an *okay, if you say so . . .* But she didn't push it. She probably knew better than most that a person is entitled to her secrets.

She slid into another one of her men's coats, smoothing it gently. It dawned on me that those coats must have belonged to her father, and her frequent absences from the apartment must have been so she could visit her mom. She wiped off her streaked makeup and straightened her shoulders.

"Anyway, see you around." She should have been sad and lonely but instead she was popular and fun-loving. And probably for the hundredth time, I wished I could be more like Emerald, someone who wasn't afraid to live out in the open and offer her heart to people who might hurt it.

Chapter 25

The next night, Melinda texted me out of the blue and asked if I wanted to eat a late dinner with her. I wondered if she had seen Emerald, too. I had been meaning to talk to her about easing up on the Emerald-hate. Between that and torturing myself with thoughts of Pascal and my second visit to Bakushan, a night out would do me good.

I wore leather Band of Outsiders pants, a slinky Alexander Wang sweater, and a Marni wool bubble coat with trumpeted sleeves that peekabooed a bright yellow lining. I rarely wore my regular clothes anymore.

Melinda had already arrived and was wearing a knitted purple tube dress and a yellow turban. She, too, was always changing her style. She wore overalls and plaid, or sky-high heels and piles of gold bangles. When she wore something glamorous and oversize, I sometimes thought she was Emerald, even though Melinda had none of Emerald's curves.

Heedless had just opened in NoHo, and served a variety of raw fish and meats in a blinding white space with scatterings of barren branches. It felt like a boutique in a desert, amplifying the chicness of nothing.

I had once suggested to Michael Saltz that we come here, but he'd thrown a fit about how he was the one in control of the schedule, not me. Fine, but there was no reason I couldn't eat there without him . . . and use his "pocket money."

"Hey. Sorry for the late invite," Melinda said, throwing her purse from my seat onto the floor. "Some guy asked me out tonight, but the fucker bailed last minute."

I smiled in commiseration. Melinda was stood up with surprising regularity. "That sucks," I said, though I thought that if the guys weren't standing Melinda up, she would likely be the one standing *them* up.

We shared some small plates. Beef with raw quail egg tasted elegant and savage, perfect with some delicate pickled chives, slicked close like veins. Bluefish came slashed with a streak of hot oil that blistered the flesh in a caramel-colored scar. The herring was paired with a curried goat cheese curd with blueberry jam. The duck breast arrived sliced like sashimi, with a smear of fresh American horseradish.

"This food is like the opposite of Cleveland fare. So sexy," Melinda said as a busboy came to refill her water glass. "But the service is eh."

The busboy, our age or even younger, drew back at Melinda's comment.

"Come on," I said. "Go easy. They're new. Every reviewer gives a restaurant at least three months to get on their feet." *Restaurant Reviewing 101,* I thought. *Give the restaurant some time, and—oh, yeah—don't be a jerk.*

"Hm, interesting," Melinda said. "So, suddenly you're a babe . . . and a restaurant expert . . ."

"Well . . . I read it somewhere," I said, shrugging as if it were some factoid on a bottle cap, not knowledge I had earned the hard way, night after night.

Melinda dropped the subject. The conversation drifted to random things like how our apartment was too hot, how she'd applied for a barista job but didn't care for the group interview process, how she had a bunch of guys she wanted to set me up with. I didn't need to talk to Melinda about my secret life with Michael Saltz or Pascal, or even my real life of family and NYU, for that matter. Our friendship was there with no pushes or pulls or obligations, which was often nice, when it didn't feel empty.

As we left the restaurant, Melinda took out a cigarette and we hung out on a bench in front of a health food store. Some guys swept the sidewalk around us, ready to close up. I meant to talk to her about Emerald, that we should try to be nicer to her, maybe invite her out to drinks or make dinner at home or something.

But something gave me pause. I was running low in the friend department and I was afraid of what would happen if I said anything. Melinda had no problem talking shit about Emerald, and I was sure she'd have no problem talking shit about me. I didn't quite care for her friendship, but she was one of the few friends I had, and I didn't want to lose her.

So we just sat on the bench while Melinda smoked. I kept looking at the burning red end of her cigarette, thinking about how to tell her, if at all.

The smoke swirled around her, caressing her with mystery and poise and sophistication. The glow hypnotized me.

"You want one?" she asked. She pulled the pack from her purse, some brand I had never seen. The cigarettes sat in a black box trimmed in silver, wrapped in a slightly textured gold foil, like expensive chocolate. She passed me one and I almost dropped it because it was so light. I had only smoked one cigarette in my entire life. I thought they were heavier.

She gave me a light and I took a breath. The smoke filled my mouth with a flavor like garbage, like bad neighborhoods and wrong corners. I took another breath, and it tasted like men in white undershirts and sweaty feet after dancing. After the third breath, I realized I liked cigarettes now.

Melinda and I smoked that one, then without even thinking, another, just sitting there quietly among the East Village's nightly parade of characters.

After a while, I stopped thinking about confronting Melinda. I didn't think about the upcoming Bakushan review or my paper or what would become of me and Pascal after that late-night kiss and the even later-night sex. I watched people pass me by—NYU students, tourists, New Yorkers annoyed at both. The smoke filled me with a soothing dumbness that fizzed into relaxation.

"Jeez, it's getting cold," Melinda said. She grabbed a scarf from my bag.

Before I could snatch it out of her hands, she peeked at the tag. "Whoa, whoa, whoa! Where the hell did you get this nice scarf? Fendi?" She put it around her neck and ran her hands over the cashmere and fur trim a couple of times. "Okay. This totally stumped me before, but the new look? The swag and restaurant stuff? You have a sugar daddy, don't you?"

I stared at her in my nicotined post-dinner buzz and smiled dully.

A big guy in green cargo pants and a peacoat walked by. "Hey, Tia Monroe, right?"

I said nothing. I could sort of hear muffled sounds in the distance, as if they or I were underwater.

"Uh, yeah," Melinda said when I didn't answer. "This is Tia."

"Oh, hi," the guy said. I raised the cigarette up to his face, as if it were a torch that could light the way. My arm felt heavy and tingly. He stepped back. "It's me, Kyle Lorimer?"

"Oh, yeah," I said, still in my murk.

"I wouldn't think a foodie like you would smoke."

"Why's that?" I said in a toothless, floating-on-the sea sort of way. "Tons of people in restaurants smoke."

"Don't you need your taste buds, though? Smoking destroys them."

Taste buds. I needed my taste.

Suddenly I felt the smoke like a gang of ghosts, terrorizing my tongue. I snapped out of it, threw the cigarette down and stomped on it.

And only then did I register Kyle.

"How's the job at Madison Park Tavern?" he asked.

"It's fine. It's coat check, so it's a riveting collection of wool," I said, knowing that my sarcasm wasn't a very subtle defensive tactic.

"You know, Madison Park Tavern was almost my first choice," Kyle said. *Ha, figures.*

He was carrying two packed-to-the-brim bags of groceries. I peeked inside and saw three different flours, cornmeal, and parchment paper.

"How is working with Helen Lansky?" I ventured.

"She's amazing. We're transitioning to a big project that will keep her occupied for a couple more months. A bit different from her other work."

"Oh, wow," I said. "What kind of project?"

Melinda put out her cigarette and nudged me. "Come on, let's go. There's a cocktail special at that Hawaiian-themed place!" Her eyes crossed drunkenly as she did a halfway hula motion. We hadn't drunk much, so I didn't know why she was acting that way.

"But wait," I said. I truly was wondering about Kyle's experience with Helen. "I want to talk to Kyle for a second."

Melinda stood and swung her purse around, bored.

"Yeah, she's working on a cookbook," he said, brightening up so much I couldn't help but smile along with him. "But she's taking a departure from general recipes and is specializing—"

My phone gave a *ping* and I looked at it while Melinda watched over my shoulder.

FREE TONITE AROUND 1?

Pascal. Even his texts had his magical smell.

"Whoa!" Melinda said. "It's that unknown number. That dude Pascal again! He wants you so hard. Is he a babe?"

He had been texting ever since our night together. Little smileys and pictures of dishes. He'd wanted to meet up, but hadn't been able to because of restaurant obligations. *Yes. You're on!* I texted back. It was already half past midnight.

"Sorry, I have to go," I said. I had to see him, especially because the review would come out soon. If he was busy now, he'd be even busier later.

"Yeah, of course," Kyle said. "You're a busy gal. Well, anyway, we should get together sometime and talk shop! If you have time."

I realized I hadn't heard what Helen was working on, though I wanted to find out. What was Kyle doing with those ingredients at this hour of the night? But he was already retreating, probably embarrassed after Melinda's boy-crazy encouragement.

"Yeah, sure," I said, and I meant it. But in the end, Pascal took precedence over Kyle.

As he walked away, Melinda pulled me by the elbow. "I don't buy that that fratty guy is into food. He doesn't look the part. I call bullshit."

I didn't think that was a fair assessment, but I went along anyway. "Yeah," I said. "Total bullshit."

I tried to sober up and concentrate. Pascal. I had to get to Pascal.

"I'm super impressed by you," Melinda said. "Say hi to your sugar daddy for me."

And with that, I left to see him.

WE MET ON the corner of Thompson and West Broadway, outside a bar. Pascal jumped at me from the shadows.

"Hello!" he said. "Sorry to scare you. Let's not go in there. The staff is . . ." He fanned the air in front of his nose. I peeked inside the bar and saw darkness. The only sensation was a full, bitter smell of weed. "Unless you want to have some?" Pascal asked.

"No, thanks. I don't do that."

He chuckled and grabbed my shoulder. "Good girl! Focused!"

"So what do you want to do? Is there another place you want to try?" I batted my eyelashes. Did he notice my new outfit?

Pascal looked at me for a long while. "Let's go to my place. If that's okay with you?"

"Yes!" I said, a bit too quickly, with a little too much blush in my cheeks. "Sure."

We were moving fast. Maybe too fast. Elliott and I had just broken up five days ago, the same night Pascal and I had had sex for the first time. But why would I slow down? He made me feel something I had never felt before. I wanted to say good-bye to that humdrum existence, putt-putting along. I couldn't wait for the next step with Pascal. Maybe we'd go out on a dinner date somewhere—where? I would let him choose. We would say hi to the chef and sit at a PX table. The waitstaff would fuss over us, but we'd be nice to them, tell them not to work so hard because we were on their side.

He held out his arm and I hooked mine in his. We wove

through the night to his place, a small but sweet one-bedroom on Mulberry. So this was what it was like to enjoy New York with a man. Bars twinkled with premature Christmas decorations, and couples smiled at us gently, like they were extras to set the scene: *A man and a woman walk out in the November air. Romantic music sets the mood.*

He opened his apartment door and let me enter first. It looked like he had just moved in, with basic furniture and nothing that warmed or personalized the space. We sat at a plastic table and he poured me a glass of red wine, then wiped the lip of the bottle with a white dishcloth and turned the label toward me. I laughed at how cute that was, this little bit of hospitality in his austere bachelor pad.

"Sorry," he said sheepishly, as he served himself a Scotch. "Still in restaurant mode."

Thursday nights were his least favorite of the week, he explained—lots of customers, often demanding and entitled. He didn't mind tourists, who were annoying in their own way, but were at least polite. I put my hand on his thigh and felt his muscles relax. He closed his eyes and took long, slow sips from his glass.

After a couple of minutes, Pascal put on some music, opened a door into a dark room, and returned with a single flower.

"For you," he said. It was an elaborate puzzle of a flower, a vermilion red the texture of crepe paper.

"Me?" Elliott had given me flowers all the time, but they were flowers from his greenhouse experiments—simple blooms that were understood with a few slices of the scalpel. This one was tantalizingly exotic. The stem was warped, the petals tangled and butterfly-wing thin, the stamens like eyelashes glooped with mascara. This strange thing was the most beautiful flower I had ever received.

"What's in the back there? You have a floral shop on the side?" I nodded over to his bedroom.

"No, of course not. I saw that flower and thought of you." He combed his fingers through my new hair and I briefly closed my eyes in involuntary euphoria. "I like your new hairstyle," he said.

He was a guy who noticed these things. I laughed. "You're pretty observant . . . for a boy."

"Haha, I'm not just any boy," he said. He fingers moved deeper and I thought that the dye may have given me new nerve endings because every hair prickled up to his touch. "We're sensualists, aren't we?"

"Sensualists?" He lowered his hand to my neck and pulled me so close our foreheads touched. "What do you mean?" I asked, the tips of my lips—just slightly—against his.

"Sensualism . . ." he repeated in his bizarre accent. He didn't press his lips against mine and I didn't dare press back. We let our mouths push and graze as we spoke. "We are passionate, you and I. We know how to give in to our senses."

Then I felt the full heat of his mouth on mine and I lapped him up greedily, my hands grabbing his face and hair and shoulders.

I had never thought of myself as much of a sensualist. I was a writer, a rationalist in a sensualist world. I was always worrying about what other people thought of me and more often than not I liked the company of babies and dogs instead of humans my own age.

But what's rational about a man's lips on you, when he's touching you in a way that makes you feel the exquisite pleasure of belonging? Everything else is a distraction.

We tussled around with our shirts off, until he pulled me on top of him and slid his hands from under my hair, to my shoulders, down my arms, and finally to the place where the top of my pants met my skin.

"Leather pants, you little minx. Shall we have an encore?" he asked.

By now my hair was a wild mess. I was red from the wine. The lights were sort of dark, but not dark enough. I was wearing some Kiki de Montparnasse lingerie, black lace with tiny bows that were at once sweet and not so sweet. You could even describe them as naughty.

He let the tip of one finger move around the edge of my pants. When he got to the button, he made a flicking motion that stressed its hold. The critical button.

I was ready to undo it for him when I spotted a plate of leftovers on Pascal's kitchen counter: the snail dumplings that Elliott had pushed aside that first night at Bakushan.

Pascal seemed to sense my hesitation and sat up. "Tia? Are you okay?"

As my eyes slid to his, I suddenly felt dizzy, like I couldn't get enough air. I jumped off Pascal. His heat, his motion, his heartbeat, it all nauseated me. If he touched me, my heart would have exploded.

"Tia?" he repeated, and that's when the panic attack took over. I leaped off the couch, opened the window, and stood there on my tippy-toes because even the floor's molecules were too much.

Pascal came to help, but I stopped him before he could touch me.

"Hold on!" I said, trying not to show how one look at those snail dumplings had sent me headfirst into a pit of anxiety. "I'm okay!"

And I just stood by the window, heaving the cold November air, wondering how long I'd have to fake it to make it.

I WOKE UP in the middle of the night on the couch, my head an inch away from Pascal's. For a second, I didn't recognize him and almost went into another panic attack. But then reality set in. It was Pascal. My Pascal. The guy I wanted. I hated my heart for being so slow on the uptake and took a couple of deep breaths.

The panic had completely subsided, and I was relieved to see that Pascal had already removed the snail dumplings. It was a hiccup, I thought. Nothing serious, just some transitional turbulence. I had to get it together for Pascal, especially before the review came out. That would be a turning point for us. Turning where, I didn't know, but I wasn't going to let some residual feelings for Elliott ruin our chances.

I watched Pascal sleep. He had long, curved eyelashes and lips that swelled with every little breath. I nestled into him, and his body responded in turn. He pushed his leg in between mine, nuzzling the top of his head against my cheek. His hair smelled like smoked wood chips.

He looked old, in a good way. Even in his sleep, he had a reassuring quality. Restaurants were about hospitality, but the chef wasn't usually the one with open arms. Pascal was, though. He was everything at Bakushan: the genius behind the stove, the draw through the door, the face on the magazine covers. He embodied so many things, and I was floored that he was the one cuddling into me. He was the one who gave *me* little kisses as he slept. I stayed up for an hour, just staring at him.

And as much as I was inspired by him, he must have been inspired by me, too.

He'd pursued me. He'd sat across from me at Tellicherry, asked me for advice at Whole Foods, and invited me to Bakushan. He'd made things better after Elliott spotted us late that night and now we were in his apartment, an apartment so barebones that surely he didn't invite people over all the time. Just ones he liked. And he'd taken care of me during whatever had just happened. He made me feel safe. It was only after I finally managed to tell my stupid, slow heart to shut up and come to terms with all that, that I was able to fall back asleep.

I WOKE UP the next morning at nine and found a note on his kitchen counter.

SORRY. HAD TO GO BACK TO BAK FOR PREP. REST UP. ILL BE THINKING OF U

I put the note in my purse as an anchor of sorts. This was where I wanted to be.

Chapter 26

TWO DAYS LATER, MICHAEL SALTZ AND I MET FOR OUR follow-up dinner at Bakushan.

We decided I would be his "companion," as he said gently. There was no other way around it—when an older man and a young woman went out to a nice restaurant, sometimes they were father and daughter, sometimes uncle and niece, sometimes colleagues. But in this town, on popular nights at popular restaurants, more often than not these scenes meant we were dating.

I wore bright red lipstick, black Rick Owens leggings, a Givenchy blazer, and a knit cap from The Row that slid over my eyebrows, hopefully masking my identity.

"You look like you're homeless," Michael Saltz said. "Did Giada give that to you?"

"Yes, of course!" I said, though I had requested it specifically. No more pant suits for me.

"For the record, I would never have *you* as my companion." He wore blue jeans, an olive green button-down, black plastic-rim glasses, and shoes that looked like they were snakeskin. This was

Michael Saltz's idea of a "downtown" outfit. He groaned wearily and snapped open the menu. "Pascal Fox . . . tell us, are you ready for four stars?"

I scanned the room for him, making sure to tuck any stray hairs under my hat. I couldn't see him in the open kitchen, so I pretended to go to the bathroom to get a better look. Nope, not there. He wasn't in the dining room, either. Where was he? Was he taking some time off? Or maybe he was with another girl? He wouldn't do that after spending a night with me . . . would he?

At first I thought I was upset because this was the last meal before the review—it didn't seem fair to evaluate the restaurant not under his guidance—but really, I wanted to see Pascal because of the urging in my skin. I *needed* to see him again, to touch him. I wanted him to want me and it killed me that I could only do so much to have him close.

We ordered around the menu, but it was all perfunctory. I didn't love everything, but it didn't matter.

"You didn't eat that much. What's with you?" Michael Saltz huddled in close to me, his fake glasses sliding down his nose. "You had me convinced this is four-star. You still feel that way, right?"

I could have said yes, I could have said no. He would have listened.

He had been surprisingly quiet during the dinner. He knew he had nothing to say anymore. Michael Saltz smelled the food, evaluated the service, but beyond that, he was just a credit card.

As it turned out, he wasn't even necessary for that. The fake name on the *Times* card, Alex Dresden, could have been either of us. And since I was the one who had ordered and asked questions and ate, the somewhat flaky waiter with the nose ring gave the bill to me and I signed for the meal that would seal Bakushan's fate.

"Absolutely four stars," I decided. World-class. Pascal Fox, superstar. Saying that in the *New York Times* would transform his restaurant and his career, for sure.

But I hoped that it would transform us.

"What does a four-star rating mean to you?" Michael Saltz asked, not challengingly, but more like an existential question between friends after dinner.

"It means you'll remember your meal forever. That the chef has advanced the world of cooking so it will never be the same. A meal you tell your grandchildren about. A meal that changes you. A meal that—"

"Okay, just checking." He smiled. "You've jumped into this opportunity. I'm proud of you."

I blushed. I had jumped in, all right.

THE REVIEW WAS basically written, but I put some finishing touches on it that night. Right before I sent it off, I received a text from Pascal.

BEEN THINKING ABOUT YOUR HOT KISSES ;) TELL ME I'LL SEE YOU SOON?

I wrote back:

Sure, but only if you're good ;)

He replied:

WHEN AM I NOT GOOD?

I hugged the phone. The heat moved across my collarbone, through my chest, and deep into my heart. *FOUR STARS,* I typed.

And though I'd like to say I did it because I believed Bakushan was one of the best restaurants in the world, deep down, I knew that wasn't true. All those complaints I'd heard had seeds of truth.

But I wasn't looking for truth.

I sent the review to Michael Saltz.

Chapter 27

I WENT TO SEMINAR LIKE NORMAL. I WALKED AMONG MY classmates like normal. But the whole day, I knew everything between Pascal and me would change forever that night.

Pascal called me in the afternoon.

"Guess what? On Monday a photographer came to the restaurant—from the *New York Times.* Just shooting around. And then yesterday a fact-checker called about some of my ingredients and methods."

"Oh?" I said, acting confused but smiling at the end of the line. "Why is that special?"

"Tia, Tia," he kept repeating, and every time he said my name, my heart clenched tighter for him. "This is it! What I've been waiting for . . ."

For some reason, he wouldn't say it. Maybe he assumed I knew what those two things meant or was afraid to jinx it.

"So that means . . . Bakushan is being reviewed?" I asked sweetly, innocently.

I could sense him cracking a smile. "Tia, Tia, Tia," he said. And that rapid-fire name-calling made my knees wobbly. "I don't want to work today, what's done is done. Let's hang out after I take care of a few quick things?"

I immediately went home and changed into the green-and-gold Hervé Léger dress from Giada's very first shipment of clothes. Before, it had kinda felt like too much, too tight, too slutty—and not like me. But tonight was the night, and I'd decided that I'd go all-out. The fabric took my breath away—as in, I could hardly breathe in it. It was all stretch, but a stretch that made you work for it, like my breathing and walking was some sort of physical therapy exercise.

I needed to be ready for his call. Instead of eating dinner, I snacked on chips. I tried to do some reading, but the review was nigh. Everything came down to that. Yet hours passed, and Pascal still didn't get in touch.

Later that night, he finally texted me.

U READY TO GO OUT? MEET ME AT MY PLACE IN 20?

I replied:

I thought u said u were taking today off. What happened to getting together early?

It seemed like the kind of complaint a girlfriend would send to her boyfriend, but I sent it anyway. Immediately I worried he'd be turned off by my tone and wouldn't respond. But to my relief, it hadn't seemed to register at all.

ONLY 8:30 NOW! THATS VRY EARLY 2 ME.

By the time I got to his place, it was a matter of minutes until the review went live. Like always, I hadn't gotten to approve the final article before Michael Saltz sent it in, so even I was eager to read it. I had always gotten so excited about my reviews, but this time the review wasn't for me. It was for him, for us. I was about to make him extremely happy, more than any other woman in the world could.

I knocked on Pascal's door, but when no one answered, I let

myself in. Pascal sat on a stool pulled up to his kitchen counter, a glass of Scotch close at hand. His face and tattooed forearm moved in and out of his laptop's light. I had already taken off my coat so the dress and I—all legs and curves and cleavage—could dazzle him. But he just nodded to acknowledge me, then looked back at his computer. I fell into a soft chair in the living room, watching him tap on the laptop's keys while crossing my legs so the dress's hem rode up higher.

Finally his click brought him to a different screen and Pascal pulled his face close. Every now and again, he tapped again, paging down. After about six long minutes—I noticed he read slowly, probably because English wasn't his first language—he looked up. He swooped toward me and lifted me in the air.

"Four stars! *Quatre*! FOUR FOUR FOUR!"

He vaulted me again and again, and I thought he must have acquired some temporary superpowers the way he raised me up so effortlessly. I squealed the whole way, propping myself up on his shoulders, feeding off his energy.

I ran up to the computer to see it with my own eyes. We'd pulled it off. The review connected us forever.

"*Out spills a green liquid, as slow and mesmerizing as lava,*" he read. "*Go on, take a forkful. Drag the finest, smoothest foie into the absolute essence of pea.*"

I closed my eyes as he continued.

"*Pick up a few pieces from the pool of accents. And taste. And put your fork down.*"

I heard him pick up his Scotch and flicked my eyes open. I took the glass out of his hands as he was about to sip and said, "Keep reading."

He smiled devilishly and continued while I drank. I swam in the rhythms of my words.

"And wonder: how could this dish seem so pure and elemental, and yet have a flavor so electric, so challenging?"

"Do you like it?" I asked. Pascal was momentarily speechless, so I asked him again. "Do you like it?"

"Of course I like," he said.

"What do you like about it?" I asked.

"I like . . . the grade, of course. And the words. The way the review captures the restaurant."

"It's beautifully written," I said, edging closer to him along the counter. "Don't you think?"

"Beautiful," he repeated. "I love it. People will love it."

I wanted him to say it again and, magically, he did.

"I love it. People will love it."

He stroked me on the head, and I nuzzled into him like a cat. I saw his chest heave, his lungs filling with his accomplishment, *our* accomplishment. I had never been so attracted to him, or any man, before.

Then he took me by the face and kissed me harder than I've ever been kissed. He kissed me over and over, his lips only loosely aiming for mine. He pulled my lips with the strong pucker of his mouth, then let them snap back. All I could do was give in. That's all I wanted to do.

We made our way to the couch, lips locked. He laid me back so my feet were off the ground and my head hung over the armrest. He massaged my neck hard, digging his fingers alongside my spine. His breathing took on a husky bite, an animal roughness that gave me goose bumps. His hands followed my curves, focusing on my hips and butt. I kicked my leg around and sat on his lap. It wasn't very comfortable, but it'd have to do.

"You are irresistible," he purred, and toyed with the straps of my dress. I took his hands in mine. I had the control. I controlled whether or not we had sex, whether or not he got his four-star.

He was begging for me. But I wanted to milk this even more. There's so much in life that is outside your control, that you accept because that's the way of the world.

But in this moment I felt influential and sexy and important and desired—the very recipe for invincible.

I held New York City and its restaurants in the palm of my hand. I could make them or break them. I'd done this for Pascal, but—I finally let myself admit it—I'd also done it for me. I liked it and I was good at it.

I started moving my hips on top of him.

He leaned back and started to groan. "Oh, Tia, you know how to move. You—"

But I put my hand over his mouth. "Shh," I said. And then I stood up and swallowed every fear and insecurity.

Never in a million years had I thought I would do anything like this—a striptease? An erotic dance? It all sounded so cliché, so tawdry on one hand . . . but on the other, bold, empowered, free. I had all the elements—the hair, the makeup, the dress, the shoes, the hot man. And the most important thing, the confidence. I couldn't control a lot of things—Elliott, Emerald, Dean Chang, Michael Saltz. But I controlled his attention, his hunger for me and me alone. For the moment, that made everything else melt away.

I shifted one strap over my shoulder, then the other. I circled my head around and swiveled my hips, creating a sort of hula hoop helix, a study in the curves of a woman's body. He reached for me, but I stepped back, just beyond his reach.

"Not yet . . ."

"*Argh,*" he said, but he said it with a smile. "Yes, mademoiselle."

I turned around and grazed the tops of his knees with my butt, then spread my legs and bent over, because I knew the dress would ride up. I'd known this Hervé Léger was good for dancing, but I hadn't known until then that it was made for holding men entranced.

I stood up while his hand moved up and down my inner thigh, and then his other hand joined in. He unzipped the back of the dress and it fell to the ground with an unsexy sandbag-like thud. I had never stood in front of a man in just a bra, panties, and heels. My first instinct was to be embarrassed, to want to cover up or turn down the lights, to jump on him so he wouldn't have such a complete view of every inch of me.

Yet his gaze only grew in intensity.

But then Pascal pulled me at the knees so I buckled and tripped on the way to his lap. He flicked my bra open and off so my arms flew wildly in front of me. Then, in a rather impressive move, he slid my panties off and circled around me so I was the one sitting and he stood over me. All of sudden, he had the control.

"Hey," I said. A quiver came into my voice now that he was on top and I didn't know what he would do.

Pascal unbuttoned his shirt and unbuckled his belt. I got the picture and began to kick off my shoes, but he stopped me.

"Leave them on," he said. "You look so fucking sexy in those heels."

I blushed, but now wasn't the time to be sheepish. He leaned over me. I squeezed his waist with my legs and held his neck in the crook of my elbows so I could keep his face to mine.

We rocked together forcefully but in sync. He swiftly slid off his boxer briefs and put my hand on him. He was even harder than before, harder than I had ever felt Elliott. Pascal was roaring in triumph as he sat over me, himself in hand.

We stayed there for a couple of seconds. And then thirty. Then what felt like millennia. His breathing had slowed and he looked distracted, in another world. Why was he hesitating? I was so scared of losing him.

"I love you!" I blurted. It seemed ridiculous to say so much, so fast, but I needed to make sure he was mine.

It took a full second for him to wake up to my words, then he pressed his lips to mine and suddenly we were breathing inside each other's mouths, sucking on each other's lips, moving our hands all over each other's naked bodies. He was lying directly on top of me when he stopped and looked me in the eye.

"I love you, too," he said.

He loved me. He loved me! I melted into the couch and let his body take me over. This man—this smoking hot, super-accomplished, nice, and considerate man—loved me.

I felt that this could be my Thing, the thing that validated me.

He held me as if he were made of mercury, strong but slippery, a touch that seemed to skim the edges of my body leaving just the pressure of desire. When he came, he looked me straight in the eye. He whispered in my ear, "You're amazing."

I didn't come that time, but I didn't show my disappointment. No good would ever come from that.

Pascal got off me and spooned me from behind, holding me with both his cow-and-pig-tattooed arm and his vegetable arm. He smelled my hair and ran his fingers up and down the front and back of my naked body. Our breathing rode the same wave, our heartbeats kept the same rhythm. First rushed, exhausted, then calm, content.

Finally, he released me and lay on his back. Or at least, tried to. There wasn't much room on the couch.

"Four stars," he said. "Wow."

"Me or the restaurant?" I asked in a voice that was surprisingly sexy.

He laughed long and hard and turned his full gaze to me. "I think you know what it means . . ." He trailed off sleepily.

I closed my eyes and ended up falling asleep, too. When I woke up, maybe a few hours later, Pascal was standing, looking out the window. I stared at his sharp shoulder blades and his beauty marks. He had a double-jointed elbow and as he leaned into the night, he looked like a fashion model doing some awkward and mysterious pose.

"Come on, let's go celebrate," he said.

It was already two A.M. and all I wanted to do was lie on the couch, or even better, see what his bedroom looked like. I wanted to know what other surprises he held for me in his four-star glow and the declarations of our love.

"Have you been to Room 113?"

"No," I said, though I'd heard of it from Carey.

I stalled putting my clothes back on, and was glad I couldn't locate my La Perla underwear because it bought us more time. "Pascal, we can't go. We need to find my underwear."

By now he already had his winter coat and shoes on. He held my head with one hand and my butt with the other.

"Hm." He smiled. "I prefer it that way."

I sighed. He could have asked anything of me and I would have done it. I wanted to have him to myself, though. So many girls wanted to gallivant around the city with him. For once I didn't care about seeing and being seen, or eating this and hating that. I wanted to hold on to this private moment, with him.

But eventually I got dressed—underwear-less—and we hopped in a cab to Room 113. Inside, in the dark, it was hard to make out any shapes or faces. There were just jeans and sweaters, jackets thrown on the couch, bottles backlit on the bar.

Pascal whispered in my ear, "No one parties like restaurant

people. These people leave the restaurant two, three in the morning. Wake up at six, then are back at it."

He walked in ahead of me, like a king. Soon, the shadows showed themselves.

"Congrats on the review, P," a girl said, kissing him on the cheek. She was graceful and polished and probably a hostess at a very fine restaurant. "You deserve it." They locked eyes in a way that told a story, like they had shared some part of their lives. She, too, had a faint French accent. I cleared my throat and tightened my grip on Pascal's hand.

A short Mexican guy with a strong, sturdy build barreled up to Pascal, pulled him down, and placed a firm kiss on both cheeks. "Congratulations, señor!" he said. "A home run!" He held up his hand and Pascal gave him a big, hard high-five. "Too hard, señor!" the man joked. "Four stars and you're too strong now!"

Then a whole posse of young guys stood up from a banquette. Most of them appeared to be around Pascal's age and had a similar, if even more ravenous, look about them. They were clearly chefs, but didn't have four stars. They patted him on the back, they punched him in the arm. One guy crossed his arms the whole time and looked like he would have killed Pascal if that would have given him a better shot at four stars. The chefs passed Pascal around, and he grabbed a shot from one guy, then turned around and grabbed another drink from someone else.

I heard little of what they said because they quickly whisked him away. I had no way of inserting myself into their group.

For a brief second, Pascal checked on me and the chefs all looked at me for an even briefer second before deciding they didn't know who I was. It was the usual restaurant once-over. People sized up your weight in the world and applied the corresponding level of attention. In another restaurant, with other company, I might have commanded more respect. But with Pascal, I disappeared.

Pascal could have invited me over, introduced me—he had said he loved me—but instead, he stayed with his friends and left me standing in my skimpy Hervé Léger. I tried to distract myself with my phone and looking through Pascal's old texts. He had been so persistent with me, so cute and loving. But now I felt abandoned. I reasoned that this was a big night and he had spent all of it with me so far. It was okay if he had some friend-time.

But I had invested so much in him and put him above everyone else. I wished I could have said I was comfortable with our "relationship," but I wasn't.

Then I heard a familiar wave of laughter, and when I looked over, my heart lifted. There sat my friends from Madison Park Tavern.

"Hey, look who made it out to 113. I thought you'd never say hi to us," Chad said.

"She's too busy schmoozing with Monsieur Pascal Fox," Angel said.

Henri and a couple of other waiters laughed.

I saw Carey in the back of a curved banquette, her knees pulled up and her feet on the seat. Angel and Chad passed me a drink, something fizzy with a lemon.

"I had no idea that you were such a climber," Chad said. The word *climber* didn't sound very nice, but I was so happy to see them, I didn't let it bother me.

"Yeah, well. We've been hanging out a little."

Chad was biting the ear of another server from Madison Park Tavern, a cute Brazilian girl named Romina I hadn't gotten to know that well. Angel had his hand on the thigh of a pretty woman sitting next to him. I figured she was from the restaurant, too, but I didn't know for sure. Everyone was paired with someone, except Carey.

So this was what they did at Room 113. It seemed like it could have been fun. Drinking after a long night at work, complaining about Jake, talking about the new dishes and restaurant gossip.

Carey peered at me from her seat, looking rather queenly and content. Carey and I never hung out outside of work, but I thought, why didn't we? She patted for me to sit down next to her and I figured out why she looked so uncharacteristically mellow: she reeked of weed. I looked back at Pascal, trying to catch his eye, but he was busy talking to another chef.

"Don't worry about it," Carey said. "He's fine without you. Pascal's in the 'cool kid' chef clique."

I stayed quiet. Lately, in my mixed-up life, I had forgotten what people knew and what I could tell them. Writing seminar papers, sure. Writing reviews, no. Eating at Heedless with Melinda, yes. Tasting menu with Michael Saltz at Le Brittane, no.

But Pascal . . . what was Pascal? He fell into a confusing middle space. Was he part of my normal, regular-girl life? Or was he somehow related to the fancy restaurant and Michael Saltz side? The questions seemed too big to untangle right then and there with Carey looking at me, her face open and friendly.

"So you're in love with a chef, too?" she asked as her straw lazily grazed her lips.

I had the impulse to buy a stronger drink. Carey's phone buzzed on the table and she picked it up, then quickly put it down.

"Join the club," she said.

"I guess we're just starting to date," I said. "But, yeah, I have feelings for him."

"A date? You've been on a real date?"

"Well, he doesn't have a lot of time. But we get together." *Date* was too strong a word, even *get together* could've been an exaggeration. I'd been telling the truth when I said I loved him, but it was so different from how it had been with Elliott.

Elliott had said it first. We were returning from a Halloween party and he was dressed as a lumberjack (a jack made of wood), and I was dressed as the game Sorry! (my body was the board and my head the bubble with the die). We'd eaten some late-night pizza with our friends, the room a cacophonous crowd of monsters and kings and characters from TV shows. Elliott and I had paid for our slices and beer and left around three in the morning. We were laughing and walking-while-hugging because it had gotten cold and we weren't wearing jackets. When we crossed the gates of Old Campus, some jerk in a Jason mask popped out to scare us and we both shrieked. The guy ran away—probably to terrorize other tired, drunk students—as we clutched each other, first frightened, then hysterically laughing. Elliot had held me close, and my heart had flown into the stratosphere, half with residual alarm, half with the expectation that he would say something important. He took my cold hand in his and said exactly what I was thinking at that moment: "I love you."

We eventually got to his room and he showed me his "59 Reasons Elliott Loves Tia" list. He had been keeping the list for himself, but now he wanted me to know all the ways big and small that he loved me.

I was starting to realize that I hadn't said "I love you" to Pascal because I actually loved him, at least not in the way I loved Elliott. Back then, he and I had just stated the reality.

With Pascal, the words had a different purpose.

"Don't tell me," Carey continued. "He's always tired and stressed and thinking about the next night's dinner. You're always clutching your phone, waiting for him to text, always after midnight."

Chad and Romina had moved into some dark corner. Angel ran his fingers through his girl's hair, undoing her low-slung bun.

I understood her implication, but Pascal and I were different. We'd had a connection, and now it was a matter of letting it blossom.

"I wish we weren't so incestuous," Carey said. She chomped on a dinner roll she must have taken from Madison Park Tavern. "But—well, you know—I guess I can't help being in love with Matthew, just like you can't help being in love with Pascal. Is this, like, a thing?"

"I mean . . . I hope?" I more than hoped. I wanted this to be a relationship among friends and equals and partners. But now I had given him the review and then professed my love. At this point, I had no more ammunition besides just being me.

And I feared that wouldn't be enough.

But Carey was on her own wavelength. She just wanted to talk about Matthew.

"I thought things were going to work out between us. I understand his hours and his passion. That's why I love him so much," she went on.

It surprised me how she said "love" so deeply and painfully. She believed in love so much it broke my heart to hear her talk about it not being reciprocated.

"Then the review came out with only two stars! Matthew changed. He became obsessed. That sunchoke thing, his new dishes—I mean, they're great. He's really finding himself. But at the same time, I thought I was becoming important to him. Ever since we got that two-star, it's like I fell off the face of the earth. That's when I realized it was always about the restaurant and building his reputation. It was never about me." She sighed and made a forlorn slurping noise with her straw.

I pinched the bridge of my nose. Great. It was bad enough

that Chef Darling had been put on probation after the *New York Times* review, but it had also had quieter, equally damaging effects. Carey loved two things: the restaurant and Chef Darling. And I had screwed up both of them.

"I bet that's not true," I tried. "Matthew had to . . . realign his priorities temporarily. The review is one sudden thing. Things might get better? To where they used to be?"

"And where's that? Me pining for him at staff meetings? Wishing he'd take off the chef's jacket and spend time with me? I never in a million years wanted to fall in love with a chef. I went to Stanford and spent two years in supposedly the best Food Studies master's program in the country. By the time I graduated I thought I'd be working on strategy with Gary Oscars, but instead I'm some pathetic boy-crazy backserver, not even a waitress!"

"But Jake likes you, Carey. He's always seen something great in you." Even though Carey was scattered, I think Jake liked the intelligent eccentricity Carey brought to the restaurant. I know I did.

"Jake? Jake's practically gone, Tia. Fall is our peak season, and we're thirty-five percent down in covers. Gary put Jake on probation right after that review. He's walking on eggshells. Matthew is, too, but he's taking the balls-to-the-wall approach with all his new dishes. I'm not sure about Jake. He's too good to pander to Gary Oscars, but Jake and his wife have the twins to worry about . . ."

"Really? I didn't even know Jake was married."

Carey looked at me without judgment, just high and sweet and factual. "Yeah, with two girls. They're toddlers now, but they were preemies, and they still have some lingering health problems."

"I didn't know," I wheezed, saddened that I could be—yet again—so dense. The restaurant was changing right under my nose and I hadn't even been paying attention.

"Well, you want to know more dirt? Angel is quitting to

become a full-time poet. And Chad already has another job at Bank Lodge. He'll be the bar manager."

"Wow. And you?"

Carey reclined into the cushion of the banquette. In the darkness, she looked prettier and more self-possessed than I remembered her. Her low-key misery, in some weird way, suited her.

"I'm attached to Matthew."

It was hard to see happy, smart Carey so dejected. But at least she recognized her own delusion. I began to feel uneasy.

"I should go back," I said. "Pascal is waiting." Carey and I looked back at him as he made a swift, slicing motion to some other younger, tattooed guys who nodded with their eyes wide open, basking in the glow of New York's newest four-star chef.

"Okay, well, it was cool seeing you out," Carey said. "But I have one more question." She looked at me with concern. "Why did Gary summon you to his office that one time?"

"Gary hates me," I said. And this wasn't even a lie.

"Oh, I see. I'll see you later, then." She lurched forward and hugged me with all her weight. Then she moved her head as if coming out of a long slumber, and brought her face so close to mine, our noses touched. I thought she would kiss me or something, but instead she turned her head and whispered with her lips inside my ear because that was the only way a whisper could be heard at Room 113. "I heard you talking to Michael Saltz that night in the basement," Carey said. "But I didn't tell Jake."

I pushed out of her arms. "Why?"

She sighed and all of a sudden became like an older sister, because she used a voice that was calm and knowing and made me want to listen to her. "You know that new staff rubric? Do you know what CTD stands for?"

I shook my head. I had no idea, but I remembered that Carey always had the highest score.

"It means 'connect the dots.' Jake's mantra and what I happen to be good at. First, I realized my algorithm was wrong. I should have known we would be reviewed in September. I wish I had been working in coat check that night so I could have ID'd Michael Saltz at the door. The night had been so busy that I didn't have time to look at the non-PX tables until late. I had a weird feeling about that guy, though, and went searching for him when I had a free second. I didn't even think to suspect he was Michael Saltz until I saw him with you. You were all fired up, like you were on a mission. Like you were fulfilling your purpose. No offense, but I didn't think Michael would listen to your thoughts on the menu. But he did. I stood there and saw him take it all in. There he was, the most important food critic in the world, listening to you. You were lucky to have that."

So Carey had known the whole time. Not the whole truth of it, but some. And to my surprise, the world didn't end. "What do you mean? Have what?"

"That moment of greatness," she said with a little smile. "It's crazy he paid so much attention to you."

Suddenly I got excited that we had this connection. It was barely anything, but at least that shadowy part of my life had gotten an inch of light. I thought about telling her everything about Michael Saltz. Unlike Melinda, she'd try to understand. I was sure she'd relate. I could tell her about Pascal and maybe mollify her worries about Matthew. Tell her that sometimes these types of guys need space and that's why you fall for them in the first place. If Matthew and Pascal were always available, would we still love them? Probably not.

She seemed to be giving me an out, a safe place to relieve myself of this double life.

But I couldn't. I had a promise to keep to Michael Saltz and he had a promise to keep to me. But more than that, I knew Carey, with her Wiki and algorithms, might see something I didn't want to see. Michael Saltz wasn't a regular *piston,* launching me into something with a minor push. With him, the rules changed. I had changed.

Instead, I backed away and said good-bye with embarrassed bowing and waving and rushed to the bathroom. I worked on plumping the volume of my hair using a circular motion the stylist had taught me. I reapplied my makeup and stared at my reflection for one beat, two, three. I didn't look like myself anymore. And that was fine by me.

A FEW MINUTES later, I joined Pascal and his friends in a semiprivate back room. Around last call, they begged him to relocate to another after-hours place. They shook him and threatened to steal his leather jacket, and Pascal laughed, which only encouraged them. I suppose they had switched from weed to coke and I think he thought about joining them, until a guy who wasn't in Pascal's group but who was also probably high out of his mind came up behind me and spun me around.

"Hey—don't I know you? I know you! I know you!"

He waved his hands in the air and with his red nose, he looked like a crazy druggie coming in from the street. Pascal's face sobered up and his stance stiffened.

"I don't think so . . ." I said, clinging to Pascal.

Pascal put his arm around me as more of the chefs crowded around us.

"You don't remember me, do you?" Then he stood up straight, took off his knit beanie, and brushed his hair back. "You know I used about five hundred dollars' worth of truffles on you and Saltz that night. But we only got three stars."

For a moment he controlled his maniacal eyes and gave me a flirtatious wink. The same twinkle he had given me at Tellicherry. Felix, our server.

His eyes blazed to Pascal. "But Chef Fox, you clearly knew what you were doing," he hissed. "She wanted more than truffles, didn't she? So congratulations on the four-star. You deserve it for fucking the slut first."

A girl next to Felix spoke up. "Hey, don't talk to her like that, asshole."

Felix laughed and I squeezed Pascal's arm, scared.

"Pascal, everyone knows your restaurant is shit. But I have to give you props. Why bother improving your dishes when you can get this?" He gestured to me, and not in the elegant way of fine dining, but with a vulgar flinging. Then he gave me an ugly look and turned away.

My mind was just trying to catch up.

Pascal took me by the shoulders and shoved me through the main room, toward the door. People still came up to him, trying to congratulate or recongratulate him in their now totally drugged and drunk states. But Pascal kept pushing me forward, bulldozing through his oncoming fans until we were through the front door and out on the street. We walked quickly toward his apartment, but my bare legs were freezing and I couldn't keep up in my heels. He kept walking, practically dragging me.

It took me a while to figure out what Felix had said. I wasn't in that mind-set.

Felix somehow knew that I was responsible for Tellicherry's three-star review. He knew that he'd been serving Michael Saltz and me. And he also knew Pascal and I were somehow involved and that . . . what?

We got back to Pascal's apartment and neither of us said anything for a while. I looked up at him, for some reassurance.

Something like, "Felix is a cokehead and everyone knows it." Or, "Baby, I love you, that guy is out of his mind."

I made room for him on the couch, but he didn't sit. He paced along his kitchen counter, wringing his hands.

And then I connected the dots.

"You deserve it for fucking the slut first."

"Pascal . . ." I started. "Why did he say those things to you?"

He inhaled and approached me gently. "Tia, I'm sorry. I shouldn't have taken you there. I think you're great but I don't want to lie to you."

I sat up and looked him in the eye. He looked away and sat down on a stool. "Are you going to be okay?" he asked.

The tears came out slowly at first. I thought about losing Pascal. The man I'd thought I loved was actually using me.

And apparently people in the restaurant industry knew about it. I wasn't just a slut, but something even worse: an ignorant slut.

I would have wanted to cry alone, but what did it matter now if Pascal saw me? Everything I had, I put into those tears. They gushed out of me like a waterfall and there seemed to be no end.

I thought about my family and friends. I thought how I had wasted this semester and important relationships so I could—what? Be a pawn in Pascal's game?

I thought of Elliott, poor Elliott. He deserved someone better than me. Of all the guys to see me kiss—this jerk? This scum who had taken advantage of me this whole time?

Pascal sat next to me and put his hand on my thigh. And even that killed because it still felt so good. Unbearably good, a touch that sizzles in your skin. Even when I knew it was a ploy, something else not anything like love.

"Christian, my friend at Tellicherry, tipped me off," he said over my crying. "We worked together at Veilleurmet Kitchen. I lied to you when I sat down at your table—I didn't have the night off. Tonight is the first night I've taken off since Bakushan opened. I couldn't rest until that review came out. You must understand that, right?

"For a while, the restaurant industry lost track of him. He went off the radar. But then we heard from some people at Madison Park Tavern that he had gotten super thin. Christian spotted him at his place and told me. I dropped everything and went to study him. He was the one and only reason I'd ever leave the line. And that night, I saw *you* there with him."

I hushed myself, hiccupping my sobs so I could hear him explain himself. He couldn't even say his name. I wanted him to just say it. To admit that he'd been using me for Michael Saltz. Say it while I was sitting on this couch smelling of our sex.

Sit across from the girl at Tellicherry, get her number, get her in bed. I had made it too easy.

"There'd been buzzing among some chefs that Michael Saltz had taken up with a young woman, which came as a surprise because everyone knows he's gay. But there was a picture taken at Panh Ho, and it's been making the rounds among some of my chef friends. I recognized you from the other time you came to my restaurant."

The click I'd heard as we left Panh Ho—I had been "made" from the very beginning. I had thought I was secret, special. I'd thought I could play NYC any way I wanted. But now I realized with gruesome clarity that the city had been playing me the whole time.

I wished more than anything that this was a bad dream. Maybe I'd had an allergic reaction at Room 113. Some high-proof lobster cocktail.

"Everything between us was a lie," I whispered to myself. "So you never liked me? All those times we went out, and Whole Foods . . . and earlier tonight, when we . . . ?" I ran my hands over my filthy dress. I looked down at Pascal's couch, the pillows we had thrown aside earlier in the evening, and the room started spinning.

"It's not that simple," he whispered back. "Not many people know, and even fewer believe you have any influence. Like, what do you do for him? Are you his secretary? His . . . cover of some sort?"

I smacked a pillow. Now he was calling me Michael Saltz's secretary? He didn't know anything. He didn't know that everything the man wrote was mine. I was no secretary. I was the one in charge.

And yet. Now I was a puppet who finally saw her miserable strings.

I lost the will to sit up and slumped over on the couch. Pascal took me by the shoulders and sat me up again. "You've probably heard how Bakushan has been getting mixed reviews. I had to do something about it."

"Oh, I don't know. . . . You could have made better food!" I screamed. "Trained your staff better. Made sure there was no sand in your fucking dumplings! What did you think you'd get from me?"

Pascal looked at me like, *Do you really want me to tell you?* But he relented.

"Tia, it wasn't just me. Didn't you notice when the restaurants always sent you and Michael a good-looking male waiter? Couldn't you tell when people played you? You knew it came with perks, right? You've always known that."

"I didn't do this for the perks!" I said in a teary, wet voice. "I did this . . . for you. I did it because Michael Saltz told me that I'd be able to work with Helen Lansky. Did you know that, too?"

He looked confused with a tinge of fear, like he wasn't sure if I'd snap. I wasn't sure, either. "Know . . . what?"

"About Helen. About why I did all of this!" I shrieked.

He backed away. "No, I didn't know anything about Helen. I just knew that you were involved somehow with Michael."

"Yeah, well, I didn't ask for that. I just wanted to work with Helen, and help her with her cookbook—"

"Wait, wait, a cookbook? That sort of recipe-testing drudgery? Tia . . ." He started laughing but then stopped himself. I realized then that even though he was just six years older, he was talking to me like a child. He *saw* me as a child, someone he could toy with.

"Maybe you thought you were doing this for Helen. But I'd venture to say you played along with Michael Saltz for other reasons." He looked me up and down: my dress, my shoes, my hair. I closed my eyes and felt as if I had vanished, become a total fabrication made of nothing but falsehoods.

I picked up my coat and started to leave. But as much as I hated him, part of me just wanted to stop time, to keep this hurt where I could see it and understand it. I knew once I walked out that door, it'd get a lot worse. I'd see the world in its true colors.

"Tia, no. Don't go," Pascal said. "Can you blame me for seeing an opportunity and taking it?"

I just stood there, tired. Tired of staying up late, for him, so I could get to know him and be in his world. Tired of standing in these stupid high heels and this tight, ridiculous dress. I wanted to go back to the way things were.

"If you're going to leave, I want to give you something." He opened his fridge and pulled out a plastic quart-size container of something bright green.

"It's my pea shoot puree. The same one encased in the foie gras."

"So?"

"I know you loved it." I had said as much in my review. "Here, you can have it."

"Oh. Oh! Really?" I started to chuckle, then giggle, then laugh hysterically. "Is that, like, a doggie bag?" My words slurred but Pascal stayed alert, even concerned.

"I could give you the recipe. Every press outlet asks me for it, but I've never given it out. Here, I'll print it out for you." He walked to his laptop. "You can reprint it in the *Times*."

"No!" I yelled. "No! No!" I smacked the container off the table and it blew open, spilling green ooze on his white rug. "You do not get to do that to me. You've fed me nothing but bullshit this whole time. How do even live with yourself?"

Pascal plopped onto the couch. "I'm sorry, Tia. This is the game. I didn't make it up." He opened his arms, inviting me to sit next to him. "Come on, please, don't take it so hard."

His voice sounded so sincere. It didn't seem like he had wanted to harm me, but what did I know?

"We were just hanging out."

I exhaled sharply. This had never been "just" anything—"just" grad school or "just" Helen Lansky. I hadn't "just" been hanging out with Pascal, and most of all, this hadn't "just" been sex to me.

When I'd said I loved him, I thought it had come true. For me. For both of us. And now this loss had gutted me from the inside out.

"Here, take this." He held out my crumpled La Perla underwear. So maybe I hadn't lost them, maybe he'd taken them from me as a kind of bounty.

I looked around his apartment. The table where he'd first poured me wine and where I'd happily—naïvely—watched him read his review. The couch where he'd fucked me. When I had first arrived, I'd thought this empty apartment was everything, that he was an open book. But now I realized that I'd never even seen his bedroom. This whole time, we had only ever stayed in his living room.

I knew tomorrow I'd see the Bakushan review in print and the blogosphere would go crazy over it. There would be lots of naysayers, but for the most part, people would take my word as truth. I'd thought that feeling would never get old, the thrill of my words rippling across the world. But now the hype terrified me. I could only wait for its crushing force, like a tsunami arriving the day after an earthquake.

"I'm sorry," he said.

I left his apartment shattered and raw. A rancid feeling started in my mouth, then went down to my stomach and finally the space between my legs. The only upside was that I doubted my heart would survive. Good riddance. I couldn't trust it anyway.

I WALKED BACK to the apartment. I had expected the sun to rise hours ago, but the night stretched like elastic, moving but not advancing. People smoked and talked on the sidewalk and cars passed in the street. I briefly thought I had been drugged because the night had become too surreal. But that was wishful thinking.

When I got to the apartment, I knocked on Melinda's door. No one answered. I waited for a couple of minutes, or maybe more than that, I don't know. I had never found our living room so mesmerizing.

Finally, the door opened.

"Tia? Tia, what's wrong?" Melinda could barely open her eyes and she hugged her arms across her chest. "What's going on? What time is it?"

I opened my mouth, but nothing came out. I had so much to say and yet to talk felt like an impossible challenge. I lifted my wrist to look at my watch, then remembered I wasn't wearing one. I opened my clutch and looked for my phone, but couldn't find it, even though the clutch was no bigger than two paperback books.

"I'm sorry, I'm sorry," I squeezed out, and the tears started falling. "I don't know what time it is."

"Oh, Tia." Melinda laughed. "That's okay."

"I've been such a bad friend."

Melinda furrowed her brow. "It's not a big deal. We've known each other for, like, two seconds. You don't have to put so much pressure on yourself."

My bawling only got louder. "Everything's gone wrong."

Melinda raised her hands. "No, Tia. Stop. Nothing is worth this much grief, okay? Whatever's happened, it'll pass. Let it go." Another one of Melinda's mantras, but now it didn't help.

"I can't. Things won't get better on their own."

We stayed quiet while she thought. If someone had blown on me, I would have crumbled.

"We all screw up, Tia. And we all get screwed, too. It's the circle of life, and it sucks. But you'll be back on the upswing soon enough. I know you will."

That night, Melinda and I fell asleep on her air mattress.

We had brunch the next morning at a greasy spoon diner with old, cranky waitresses. My chair was still warm from the man who'd sat in it before, and I had to wipe his crumbs off the table. Melinda had a chocolate chip muffin and a side of bacon, and I had an omelet filled with onions, white mushrooms, and green peppers.

Every now and again a little sob would make its way into my breathing, but Melinda never once called attention to it. I smothered my omelet with ketchup and black pepper, took one bite, then decided I didn't have an appetite. I didn't feel like eating now. I didn't feel like eating ever.

Chapter 28

FOR THE NEXT THREE DAYS, MY BED BECAME MY BEST FRIEND. I didn't go to my internship seminar. I planned to watch the livestreams of my classes, but instead fell into an agonized sleep with my jaw clenched and my chest heaving on cruise control. When I woke up, I never felt rested. I called in sick to Madison Park Tavern and I didn't care about what Dean Chang would say about my scholarship. No one from the restaurant had contacted me, so I figured that they hadn't seen my episode with Felix and Pascal. I didn't answer Michael Saltz's calls, but I read his emails. Surprisingly, he didn't raise a fuss about my disappearance. I passed on a re-review of The Oak, helmed by a dangerously sexy, tattooed chef-wunderkind. I finally saw that sexy chefs were a dime a dozen. But that didn't lessen the hurt.

An email from Carey finally got me out of my funk.

> Hey, how's it going? I heard you've been sick. I hope you feel better! I can't wait for you to come back to the restaurant. Chef has some new dishes and they

are to die for. (I know I'm prone to exaggeration, but this time I'm SERIOUS.)

See you soon? Before Thanksgiving for sure!

Carey

XX

I read that email ten times, hearing Carey's voice in my head. Every time I read it, more of the restaurant fleshed out. The late-afternoon light shining through the dining room window. The rotation of beautiful flowers at the entrance. The elegant clockwork of the kitchen, the dining room, and even the coatroom. Plus, all my friends.

The next day, Saturday, I went back to work. I missed those guys, and more than anywhere else, the restaurant was my home.

"Tia!" Jake called to me.

I ran up to the dining room wearing my old Jil Sander. What can I say—it was a good suit and didn't raise any eyebrows.

"Gary is in Miami this week, so I'd like you to help in the dining room tonight. Would that be okay with you?"

"Yes!" I said. "I'd love to." The Pascal episode had weakened me a lot, but I felt myself reenergizing the second I walked into the restaurant. Here I'd be useful. The tasks were straightforward, elemental. Bring food, take away food, clean. I had never fully appreciated how pure this job was. People want to be nourished. To be welcomed. To be known. That's what the best restaurants provided.

Jake grinned and handed me an apron. "Come on. You're getting your hands dirty tonight."

Carey wasn't kidding about the revitalized menu. In his rush of post-review inventiveness, Chef Darling had introduced a dish of "crushed autumn duck" in which the waiter presented a clean, lovely plate of carved duck and vegetables. Then a backserver—

me—used a medieval-looking instrument to crush the carcass so the remaining juices dripped down a spout onto the plate.

The machine was massive. Every time I crushed a new carcass, I had to degrease the nooks of the intricate carvings. The crank was so tall I had to stand up on my tippy-toes. I tried with all my might to avoid sticking out my tongue in intense concentration.

Halfway through the night, Angel pulled me aside. I was briefly scared that Carey had told him something. Or maybe word had gotten around about Pascal and Felix. But instead he took out a tasting portion of the duck I had been serving.

"You have to try this. This is one for the Madison Park Tavern Hall of Fame."

It was incredible—especially the carcass drippings.

By the end of the night, my apron was soaked with duck fat. I loved every minute of it.

Carey ran up to me. "Hey, amazing work with the duck press! Do you want to go to Room 113?"

"I'd love to," I said, "but I have some schoolwork I need to do." I'd also vowed to never step foot in Room 113 ever again.

"Oh, yeah, I forget you're still a grad school intern. I always think you're one of us."

"Aw, Carey . . ." I said.

"Well, you should come out with me and Romina on Monday. It's industry night at Kel Jabone."

Industry night at a nightclub? That seemed like the last place I wanted to go—as bad as attending a Food Studies graduate reception as an anonymous restaurant critic.

"Come on," she implored. "I know I was out of it at Room 113, but . . ." She shrugged and gave me a look that implied Chef Darling had rejuvenated more than just his menu.

I had holed myself up for days already and I could have done that indefinitely. Yet Carey's kind eyes finally convinced me. I could be a pathetic moper, or I could go to Kel Jabone.

"Sure," I said. "I'm in."

Carey looked surprised that I had agreed. I had never taken her up on her invites, but she never gave up on me and I was glad to have someone like that.

I was about to leave when Jake met up with me in the entryway. "Thanks for pinch-hitting with the duck press. That's difficult work, but you did a great job. Sorry about the grease." He gave me a twenty-dollar bill.

"What's this for?"

He looked down at my outfit and for a split second I thought I had worn the wrong thing and he suspected something. But then I saw that the duck fat had soaked through my apron, onto my skirt.

"Dry cleaning." Jake smiled.

Chapter 29

MONDAY NIGHT, I WENT TO CAREY'S APARTMENT ON AVENUE C to pregame. Melinda even joined me. I'd never liked big contrived social events, but dancing I could do.

I still hadn't responded to any of Michael Saltz's emails, even though they bore down on me more with every passing second. A review had come out that I didn't write, so I guessed Michael Saltz had summoned the bullshitting skills he'd used during the three months before he'd found me.

"Hey, guys! Thanks for coming," Carey said as she laid out a plate of cheeses, charcuterie, crudités, and homemade cookies. Romina put Nina Simone on the record player and the wintry late November chill slid off us.

Carey's place was cute and eclectic. She had African baskets in one corner, glass sculptures on her tables, and funny weaving experiments on her coffee table. But the most impressive thing were her bookshelves. She must have had a thousand books in her tiny one-bedroom. I went to inspect them, trying to figure out how they were organized.

"By region, then by time period, then by author last name," she said, barely looking up from the kitchen counter, where she was mashing some berries and mint in our Champagne flutes.

"Ha!" I said. "Of course. Carey . . . you are amazing."

"No, I'm not," she said loading her Champagne concoctions onto a tray she had découpaged, thus negating her insistence about not being amazing.

I tried to get Melinda to come join us on the couches, but she lingered by the windows. She hadn't spoken to anyone, then all of a sudden, as if she had just gotten a phone call or woken up, she turned around and said, "Hey, guys? You guys should go without me. I feel weird since I'm not 'industry.' "

"Are you sure?" Romina asked, nibbling on a lemon-poppy square. "I just got a text from my friend at Hellenica. He's bringing his crew. They're Greek and so gorgeous."

Melinda smiled, but I could tell she was rolling her eyes inside. "I appreciate your invite!" she said in a fake, cheery voice that was patently not Melinda. She was mocking Romina right to her face. "I think I'll sit this one out."

"Okay then," Romina said. "See you later." Carey waved goodbye from the kitchen. Before she slipped out the door in her trench coat dress and red coat, Melinda gave me a pitying look and shrugged. But there was no need—I was having fun.

After another glass of Champagne and ten more bites of Carey's delicious hors d'oeuvres, we made our way to Kel Jabone. I had never once been to a club before but I imagined it as a room packed with beautiful, intimidating glamazons. No thanks.

But here on industry night, there were no glamazons in attendance. Everyone was basically in after-work, comfy-casual clothes. I had heard that Kel Jabone was a pretty hot club, but inside it didn't look like much—basically a black box with low-slung tables and couches, a dance floor, and a DJ booth.

Carey said she didn't like to dance, so Romina and I took to the floor while she hung out with a friend who used to work at Madison Park Tavern, but was now training to be a sommelier. A group of girls and guys who Romina knew joined us, but it was so loud I didn't catch their names or their restaurants.

The DJ was an excellent crowd-pleaser. At first I started with some classic, conservative moves—the shoulder sway, the hands getting into it. And then later in the night, my hips started circling. Jumping was involved. I may have imitated a person putting groceries in her cart, a television news anchor, and a plastic bag blowing in the wind.

I probably looked ridiculous, but it was so silly and fun. The club was now speckled with red and white lights as more people crowded onto the dance floor.

Finally the DJ said he had one more song, and "Sweet Caroline" came over the speakers, a far cry from the hip-hop he had been playing. Romina and I put our arms around each other. Then everyone joined in. Even Carey removed herself from the wall. I threw my Manolo Blahniks underneath a chair and danced barefoot.

There were probably people there who knew about Michael Saltz's mysterious companion. Most definitely people who had been at Room 113 when Felix had caused our quick exit. Maybe some people even knew the exact nature of my relationship with Michael Saltz. I didn't rule anything out.

But I didn't care. I didn't *want* to care. Michael Saltz said he could have destroyed my career if anyone found out about him, but he couldn't destroy this: pure fun with people who liked me for me.

We were all screaming and jumping, and just as I closed my eyes, really getting into the music, I felt a heavy arm around me.

"Oh, hey!" I said.

"Hey there yourself," Kyle Lorimer said. He wasn't wearing plaid or those big, boxy cargo pants I'd seen him in. Tonight, he wore a white button-down and jeans. I started jamming and he joined me with surprising rhythm.

"Ha, you can dance, Kyle Lorimer."

"*Pff,*" he said, and then he busted out this move where he rubbed my shoulders and shimmied down until he was squatting on the floor. It would have been sexy, if he hadn't looked so hilarious doing it.

"Help me up!" he screamed, and when I held out my hand, he pulled me down with him onto the dirty floor. I laughed anyway.

"*Sweet Caroline! Good times never seemed so good!*" he yelled into the air. He was sweaty, but we were all sweaty. He was actually a pretty good singer. We helped each other stand up and then jumped up and down.

"*Oh! Oh! Oh!*"

"That's it, lovers," the DJ said as the song finished. "You guys rock. Be safe, and good night!"

Kyle put his arm around me and I swiveled to look up at him. His touch had startled me, but it wasn't unwelcome, either. "You're a wicked dancer!"

"Wicked?" I laughed. The weight of his arm sank into my shoulder.

"Yeah, yeah. *Pahk* the *cah* and all that," he fake-protested. "I'm from Boston, what do you want from me?"

"You're so *exotic,*" I said.

He batted his eyelashes. "Exotic indeed. My family owns a lobster shack. Lorimer's Lobsters."

"I'm allergic to lobster," I said as a playful dig.

But he didn't get it and looked legitimately concerned. It was kinda cute. "Yeah? Like how allergic?"

"Never mind." I laughed.

At this point, everyone was gathering up their coats and leaving. We were the only ones on the dance floor besides the guy cleaning up the confetti. Kyle had dimples in his big, soft cheeks. I thought he smelled a little like bread. Really good bread.

"Well"—and he hooked his elbow around my neck, whispering to me—"just coleslaw for you, then."

Though the speakers had long gone silent, I could still feel the bass in my bones. My muscles ached. They turned the lights on and we blinked into consciousness. I didn't want to step into the city streets again. I liked this: happiness. No one to fear. No concern for being "made." This night had been so nourishing and real, I didn't want to go back to my paranoid life now. Or really, ever.

I tiptoed to my shoes and coat. Kyle seemed like he wanted to talk to me, but he didn't say anything else.

"Okay, I'll see you?" I said when I was properly bundled.

"Yeah," he said warmly. "Don't be a stranger."

Romina, Carey, and I walked back to Carey's place to have one last drink.

"Tia! You're such a good dancer—like, super sexy," Romina said once we arrived.

I laughed. Yeah, the last time I'd danced with a guy—for a guy—it hadn't turned out so well. But at least this time, I'd remembered everything I loved about moving.

"You're so mysterious," Romina continued. "Like, what's with you and Kyle Lorimer?"

"You know Kyle?" I blurted.

Romina looked at Carey like I was crazy.

Carey saw this as some sort of opportunity and walked me over to her desk. To my surprise, she opened her Wiki, typed "Kyle Lorimer," then walked to her room.

Up popped an entry: *Kyle Lorimer, son of Claire Lorimer, owner of L&O Clam and Lobster. Supplier. PX.*

Kyle was a PX? I had always thought of PXs as demanding bigshots or celebs. But there were also people like Kyle and his family. The restaurant could do without yet another investment banker, but they couldn't do without L&O Clam and Lobster.

Romina was still looking at me expectantly. "So? Tell us what's going on there."

"Um, nothing. He's just a classmate of mine."

Carey came out of her bedroom, already in pajamas and glasses. "Tia's with Pascal Fox," she said while snuggling into the couch and paying no mind to the fact that Romina and I were still very much dressed and awake. "And she's also chatty with Michael Saltz." She lay her head on a cushion and within seconds her curls gave a bounce as she nodded off.

Romina gave me another look and yet again I worried that I had been made. I didn't remember Romina's CTD score, but connecting any dots could have been bad when it came to Pascal Fox and Michael Saltz.

But instead she just laughed. "Carey is so wasted." I laughed along with her, but Carey's words still rang in my ear. *Tia's with Pascal Fox. And she's also chatty with Michael Saltz.*

Those words soured everything that had gone well that night, and I suddenly wished for a total reset on the school year:

Accept the internship.

Wait patiently for Helen.

Make friends.

At one point, that had all sounded so mundane, but now I couldn't think of anything better.

I GOT BACK to my apartment around five A.M. and woke up three hours later to a phone call from Melinda.

"Hey . . . Tia?"

"Hey," I whispered, barely conscious and still very much buzzed. "Did you have a good night?"

"Yeah . . . about that . . ."

The phone went dead silent and I immediately knew something was wrong.

"Melinda? Hey, are you there?"

"Yeah . . ." she said. "I . . . um . . . This is sort of hard for me, so I'm just going to say it."

Someone on the other end of the line—not Melinda—yelled, "Hey, baby! Where did you go?"

Melinda spoke up before I could hear any more. "I've sort of gotten myself in trouble. I need the morning-after pill. The condom broke." Her voice cracked and for a while neither she nor I said anything.

"Of course I'll help you." I tried to stay calm. Someone had to, for Melinda's sake. "Can't you get it at the pharmacy? It's over-the-counter, right?"

"Come with me?"

"Um, okay. Sure," I said, though I never would have pegged Melinda as someone who'd be prudish about emergency contraception.

In the background, I heard that guy's voice again. "Hey! Melissa! Come back to bed, baby."

He didn't even know her name. I understood right away and started putting on my jeans.

Melinda said to me softly, "Can you be ready fast? I'm gonna try to get out of here now. I'll meet you outside the apartment in five minutes."

I SAT ON our steps for five minutes, then ten. The sidewalk was oddly barren—only pigeons and a mother taking her baby out for a morning stroll. Then I saw Melinda walking toward me and I got up to meet her halfway. At first, I spotted her red coat. Then, her trench-coat dress. And finally, her face, wrenching in pain.

"Melinda! Are you okay?"

"Yeah, yeah. I don't want to talk about it yet," she said, shivering and refusing to meet my eyes. "Let's go to the Duane Reade on Tenth, 'kay?"

"Okay," I said. She held me by the shoulder and slipped a couple of times, almost knocking me down. I made sure we steered clear of any newsstands. The *New York Times* masthead just reminded me of Pascal.

I didn't mind taking her to the pharmacy, but I also wondered how things had gone down last night. Even if this was a one-night stand, the guy should have seen how freaked out Melinda was and had the decency to get the pill with her.

Melinda didn't say anything for a while, so I started talking. "Carey's was fun. She and I have been working together for three months, and I've never hung out with her. But I guess I could say she's my best work friend."

"Yeah . . . interesting," Melinda said, staring at her strappy-sandaled feet, blue from the cold.

"And Romina is taking a year off before going to grad school in Brazil. She's studying art restoration. Doesn't that seem cool?" I knew my words meant nothing to her, that I was just spitting them out for the sake of distraction, like music in an elevator. It was uncomfortable to fully realize that. Our empty friendship wasn't something to be proud of. Why did I seek out distance rather than connection?

Melinda stopped in the middle of the sidewalk, right before we reached Duane Reade. Her face was blanched, but her lips were still stained red from her lipstick. "Tia? I'm scared. What if

I'm pregnant?" She sounded like a little girl, not the take-no-shit woman I knew.

"Well, that's why we're getting the pill now." I didn't know the exact mechanics of the morning-after pill, but I knew time was of the essence.

Inside, the pharmacy already had a line: a few elderly men and women, and even two couples, maybe there for the same reason Melinda and I were. One couple was taking it all very seriously and resting their heads on each other somberly. The other couple stood with their eyes averted and arms crossed.

Melinda turned around to leave.

"Hey, what are you doing?"

"Sorry, sorry," she said. She stepped back in line with me but couldn't keep still.

"Tia?" Melinda whispered, not in my ear, but to my shoulder. "Hey, can you get it for me? I can't do this, I'm sorry. I'm freaking out." She scanned the floor, as if she'd lost an earring. "What if someone sees me?" She had a tear in her eye, cradled in the corner.

"Sure, but who's going to see you? And even if they did, they wouldn't know what you were getting."

"Can we go to another pharmacy, somewhere farther from the apartment?"

The line moved forward. "Just wait here. We're almost there, okay?"

"I have a boyfriend," she blurted. "What if he sees me here? In this?" She gestured toward her dress, her high-heeled sandals. "He'd figure it out."

"And the person you were with last night . . . that's not your boyfriend," I said, making sure I'd heard correctly. I meant to say it like a question, but it came out like a statement, flat and disbelieving.

"Yeah. My boyfriend is visiting New York today. Like, now."

"So who were you with?"

"I don't know!" She was already slipping away from the line, but I grabbed her closer. Only one person and one couple stood ahead of us. "I mean, I know, but it's not important."

"Stay with me. It'll be okay," I said. I tried my best not to sound like a disapproving parent. After all, I wasn't much better in the cheating department.

She sulked beside me. I had stepped in a puddle on the way over, and the wetness was creeping up my pants.

"What can I do for you?" the pharmacist asked robotically when we reached the counter.

"I'm here to get the morning-after pill," I said. Then as I reached for my purse, Melinda bolted. If that's how it would be, fine.

I showed the pharmacist my ID and she reached below the counter and handed me a small cardboard box, the size of a deck of cards.

"Twenty bucks," she said. I handed her the money and tucked the box into my purse. I found Melinda by the magazines. She'd already bought a new pair of flip-flops and changed out of her heels.

"Okay, you're all set," I said. "You should take the first pill now."

"Jesus, Tia! Can't you wait until we get outside?"

Once on the sidewalk, the pill calmed her immediately. We walked back to the apartment and Melinda changed into some comfy clothes and took off her makeup while I stood in the doorway. Her phone rang as she was brushing her hair.

"Hey, Adam!" she said. "Yeah, I had a great time. Tia brought me over to meet her work friends, Carey and Romina." She said their names as if reading from a script. Her acting classes were coming in handy.

My stomach soured and I bit my lip. I wanted to be a good friend to Melinda, but I didn't like being complicit in her lie.

"You've never met Tia, but she's great . . . What did you do? Oh? Haha . . . That's funny."

She actually said "haha." She didn't even laugh. I was beginning to feel nauseous.

"Okay, sweetie," she said. "Okay . . . okay! I'll see you soon. I missed you so much!" Then she hung up and heaved a big sigh. "He's so stupid," she said in a voice the exact opposite of the sweet tone she had used on the phone.

She put her hair up in a ponytail and took a picture board out of her closet, propping it up on the floor, next to her air mattress.

The pictures were of Melinda and a guy who looked cheery and high-spirited. In one, they were on some tall building that may or may not have been in New York. Another captured them eating a giant ice cream sundae. There were a couple of different shots showing them having a picnic under an ancient-looking tree.

"How long have you been with this guy?" I asked, again trying to play it cool, to not care one way or the other. The Melinda way.

"Two years?" she said, like all that time was nothing.

"Two years! But you . . . last night . . . and how did I not even know about him? Did he go to school with you in Cleveland?"

"Yeah, he did. He's still there. He'll probably try to convince me to go back with him. It's our *home,*" she said mockingly.

"So . . . you cheat on him . . ."

"Yes."

"And you lie about it?" By now my voice was into full-on what-the-hell-were-you-thinking mode.

". . . Yes."

"And you don't feel bad . . . at all?" I thought back to my time with Pascal in the kitchen. Had I felt bad? No, not really. I could have ignored his texts. Politely excused myself. But I'd let myself get sucked in by his spell, as if the rules of trust and morality hadn't applied with him.

Melinda looked at her photo board. "I guess I feel bad."

My stomach somersaulted and a knot caught in my throat. Melinda had said it so easily, with so little heart. And yet, looking at her now, I knew I couldn't be so haughty. It was fine when Melinda and I were vapid and petty about our lives. No one got hurt.

But the cheating part? I could convince myself that at least I'd actually loved Elliott and that Melinda had probably never given this guy a true chance . . . but what did I know? All I knew was that I had betrayed Elliott's trust and friendship. I had lied to my best friend. Yeah, maybe we weren't meant to be together, but I didn't have to take the low road. Cheating. Lying. Avoiding hard conversation for some cheap thrill. Melinda lived her life on the surface, never getting in too deep with friendships or commitments or passions. At one time, I had liked her shape-shifting nature. But now I could see that you couldn't live life that way. People got hurt. Promises got broken.

Shape-shift enough, and you lose what shape you were in the first place.

I picked up my purse. "I'm gonna go work on a paper now."

"Oh, okay. Let me know if you want me to take a look at it or something." I could tell she was trying. But I didn't want her help. Not now.

"Sure, thanks."

"Okay . . . well, thanks for coming with me today. You're one of the five people in the world who've seen me cry."

I'd barely seen a tear from her, but I wasn't going to point that out. Who was I to lecture her, anyway? Melinda's lies paled in comparison to mine.

"Hey, how much do I owe you?" Melinda asked.

"Don't worry about it," I said. "You don't owe me anything."

Melinda cracked open her sketchbook. She placed her hand on the pages as if pledging an oath. She didn't look back at me.

"I'm not a bad person, just confused. I'll figure it out."

"Yeah," I said. "I know you will." I really hoped she would. I really hoped I would, too.

WHEN I GOT back to my room, all I thought about was starting over. No more lies. No more cheating.

And the first person I needed to talk to was Michael Saltz.

I picked up the phone.

"Tia! Well, well, well. You've come out of the woodwork," Michael Saltz said, surprisingly not angry, and suspiciously cheery. "I'm glad you got a break. Are you okay now?"

His kindness caught me off guard. "Yeah . . ." I said. "I'm okay. But I wanted to ask you about the rest of the year. It'll be spring semester in a month and you haven't told me when I'll be transitioning to Helen."

"Oh, yes. Of course. First, I want you to know I wholly appreciate what you're doing, Tia. I suppose I don't tell you that enough. The Bakushan review went over so well. Everyone loves a new four-star. I do hope you realize how grateful I am."

"Okay, thanks," I said, glossing over the review I was trying to forget. "And . . . Helen?" I wanted him to address my concern, not stroke my ego.

Michael Saltz laughed uncertainly. "Yes, yes, my dear, I've already spoken to Helen on your behalf and . . . uh . . . she's very excited about working with you next year."

But what was that in his voice? Just a couple of months ago, he had said those words with such confidence. But now . . . was it hesitation? Or maybe that was just me. Maybe his tone hadn't changed—maybe my outlook had.

"So, do I start with her right after your surgery?"

"Yes, after the surgery. In the interim, she wants you to read up on different kinds of flours and ancient grains." I heard nothing on his end of the line, not him fidgeting with some jar, no sounds of feet on kitchen tile, no refrigerator opening. Not even breathing.

I tried to steady myself. The grains homework fit with what I'd gleaned from peeking in Kyle's grocery bag. Everything seemed plausible and legitimate. This was good. Something stable I could look forward to.

"Just four or five months," he said.

"No way," I shot back. "Four or five months? It'll be December in a couple days. You said it would start in the spring semester. I.e., in a little over a month." Of course. Nothing was ever straightforward with this man.

"Patience!" Michael Saltz said, and this time his voice was much stronger. "You know that Helen's time is valuable. You're a student, for god's sake!"

"Why are you talking about this in terms of school? I *thought* this was outside of that. Remember, grad school is for amateurs? You wanted me to quit Madison Park Tavern so I could embark on this very special, very elite program of yours?"

Michael Saltz didn't hesitate now. "I'm not talking about *grad school.* I'm talking about working within the confines of your life, my life, and Helen's life. I'm asking her to carve out special time for you, and that simply won't happen until the summer. That's when she does all of her best work, anyway, and she's even said that if you're as good as I've *insisted* you are, she will consider keeping you on indefinitely. This is your chance, Tia, and I want to give it to you. Except I need you in the short term. The FDA has approved the surgery and my doctors have given me the go-ahead. My surgery is scheduled for February fifteenth, and as I've told you, it's a complex recovery. I'll require a cushion of several months before I can return to work in full force. I'd like you to do this for me out of compassion and charity. My professional standing—my life—is at stake here."

I saw his point. Sometimes these things took time. But could I do this longer? More clothes, more dinners, more lies? Could I survive another Pascal? Would I even see the warning signs if someone like him came up to me and said the same things, touched me in the same way?

Call it desperation, inertia, or willful ignorance, but I decided I'd do it. I'd last.

There was a light at the end of the tunnel. A far-off flicker, for sure, but I couldn't bear to let it go. I had lost my boyfriend and been used by a celebrity chef. I had missed the little parts of graduate life and my internship that I could never, ever regain. But something in me told me to keep going.

I hadn't learned that much from my college econ class, but I remembered what sunk costs were. All that was in the past. As long as the future with Michael Saltz stayed relatively bright, then I should keep on going.

If restaurateurs knew who I was, then I'd apply more makeup and wear different clothes. If I wanted my words in the paper and later my name on the cover of Helen's book, then I'd have to write more. If I wanted Helen, then I'd have to bear through this.

As for my broken heart, there wasn't much I could do about that besides file it away as another casualty.

"Okay," I said finally. "I'll work with you until the summer."

"Wonderful," he replied. "I'll be in touch after the holiday."

I made some vague sound of agreement, but I didn't feel good at all. At least I had Thanksgiving to clear my head.

Chapter 30

I WALKED HOME FROM THE TRAIN STATION WITH ONE SMALL duffel bag filled with normal clothes that I'd had to dig out. Bergdorf clothes were most definitely not an option.

Mom answered the door. "Tia! Happy Thanksgiving!" She wore an apron, sweatpants, and just a T-shirt, even though it was freezing that day. "Gotta go, I've got some lotus root that's almost done frying!"

I walked in and almost broke down in tears. Everything was as I had left it. I hadn't been home since the summer, but now that I was back, I realized how much I was missing, how much of me I was pushing away.

There were the Chinese embroidered silks, Grandpa's Senegalese statues, and Mom's curious multimedia artwork. But the smells did me in. On top, notes of brightness—scallions, lemongrass, ginger. Underneath, a blend of musty flavors—dried mushrooms and smoked peppers. Then, something that came from Mom's frying pan, that caramelized sweet meatiness, and the character of whatever was in Dad's broth on the stovetop, chicken and carrots and roots and sticks and pods.

Most people do the turkey and mashed potatoes thing for Thanksgiving, but why bother when you can have something so much better?

Grandma sat at the dining room table peeling knobby Jerusalem artichokes. They were so fresh and crisp, I heard the brown hairy outside separating from the flesh, a sound like paper ripping. Mom stirred her wok while Dad walked around the kitchen, opening cabinets to see what other weird things he could throw into his pot. He loved being the unexpected, underestimated white guy.

I'd always been impressed with Mom's kitchen choreography. She never used cookbooks, yet moved with purpose. If she was sick and I replicated her meals, it always took me twice as long and the dishes had none of Mom's depth.

Mom was an O.R. nurse who had long, hard days with sometimes no thanks. So at home, Dad treated her like a queen. If she wanted to cook, he played sous chef. If she preferred to make art, he'd get her the necessary supplies, and then some. If she needed a pick-me-up, he'd cook lavish, adoring meals that were indeed better than any restaurant around.

Being an only child, I'd sometimes felt oppressed by their love, but now I could see it for what it was: rare and real. I could do a lot worse than look to them as a model.

Dad nudged me on the shoulder. "Come on, are you going to help?" I jumped into the action with no further instruction.

We started eating while the turkey finished resting, so the juices that had rushed to the inside could seep their way back out. First came a foie gras chunk with the clear layer of fat still on top. Mom usually took the fat off and saved it for frying other things, but she had left it on this time because it was a special occasion. We also had cold salmon, which Dad had cured in sugar, salt, and caraway seeds.

Mom was looking older than usual. Her eyes, usually sparkling and curious, were now a little more downcast. Her shiny loose ringlets had gone frizzy and dry and she spoke with 90 percent of her regular energy. Dad of course tried to compensate, booming about certain ingredients and some of the happenings around Yonkers. But he, too, looked older. He had stopped shaving his head and now you could see the deep retreat of his gray hairline.

I tried to avoid talk of NYU, and thankfully they didn't seem to notice. I didn't want to stress them out.

After we finished our appetizers, Mom came out with the turkey, and our version of stuffing: saffron-scented rice, dried fish, pickled radish, toasted peanuts, scallions, and a poached egg on top for good measure. Grandma butchered the bird tableside with a huge meat cleaver that had been around for as long as I'd been alive. Dad scooped some roasted yucca mash onto his plate. I served myself steamed skate with ginger and soy.

They were pulling out all the stops for me. I had come home for Thanksgiving during college, but always arrived at the last minute and left as early as possible. After Grandpa died and my column picked up, I'd felt like I had to be around for the paper and school and Elliott.

But none of that had gotten me anywhere. I should have come home more often.

By the time dessert came around, I was fuller than I had been in a long time, even considering all those multicourse dinners with Michael Saltz. But this food was clean and familiar, and I couldn't get enough.

DAD KNOCKED ON the door as I was getting ready for bed.

"Hey, Dad," I said from underneath the covers. "I'm so full. I missed home cooking."

"Well, I've told you a million times that there's plenty of food for you here," Dad said, coming in and settling on the chair next to my bed. "We're just a short train ride away."

I groaned good-naturedly and cuddled even deeper inside the blankets.

"But that's not what I want to chat about."

"Oh?" I asked, too stuffed to question his motives.

"I wanted to check in about school. How's it going for you?"

"Oh, it's okay," I said, trying to emulate the hundreds of times I had said that before.

"Well . . ." he replied. "I want to say that I'm proud of you." He looked up at a framed newspaper clipping on the wall, my Dacquoise Drops on the front page of the *New York Times* Food section. "But I'm surprised you haven't told us more about it. Are you happy?"

He had no idea that I was on the verge of losing my scholarship and that my chance to work with Helen—my guiding star—was now buried under some nasty complications.

Outside it had just started snowing, a pristine suburban snow that didn't turn black the second it hit the ground.

"Okay, I'll let you rest," he said when I didn't answer.

I wondered what he saw when he looked at me. Based on the way he was talking to me, I knew he couldn't have known anything. Dad would've wanted to rescue me from Michael Saltz and his shifty talk. He'd want to separate me from Melinda and kill Pascal. He didn't know the people or the facts, but he was my dad. And the longer I lay there and looked out the window, the more I could tell he was looking into my heart, the same way he had for the past twenty-two years.

In my mind, I told him. *I had my heart broken. I'm confused. I feel trapped. I thought I was gaining power, but now I feel powerless.*

We sighed in sync, and as if he had heard every word, Dad

leaned down and broke the spell. "Mom and I love you no matter what."

"I just . . . don't want to mess up anymore," I said, apropos of nothing that had been said and everything that wasn't.

"There are no mess-ups. Only opportunities to do better."

"Thanks, Dad," I said, holding back my tears.

"Of course, Tia," he said. "I love you."

THE NEXT MORNING over breakfast, I asked Mom a question that had never even popped into my head until last night. Mom's cases were in pediatrics—which was definitely different from taste-correcting brain surgery—but, who knew, maybe she'd have something to say about this new suspicion.

"Hey, Mom? How long does the FDA take to approve surgeries?"

She looked up from her newspaper. "Surgery? FDA stands for Food and Drug Administration. They regulate medication, not approve surgeries." Then she took a sip of coffee.

And I lost it.

How could I have been so stupid?

Chapter 31

THE SECOND I GOT BACK TO NEW YORK, I CALLED MICHAEL Saltz and told him I needed to see him. He suggested we meet up on Saturday at Bay Derby, which I assumed was up for review. He even gave me the whole pre-review spiel: the chef was Zinc Varley, he had five other restaurants in San Francisco, this was his only place in New York City. I asked to move the dinner to Tuesday, when I knew the restaurant would be quieter.

I would play along for the time being, but my days of doing his work were over.

It all made awful sense. Maybe a couple of months ago I would have made excuses for him. Perhaps he'd misheard a doctor, or the FDA had some covert surgery division. But I wasn't that naïve anymore. All those sleepless nights spent researching restaurants, not once had I ever thought to google taste-correcting surgery. It had taken two seconds to see that New York–Presbyterian had stopped their experimental trials a year ago. Apparently the early patients suffered a drastically increased risk of schizophrenia. I also learned that taste-correcting surgery was widely considered to be bad science, likened to crude and cruel lobotomies.

Then I emailed Kyle Lorimer.

> Hey—good to see you the other night! I totally forgot to ask you at Kel Jabone, but do you know when Helen will take on new interns?

Kyle got back to me right away.

> Hey there, dancing machine. No interns for the rest of the year. We're wrapping up some things before Christmas, and then she's off to Paris for the spring and summer. That's where she's doing more cookbook research and testing.

Helen had never been a possibility, spring or summer. The surgery was never in the cards. I half expected the clothes in my closet to disintegrate into ash.

My anger burned up so much that my whole body shook. I knew Michael Saltz was unreliable, but I had never suspected anything on this scale. Though if there was one thing I had learned from him, it was the capacity to lie when the situation demanded it. My ignorance would end here. Starting with this dinner.

On Tuesday, once again, I transformed myself.

I knew my picture had been circulating, but it was of me at Panh Ho, wearing my first designer dress and stumbling in my new heels.

I put on a white knit Chanel dress, black knee-high boots, and the New York woman's armor—a black leather jacket. I crowned the whole thing with a flawless chin-length wig and a pair of German eyeglasses that looked like tortoiseshell but were made of a metal reserved for spacecraft. I had erased myself.

When I arrived at the restaurant, Michael Saltz was already seated, munching on something fried. The waitstaff snapped their heads toward me. Did they already know who I was? I immediately regretted coming and yet the sight of Michael Saltz smugly chomping away revved me up again.

"There you are!" he said, mid-munch. "The evasive Tia Monroe shows her face."

"*Shh!*" I said, not wanting anyone to hear my name. I pushed my wig in front of my eyes. Even though I cared little about Michael Saltz's anonymity anymore, I still needed to stay discreet for the next phase of my plan.

I put my phone on the table and eased in. Busboys squeezed behind me; the kitchen's steam and smoke filled my lungs. A table of frat-boys-cum-bankers toasted with tall glasses of beer. I ordered a Cabernet from our handsome waiter and forced myself to look Michael Saltz in the eyes.

"Here," he said. "Try one of these." He handed me a wrinkled deep-fried clam.

"Bivalves? Remember?" I said.

"Oh, yes. Sorry." He could hardly keep his hand out of the red plastic bowl, the type you get at roadside New England fry houses.

"These clam strips," he said between chomps. "You're missing out." I had never seen him eat with so much enthusiasm. "The batter is perfection. It's a panko beer crumb with a double pancake batter! Do you know how I know that?"

One of the frat-boy-bankers ordered another round of beer, and the guys cheered, filling the restaurant with their voices. I pushed my phone closer to Michael Saltz.

"Why do you know about the batter? Did you ask a twenty-two-year-old girl?"

"No!" Michael Saltz said, brushing my comment aside. "I tasted it."

"Your taste is back?" Relief instantly, instinctually, washed over me.

"Well," he elaborated. "Not like that. It's the texture. It's as forceful as a flavor."

I took another sip of wine as our waiter approached. So his taste hadn't returned. But that was okay. Better, in fact, for my plan.

"I already ordered the whole menu," Michael Saltz said.

"But I can't eat some of these shellfish courses."

"Oh, yes, I always forget about that allergy."

After the scare at Le Brittane, you'd think the knowledge would have been seared into his mind. But of course he wouldn't remember it. I was just a disposable pawn in his plan. *Who cares if you lose Tia to a deadly allergic reaction?* There were plenty of others who'd take my place.

"We'll have the waiter identify them," he said. "I have a good feeling about this place." He took a deep breath, as if he were at the top of a mountain and Bay Derby's smoky, garlicky air was invigorating his very being.

"Right," I said, rolling my eyes. "Maybe I should write the whole review right here on the spot. Without tasting a thing. Just like you."

"Tia, watch yourself."

The wine rushed to my head. "Why bother eating anything? I'm better off without all the calories," I growled. "Let's see . . . *The crab cakes offer a luscious bite of the seashore, a satisfying blend of citified grade-A sophistication and down-home buttery crumb . . . the goat meat and goat cheese ravioli is a rustic, sloppy dish with a papery-thin dough encasing a burst of savory decadence."*

"Tia, I'm warning you."

"No, really, Michael, I can write these in my sleep." Rage bubbled up inside me and my volume rose. "It's a fun game. You can play along, too! *The foie gras, flown in from Marin Cress, the famously sustainable farm in Sonoma, had piercing earthy undertones, but a grainy texture I found off-putting . . . the quail with rosemary and red grapes felt like supper in some Tuscan wonderland, though the bird would have benefited from a couple more days on the feedlot to fatten itself up."* My voice carried through the restaurant and now I knew for sure that the staff was looking at me, my face wide open for everyone to see.

"Tia, please."

"It's all bullshit," I said. I glared at him, but he looked at me with such horror I had to look away. "You must think so, too, if you wrote reviews for so long with a dead, burnt-out palate."

"Shut up, will you?" he said. "What's gotten into you?"

He still wasn't giving me what I wanted. I kept silent and thought as the waiter brought us our meal, dishes upon dishes, like some gag assembly line where the food just doesn't stop: oysters with five mignonette sauces, the crab cakes, rabbit sausage with kale chips, goat ravioli, chicken under a brick with warm bread and dandelion salad, a strip steak with horseradish-scallion mousse, grouper with carrot and pine nut risotto, pork shoulder with a caramelized potato and apple galette, and finally a bowl of classic San Francisco cioppino, a rustic seafood soup.

When the waiter left, I went on the offensive again. "Tell me the truth—is this surgery ever happening?"

Michael Saltz furrowed his brow and took a sip of his wine. "Why would you ask such a thing? You know it is."

"I saw that New York–Presbyterian canceled their experimental trials a year ago. Were you planning on stringing me along forever or just dumping me on the side of the road?"

"Tia!" He kept shaking his head, confused, even aggrieved by my accusation. But I didn't back down.

"I don't know the whole story, but I know you've been lying. The FDA has nothing to do with experimental surgeries."

Michael Saltz put his hands in front of him, as if I would flip the table on top of him. But he didn't have to worry about physical assault. I'd flip the tables another way.

"Now, Tia. Please don't get ahead of yourself. There's an explanation. You are . . . not incorrect about New York–Presbyterian. But experimental surgeries aren't like haircuts. You can't walk in, pick from a celebrity gossip magazine, and get one. So, yes, there have been bureaucratic complications. And, yes, I haven't been totally honest with you. I'm rather embarrassed that I cited the wrong government agency. But . . . well, I suppose this is as good a time as any to tell you."

Michael Saltz pushed the bowl of cioppino toward me. "Can you try a bit of this? Here, I'll take out the shellfish."

"I asked you about your surgery, and now you're giving me soup you know I'm allergic to?"

"Tia, please. You would help me immensely."

I crossed my arms and leaned back in my seat. His face had gone pale and his eyes—normally beady, precise—were big and mournful.

"We will review this place," he said, "but I also brought you here for a personal visit . . . as a friend."

"Personal how?"

Michael Saltz sighed. "This cioppino was my last meal before I lost my sense of taste. I was sitting in that back booth over there. Every now and again, I still experience the phantom taste of it. It's true that the New York–Presbyterian trial suffered setbacks, but I have five other hospitals I'm talking to. Just a couple more months of this charade. Think about how much you want me to get this surgery, how that will help you start your life. Now think about me. You're not the only one who wants to start their life, Tia. We're on the same team. Yes, once in a while I might *lie.* There might be *secrets.* The world runs on secrets, and the sooner you understand that, the better. Your writing—*our* writing—is essential to New York. You go to any restaurant and ask them—would you rather the *New York Times* come to your restaurant and judge you anonymously, or would you rather be passed over—neither forgotten nor known, but never was?"

I stammered for an answer. I hadn't made a career out of secrecy and I obviously couldn't weave in and out of the shadows like he could. But I also didn't want to.

He pushed the bowl closer to me. I eyed it but kept my hands on my lap.

Just a little more information. I already had enough for my other purpose, but this I wanted to hear for myself.

"Answer one question and I'll taste the soup for you," I said.

"Okay, you taste the soup and then I'll tell you what you want."

"No," I said. "You answer me first."

". . . Or what?" Michael Saltz said.

My nerves picked up. I wasn't as sneaky as Michael Saltz. Lying would never be second nature to me, and for that I was grateful. I wouldn't take him down with lies—the truth was better.

"Or nothing," I fake-demurred. "It's an easy question. Did you ever talk to Helen about my interning with her?" I asked.

"Tia, of course I've spoken to her. I told you I'm a man of my word." He sighed, and I assumed he was happy that he could just flick my question away, but he was too skilled to show any triumph.

"And she knows that I'm supposed to work with her this summer?"

". . . Yes," he said. "That's exactly what I said."

"But she's going to be in Paris." Then I stood up and leaned over the table, my face a foot away from his. "You're full of shit."

And now—finally—I saw panic on his face. The moment when he realized that he couldn't stay two steps ahead of me. That I had caught up and wouldn't back down.

"Well . . . she is a busy woman. These things take finesse. I was meaning to email her about it."

I wanted to spit in his face. I wanted to swipe every one of these plates onto the floor.

"You lied. She was never planning to be in New York in the spring *or* in the summer. You probably never even gave her my essay. You probably made sure I was placed at Madison Park Tavern so you could corner and con me."

He pursed his lips and sat up in his chair. "I planned to do it soon enough, Tia. I would have made it happen given enough time."

"You *robbed* me," I said, disgusted.

"I gave you all the food, those clothes, an opportunity of a lifetime."

"You gave me misery! I don't even know who I am anymore!"

"I will admit to manipulating you. But you must own that you wanted this for yourself."

"What are you talking about?"

"Come now, Tia. You wanted the power."

"No, I didn't," I said. "And I never wanted to lie."

"Maybe not. But you *loved* taking restaurants down. Madison Park Tavern. Le Brittane . . . you did it without flinching. And you loved bringing them up. Bakushan?"

Just hearing the name sent me backward into my chair.

"You cannot tell me that you didn't like benefiting from that, too."

I realized with a sting that what he said was all true. I sat and thought and started idly spooning the cioppino, letting the broth's scent fill my nose, a rich tomato infused with fish and shellfish, salt and seaweed. I imagined what it would be like to have this as my last meal, an ocean of bloodred soup, vast and complete and deep.

I could have tasted it, as he had asked. Part of me wanted to. I could've cleansed myself of every awful and fraudulent thing I'd done over the last few months. Tasting this soup would've destroyed me, and that's what I thought I deserved. I could gulp the cioppino until that point where consumption was no longer about pleasure but about filling your belly and thumbing your nose at hunger, as if it was some childhood lisp, some mean friend, some sadness that thought it could get the best of you.

"So there, Tia Monroe. No secrets. We're truly on the same team."

But we were never on the same team. Not now, not ever.

I put the spoon down, picked up my phone, and got up from my chair.

"Where are you going?" he said, standing up. "Did someone call?"

"Yes," I said, then showed him the screen. The last forty-five minutes, recorded and still going.

"Our lovely conversation has been uploaded into the cloud, out of your reach no matter how hard you try, or whatever bullshit you spew."

Then I walked out, leaving Michael Saltz slack-jawed at the table.

I WENT STRAIGHT home, closed my bedroom door, and listened to the entire conversation. Some parts were hard to hear, but the story line was intact.

Journalistic fraud. Exploiting and intimidating a young

woman. Even insisting she eat a dish he knew she was very much allergic to. That one was a bonus.

I edited out my name and everything about Helen. I was just a female voice, a nobody, but Michael Saltz's arrogant lisp came in loud and clear.

This was nothing like sending my reviews to Michael Saltz. This wouldn't go out to the entire globe. The recording had no sense of art, and in fact was rather disturbing to listen to. But Carey's Wiki reached the right people and I knew this news would ignite their world.

I titled the entry: *Michael Saltz exposed as fraud, using young woman as ghostwriter for three months.*

I wrote an overview, so people could make sense of the conversation more easily. As further evidence, I also included screenshots of the reviews I'd fed to Michael Saltz, with my name and email blocked out. I signed it "Guest 59."

Finally, I uploaded the file.

I wanted to bring Michael Saltz down without taking myself with him. I had a name to protect and to build. Though there was a chance that Felix or someone else would reveal me, I hoped that Michael Saltz would be destroyed before that happened. He could try to bring me down, but who would listen to him or take his side when he himself had disrespected his craft and his peers so egregiously? That's what I kept in my head as I pressed Publish.

I kept waiting for freedom to wash over me, but it never did. Like always, I had sent my words into the world and all I could do was wait and wonder if people would believe me, if I had cut to the bone of truth.

Chapter 32

By the next day, the news had gone viral. Really viral.

Based on what I could see, first a couple of waiters tweeted something about it. Something to the effect of: *What the fuck?*

Then more people tweeted. *Grub Street* picked it up first, but just a couple of minutes before *Eater.* By ten thirty a.m., the *New York Times* had issued a curt, inscrutable tweet: "Since 1851, our number one priority has been journalistic integrity."

Other national newspapers jumped on it next.

From the *Washington Post:* SECRETLY HANDICAPPED *NEW YORK TIMES* RESTAURANT REVIEWER CAUGHT IN EXPLOITATION SCANDAL.

From the *L.A. Times:* INTERNET RECORDING SUGGESTS MICHAEL SALTZ, *NEW YORK TIMES* RESTAURANT CRITIC, FALSIFIED 6 MONTHS OF REVIEWS.

From the *Boston Globe: NEW YORK TIMES* REVIEWER DISGRACED AFTER LEAKED RECORDING ON INDUSTRY WEBSITE.

As an admin, I could also see that the Wiki's traffic had spiked to ten thousand unique views, fifty times what it normally received.

Yet no one had come close to guessing that I was Guest 59. Thankfully, my payback had been bloodless and quiet. I got no phone calls or texts or emails for the first half of the day.

I imagined Michael Saltz in his apartment, watching everything escalate. Him and his jars and his one coaster and his huge dining room table with every chair but one buried under a pile of books. Why had I thought following Michael Saltz would lead me to the life I wanted? Thinking about his apartment, that life was everything I feared.

I wanted to call Carey, but figured it was better to wait, to pretend I was just as surprised as everyone else. But I didn't have to wait long. She called me around noon, right as I stepped out of class.

"Hey," she said. "Do you have a sec?"

"Yeah . . ." I thought she'd be excited that her Wiki had made it into the mainstream. But instead, her voice was strangely level. "I guess you've heard about Michael Saltz?"

I could hear her take a breath. "Yeah. I have. I'm at the restaurant now and Jake wants you to come by. Michael Saltz is here." Then she hung up.

I WAS THERE in less than ten minutes, checking my phone every couple of seconds for new articles about the revelation, but they had slowed down.

The lunch crowd at Madison Park Tavern was still going strong, a mix of early Christmas tourists and businesspeople taking extra-long meals in the wintry chill.

So Michael Saltz wanted to meet in person. Maybe he was

afraid of emailing or calling me. Smart. I knew he'd want to intimidate me, to tell me I was done for, but so far only he had suffered, not me.

I saw him sitting at the bar, drinking a martini. No one would have suspected that he was a man at the edge of his demise. In fact, he looked downright cheery and I hated him more for that. When could I actually be rid of this man?

I took the seat next to him and saw Carey and Jake from the corner of my eye.

Michael Saltz took another sip of his martini, then slowly lowered it down to the bar.

"Tia . . ." he said, still looking forward at the bar and not at me.

"Michael . . ." I was glad we were in a public place now. No more clandestine conversations, no more hiding our identities.

We sat there for two more minutes while my mind raced. Was he losing his mind? Would he lash out at any second? I had come in thinking that this would be our showdown, and yet he had barely looked at me.

Nearby, Angel was giving me looks like, *If he does anything, you just holler.* Jake and Carey were circling around us.

Finally, I spoke up. "Michael . . . why did you ask me here? I'm done with you . . . with this." I moved my hand in the space between us.

He turned his head and seemed to let the thoughts in his head boil over. "You silly, stupid girl. The recording was a waste of your time. The *New York Times* is never going to fire me based on some anonymous posting on some no-name website." In this beautiful bustling room, his words oozed like venom.

He wasn't bothering to take me down because he didn't think I was a threat. I loathed his egotism, that he was so sure he was above justice.

"You missed out on your one chance. You had it so good with

me and you ruined it. And now you'll never get Helen. You'll never make it in this industry. Done before you even started. I'd say it was tragic, but you deserve it. Good-bye, Tia. Good luck getting on without me."

He downed the rest of the martini and got up from his seat. "I'll leave you the bill. God knows you owe me." He put on his cashmere coat and swaggered away.

I sat at the bar, frozen.

Angel ran over first, then Carey, then Jake.

"What did he say?"

"What did he want?"

"Are you okay?"

I came to the sickening realization that he was probably right. Who would side with the anonymous Guest 59? Sure, some people knew about me and my "special relationship" with Michael, but they didn't know the exact nature, and even if they did, would they risk coming out against the most powerful man in NYC food?

Restaurants were a world of PXs and status codes, rooms where your worth was explicitly mapped in seatings and servings. I had seen disgusting, terrible men being treated with the utmost respect at Madison Park Tavern. Who was I kidding? Restaurants didn't care about character or even truth. They cared about influence. And by that score, it was no contest. The press may have jumped at the story, but at the end of the day, he was still the powerful man; I was the "silly girl," that "ignorant slut."

I racked my brain for ways I could double down. Maybe send something to his editors? Or stake him out at a new restaurant with his inevitable new "protégée"? Or maybe I could work for him again, and take him down from the inside? I'd build up more evidence and post it online. I'd have to live in the shadows again.

Or perhaps I could let him win. What good would it do me to speak up? He'd just deny it and drill me into the ground.

"Listen," Carey said. "Let's just get this out in the open. We know you were the one who posted that recording on the Wiki."

Of course she would know. I felt a surge of resistance, but before I could make any excuses for myself, Carey spoke up again. "I own the site and know who posts what."

Jake stepped closer. "And this morning, I checked Michael Saltz's bill. I saw that he didn't order the pork with ras el hanout, as he had said in the review. Is that what you were talking about in the basement?"

I clenched my jaw and instinctively wanted to deny everything. I had been doing it for so long, thinking that playing dumb and keeping silent would protect me.

"*You must be incognito, discreet.*" The words panged in my head.

But if I didn't come clean now, with people who were offering compassion—and maybe even understanding—then when would I? I didn't want to be alone anymore.

I had to accept their help, but before that, I had to accept that I had failed, too. Lied, cheated, deceived. I had done it all and I had to own up to it. I didn't want to drag myself and my name into this, but if I wanted to bring him down, I had to take the stand.

"Yes," I confessed, feeling my body rebelling against my words. "I was the one who loaded that recording on the Wiki. And I spoke to Michael Saltz about his dinner. It started off innocently. He asked me what I thought of some dishes. I never should have told him—"

Jake stopped me right there. "You're entitled to your opinions, though I wish you had channeled them differently. But let's focus on Michael Saltz, the real bad guy here."

Angel crossed his hands over his chest and said, "He's not

the only bad one. Today I heard what happened at Room 113. I wasn't sure what to think of it, but now it's clear. I always thought Chef Pascal was an upstanding man, but not anymore."

I heaved and tried to control my shaking body. Lunch service was getting a bit sloppy. People were sitting up from their chairs, looking for help. People were standing in the foyer, waiting for tables. And yet Carey, Jake, and Angel stayed with me.

I had been "made," and it felt great.

I looked them each in the eyes, wondering how I could thank them for believing in me and sticking up for me, even when I'd done Madison Park Tavern harm.

In his expert maître d' way, Jake read my mind.

"I know you're no angel," he said. "I cannot fathom the lies you had to tell to get in this position. But I'm sure you've paid the price personally and we all agree . . ."

Carey grabbed Angel's sleeve so we all stood in one tight circle. "We all deserve second chances," she said with a swift and certain nod.

"Right," Jake said, smiling. "And now we'll help you get yours."

"A second chance?" I asked, bewildered. That was the best I could have asked for. A do-over.

Jake pressed his palms together. "Yes. Come back in an hour so we can finish up lunch service. And then it's on."

That gave me just enough time to talk to one more person who I thought could help. I rushed back to the apartment, and thankfully, Emerald was there.

"Hey," I said, catching my breath.

"Hey," she said curiously, because we still weren't quite sure how to interact with each other after her confession about her mother.

"Emerald . . . I need to tell you something."

I told her everything. My heart beat faster after every sentence.

Showing her myself wasn't easy—I cringed at every word—but I wanted to do it.

I had never spoken so much to Emerald. She stayed quiet until I finally said, "And I'm sorry our friendship got off on the wrong foot. I'm glad you were a good friend to Elliott. Better than I was. Can we give us another shot?"

Emerald chuckled darkly, and I realized that maybe the friendship boat had already passed us by. "It's funny," she said. "I've thought about why we were never friends, even after you found out about my family. People think secrets bring them together, like they've made some sort of promise to one another. But that's not true, is it?"

"Yeah," I said, staring at the wall. "I guess not." I tried to smile, but it was hard in the face of rejection. "Okay, see you later, then," I said, sorry and resigned. I couldn't blame her for not wanting to get involved.

I turned around to go back to the restaurant, then felt a tap on my shoulder. I turned into Emerald's hug. For a split second, I resisted. But then I couldn't hold it anymore.

I hugged her back and started to cry, not individual tears but a steady sheet that washed everything away.

"You'll be okay," she said, and her voice was that same Emerald honey, soothing and sweet. "I'll help you out because I know how it is. You think you're the one who keeps the secret, but really it's the secret that keeps you."

Chapter 33

After some planning, Jake, Carey, Angel, Emerald, and I went to the *New York Times* office the next Monday. Jake had a connection to the food editor, Jay Garvey, and all he needed to say was that he had information about the Michael Saltz incident.

Jay took our meeting right away. I had never stepped inside the *New York Times* building, and as I walked through the doors, I felt my college self clinging to every wonder: the bold *New York Times* logo over the front desk, the hallway lined with more than five hundred little screens displaying snippets of the day's news. My heart gripped itself just as it had when I'd first seen my name on the front page of the Food section almost three years ago.

We rode the elevator to the sixth floor, where the Food, Home, and Style sections had their offices. I saw cubicles filled with nothing but pillows, candles, and huge coffee table books. Over on the left, a team of stylish, animated people argued over a fashion spread.

Jake led the way to Jay Garvey's office. He had floor-to-ceiling windows that made it seem like you could walk right into the air. You were at the perfect height for Times Square: close enough to see people's faces, and yet far enough to view the patterns in their movements.

We sat and I briefly introduced myself and explained my relationship to Michael Saltz. I said that I was Guest 59.

Jake spoke about how odd it was that I had been placed in the Madison Park Tavern NYU internship. I had expressed no interest in it, and so many others had. After discussing with Dean Chang, he believed Michael Saltz had altered and resubmitted my application materials under a false email address so I'd be placed there and he could "accidentally" bump into me. Then, he described the basement tapes and the wrong pork, how the restaurant didn't get a fair review. He didn't say it explicitly, but he implied that the *New York Times* had already lost some credibility among restaurateurs. If they didn't take action against Michael Saltz, they'd lose it all.

Then Carey explained her Wiki and showed a graph of Michael's irregular patterns. Usually critics wouldn't select a restaurant that had been reviewed in the last four years, but Michael Saltz did, likely because he was relying on his previous visits. She had also asked for private Wiki access to all the restaurants reviewed by Michael Saltz in the past eight months. Besides Bakushan, every single restaurant surmised they had only served Michael Saltz once—a clear departure from previous critics, who would each go at least three times in order to deliver a well-considered review. The *Times* hadn't seen the clues in his expense reports, but Carey's data didn't lie.

Angel spoke of the stories circulating about Room 113, where a waiter had turned on me and called me—he said this in a whisper—a slut. A pocket of the industry already knew that Michael Saltz had a female companion. Some, like Pascal and

Felix, had attempted underhanded means to use that to their advantage. But as Angel said, restaurant people protect their own, and that's exactly what he was doing.

Finally, Emerald spoke up. She talked about seeing me with a personal shopper at Bergdorf Goodman, after she had personally witnessed my nonexistent fashion IQ at Trina. She said when we had first corresponded, I was cheery and bright, but once I moved to New York, I had gotten furtive, holing myself up deep into the night, disappearing without telling anyone where I went. She said my ex-boyfriend Elliott used to call her to find out where I was and she'd never known what to say.

I looked at everyone as they spoke about me. Flickers of pride and shame and embarrassment flashed inside me, but I tried not to flinch.

Jay listened to everything with little reaction: a true unbiased newsman. He was a tall, middle-aged man with thick, wavy blond hair. He wore a stiff powder-blue dress shirt, opened at the collar and at the sleeves. The light from outside gave him a golden glow, and he looked like a decent family man, the opposite of Michael Saltz.

Everything Jake, Carey, Angel, and Emerald had said was true. A painful, blinding truth that humiliated and condemned me. But my heart was filled with gratitude and love. Michael Saltz could never bring me down, not when I had friends like these.

"Mr. Garvey," I said finally, "that's my story."

He shook his head. "Okay, thank you all for coming. I'll need to process this, but I'll be in touch if I have questions."

We thanked him and put on our coats, but not before Jay asked me one last question. He had just heard the story from every angle, from a range of trustworthy people, but he questioned one small detail.

"Why did you call yourself Guest 59? Why not 'Jane Doe'?"

I did it, of course, because Elliott had once told me fifty-nine reasons he loved me, and I had given him fifty-nine reasons back. It was a real number, solid and true.

If things had turned out differently, he would have been here at the *New York Times* office with all of us. But I had betrayed him—plain and simple. Not because I was tricked or intimidated. I did it on my own. It was my way of having him there: his love and his support, his essential *Elliottness*.

"Oh, no reason," I said. Some things were better kept private.

Chapter 34

FIVE MONTHS LATER, I WAS STILL WORKING IN A RESTAURANT.

"Right this way, sir," I said to a man standing in line at Reststop. He slung his tweed jacket over his arm. It was too warm and beautiful a day for cold-weather fabrics. Memorial Day had just passed and the wait for brunch was more than an hour and a half. Brooklyn had officially shifted into summer. I brought out some lemonade and iced tea to those waiting and bowls of water and bones for their dogs.

Reststop had started as an experiment in January. Jake, tired of being harangued by Gary Oscars, had quit. He'd wanted to test a new restaurant concept before trying to get investors for a full-time place and opened a temporary spot in a Brooklyn restaurant that had gone out of business, but still had some months left in its lease. By February, the place was packed.

At first, Reststop hadn't gotten the greatest reviews. People had said the food was too simple, or too greasy, or the service was too friendly or absent-minded. Of course, Jake had freaked out and started rethinking the whole concept. But eventually, he'd realized that the reviews meant nothing, not to the neighborhood people who brought their family, friends, and business partners and considered the restaurant an extension of their home. After a couple of months, investors were pushing to open a permanent location as soon as possible.

I had decided to take spring semester off and wasn't sure I'd return to grad school at all. I don't think they would have taken me if I'd wanted to, though. Because of me, the program had been shamed in the most public way possible. Dean Chang stopped talking to me altogether and corresponded only through her assistant. She didn't want to stick her neck out for me, and I didn't blame her.

After our visit to Jay Garvey, the *New York Times* had published a short update to the allegations and the press jumped on me. I released one statement that confirmed everything and tried to suggest that was the last I ever wanted to talk about it.

But that didn't stop the blogs and food pundits. Pictures of me at various restaurants surfaced. Some people called me a slut or a spineless opportunist. Others came to my defense and said that they would have done the same in my situation or that Michael Saltz had brainwashed me and I was lucky to have made it out alive. After a while, I stopped reading the articles. I had already spent my fair share of time obsessing over Internet chatter.

Jake had suggested I get a publicist for the short term, and I even interviewed a couple. But they were interested in the spin, casting me as a naïve victim, the talented ingenue run over roughshod by the greedy and impotent older man. I could see why the story had appeal, but I didn't want to take that way out. I had done enough spin on my own and now I just wanted to take what was coming.

The *New York Times* hired an outside investigator who spoke to me for an entire afternoon. I thought she'd come with some agenda to protect the *Times,* but she was more pleasant and curious than judgmental. She even told me, off the record, that Michael Saltz had always been a polarizing figure at the *Times* office. Even when he'd allegedly had his sense of taste, he was always getting people to do things for him, preying, she said with downturned eyes, on the vanity of newbies.

Michael Saltz, of course, was fired.

Two weeks after, a full debrief was published on the front page of the A section, which included action steps the paper was taking. They would revisit all the restaurants that had been reviewed while Michael Saltz was incapacitated: Madison Park Tavern, Le Brittane, even Bakushan. The whole lot of them. Part of me was sad that all my work was being undone, but I also knew that it was the right and fair thing to do.

Pascal had texted me:

A RE-REVIEW? I COULD USE YOUR HELP BRAINSTORMING IN THE KITCHEN. ;)

I deleted our chat history, then blocked his number.

My name was finally in the *New York Times* again, but not for the reasons I wanted. The article had said I was his "unwilling accomplice" and that I had been coerced with "bribes and intimidation." There was truth to that, but even the *New York Times* couldn't get to the heart of the matter: that coercion had only gotten me halfway. The article didn't delve into ambiguities, preferring to neatly pack everything in black-and-white so the scandal could be easily buried. I got away, while the public cast Michael Saltz as the pariah. He became the villain, and I the clueless victim. In the end, I didn't even need a publicist.

I knew it was unfair, but I had already confessed to the people who mattered. My parents took it hard and had a difficult time wrapping their heads around my double life. They never would have expected that from me. I tried to ban them from ever googling my name, but it didn't work and I had to spend a lot of time on the phone trying to convince them, at the very least, not to read the comments.

The paper named an interim critic, the woman who had been doing the excellent "$25 and Under" column for five years. Eventually, she officially got the job.

It took about six weeks for things to settle down. The moment that happened, Jake emailed me and asked what I was up to. I would have thought I'd be the last person he'd want working at his restaurant again, but he was having a hard time getting competent waitstaff at a temporary restaurant.

So I helped out. Finally I was done hiding, done explaining. Now I could just work.

I worked with Jake to develop the full Reststop concept in addition to playing hostess, coat check attendant, waitress, and sometimes sommelier. I worked in the weeds with everyone else, and also got to take a bird's-eye view of the business itself. I liked throwing myself into restaurant life, though it didn't satisfy my desire to write.

Still, it was a totally different place and had totally different clientele than Madison Park Tavern or any of the other places I had been to with Michael Saltz, and I liked working there. Eventually Jake had let go of any hesitations about me and became a mentor and a friend.

Just as brunch was slowing down, Carey dropped by, hung up her coat, and started making herself a latte, as if she worked there. Jake had tried to poach her from Gary Oscars, but she'd stayed on and was now working on Gary's business development team.

"Here," she said, and handed me a thin book decorated with

small green flowers. The only words I could understand on the cover were *Angel Martinez*.

"What is this?" I asked.

"It's Angel's self-published collection of poetry. It's in Spanish but I wrote in some translations for you." She opened to a random page and I saw she had written, in purple pen, every single line for me. "It was fun. A good break from restaurant stuff."

"Hey!" Jake called from the kitchen doorway. "No moles in the restaurant!"

"I come in peace," Carey said.

"Does Gary know that?" Jake said under his breath, but loud enough that we could hear.

Carey and I giggled to each other.

"I get off at three, then we can go," I said. Carey gave me a thumbs-up and went back to her coffee and book. That afternoon, we planned to make and photograph a peach tart for my new blog. It covered recipes, restaurants, New York, and writing. Barely anyone read it, but I did it anyway.

I picked up some bread baskets and gave a piece of blueberry–sour cream coffee cake to each of Jake's twins, Natalie and Leslie. The powdered sugar snowed down my blouse, an old Helmut Lang I loved and wore almost every night at Reststop. After the exposé, I kept expecting Michael Saltz or even Bergdorf to come after the clothes, but they never did. I gave some to Emerald so she could study the seaming and draping, kept some for myself, then sold the rest to Sherri at Trina. Since our Jay Garvey visit, Emerald and I had hung out more. Melinda joined when she felt like it.

As the day's last matter of business, I reviewed the watchlist of PXs. Same as in Madison Park Tavern, there were vendors and friends and family that Jake wanted to give special service.

Officially, we didn't take reservations for brunch, but Jake always made exceptions, and I wanted to update our records with new guest notes. I knew most of the names, but didn't recognize one set of initials that had three asterisks and my name beside it.

"Jake! What does this notation mean?"

"Don't worry about it. Do your work."

"Did you write this? Or did Lexi?"

"I don't know," he said. He brought his cell phone to his ear and moved behind a curtain into the nook we used as the coat closet.

Around 2:45, one of our waiters told me a woman had come in with a bread drop-off. At first, I just saw her from the back. She wore a delicate blood orange–colored shawl and a big bun on top of her head.

I told him to send her to the kitchen, then tried to find the delivery clipboard, which wasn't on top of the ice machine where we usually put it. I didn't mean to ignore the woman, but I needed the clipboard before I logged her bread into the inventory. Besides, we typically got our bread from Graham Street Bakery, so I wasn't sure what Jake was thinking.

I was crouched down lifting a hotel pan when she spoke.

"Hello?"

Her face radiated with warmth and positivity. The world stopped. I had imagined this moment a hundred times, but had never come up with a satisfactory interaction. I'd always played out the situation with me too fawning, or her disinterested. She had become a far-off dream I sometimes indulged in, like imagining you won the lottery.

"Oh! You're Helen Lansky!" I couldn't help but say. "Sorry." I gulped, each word walloping me with a sense of The Moment. "I'm just so happy to see you."

"Miss Monroe," a busboy said, handing me the clipboard. "You were looking for this?"

"Thank you, Pedro," I said. I pulled the clipboard in front of me, but the words went all blurry.

Helen laughed. "Is your name Tia, by any chance?" She looked like a jewel-toned sprite, a person from another time, another place.

I had spent years pining for her, getting to know every lilt and nuance of her writing. I heard her voice in my ear and her stories in my heart. She had entered my life in the deepest way, like a language or a country, a thing that touches your every thought.

After I had become known as Michael Saltz's lackey—coerced or not—I was convinced that I would never get to work with her. I had already abused the trust of millions of readers all over the world. Why would she trust me?

But now she stood in front of me—all five feet of her—guileless and gleaming, and every nasty thing that had happened with Michael Saltz disappeared.

"Yes, my name is Tia." I looked to Jake, who'd returned from his phone call, and saw him grinning ear to ear. "What can I do for you, Ms. Lansky?" I asked, my voice trembling.

She gestured to the baguettes, boules, flatbreads, and even some crackers in front of us. "Well, first, I have bread!" she said. "I've become obsessed with the most wonderful baking method, one that few people in the States know about. After so many years in Paris, I knew I had to write about this craftsmanship firsthand. It's the ease of commercial yeast, with the taste of a wild yeast starter." She waved her small but strong-looking hands in the air. "They're for my latest book, *The Bread Worth Eating: Loaves, Buns, Pizzas, and More.*"

"That sounds like an amazing project," I said.

"Would you like to try a piece?" she asked. "I emailed some local contacts and Jake was the first one to respond. So he gets all my bread experiments. Too delicious to waste." She chuckled and tore off a piece of baguette and another piece from an identical loaf.

"Tell me what you think of these." The pieces had the same hardened brown exterior, the same spongy give that let out a sweet-sour smell.

I took a bite of one, then the other.

"This one," I said, "tastes smoother. More refined. And this one, I guess you can say it's more rustic. It has a mineral depth to it."

Helen nodded and her bun bobbed along with her. "Yes, the first bread is from a mother starter cultivated in Paris. The second one is a New York mother. I started it last week when I came back, so it's a little underdeveloped, but I think it has a lot of character."

She picked out a quart-size container from her tote bag. "See?" she said. "I brought some New York mother starter for Jake's guys to experiment with." She lifted the lid and it opened with a pop. Whatever was inside was clearly alive.

"This one's a kicker," she said. "Here." She scooped out a pinch and held it in front of my nose.

"Wow, that's really interesting," I said. "It smells so . . . primal."

"Indeed," she said. "It's an expression of its surroundings. The wild yeast lives all around us." She wiggled her fingers above her head. "The character of the loaf comes from the air."

I inspected the sourdough starter again and it fizzled and popped its singular scent.

"Paris, New York . . . Brooklyn," she continued excitedly. "After discovering this method, I've almost stopped adding other accoutrements to bread. The bread speaks for itself. Olives, raisins, nuts—they're nice, but distractions, don't you think?"

"I've never thought of bread like that. But I get it. It doesn't need a lot of ornamentation. Maybe the best flavor . . . is itself."

"Brava." Helen clapped, impressed. "The best flavor is *always* itself. That's taken me a lifetime to figure out."

I thought I might cry.

"And now my second matter of business. I'm leaving for Paris in a couple days," Helen started, "but I'm coming back in the fall and will need a New York assistant as I finish my manuscript. Do you know what you will be doing then?"

"Oh! Next fall . . . I haven't thought about it yet. I'm not sure I'm going back to grad school, so would you consider a nonstudent?"

Helen Lansky leaned toward me and grinned. "Well, if *you're* a nonstudent, then I'll say *yes*."

A waiter poked his head into the kitchen. "Ms. Lansky? Your table is ready now."

She reached out for my hand and gave it a squeeze.

It wasn't the first time Helen Lansky had given me something to hold and hope for. But this time felt different. I felt different.

Jake came up behind me. "Who was that?" he asked mischievously.

"As if you didn't know." I swatted him with a dishcloth. "I've actually never spoken to her before. I didn't know what to do with myself. She said she's coming back to New York in the fall. That means, after everything, I might actually have a shot . . ."

Jake rolled his eyes at me. "Tia, you've done your fair share of bad. But I know there's a lot of good in you."

I gave him a huge hug. I couldn't thank him enough. Jake had believed in me, and I hoped that one day I could return the favor.

A little while later, I walked up to Helen, who was amiably eating poached eggs in a bed of kale and blistered berbere chick-peas.

"Um, Ms. Lansky?"

"Yes, Tia?"

"I'd love to be your assistant next fall. Please let me know how I can officially apply."

Helen put down her fork. "Tia, that is wonderful news. But I already know you're the woman for me. It was your choice to make and I'm so happy that you made it!"

I hurled myself forward and gave her a hug. "Thank you, thank you so much. I'm so grateful to you, and to Jake for helping connect us."

"Oh, it wasn't just Jake who put in a good word. I've been out of the country since Christmas, and I've missed most of the hullaballoo around your past. But let's just say you had another ringing endorsement from . . . an anonymous fan."

I released my embrace and sat down across from her to gain my bearings. Michael Saltz. He had said I'd never work with Helen, and now he had endorsed me? Either he'd had a change of heart, or he was planning something. But at least now I knew not to fall for his games.

"Well," Helen said, dragging a piece of bread over the last smear of egg yolk. "I won't be back in New York until September, but perhaps we can correspond via email until then. Would that be okay with you?"

I couldn't help but laugh. "Of course that'd be okay," I said, and a million pounds of secrecy and shame and deception and doubt evaporated off me. "That's what I've always wanted."

After work let out, Carey and I walked to a gourmet market on Grand Street to pick up a few things for that afternoon's tart project. I bagged some gorgeous peaches, then turned to suggest to Carey that we add some pears to make the flavor profile more complex. She had disappeared.

I walked through the olive section, the cheese section, then the prepared food section. It was then that I noticed a couple sitting at the little café on the side, sharing a semolina cake.

The moisture in my mouth dried up. The girl was petite, and wore a purple flowered top and a bouncy ponytail. It only lasted a couple of seconds, the two of us seeing each other. He nodded to me and a smile spread on his lips. I nodded back, then escaped around the corner.

Carey tapped me on my arm. "Hey! Sorry, I got distracted by the spices." Then she waved her hand in front of my eyes. "Hello? Are you okay?"

I shook my head and looked at her. "I'm okay," I said, more out of reflex than actually feeling that was true. I picked up some pears.

"Are you sure?"

I studied the pears in the bag.

"Come on," Carey said before I could answer again. "Let's go. Don't you want to shoot this with natural light? We've gotta get this in the oven."

We took the subway back to Carey's place and made the tart, getting the perfect shot in the day's magic twilight hour.

Afterward, while Carey hung out in her bedroom, I sat down in her living room to work on the blog post. Alone, I finally let my mind rest on that moment seeing him. Elliott and his new girlfriend. We hadn't spoken since the night he broke up with me, not even during my public flogging over Michael Saltz.

I had thought it would hurt—tremendously—knowing that he was with someone else. I played the scene over in my head. I heard Carey tapping on her keyboard. I listened to the traffic noises outside the window. And I realized that I was fine. More than that, I was happy in my own life and happy for Elliott. Truly.

I loaded the pictures on my computer and attached a couple in an email to Kyle.

> Hey—I wish you could have a slice of this with me, because I have something to celebrate. I saw your old mentor today. We're going to work together. Maybe you can give me some tips.

Kyle Lorimer. He was a great guy and I found myself hoping that we'd get to spend more time together. After all, we had a lot in common.

The blog post included the peach-pear tart recipe and a meditation on what you want versus what you get versus what you fight for. I finished the post as I always did, though the first time had been strange. After all that writing under Michael Saltz's name, it had felt foreign to see those two words together, though I've had them my whole life:

Love,
Tia Monroe

Acknowledgments

I NEVER READ ACKNOWLEDGMENTS UNTIL I STARTED WRITING this book. I was hungry for clues: Who are the people who help make books happen? Where can you find support? How solitary is writing, really?

Aspiring author, you're not going to know most of the people in this section. So I'll say: Surround yourself with positive people. Share your ideas. Be generous with your time. Thank those who give you theirs. Work hard. Persist.

THANK YOU TO my agent, Stefanie Lieberman, who has guided me with patience, understanding, and a razor-sharp intelligence. My gratitude to my editor, Chelsey Emmelhainz, who made this story deeper, stronger—a "real book." Additional thanks to Megan Schumann, Laura Cherkas, Ivy McFadden, and Diahann Sturge. Thank you to Connie Gabbert for the luscious cover. Go Team *Food Whore*!

To Amy Bloom, who awakened a passion for writing and

taught me lessons that'll last a lifetime. And, simply put, this book wouldn't have existed without Amanda Lewis.

Thank you to my advance readers: Jen, who tells it to me straight, and Lin, who shares my love of the juicy page-turner. Thank you to Cam and John, who in addition to being amazing writers and readers, are also savvy marketing minds.

And then there were friends who kept encouraging me, even when this book was just a file in my computer, a line to say at a cocktail party. An incomplete list: Andrea, Lauren, Allison, Amara, Alex, Bill, Jay, Sherry, Karen, Leiti, Liz, Matt, Meredith, Michael, Julian, Rosemarie, Randall, and Brian. You treated my little nothing like a Something, and that made a huge difference.

Thank you to my family—Mom, Dad, Andrew, Chris, and Uncle Jerry. I know my pursuits might seem strange, even disruptive, and yet you still support and celebrate them.

And thank you to Dave, the water ox to my wood rat.

About the Author

JESSICA TOM is a writer and food blogger living in Brooklyn. She has worked on initiatives with restaurants, hospitality start-ups, food trucks, and citywide culinary programs. She graduated from Yale University with a concentration in fiction writing and wrote the restaurant review for the *Yale Daily News Magazine*. *Food Whore* is her first novel.